LUKE CARTER

AND THE SWORD OF KINGS

LUKE CARTER
AND THE SWORD OF KINGS

A.J. ENSOR

WinDruid Publishing
St. Louis, MO

Published by WinDruid Publishing
P.O. Box 25008
St. Louis, MO 63125-5008
www.windruidpublishing.com

Publisher's Cataloguing-in-Publication Data
Ensor, A.J.

Luke Carter and the sword of kings / by A. J. Ensor. -- St. Louis, MO : WinDruid Publishing, 2004.

p. ; cm.
Summary: A 12-year-old boy born into a magical family struggles with his family's legacy in the American Magical Realm.

ISBN: 0-9758943-0-7

1. Magic--Juvenile fiction. 2. Responsibility--Juvenile fiction.
3. Fantasy fiction. I. Title. II. Luke Carter and the sword of kings.

PZ7.E576 L84 2004
LCCN: 2004108616
813.6--dc22
0409

Interior design by Linda Powers/Powers Design • www.powersdesign.net
Jacket design & illustration by: Jenniffer Julich, JNNFFR productions
Jacket title & graphic effects by: Eric Tufford, rocket88@vaxxine.com

Printed in the United States of America
08 07 06 05 04 • 5 4 3 2 1

To Mary and in Memory of Melvin Ensor
My Parents, originally from Jersey City, and now Lacey Township, New Jersey.

Susan Whinnery
Originally from Lebanon, Illinois, and now St. Louis, Mo.

Claire Weir
Of Glengormley, Belfast, Ireland.
A Master of Continuity and Naturally Talented Literary Critic.

Thank You will never be enough. So I dedicate this book to you.

AJE

CONTENTS

Return Of The Darkside

CHAPTER 1

ALONG A NORTHERN mountain pass, a very special train moved along a very special track at a slow pace through a heavy rainstorm. While there were many other tracks through the mountain passes with many other trains, this train had its own track, and no other trains could ride on this track except for this very special train. The Griffin Express had moved along this track many times for many years, and never had there ever been a problem. Nearly five times a week, the Griffin Express had moved between New York City and the Griffin Valley. The trip was always swift, and the train was always on time. For reasons yet unknown, this night, things were very different. It seemed that for the very first time, the Griffin Express would not meet its schedule. Its movements were slow, and rumors of explosions and fire on the track ahead had been heard across the engineer's radio. He was not sure what to make of it. No other train was allowed on his track! The communications were so garbled the engineer was uncertain whether the radio noise was about his track or a different track. He called for more information but received no directions to stop from the central dispatch, so he continued, slowly and cautiously. He was very upset, for the first time ever in his career his train was not going to be on time.

The passengers had more than noticed the slow pace of the train. They kept up their complaints to the conductor each time he passed. Many doubted that they would make it to the valley by the next morning. A few of them warned the conductor about all of the complaints they would make when they finally reached the valley. Most passengers just stared out into the heavy falling rain and were amazed by the reflection of the lightening off of the sides of the mountains. Some of them sensed there was something very wrong.

Into one of the train cars entered a lovely woman. She glanced at the other passengers staring out the widows as she searched for her seat. Her hair was red, her eyes were blue and sparkled in the flashes of lightening that filled the car, and she had a cloak draped over her arm. She sat and like everyone else began to stare outside. To anyone who noticed her, it was obvious she was both anxious and worried. The woman whispered complaints to herself about how slowly the train was moving. She also thought out loud about the rumors she had heard. In all fairness, they were just rumors—nothing anyone would have taken seriously. She and the rest of the passengers had no real knowledge of any problems ahead. Still, the rumors haunted her, and she had only to worry as the train continued onward through flashes of lightening on a black, almost evil, dark and rainy night.

The woman's name was Claire. Claire Cohan was the wife of Harry Cohan. A few times a year, Harry lectured at the Citadel University in upstate New York. It was the place that Claire first met Harry, and she was now returning there for the first time since graduation. She received word of a possible accident at the school. There was nothing in the message that made her worry, and she remained unconcerned until she lost contact with Harry. As the train slowly rolled on, Claire had a terrible feeling inside that something dreadful might be going on.

Before leaving New York City, individuals on the train platform spread gossip of large explosions at the university. They also said that fires could be seen burning in the Griffin Valley where the Citadel was located. "How strange—fires burning in this kind of weather," Claire thought. All roads were blocked by mudslides caused by the heavy rain, and the only way in was by train.

Suddenly, and so abruptly that Claire had to hold onto something as tightly as possible, the train attempted to screech into an emergency halt. Then, there was an enormous flash of light and a tremendous explosion, and the train began to roll over on its side. Screams were coming from every direction! Claire screamed. The sounds of metal being crushed and broken surrounded all of the passengers. Soon, Claire found herself lying on what used to be the ceiling of the car and was now its floor. People moaning could be heard everywhere. Individuals were calling for help, but Claire couldn't see anything—it was too dark. She struggled onto her knees. She felt her arms and legs and knew everything was still working. "I'm not hurt," she thought. There was mass confusion around her. She felt along the floor and searched for a direction to move in. By accident, she laid her hand on what had been one of the car ceiling lights. She looked around her as best she could and then bent over close to the lamp. With her lips nearly touching the light, she whispered, "Solas!"

The lights in the car came on. People could see one another as they began to stand up. The car began to turn again from the motion of people standing inside. Soon, it began to roll over on its side. Panicked, screaming people could be heard as the car came to rest on the next set of rail tracks. Now, the ceiling was a set of windows, the lights were part of one wall, and the seats made up the other wall. Men tried to open the car doors to get out. The doors were bent and would not budge.

Claire looked around for her cloak. If she could find it, she could help, but she had to hide as best she could what she was up to, and she needed the cloak to do that. She spotted it hanging from one of the seats and quickly put it on. Claire looked around. There was no doubt that everyone in the car was trapped. Something drastic had to be done, so she pulled the hood of the cloak over her head and turned to face the wall. She hoped no one could see what she was doing. There was a flash of light that scared everyone. No one in the car knew what was happening or where the flash had come from.

When Claire turned back away from the wall, she had a long broad sword in her hand that hummed a little and had a slight glow to it. The sword shimmered brilliantly and was stunning to look at. It almost seemed as if the sword was made of light. When she raised it up, a woman began screaming out of fear.

"Will you shut up?" Claire shouted at her.

Claire jumped upward and swung the sword at the emergency releases on the windows above. The window, still inside its frame, came crashing down as Claire jumped out of the way. She then sliced the supports off of one of the car seats and braced it under the now open window. Once again she turned away toward the wall and placed the sword under her cloak. Another flash was seen and when she turned back the sword was gone!

"Get on with it now!" Claire shouted desperately. She used the seat and climbed to the top of the rail car and out the window. The rain poured down, and the lightening flashed as she knelt and helped one person after another climb out of the car. From a distance, there was a noise—then, it repeated itself.

"Oh, my God!" Claire thought out loud with fear in her voice. There was another train coming along the secondary track! It was heading right at them.

"Move! Move! Move!" Claire screamed at the other passengers in a panic. The men helping her began to yell the same. There was an old couple walking along the bottom of the car and gathering their personal belongings.

"There's another train coming!" Claire screamed at them. "Get up! Get out! Now!"

The men helping Claire got up and ran in a panic.

"We're coming!" the old woman shouted back, but she didn't move to climb up. She was too busy shouting at the old man to come along. The train was so close its nose light was racing down at Claire.

"Come on!" she shouted again desperately.

It was too late! Claire stood, ran, and jumped off of the far side of the car and leaped into the air as the two trains collided. There was a tremendous explosion and a stupendous fireball as she rolled down the side of the mountain and onto an access road below. There were several loud explosions, one after another, as the new train was pushed off of one track and onto the other. Claire rolled over behind a large bolder as fire and large pieces of train parts came raining down on her!

Claire braced herself beneath the rock and prayed for life! Then, everything stopped as time seemed to stand still. There was nothing crashing down around her anymore. A strange calm began as Claire lay on the ground. At first she was too scared to move. Her back and legs were in pain. As she looked up, it was clear she had been cut in the fall. Rain washed away the blood as fast as it appeared on her face. The rest of her couldn't be seen from behind the cloak.

Shaking, Claire pushed herself up onto her knees and then rolled over with her back against the rock. As she looked up, there lay the engine from one of the trains. Had she chosen the other side of the road to seek cover, she would have been crushed! She looked down the railway access road. There were utility lights once every 50 yards or so. The road back to the city was blocked by train wreckage. Claire sat there for a moment with her head on her knees and tried to think of what to do next.

She felt pain but decided to try standing to see what did or did not work. Bracing against the rock, she lifted herself onto her feet. Standing for a moment in the rain, she then took a step and another. The pain continued as she moved. Though still shaking, Claire had survived with only bruises.

She took a few steps toward the other side of the road. With the light from the burning wreckage, she could see up the side of the mountain. She was amazed to have survived the fall, but the climb was clearly too steep to go back up. Pausing for a moment to look around, she didn't see many options. So with the rain coming down so hard that Claire could barely see the next utility light, she turned north and began to walk along the railway access road. At first she limped a bit, and then slowly, the pain seemed to subside some. The rain did not penetrate her cloak. In fact, the cloak dried her clothing beneath it.

After walking for a time, Claire began to notice voices coming from above her on the main tracks. There were calls for help, and others just seemed to be moaning. Voices shouted for everyone to keep moving. Claire assumed it was survivors from the train wreck. After a mile or so more, a railway supply shack appeared. It was surrounded by wire fencing. A sign on top was marked "Chattanooga Pass Supply Substation 1."

Everything was locked. Claire looked around for a moment carefully as if to make sure no one was watching. Raising her right hand, there was a flash of light, and her sword appeared again. With a few swings, Claire made short work of both the fence and the locked door.

Inside, hope of calling for help faded. There was no phone. There were several hand lights with extra batteries. Claire borrowed one. Staring out the door and into the rain, Claire could not help but think how she had managed to get into this mess!

The situation presented few options. Still shaking a bit, Claire kept reminding herself about Harry. There was a really nice train station at the entrance to the Griffin Valley. It couldn't be far now. Once there, she could call for help, and even if she could not, the tunnel entrance to the Valley was but a short walk.

The rainfall was unbelievable. It was coming down so hard that raindrops bounced off of the ground as they hit. As hard as her night had been so far, Claire was still sick with worry about her husband. A nightmare of him lying somewhere, calling for help, and no one answering his call haunted her—odd thinking for someone who was nearly in that very same position not an hour before. Claire was both beautiful and odd.

Soon, Claire was walking again. She came on an access trail that wound itself up the side of the mountain to the track level. The borrowed light was quite powerful and cast a long and brilliant beam. There was no problem finding her way. Claire was not, however, prepared for what she found at the top of the trail. There was a long line of people moving out of the north and heading toward the train wreck.

Many of the passersby were limping, and others were being carried. People's clothes were dirty, torn, and stained with blood. Many were crying, and others were covered with dirt and were near the point of exhaustion.

"My God," Claire thought. "What has happened?"

Fear and alarm now replaced reason in her mind.

"Where is Harry?" she muttered.

If he were in the same condition as these people, then he would need her now. Claire began to move along the edge of the tracks against the flow of people. It was so dark that only the light she carried illuminated anything. Endless questions possessed her, but each time she approached someone, he or she moved away in fear. Claire was desperate and needed to make her way into the valley. She shouted at the crowd of people walking, "There's a train wreck ahead! You can't go this way!"

The rain was so intense she doubted many had heard her. One man walking by looked at her. She could barely see his face in the dark. He said in a broken voice, "There's nothing but death in the other direction." He just kept moving.

The tide of people seemed endless. By their clothing, Claire knew they had come out of the Griffin Valley. She just didn't understand why no one was willing to volunteer a few answers. Some were dressed in school uniforms, and others were members of the Citadel staff. She kept asking what had happened, but everyone refused any conversation with her. Clearly, they were gripped by fear, but they were also outside the Realm. All of these people, including Claire, were members of a society that was distinct and apart from the rest of the world. Their society had its own rules, places, and government. Among themselves, their world was known simply as "the Realm." The valley, the university and its prepschool were all parts of it. All of the people on the tracks were members. Claire had not been to this place in many years, and she was a stranger to these people. There were rules against talking to strangers about the affairs of the Realm, which was why they avoided all conversation with her. But there was something else — something so bad and inflicted so much fear that there seemed to be no way of reasoning with anyone.

Some of the people passing were moaning and asking for help. Claire truly wanted to help. Indeed, she wanted to stop and help all of them, but fear possessed her now. She had to find Harry! Nothing was going to distract her from that objective. Helping such a huge tide of people was beyond any one person's abilities. She could help Harry, however, if she could find him!

Claire had walked along the track for nearly five miles before she spotted the lights of the Chattanooga Pass Station. The station itself was gone, but the streetlights remained. The station had been burned to the ground. The tracks that ran in front had been torn apart by what appeared to have been explosions.

Turning to follow the flow of people back toward a tunnel in the mountain, she found the entrance had been scorched by fire. The signs that hung over the entrance were in pieces and were still burning. Claire began to make her way back through the tunnel. Having to maneuver around one person after another was exceedingly difficult. One old man grabbed her by the arms and caused Claire to scream.

"Don't go back there!" he shouted. "Leave here while you still can! The armies of the Darkside are on the move!"

Claire shoved the man away from her. She said nothing as he stumbled away. He had really startled her, and she stood for a moment to catch her breath. People just kept walking around her in a mindless daze as if no one was there. Claire knew staying focused was what she needed. Continuing onward, after about a mile, she entered the northernmost edge of the Valley of the Griffin. Things seemed very strange and out of place. The tunnel was only mile long, but at the other end, there was no rain falling.

As Claire moved out of the tunnel, the sound of rushing water could be heard. At the extreme northern edge was the waterfall that fed the valley. In the dark, she could not see the towering mass of water moving over the cliff, but the area was heavy with mist from where the water fell on the rocks. The sound it made was deafening but beautiful and seemed out of place given the horrors around her. The river it fed flowed into the Griffin Valley and directly past the university. A human tide of people desperate to leave covered the entire trail leading out of the valley. The path was too narrow, and the volume of people was too much for Claire to try to walk against. Near the river shore were small abandoned boats. They had obviously been used to move people to the tunnel. Climbing aboard one, she threw off the anchor line and began to float downstream.

Sitting in the rear of the boat, Claire used a small wooden rudder to steer. She watched as people onshore struggled to keep moving. Some were calling for help. Others were helping, but most just ignored the pleas for help. Claire was completely baffled by this behavior. The people of the valley were good, caring individuals. She did not know what to think of the behavior she was witnessing. Fear kept her mind focused on the nightmare of her husband lying on the ground. It was a horror unlike anything she had ever experienced, and it was now reinforced by the smell of death that seemed to come from every direction.

On the horizon, things looked even grimmer if that was possible. Light from an enormous fire reflected on the clouds above and fanned out in every direction. The woodland around the university was burning in a firestorm. Her small boat floated past the trees on shore and into a clearing.

"Oh, my God!" Claire gasped.

The scene on shore was one of mass destruction. She stood on her small boat in total shock. Claire wanted to cry! This valley had been the most beautiful place she had ever lived, and now it was in ruins. She had spent 11 years there as a schoolgirl. The beauty of this place had been so possessing its images filled her dreams long after she had left. Now ... now it was scorched earth in every direction! Sorrow turned to anger as Claire filled with rage at those who had destroyed her schoolgirl home. Suddenly, there was an enormous explosion whose shock wave sent Claire crashing onto the deck of the boat.

Claire had been knocked out. When she came to, she found herself face down against the wood of the boat. Some time had passed, for on the horizon, the slightest hint of sunlight could be detected. Claire struggled onto her knees. She knelt there for a moment before she noticed the sound of steel breaking against itself in the distance. When she turned in the direction of the noise, the look on her face turned from pain to shock and then fear.

In the blue-gray murky reflection of dawn's early light, the Citadel could be seen in the distance. Its massive stone walls gave way to a large field. Beyond the field was woodland consumed by firestorm, and on the field, students were in full battle against creatures dressed in blood-red cloaks. The students were not winning. They were obviously worn out and too tired to fight. They would cross swords, run, and then turn and fight some more. Each time, the creatures would pursue. There were no firearms in the valley. Unless enchanted somehow, simple guns, pistols, and rifles were useless against members of the Realm, good or bad. Each time the students stopped to fight, one or more them fell by the sword of their attackers. These creatures were the Army of the Darkside the old man in the tunnel had warned Claire against.

Suddenly, a loud and penetrating roar could be heard. It seemed to come from the sky. In the next moment, lions with wings flew in and landed behind the Darksiders on the field of battle. These creatures stood five times the height of a man, nearly as tall as the trees. They had enormous claws or talismans. Their roar, or their scream, or whatever the sound they made, was painful to hear. Claire was forced to cover her ears. Even with her ears covered, the sound of the creatures sent pain up and down her spine. In the 11 years she lived in the Griffin Valley, Claire had never laid eyes on a real griffin. Clearly, they were real and now infuriated! They had left their sanctuary and were seeking revenge on those who had wreaked destruction inside their valley!

The scream of the griffins had the same impact on the Darksiders as it did on Claire. The ones who had been fighting with the students now turned to face the griffins. Their leader ordered the griffins to withdraw or be destroyed. The griffins just roared again, and the Darksiders held their ears and bent over in pain. Then they raised their swords at the griffins, and bolts of energy flew at the creatures! It was a desperate move. Throwing high levels of raw power from a sword would weaken the bearer very quickly—particularly after battling all night long! The griffins were thrown into the air and crashed down on their backs. The matriarch of the griffins recovered, and rolling quickly, she jumped up again. This time when she went after the Darksiders, she bent forward and kept her head low to the ground. When the Darksiders sent bolts of energy at her, she roared in pain but did not stop her forward attack. When she was close enough to strike, the other griffins roared, forcing the Darksiders to hold their ears rather than their swords. When this happened, the matriarch reached out with her claws and began to cut the Darksiders in two. Again and again she swung! With each swipe, dozens of Darksiders were vanquished. The students who had run now came back in force and joined the battle. They attacked the Darksiders while trying to protect the griffins from counterattacks.

Without warning, a new wave of Darksiders came running out from the burning forests. They blasted the closest griffin off of its feet, and closing quickly, they overwhelmed the students that were protecting it and drove their swords into the griffin! The griffin screamed in pain and was instantly reduced to dust and ash. With just two mighty leaps, the matriarch crossed the battlefield and faced the new column of Darksiders. She roared so powerfully that the fire in the forest behind the Darksiders rose high into the air from the blast of her lungs. The Darksiders were forced to their knees in pain. Then, the matriarch inhaled again, stretching her body wide, and when she exhaled, fire flew from her mouth, and everything in front of her, including all of the Darksiders, was reduced to dust!

Now very weak, the matriarch collapsed onto the ground. Unleashing her fire had used up her remaining strength. Using direct energy always made members of the Realm very weak. Using too much at once could kill a person. Three of the other griffins came and surrounded her to protect her. Then two other griffins spotted Claire floating down the river. They made a loud noise, but they didn't roar. They ran to the river to see who was on the boat. Within moments, they stood high over Claire. Their teeth were exposed as they prepared to attack. Claire stood as high on the small boat as she could. She pulled down her hood and removed her cloak so that the griffins would see who and what she was—just a girl dressed in a brown sweater and blue jeans. She wasn't a threat to anyone. In a gesture of respect, she bowed to the powerful griffins. In that moment, the griffins relaxed from the attacking position. They made sounds to each other and then turned and walked away. They knew the woman on the boat was no Darksider.

Soon Claire floated up to the river dock near the main entrance to the once great Citadel. Since the American Revolution, thousands of members of the Realm had come to this place to be educated. Here they did not have to live in fear of being discovered. They could practice their art without their lives being threatened. They could learn to make a contribution to society without being isolated by it. They made lifelong friends, and some even fell in love. Now, the enormous 250-year-old doors that marked its great entrance lay crushed and burning on the ground.

The Darksiders had planned well for this attack. It made Claire suspect that they had inside help. The once proud tall stone walls had enormous gapping holes in them. Everywhere people lay about, but no one was moving. Darksiders lay face down next to the students or staff members who had vanquished them. Brilliant lives with everything to live for were cut short for reasons that went beyond comprehension. Now all they were or might have been was gone.

Claire felt ill. She had a lump on her head from where she fell onto the wood of the boat. Cuts and bruises covered her body from when she jumped from the train. She had been traveling all night. She was having trouble breathing. Tears filled her eyes as she stepped over one person after another and made her way into the common grounds. The sight of what true evil could do overwhelmed her.

These creatures, as evil as they were, were still part of the Realm. They were just the dark side of it, which was why they were called Darksiders. "The train," Claire remembered. There was a flash before the accident just like the one that knocked her out on the boat. The Darksiders had launched an attack outside of the Realm! Claire was just now realizing all of this. "Oh, my God!" she thought. "If the mundane world felt threatened by the magical realm, they might send in their military and destroy everything!"

Soon, Claire was walking through what was left of the door to the main castle. The great halls and classrooms were empty. Smoke still rose from the ashes. The stench of death was everywhere. The sun began to rise as Claire walked across the breezeway that connected the castle to the main living quarters.

She entered the main hall and moved with caution. Something was wrong. It was close, and it felt very cold to her. Claire reached out with her mind, and her senses became alert. As she moved past one of the rooms, a creature in a red cloak lurked from behind the door and watched. Claire didn't see it, but she could feel it. The thing crept out of the room and silently began to stalk her. She walked from room to room and searched for anyone who might be alive. She walked past another room, and she didn't notice, but a pair of eyes watched her. They blinked as she finished passing by. Again, Claire couldn't hear or see anyone, but her senses were alert. She could feel they were there. Three creatures now cautiously stalked her from behind. Each time Claire looked around, they hid themselves. They wanted her, but they were also afraid of her.

The one thing Claire could not feel was Harry. At such a close distance, if Harry were anywhere to be found, she would have been able to sense him. His essence was gone. For that to happen, someone must have vanquished him. That's how powerful a witch Harry was. No one could have taken him by the sword alone. Claire would be lucky if she could locate his ashes. Neither could anyone have taken Harry's brother, Philo, or his wife, Sara. Philo was High Chancellor and the single most powerful individual magical force on the planet, a person referred to simply as the White Robin. Sara, like Claire, was an Alfa-Omega witch of the first order. No one could have taken her by the sword either. Claire could not sense either one of them. In the case of Philo, this was simply impossible. The only thing that could have terminated his existence was old age. Something very new or very ancient had stepped into the Realm. There was no logic to what had happened here. What Claire could sense were the children.

Claire walked halfway through the next hallway to the point where it connected with another corridor. Each time she moved forward, the creatures in the red cloaks got closer and closer. They were being so careful. Like wolves, afraid their prey might run off if discovered, they kept as silent as possible.

Through the doorway, at the far end of the adjoining corridor, appeared three Darksiders who stood in their blood-red cloaks and stared at her. Their dark deformed faces were slightly illuminated by the rising sun. Claire was about to move on, but she thought it was odd that these creatures would show themselves. In small numbers, they were no match for a fully grown witch. They knew that, she knew that, and their daring and sudden appearance changed nothing. So Claire chose to ignore them and tend to the needs of her family. Besides, in time they would see justice!

Originally, Claire had come for Harry. Her soul felt empty knowing he was almost certainly gone. She would have come sooner had she any hint of what was happening here. As for the survivors, she still sensed the children. "I need to find them," she thought. She was about to move on when three more Darksiders entered the hall and blocked her path. Then the ones who had been stalking appeared from behind. Claire was trapped! But at the sight of the first three Darksiders, fear had gone away and was replaced by anger and hate.

Claire's fear was for the lives of the people she loved. Claire wasn't afraid of anyone or anything—least of all nine evil, worthless dark creatures arrogant enough to think they could take on a full-grown witch! The three in the adjoining corridor pulled out their swords and charged at Claire. They yelled words she had never heard before. Claire gave an evil glare of her own but made no move at all. Then the three behind her drew their swords and charged, followed by the three in front who drew theirs and charged.

When the first three got close enough, Claire pulled the hood from the top of her head, raised her left hand at them, and shouted, "I steach I An Fear Aer!"

The three went flying into the air backward, across the entire length of the corridor, and crashed hard on the doors at the far end. Then, Claire quickly raised her right hand inverted, and with a flash of light, her brilliant sword appeared in it. She pointed it at the three charging her from the front and shouted, "Cumhacht!"

A bolt of power flew from the end of the sword and struck the three, instantly reducing them to dust and ash. In the very next moment, Claire spun backward and cut in half the swords of the three Darksiders who were attacking from behind. She cut their swords like they were toys an instant before they would have killed her. Claire's fury knew no mercy. She swung her sword with amazing speed. She cut the dark one to her right in half, and he became dust. She spun around the middle one and lopped its head off from behind, and it too burst into ash. The remaining one she ran through, and in the same moment, it also was reduced to a pile of ash on the floor.

The three at the far end of the adjoining corridor had made it back to their feet. Once again they charged. "One would have thought they would have learned their lesson," Claire thought.

"Cumhacht!" Claire shouted. The remaining three were reduced to a dusty memory. Bitter anger raged from Claire's soul.

"I am the light, says the Lord. Those who believe in me will fear no evil and cannot die!" Claire screamed and cried "cannot die" at the top of her lungs furiously as her eyes filled with tears.

There was so much pain in her voice! Claire was so angry! She stood for a moment in the hallway. She felt the effect of tossing raw power from her sword, but she was a very powerful witch. It would take several dozens of power strikes before it had any real effect on her.

Responding to the sound of her furious scream, a boy and girl came rushing in through the far doorway. Claire immediately took a defensive posture with her sword. Then she realized that they were wearing student uniforms. They looked terrified. Their clothing was torn and covered with blood and dirt. She relaxed her posture.

The two walked up to her. "I am Jason Fesserack," the boy said. "I'm Lisa Barns," the girl told her.

"I am Mrs. Harry Cohan. I came to search for my husband, Professor Cohan. What happened to you two? What happened in this place? What is this blood on you two?"

"We've been fighting since sunset yesterday," Lisa told her. "Many of us are gone, and most of the blood was splattered on us when they fell." The girl seemed distant, and she didn't blink much. She constantly stared, never looking at anyone, just looking around expecting another attack.

"I know your husband, Lady Cohan," Jason responded.

"Can you tell me where I might find him?" Claire inquired with a voice that had a sense of hopelessness in it.

"No, my Lady," Jason responded. "Shortly after the first wave of attacks, the first Lady sent him off to seek out the Alfa male of the griffin pride to warn him that Darksiders had entered his valley and to ask for help."

"What happened to the Lord White Robin?" she replied.

"He went off with the members of the Board of Trustees and the White Robin's cauldron to perform the equinox visual. Then the group would have fasted until sunset, when the Robin would perform the passion to reveal his soul," Lisa told her.

"Which way did they go?" Claire asked.

"No one knows, my Lady," Lisa responded. "The ceremony is performed in a cave that is lit only at sunrise on the morning of the equinox. Because of the passion, the location is always kept secret."

Claire leaned against the wall. Emotion was replacing reasoning again. Her chest tightened, and she was having trouble breathing. The situation was so desperate. Claire turned and rolled against the cold stone wall.

"No one survived?" Claire asked.

"Three made it back," Jason answered. "One of the members of the Robin's cauldron was carried by two others. The one they carried was already mortally wounded. The other two stood and fought with us. They vanquished hundreds of Darksiders before they were worn down by the overwhelming numbers and were in the end vanquished."

"They said," Lisa added, "that a dark lord using a wand and wizard's craft attacked them by surprise, that he trapped the White Robin in a Merlin's cave! Do you know what a Merlin's cave is, my Lady?"

Claire shook her head no. "I know who Merlin is, of course, but I never heard of such a cave. A dark lord wielding a wand and using wizard's craft," she thought out loud. "That's a warlock! A warlock in America? How did this happen?" She looked up at Lisa and Jason.

"What of the first Lady Sara and the children?" Claire asked.

Jason answered her with pain in his voice as Lisa began to cry. "Lady Sara led the student attack against the Darksiders when they breached the main gate. She and the student senior class fought them to a standstill and blocked them from invading the commons. But they breached the walls, and she and all of the rest of us were overwhelmed!" Jason bowed his head and began to cry.

Claire looked at them. "She led the charge, did she?" Claire asserted loudly. "You're bloody damned right she did!" Claire spoke loud with pain and pride in her voice as tears came to her eyes. "What about the children?"

Lisa looked up. "They are trapped inside the Robin's quarters. There are nearly three dozen Darksiders outside there trying to get past the Robin's barrier."

"The barrier is holding?" Claire asked quickly.

"Yes, my Lady," Lisa replied.

"Do you not know what that means?" Claire told them as both looked up at her. "That means that where ever he is, the White Robin must still be alive! Thank God for that!"

Claire looked across to the window on the opposite side of the corridor. She stood upright and walked across. After waving her hand, the window abruptly opened. Then she shouted out, "Cara, Cara duinn An seo mo Glaoigh An seo mo guth Tabhair aird uirthi mo Amhran!"

Claire pulled a pen and paper from her robe and began to write.

Cohan,

There has been a battle. Many dead from Darksider attack including most of staff and many students. Harry and Sara lost. Philo is missing. Board and cauldron wiped out. A dark lord using a wand and wizard's craft is thought responsible.

—Claire

As she finished writing, a large bald eagle appeared at the window. It screeched an eagle noise at them. Claire rolled up the note and handed it to the bird.

"Take this to Lord Cohan," she told the eagle.

With the note, the creature jumped into the air and disappeared into the sky.

"I have to go and help the children," Claire said.

"You can't!" Jason asserted.

"It's impossible!" Lisa said, agreeing with him.

"A large group of Darksiders has been outside the apartment all night. They are still there! There are dozens of them pooling their powers and trying to get through the magic protecting the children!" Jason was trying to make certain Claire understood the situation was hopeless.

"Dozens, you say?" Claire asserted with anger in her voice. "Well, then—good!" Claire's face began to turn red. "'Tis about time for some payback, I am thinking!" she said, raising her voice.

Claire walked past the students and headed for the children. But before she went through the door, she turned back at them and said, "Off with you both, now. I'm telling you to leave!"

Then, Claire kicked the door open and began to make her way into the next tower. She waved her hand and opened the next door and walked in, at which point Lisa and Jason caught up to her.

"My Lady! It is too dangerous! There are too many!" Lisa insisted that Claire come with them.

She stopped walking and turned to both the students.

"Listen carefully, you two," Claire said sternly. "I am ordering you both out!"

Lisa, clearly very uncomfortable with having to stand up to Claire, said in a reluctant, weak voice, "No! I'm staying!"

"I'm staying too!" Jason added.

Claire looked at them as if they were fools.

"Alright then. Stay behind me, listen to what I tell you, follow my lead, and don't help me unless I ask for it!" she said with a stern but frustrated voice. "Do you understand?"

The two nodded their heads, and Claire walked off to where the children were trapped.

"Bloody damn students have a death wish," Claire thought.

The sun had risen and began to strongly illuminate the hallways. She approached the adjoining corridor and paused before she reached it. Slowly and carefully, she let her right eye peer around it. Sure enough, at the end of the corridor were several dozen Darksiders. Their swords were drawn, and they were all taking turns directing bolts of energy toward a doorway. Their power kept hitting an invisible barrier that was made visible only when their bolts of energy bounced off of it.

She backed away from the corner for a moment and looked at the two students. She whispered, "Last chance! It's about to get nasty and dirty in here, and you're already both covered in it! Are you sure you want to stay for this one? Maybe you should go and rest up."

They both insisted on staying. "Fine," Claire whispered as if they had made a big mistake. "Stay behind me! Watch my back!"

Once again, she peered around the corner.

"Let's get this over with!" she said.

Claire summoned her sword and walked out into the middle of the corridor. She shouted at all 30 or more of the Darksiders, "Good morning, dark and evil members of the Realm underworld! Can you not see the sun has risen?" She raised her sword and pointed at the windows. "'Tis time for your wake-up call!"

The entire back row of the Darksiders began to turn and raise their swords at her. Before they had a chance to do anything, Claire launched a bolt of power at them. Eleven or so of them were instantly reduced to dust.

Jason and Lisa were stunned by the display of firepower. They also could throw bolts of power and did. They were only able to knock Darksiders to the ground with them.

Now half of the remaining Darksiders turned their attention to Claire as the rest continued to try to break through the barrier. They began to launch bolts of power at Claire and the students. To Jason and Lisa's amazement, Claire's sword was able to absorb their attacks. Claire moved her sword in an arch from side to side and absorbed everything they could throw at her. The Darksiders were bewildered by her ability to defend against them. One by one, more of them turned from the barrier to attack Claire.

Finally, Claire looked at the students and said, "Turn away!"

This time, they listened to her, and with that, she raised her left hand inverted toward the ceiling and shouted, "Laith roid Cara duinn Solas!"

As she continued to defend against the Darksider attack, a brilliant bright ball of light appeared in her left hand. She threw it at the Darksiders, and turning away, she closed her eyes tightly. The ball of light exploded, blinding the Darksiders, and sent so much pain into their heads that they dropped their swords. The brilliant flash of light overcame even the ones who were facing away.

Claire turned back and just screamed as she charged and attacked them. She swung her sword again and again, and the students charged too. Whatever the students cut apart fell to the ground and died. Whatever Claire cut into was reduced to dust! Lisa and Jason had never seen anything like Lady Claire before. She fought like an avenging Angel.

All of the Darksiders were done in! Now, Claire approached the barrier, and with only a slight spark of light, she passed right through it. When the two students approached it, they were stung and stopped. It hurt! Claire turned around, and with a wave of her hand, she said, "Lig Teama Teigh thar!"

With that, Lisa and Jason followed Claire into the home of the White Robin. Claire opened the door very slowly and peered ahead as best she could. Carefully, she moved from room to room. She could feel the children near. Then, she heard a baby crying. She opened the door to the baby's room, and a sword came flying right at her face! She blocked it and blocked again!

"Laura!" Claire shouted.

But the 12-year-old blonde girl didn't hear her. The girl was deaf from fear. If one of the students had come in first and tried to block her with their swords, she would have cut them in two.

Laura struck again and spun and swung again and again. It was as if she was avoiding counterattacks, but no one was attacking her! It was eerie to observe, but Claire also understood now why Sara hadn't survived the battle. Obviously, she had given her sword to Laura to protect the baby. Claire continued to shout Laura's name, but the little girl was just scared out of her wits! Finally, Claire grabbed her by the wrist of her sword hand. The girl struggled to get away, but Claire shook her as hard as she could.

"Laura!" Claire shouted. "'Tis me, Aunt Claire!"

Laura stood silent for a moment. She began to focus. She whispered ever so slightly, "Aunt Claire?"

"Yes, dear, 'tis me!" Claire responded with a sweet, affectionate voice.

Laura wrapped her arms around her and began to cry. Then, she whispered in a panicked voice, "We have to be careful! The Darksiders are attacking!"

With a flash, Claire's sword vanished, and she responded by pushing the girl's hair back across her head. "Aye, lassie, they are gone now!" Claire held her head and looked deep into her eyes.

Laura looked back at Claire, and in a voice so cold Claire never thought she would ever her it come from a child's mouth, Laura said, "Mama is gone. The Darksiders took her!"

Claire picked her up and hugged her tightly. All Claire could do was cry and hug the little girl. Lisa came in and took her from Claire's arms. Claire moved to the crib where the baby lay crying and lifted him up into her arms. She gently held the child, and walking around, she tried to calm the baby. She walked out of the bedroom and into the main living room. When peering out the main picture windows, it became obvious that the hallway wasn't the only way the Darksiders had tried to break in. It looked as though they had tried to blast their way though the wall.

Laura came out of the bedroom, followed by Lisa. She walked up to the great picture window and peered out of it.

"That is where Uncle Harry died!" she pointed and told Claire as she stared at the courtyard below.

Claire walked up to view where she was pointing. There was only scorched earth below.

"He tried to protect a great animal with wings." Laura's voice was filled with pain. "The animal fought the dark ones as fire burned around them! I yelled at Uncle Harry to run, but he couldn't hear me."

"The Alfa male of the griffin pride," Jason said, thinking out loud.

"Aye," Claire said in sad agreement as she stared at the burnt courtyard blow. "No wonder the matriarch griffin fought as though she were possessed. They killed her mate."

Claire could not talk about Harry. She could not even say his name. She wasn't sure they were safe and couldn't handle the emotions she knew would flood her mind if she thought about him. The hope that had filled her heart and had driven her into the valley in search of Harry was replaced by an empty space.

Suddenly, the window began to open on its own. Everyone in the room backed away, not knowing what to expect.

"Laura, get behind me!" Claire said as she handed her the baby to hold as she prepared for an attack.

Then, the screech of a bird could be heard loudly as a great bald eagle landed on the windowsill. It was carrying a note.

"It's all right everyone," Claire said. "Lisa, take the baby from Laura," she instructed as she moved forward to greet the large bird.

Claire took the note from the bird. Then, it jumped back into the air, and the window closed by itself. Claire sat down on the couch and read,

"Claire,
Bring the boy back with you. I've appointed Phineenous Dickelbee as acting chancellor. He should arrive there by noon. Laura is to stay with him. He will hold the post until a new board can appoint someone of their choice. Send out a search party for Philo and retrieve Harry and Sara's swords!
—Cohan"

"Bloody hell, Cohan!" Claire said with anger. "You're a bloody coward!" she thought. "Your baby brother and sister-in-law are dead, your other brother is missing, and all you can do is write a note!'

"Bustard!" she said out loud.

"What's wrong? What has happened?" Laura asked. She had walked up to Claire.

Claire wrapped up the note and placed it in her pocket. Then, she looked at Laura.

"Lord Cohan has appointed a good man by the name of Doctor Phineenous Dickelbee as acting chancellor," Claire told the little girl. "He will be here by noon. He has ordered you to stay with him—" Then she paused. "—and to protect him."

"How am I supposed to do that?" the girl asked with a bewildered look on her face.

"You'll do as your mother taught you—the same way you protected your wee brother!" Claire looked into her eye. "We're all very proud of you, Laura. Lord Cohan is very proud of you! That is why he has given you this assignment."

Laura stared at her for a moment and then responded with a sincere voice of respect. "Yes, my Lady, I will do my best. Tell His Grace that no harm will come to the chancellor. Tell him I swear this!" She paused for just a moment and then asked, "Can we go and look for Daddy?" Then, she broke down and began to cry.

The little girl was a mess and yet so brave. Her tears dried on her face, and yet she chose to be brave. No wonder she had survived the night! Claire looked back at her very sadly and said, "I will see about your dad and tend to your mom and Uncle Harry."

The two hugged.

THE TOWN OF SUGARLOAF
CHAPTER 2

MARTIN MADE HIS days on his fishing boat and managing the family businesses. On this day, Martin, a tall older man well past 70 years in age, was making his way across the inlet of Sugarloaf Sound, a bay between the islands of the Florida Keys. The sun was low in the west as his long gray hair, held by a black band tied behind his head, blew in the wind. Carefully, his dark blue wrinkled eyes watched as his boat made its way past the reefs that were covered with many old wrecks—boat wrecks whose former captains were not nearly as experienced as himself.

To his back, several men on the lower decks talked over the day's catch. Three long swordfish hung by hooks in the breeze as the men toasted the day's victory with bottles of beer. Tall tales filled the air as to how hard each of the fish had fought and how long it took each of the day's fishermen to pull the fish in. For these men who spent their vacations chasing fish off of the coast of Florida, it was glorious, and Martin took some small pleasure in hearing their joy and funny tales.

Martin yelled out, "Jimmy, stand on the point now! I'm cutting the speed! Make sure the reef hasn't drifted inside the channel markers!"

Martin had a strong, hefty voice with the sounds of Ireland in it. Ireland was where he was born and where he learned to work the sea. In those days, fishing was a job that helped give him something separate from his family's world. Now, it was a great joy to teach so many thrill seekers the art of fishing. Martin gazed out across the water as he remembered how long ago that was and how much had changed since then. All he had ever wanted to be was a fisherman. But Martin was not born into a family of fishermen. He was born into a family with many responsibilities. As a boy, and then as a young adult, Martin had turned his back on those responsibilities. He pondered as he gazed at the silvery blue sea how different life would have been had he grown up a little sooner than later and had accepted rather than run from those responsibilities.

Jimmy, the deck hand, an older looking thin fellow with unusually long black hair with white streaks and the look of an unshaven overly tan pop star, now stood all forward and kept a keen eye as they moved closer and closer to shore. "I don't trust those channel markers!" shouted Martin.

He shouted the same thing every time the boat came in. Coral reefs were unpredictable, and in Florida they were everywhere. While the markers said it was safe to move through, the truth was that a shift in the current could pile sand up on any one of them in just a few short hours.

The boat sailed on as the small town and harbor of Sugarloaf began to fade in the distance. Like so many others in the Florida Keys, Sugarloaf was a tourist and fishing town. The landmass was so narrow there wasn't any room for a hotel near the road, and the environmentalists would not permit one to be built anywhere else. This was not really a problem because there were several bed and breakfasts, and Sugarloaf was easy to find. The harbor sat on the western side of U.S. Route 1. "The Big Red One," as some called it, was a road that began in Maine and ended in nearby Key West, Florida. It was one of the most-traveled roads in all of the Americas, and just like Martin, the people of Sugarloaf made their living from it. On the east side of the road was one of many beaches that lined the Florida Keys. Families would drive down for the day. Typically, fathers and sons headed for the boats, and wives and daughters headed for the beach.

Off to the north, the mainland and the sea channel ran close together near the mouth of the harbor. Standing in the distance was a young blond-haired boy of 11 or 12 years. Near him sat two cats and a dog. From the point of view of the people on the boat, the boy and animals didn't seem to be doing much of anything. The boy, whose name was Luke, was playing with a small sand crab. The rocks that marked the entrance to Sugarloaf were enormous. Their sizes were meant to keep the harbor safe from bad weather. Each time the crab moved away, Luke would push it back just to watch it crawl back down the rock again. Luke was just curious and entertained by the crab's reaction to being pushed about. The animals that surround him, on the other hand, two cats, one brilliant white and the other solid black, and a brown and white boarder collie, just sat and watched. A cat might have been expected to attack the crab. The dog might have been expected to chase the cats. Together, the three sat on different sides of the boy and looked around. Their ears were constantly rolling around in different directions.

Martin spotted the group and sounded the boat's horn. Luke looked up with a sign of happiness and smiled a big smile, began to wave, and watched as Martin, who was Luke's uncle, passed on by. Then, suddenly, a cat that had been sleeping inside the cabin of the boat came running outside and knocked into various items as it went in a big hurry up onto the boat's railing. The passengers were all surprised by the cat's sudden moves. All day long, the hairy brown and white cat lay around the boat as it ignored all but Martin. Now, it seemed to come to life and let loose with a very loud "meeeeeeooooooow!" to which the two cats onshore took immediate notice, looked directly at the boat, and responded with their own cat sounds. Then, the dog joined in with a single loud bark.

This animal talk amused the passengers, with one fellow turning to the other and remarking, "Now, I wonder what that group is going on about?" All of the passengers smiled in wonderment. Above them on the quarterdeck, Martin turned back away to resume steering the boat. He giggled almost silently under his breath at the passengers' reaction to the animals talking to one another. Talking to himself in a whisper, he said, "All of these Bennies. They have no clue about the world. They are just such a joy to watch."

Luke rose to his feet onshore and began to follow the boat as it made its way to the docks. He was tall for a boy of 12. His blond hair blew in the breeze as he jumped from one rock to the next, pacing the boat as it sailed into Sugarloaf Harbor. The animals ran with him and began jumping from rock to rock to keep up.

Part of the land near the harbor entrance was taken up by a baseball field, in which many boys and girls were involved practicing and were preparing to try out for the summer's Little League teams. In an effort to keep up with the boat, Luke moved along the edge of the baseball field. One of the boys pointed Luke out to some of the others. They turned to look, and then one of them shouted, "Look! It's the animal boy!"

It was a name Luke had heard before. The local boys didn't like the fact that he was followed about by cats and a dog. "Nature boy" and "freak" were also common reactions people had to him and his animals.

A few moments later, the boys started to pick up stones and throw them at Luke. One of the girls with them—a very pretty girl named Susie Wine, with light dusty brown hair—began to demand they stop such behavior.

"That is so immature!" she shouted.

As she repeated her demands, one of the cats with Luke stood upright on its hind legs and faced the boys.

"What a strange reaction by a cat," Luke thought.

Several of the rocks began bouncing off of the baseball backboard and right into the heads of the boys throwing them. It was silly to watch. The boys found themselves dodging their own rocks.

The girls laughed at them, and Luke found himself laughing. The cat went back to normal. "How odd for a cat to behave that way," Luke thought. It was as if someone had dangled a string in front of it. The boys, on the other hand, weren't throwing any more stones. They were off to treat their now bleeding heads.

"Well, that's the end of that," Luke thought. As if nothing at all had happened, he returned to pacing the boat into the harbor. As he began to walk, he heard a girl's voice.

"Hi, Luke."

Luke found himself face-to-face with Susie Wine.

"Hi, Luke," she repeated as if Luke had not heard her the first time, which wasn't true.

Luke had heard her; he was just surprised that the most popular girl in school would care to speak to him. She never had before. Luke always seemed to be surrounded by girls at school, just not Susie and her groupies. The truth was most of the time it was just girls who spoke to him—Luke didn't do much talking back. Mostly, he listened and nodded his head at them from time to time. But the girls from the most popular group never came near him. Now he was face-to-face with their fearless leader.

"Hi, Susie," Luke responded.

Luke neither liked nor disliked Susie. There was a reason she was most popular. She was an amazing combination of pretty, direct, playful, and possessed, with perfect timing when it came to being rude.

Each of the girls with Susie said in succession, "Hi, Luke," as if attendance in class was being taken. Luke nodded his head and smiled. They all seemed so happy to see him. It was all more than odd, which made Luke wonder what was going on.

"You shouldn't pay attention to Ralph and his male challenge groupies!" Susie announced. She was talking about the boys who were tossing stones at him.

"Ralph is a bootie brain!" a voice from behind the girls announced.

The girls turned, and Luke glanced over to see his one true friend, Buddy Sanders, arriving on the scene.

Susie squinted her eyes and smiled an evil smile as she inquired, " Buddieeee! It's almost supper time! Does your mommy know you're still outside?"

Buddy's hair was as dark as Luke's was light. He had freckles and green eyes, and he wore a T-shirt that said "Eatme."

"Susie, you must be having a bad day if you have nothing better to do than harass Luke here," he said smugly.

"Well, it's none of your business, but he was attacked!" Susie responded.

"Hi, Buddy," Luke quickly muttered between the verbal jousting.

"Whatzzzup?" Buddy responded before turning back to Susie.

"The bootie brain and his groupies already got to Luke once! That's why they throw stones when they see him instead of running after him!"

"What?" Susie sounded surprised. The group of girls just turned toward Luke, with their mouths wide open. Buddy began to laugh, and Luke was nodding his head with a smile on his face, not bothering to look at anyone because he knew he was turning red. Then, reluctantly, Luke stood upright, continued nodding his head yes, and stuttered, "Yep," followed by a brief pause. Then, when it seemed he wasn't being believed, he said, "Yes! About a year ago. School had let out early, and I knew no one would be waiting for me, so I decided to walk home. I had to cross Parker's Field. They just followed me. I think they were surprised that I was alone. When I reached the end of the field, they surrounded me."

"Surrounded you?"

Surprisingly, Susie had the sincere sound of distress in her voice. Buddy was equally amazed. "She's either for real," he thought, "or she's been a girl groupie leader for so long that no one can tell anymore when she's being real." Oddly, all of the girls were just staring at Luke.

"What happened?" Susie demanded.

"I'm not sure I should tell," Luke responded.

"Why?" several of the girls said in unison and then looked each other.

"Good question," Buddy added, drawing a look of distress from Luke.

Luke and his friends were so wrapped up in their conversation that none had noticed the appearance of a falcon overhead. Falcons were a rare sight in the Keys. It was moving at an unusually high rate of speed and circling as if it were preparing to attack. The two cats and the dog were paying very close attention. They were all alert with their tails in the air. The dog moved to position itself close behind Luke and then turned to keep his eye on the bird.

"If I tell you," Luke insisted, "the tough guys will find out, and they will come looking for trouble again." Luke thought that was the longest sentence the he had ever shared with any girl ever.

"So what?" Buddy said smugly.

"Don't be silly!" Susie replied. "We're all friends here, right?"

The girls with her simultaneously nodded their heads yes and said, "Right!"

"We are?" Buddy looked bewildered.

Susie gave Buddy a very grouchy look.

"Buddy, I hear your mommy calling. Go see what she wants so we can have an intelligent conversation here! It will be all right; you're not qualified to have such conversations anyway!"

"Susie has perfect timing when it comes to being rude," Luke thought.

The white cat stood on a railing. The group of kids still had not noticed their behavior. The cat looked over at Martin's boat, which had docked and was letting the remainder of the day's fishermen off. The cat that was on Martin's boat was lying on the top deck and not paying much attention to anything. The white cat looked at it and made a noise. The one on the boat looked up abruptly and jumped to its feet. It scanned the horizon with its eyes and ears and spotted the falcon almost immediately. Luke gazed over at the cat for a brief second but paid little attention.

"Ah ... well," Luke muttered with obvious apprehension. He wondered to himself whether this was a really good time to start listening to girls. For a brief moment, he gazed into their eyes and then volunteered, "They tried to beat me up!"

In that moment, the falcon dove for Martin's boat. The cat onboard let out a mean hissing noise, showed its teeth, and then leaped off of the top deck and headed for the bottom one, but where it should have landed, two human feet appeared instead. A young woman, tall in stature with deep, dark red hair and an angry look on her face, stood where the cat should have landed, but her eyes—her eyes had not changed! She had cat eyes! No! They changed! Now she had deep blue eyes. The falcon landed on the forward deck, and as it did, the tall redheaded woman raised her right hand inverted, and with a flash of light, a long bright shimmering sword appeared as if out of thin air! Then she shouted, "Martin! Watch your back!"

Martin was on the opposite side of the boat. The woman's alarm drew his attention, and a look of serious concern came over him as he moved to see what was happening. He paused a moment, looked back, and saw Luke and his friends at the edge of the dock. Edgy and sharp, the animals with Luke looked back at him. He raised his hand signaling to stay put.

In that moment, the falcon landed on the forward deck, transformed, and became another young woman. She wore a dark blue cloak with yellow trim and had black hair and black eyes. The redheaded women drew back her sword as if prepared to strike. Martin walked up from behind her.

"Wait, Marta!" he told the redheaded woman.

The girl in the cloak raised her hand as if to say hello. But in a rather sweet-sounding voice she said, "Please! There is no need for apprehension!" She shook her head slightly as she took a step forward. She seemed to recognize Martin, although he didn't think he had ever laid eyes on her before. She bowed to him and then looked him in the eye.

"Your Grace, I have been sent with an urgent message from the chancellor."

"Around here or around any place where there are Bennies about, I am called Martin!" he replied.

Marta still stood between the black-haired girl and Martin. She watched her every reflex, her every motion, ready to strike!

"Marta, put the sword down," Martin directed her.

"But," she responded with apprehension, "we don't know her!"

Martin turned and looked at her sternly and in a deep harsh voice said slowly and directly, "Aye, did you not hear what I told you, girl?" He glanced at her and wondered what her problem was.

In a reluctant voice, she responded, "Yes, Martin," and then lowered her sword and stood easy.

"Your Grrr–" the girl in the cloak stopped herself from muttering "Grace" again and then started her sentence over

"Martin," she said slowly and with a certain discomfort in addressing him that way. "The chancellor sends a warning, sir! For the past three days, black condors have been spotted in the northern counties, and they are flying search patterns. He thinks they are looking for you, your people, and the boy!"

"Who are you, girl?" he asked.

"I am Lieta sir, of the House of Cameron."

Martin didn't really seem to care about the message, or if he did, he wasn't willing to let on that he did.

"Well, Lieta," Martin said, "someone needs to instruct you better about what clothing to wear when you're out among the real world." Martin was deliberately changing the subject as if to distract her. "You need to draw less attention next time someone gives you a message to deliver. Mundane people are paranoid and easily frightened by us. Do you understand?"

Lieta bowed, "Yes, Your Gra–" Again, she stopped herself from saying it. "Yes, Martin!"

"Now," Martin said in a somewhat friendlier voice and taking a few steps toward her. "Go give my compliments to the chancellor and thank him for his warning."

"Yes, sir," she responded as she stepped backward, bowing yet again.

But just before he turned away, Martin said, "And Lieta— fly a wide route back away across the northern counties and be weary of black condors. Understand?"

"As you wish, sir," she responded. But this time as Lieta went to bow yet again, the falcon appeared, and Lieta was gone. The bird lifted off from the railing of the boat and into the sunset.

Concerned, Martin looked over at Marta as he walked past her and headed off the boat. "Go and tell the others the message," Martin said to her.

Marta smiled a big smile and giggled slightly as he walked by, and then she bowed to him. "Yes, Your Grace," she laughed.

"Go on with ya already!" He was abrupt, not thinking she was terribly funny.

With a short flash of light, her sword vanished as she responded yet again with a giggle and an even shorter bow. "Yes, Your Grace!" she said.

This time, Martin ignored her, and where Marta once stood now appeared a seagull. The gull leaped into the air and flew off.

Martin headed for the gangplank to go ashore. Jimmy was coming the other way, and he seemed very happy.

"Martin," he said, "the larger of the three fish weighed in at 71 pounds. Can you believe it?"

Martin smiled at him.

"That means," Jimmy continued, "that not only did we win the week and the month, but we also have a real chance at the summer's cup!"

"That's grand, Jimmy," Martin replied with a smile on his face. "Aye, 'tis something to be proud of!" Then Martin's face turned more serious. "We've had word from the chancellor," he said.

Jimmy became wide-eyed and very concerned. "The chancellor himself? Sent us a message?" Jimmy whispered in a serious tone.

"Aye," Martin replied. "He sends us a warning that black condors have been spotted circling the northern counties."

"Black condors!" Jimmy looked at Martin with fear. "I thought they were extinct!"

"Aye, suren they're supposed to be!" Martin replied. He looked around to see how Luke was getting on.

"Come fall, the chancellor is going to want that boy of yours in school—and we're not talking no Bennie school either!" Jimmy's tone was most serious.

"Yes, I think you're right. They could protect him better than we could, I'm believing. But I don't like the idea anyway!" Martin didn't sound sure of himself.

"But what about the condors?" Jimmy replied. "They are just the scouts! If the dark ones find the boy, they'll make a move on him, Martin! And all of us!"

Martin looked at him in the eye and said, "We'll just have to stand our ground."

"Stand our ground, is it?" Jimmy replied abruptly. "I stood up in the last battle against them! We didn't do so well! Oh, but that's right, Martin! You wouldn't be knowing that, would ya? You've never stepped inside the valley, has ya? Not even when your own brother needed ya!"

"Mind your attitude!" Martin said sternly.

Jimmy paused for a second while he glanced over at Luke and then back at Martin.

"Martin, you're 70 years in age! And I haven't fought anything bigger than a 71-pound fish in 12 years, not since you brought

the boy here! General Armstrong Custer had a better chance!"
Jimmy seemed to be trying to remind Martin of something.

"Maybe," Martin replied. "I promised my brother if anything happened to him, I would protect the children. I've let
my family down before. This time will be different! The dark
ones will do this boy no harm. On my life I swear that!"

Again Martin had turned to look at Luke. Jimmy was looking at Martin as if he had gone mad.

"We have to move the boy!" Jimmy insisted.

Martin didn't even look at him. "No," he replied. "There
is no place safer before the fall semester than here."

"The fall semester?" Jimmy replied in disbelief. "That boy
isn't trained in anything. He doesn't even know who and
what he is! He'll be lucky to make it through next week, let
alone to the fall semester."

"Not true," Martin insisted. "Sam has been training Luke
in the martial arts since he was less than five. He has even been
trained in the sword. True, the boy thinks that it's all just a
wee dance. But if he gets into trouble, his power will center,
and the strength he draws from that will turn any dancing into
a weapon. That should be enough protection for now."

"You underestimated the Darkside, Martin." Dismay filled
Jimmy's face. "They will do what they have to do to get to
that boy, and they will kill anyone who gets in their way!
They've done it before, and they'll do it again! And let us not
forget—you're the one who created this situation!"

"That's enough!" Martin had anger in his voice and his
eyes. "The sun is almost down. Go now! Give the boat a
wash down, fill the tanks, and check the oil, and then come
and get your supper!"

Jimmy just looked at him with continued dismay and
walked off to the boat.

Martin walked ashore and stepped up onto the main dock
that ran along the convenience store behind which most of
the boats in the Sugarloaf fishing fleet were kept. He made his
way toward Luke and his friends. Luke had not spotted him.
Martin was slowly moving up from behind, and as he did, he
began to overhear the conversation Luke was having.

"That's amazing, Luke!" Susie said. "So what happened?"

"Well," Luke responded reluctantly, "they kinda took turns rushing at me, and they kinda got tossed all over the field like rag dolls." Luke smiled a silly smile. "When they finally gave up, I left. I don't like fighting really or violence. If they had just let me pass, I would not have done anything."

Susie and the girls just stared at Luke for a moment. It was an awkward silent moment. All that could be heard was the wind, some seagulls, and a boat horn off in the distance. Then, the cute little 12-year-old Susie looked Luke in the eye and said, "You're lying!"

She posed for just a moment more, and then without saying another word, she turned and walked away. Then, just like dominoes falling, each of the other girls took their turn calling Luke a liar and then walked off to join Susie. Luke and Buddy just stood there and watched them walk away without saying a word. Then, they noticed that Martin had walked up from behind them.

"Have you been telling tall tales, Luke?" Martin sounded both friendly and curious.

Luke turned around and greeted his uncle with a big hug. "Hello, Uncle Martin," Luke said with a sense of happiness in his voice. "No, not this time," Luke responded. "I was actually trying to tell them the truth. But they are just girls, so what's the point anyway?"

"Yeah," Buddy said. "I've seen better heads on glasses of beer. Hello, Mr. Cohan!"

"Hello, Buddy," Martin responded. "I didn't know your parents let you drink beer. Are you coming for supper?"

"Ahhhhh, no, sir," Buddy said. "My mom has dinner, and that's just a saying! I don't drink beer. Well, not much anyway."

"Very well, then, you have a good night. Luke, say goodbye to Buddy. You'll see him tomorrow, I'm sure."

With that, Martin began to walk off toward home.

"Later, dude," Luke said.

"Later," Buddy replied.

Luke quickly caught up to his uncle.

"So you've been fighting, have you, Luke?" Martin inquired.

"Not really," Luke replied.

"Then, what was it you were telling the girls?"

"Well, last year when I was walking home, some of the jocks came at me in the field. It wasn't really a fight, not really." Luke didn't know whether his uncle would approve. He suspected not, but they had never talked about it.

"Well, Luke," his uncle began, "your name is Carter, but you're as much a Cohan as I am. When we get angry, we become strong. That is just part of who we are. We keep it to ourselves, and we don't share that fact with anyone. You understand?"

"Yes." Luke had never had occasion to argue with his uncle, but he had seen what happened when other people tried. It was pointless.

"You are right to avoid fighting, Luke. I heard what you said, and I was very glad to hear it!" Then, Martin turned and stopped and looked Luke in the eye.

"Always avoid fighting if you can, boy. If one comes your way, always make sure you're the last one standing. You are to protect yourself and your family and people who are too weak to help themselves. Do you understand me, Luke?"

"Yes, Uncle Martin!" Luke looked the old man in the eye. He was just happy not to have made his uncle mad at him. Luke was certain that telling girls the truth was going to get him into some kind of trouble.

The two of them made their way along a path to a small mini-island separated from the mainland by a short footbridge. The light was nearly gone as Luke and Martin moved toward a tall wooden house in the center of the island. Along the waterways, pelicans skimmed the surface of the water as they searched for a meal. The breeze was strong, warm, filled with the scent of salt, and very friendly.

The two cats and the dog were no longer keeping up with the boy and his uncle. They strolled slowly and divided their attention between watching the birds move across the water and Luke and his uncle walking home. They arrived at the island footbridge in time to watch Luke turn the corner to the house. Martin turned very briefly to look at the animals, nodded his head at them ever so slightly, and then followed Luke.

The animals looked around and then at each other. In that moment, the white cat changed. Where a small cat once stood, a tall, stern-looking sandy blonde–haired woman in an earth-colored dress that reached to her ankles now revealed herself. She stretched her arms as if she had just awoken from a sleep. The black cat became a woman of India who wore blue jean shorts and a white long-sleeve top. She also began to stretch. Then, the dog became a man from Asia in long blue jeans and a red top. He just stood there looking at the women.

The Indian woman looked at the others and said, "It's time for supper." She had an Australian accent.

They began to walk toward the house. "I thought we were in for real trouble when that falcon showed up," the woman in the dress commented casually as they made their way toward the house.

"Yes," the man replied. "If something had happened, you seemed well dressed for a fight."

"I can handle myself fine," she replied, seeming bored with his criticism, as if she had heard it all before.

"Yes, I am certain you will impress some Darksider with your fashion sense," the Asian man stated with an attitude as the three of them finished walking up to the front door of the house.

"Enough!" the Indian woman insisted, pausing at the door. "It's time to eat. Let's go in here and act like Bennies and not get heartburn in the process!"

"You don't think Bennies get heartburn?" the tall sandy-haired women smartly commented. Then the Indian woman turned and exhaled in a sign of frustration as she went, and the others followed her in. The last of the day's light shone on Sugarloaf, and then it was over.

AND SO IT BEGINS
CHAPTER 3

SCHOOL HAD FINISHED for the summer, and it was hard to sleep when the sun broke the horizon over Sugarloaf. Luke's friends liked to sleep in, but his bedroom faced the sunrise, and the window was always open. The sound of the sea and its birds were great to wake up to. This morning there were voices beneath the window that seemed to be walking away.

Luke jumped out of bed and moved to the window in time to see his uncle, Jimmy, and Marta walking across the footbridge to the mainland. It was Sunday, and everyone was off. Still the boat had to go out because the tourist season had begun and the weekends were all booked.

Luke knew Jimmy and Marta very well. They worked as deck hands for his uncle and lived in what was called "the little house." The little house was where all of the workers lived. Luke wasn't sure why they called it the little house. It was nearly as large as the main house and sat on the far side of the mini-island that his family owned. The island had no name. It sat at the edge of a small river that fed into Sugarloaf Sound. At the point near where the river met the Sound was where Uncle Martin had his pearl farm. It wasn't much to look at, just several sets of docks lined with cages that were below the water level. The average passerby would not even recognize what it was.

Luke put on a pair of shorts and a T-shirt and made his way down the stairs. He was being very quiet, or at least as quiet as the squeaky floorboards would allow him to be. He did not want to wake Aunt Claire. Aunt Claire was not Uncle Martin's wife; she was his sister-in-law. Her husband, Harry Cohan, was someone who Luke had never met. No one seemed to talk about him much. Beyond the picture that hung on the living room wall, Luke really didn't know much about Harry.

Luke made his way down the stairs and into the great hall. The great hall was an unusually large room with a dining table in the center and enough chairs to seat 30 people. Next to it was a kitchen large enough to feed 30 people. Believe it or not, during the pearl harvest, there were at least 30 or more people to be fed every day.

Luke moved toward the door beyond the great hall. To the far side of the door was the large living room with Uncle

Harry's picture hanging in it. Uncle Harry always just seemed to be staring straight ahead, usually right at the door. But this morning, he seemed to be staring at the window beyond the great hall. Luke thought this was rather odd. "Pictures must look different in different light," he figured. So Luke thought no more about it as he opened one of the twin doors that led out to the front yard. The door closed, Luke was gone, and the eyes in Uncle Harry's picture blinked.

When Luke stepped outside, he faced the sunrise. It was just about breaking the horizon. To the east of the house, on a very large flat top rock, was Sam. Luke was told that the rock was something left behind by the Army Corps of Engineers way back when they cleared the channel into Sugarloaf Sound.

Sam is a man's name, but Sam was a woman. Originally, she was from China. Sam was rather short, with a slender body and deep dark black hair that extended below her waist. She had worked for the Cohans for nearly 12 years. Like so many others who were employed there, Sam arrived shortly after the Great Holocaust of the Griffin Valley. Sam was a survivor of many battles of that dark night, which never really left her mind, particularly when she looked at her scars or awoke from a nightmare. Sam found a haven in Sugarloaf. One of the ways she treated the pain of that night was with a regiment of meditation and the discipline of the ancient Asian arts her father had taught her as a child.

Most mornings Sam could be found on top of the great flat rock on the Cohans' little island. She sat on the rock and faced the sunrise. Her legs were crossed, and her arms lay on her legs with her hands facing upward. Her real name was Pei Shan Shih, or in English, "Stone Jaded Coral." It was a name given to her by her father. But even in Chinese, her name was difficult to pronounce, so her nickname was Sam.

Every morning Sam climbed on the great flat top rock and faced the sun. She told Luke it was her way of saying good morning to God and thanking him for another day. She of course never explained why it was so important to do so. Every morning Sam also danced on the rock. Well, that is what Luke thought it was. Every morning Luke would join in. By example Sam would teach Luke the dance, which in reality was an ancient martial art. Sam was teaching Luke how to protect himself without having to explain why it was so important that he learn.

The dance was precise and full of flowing moves that caused the body to move in every which way it could. To do the dance, the mind had to relax and focus at the same time. Luke started when he was just four years old. He was six years old before he could perform the dance on his own.

Now Luke climbed on the rock, and Sam was standing motionless facing the sunrise. Without looking at Luke, Sam said, "It's a good day to be alive, Luke."

"Yes," Luke replied with a happy voice.

Sam struck a pose and gripped her hands together and then pushed them out in front of her. Luke closed his eyes and struck the same pose and likewise locked his hands and pushed them in front of him. With their eyes closed, Luke and Sam unlocked their hands, and with their palms moving outward and inward, their arms stretched from side to side in every which way one could imagine. The motion was completely synchronized, and every motion that followed the last became more and more complicated. Yet Sam's and Luke's eyes remained closed. Soon the motion extended to their legs. They turned and stood on their toes and then changed from foot to foot and turned around slowly. Against the sun, the two cast a stunning ballet, sometimes blocking the light, and long morning shadows danced on the waters of Sugarloaf.

From behind them came three individuals. There was the Indian woman whose name was Lorraine Paul, the sandy blonde woman whose name was Boozu Omak, and the Asian man whose name was Sonny Kim. Sonny was Sam's husband. Lorraine and Boo, as she was called, worked for Luke's uncle on the pearl farm. They had been there as far back as he could remember, and everyone was treated like family.

The group climbed on the great flat rock also and lined up behind Sam and Luke. Once again Sam struck the starting pose. This time all five of them closed their eyes and began to move in unison. For nearly a half-hour, the five of them created a perfectly synchronized ballet on the rock. Then Sam struck a final pose and turned to face the other four. She bowed to them, and they bowed to her. Without a spoken word, the five of them picked up long straight sticks that had been left on top of the rock.

Luke faced off with Lorraine and Boo with Sonny. They drew back into a striking pose, and when Sam lowered her stick, they began to strike at each other. It was a continuation of the dance. The moves were the same, but now they had sticks that tested and improved each other's reflexes.

For each lunge of the stick, there was a countermove and a dance move that one had to perform to prevent oneself from being stung by an opponent's stick. Luke had been stung many times before. He knew Lorraine would test his reflexes as he would test hers. The point was to feel the control and coordination of one's mind over one's body. To Luke, it was also a game and a competition. Luke did not like to fight, but he loved to win.

"Today," Luke thought, "Lorraine is not going to sting me!"

Lorraine continued to strike, and Luke defended. Then Luke began to spin after each strike. This left Lorraine outside of her range to strike back. Soon Lorraine was on the defensive and was unable to counter Luke's strikes and spins. Just when Luke thought he was winning, Sam made a strike at him. Luke was stung and thought, "Whatzup with that?"

He ignored the pain, and when Sam tried again, Luke successfully blocked her. Now he had Lorraine to this left and Sam to his right striking at him. He was fully defensive until he began to jump and spin between them, forcing the girls to shift their positions in order to strike at him. Now Luke had both of the girls on the defensive. They were unable to shift positions fast enough to strike at Luke. They could only protect themselves.

"Kewl!" Luke thought.

Then, Luke was stung again. This time it was Sonny!

"Sonny!" Luke shouted. But Sonny just smiled at him.

Luke's choice was to give up or defend against Sonny. He began to spin-dance and circle the top of the rock. He kept his opponents in motion and forced them to correct their positions to get at him. The speed of motion was amazing to watch. One wrong move and Luke would be stung three times as hard! Then, he was stung yet again! This time it was Boo!

OK, now he was in real trouble. He wasn't going to win anything today! He wanted to get mad, but that would break his concentration. All he could do now was spin, step, circle, and turn. He couldn't lunge at anyone. He could barely move his stick fast enough to defend himself! Then suddenly a loud female voice shouted high and clear, "Enough! Enough, I said!" It was Aunt Claire.

Everyone stopped right away. A tall redheaded woman of about 38 years of age stood on the sand below the great rock and looked up at them.

"Go on with yas, now! The breakfast is on, and then we need to dress for church!"

The five on the rock had finished their dance and were now staring down at Claire and were breathing very heavily. They stood there for a moment and nodded their heads in agreement. Then they turned to one another and bowed. They dropped their sticks and jumped to the sand below and slowly began to move toward the house.

"Luke!" Aunt Claire shouted. "Look at you! Hot and sweaty! You are to have a shower before you dress for church!"

Luke was out of breath and simply nodded his head in agreement. Then he looked over at Lorraine and Sam and smiled and seemed to laugh a little. They just smiled back at him and each other. Luke knew that they tried to get the best of him and failed. Luke had gotten what he wanted. He wanted to win, and he did. He did it by not losing. Still, he said nothing because tomorrow was another morning, and they would certainly try to make sure it didn't happen again. Sonny put his arm over Luke's shoulders. He was also out of breath. He smiled at Luke, gave him a quick hug, and then rubbed the top of his head as he moved off toward the little house. Sonny didn't like breakfast.

Luke finished his breakfast and soon he, Aunt Claire, Boo and Lorraine were on their way to church. The church wasn't far, just on the other side of the convenience store. Sonny and Sam didn't go to church. They usually took Sunday off.

As the group moved across the footbridge, there on the far side just waiting was the Border Collie that followed Luke around everywhere. They walked past the dog as if he wasn't even there. The dog just stared at them as they walked by, waiting to be recognized. Nothing happened, so he began to follow.

They passed the docks and the Sugarloaf Convenience Store. On the far side of the main road sat the Old Sailors' Prayer House. It was a small church that marked the beginning of the main beach, an old wooden structure that had been painted white. It was also raised off of the ground by several pillars. The pillars were typical seaside construction. They permitted water to flow under the church during bad weather. Combined with the single steeple and bell tower, they gave the church an imposing look.

Every Sunday as far back as Luke could remember, he came to this church, and like every other Sunday, an old retired priest by the name of Father Penniccini stood out front and greeted worshipers first as they entered and again as they left. The priest was a short gray-haired Italian fellow who had made it into his eighties. Every weekend he had four services: one after sunset on Saturday—that was the one Uncle Martin always went to—one Latin service at sunrise, one in Spanish, and finally the one Luke went to. It was simply known as the "eleven o'clock service."

Luke, Aunt Claire, and friends walked in and took their seats. The service began, and on the first sound of music, outside, a very small man dressed in green, with pointed ears, bright red cheeks, and a thick, short walking stick, appeared and began to make his way around the pillars beneath the church.

The dog sat on a sand dune and watched this amazing and peculiar little man moving around. He also observed the arrival of two bald eagles high in one of the trees opposite the church. They also seemed very intrigued by the arrival of this small and unusual person.

The very short green-covered man made his way first to the back of the church, climbed on the windowsill, and began to carefully scan the people inside. He was also able to jump silently from one window to the next as he continuously observed the service. Nobody noticed him.

When it seemed he was finished, again at the backside of the church, he jumped down to the yard below. Well, rather, he floated down. The little man was about to walk away when he heard a sound that caught his attention. It was a dog sound from behind him. He turned around to discover Luke's Border Collie directly behind him, standing nearly as tall as himself and looking him right in the eye.

"Oh," he said in a deep Irish sounding voice. "Suren you'd be a fine looking puppy!"

Calling a dog nearly his own size a puppy seemed a little bizarre. As he reached out to give the dog some friendly petting, the dog began to change! Rising above him, the little man watched in amazement as Sonny appeared and the dog vanished. Sonny didn't look very happy.

"Who are you?" Sunny said in a voice certain to lead anyone to feel they were in deep trouble.

"Well, now," the short little man answered, seemingly unperturbed at Sonny's sudden appearance. "Suren that was a really neat trick. What have we here? Sonny Kim, is it?"

"You know who I am?" Sunny was surprised.

"Aye, yes, of course, but you don't have to worry; I am not a Darksider," the little green-covered man replied with a smile.

"I already know that," Sonny said. "The church has a gargoyle on each corner. If you had been evil, they would have brought you down the moment you came onto holy ground." Sonny then bent his knee to look in the little man's eyes. "It's the only reason I haven't cut you into little pieces yet!" Sonny was very serious, and the tone of his voice made this fact very clear to the little man. Sonny stood again, held up his hand inverted, and with a flash of light, a sword appeared in it.

"Last warning, little man! Who are you, and what are you doing here?" Sonny had anger in his face and began to raise his sword.

"Stop!" The wee man said, raising his walking stick. "I'll be telling you my name," he said, seemingly to show respect. "My name is Michaleen Og, and I am a leprechaun."

Then as if he wanted to share a secret, he leaned toward Sonny, and raising his hand to his mouth as if he were preparing to whisper, he said, "I am not the one you should be worrying about, now am I?"

"A leprechaun?" Sonny seemed confused. "Why should I or anyone else not be worrying about a leprechaun who just happened to show up in the middle of the state of Florida?"

"No, no, not me you should be worried about," the leprechaun replied. "Michaleen Og would never hurt a fly! But me brother, me brother is the one you should be worried about!"

"Your brother?" Sonny seemed confused.

"Aye, yes, me brother, Shamus Og. He's the naughty one!"

"Why?" Sonny demanded.

Michaleen leaned over once again as if he wanted to share a secret.

"You should be worried about Shamus because Shamus is right behind you!"

Sonny turned sharply, and there behind him stood yet another leprechaun. His walking stick was fully extended and pointed right at Sonny. Before Sonny could say a word or make a move, a burst of smoke jumped out from the end of the leprechaun's stick. Sonny was frozen solid. He fell backward and lay there like a statue that had been pushed over.

Inside the church, both Boo and Lorraine sensed there was something wrong. They looked at each other and then got up from different sides of the same pew and made their way out the back. Luke watched them leave and was surprised by it. It was very uncharacteristic, especially for Lorraine, who loved attending church services. Aunt Claire knelt with her head down as she prayed, completely unaware of what was going on around her. So Luke got up and followed the girls out to see what was up.

Luke watched as Boo and Lorraine spread far apart across the churchyard. At first they were very silent and took careful steps so as not to make a sound. They seemed to be searching for something, but Luke did not understand what it might be. Finally, they stopped and looked at each other and then began again. This time Boo began to shout slightly, "Sonny!"

Then, Lorraine did likewise. "Sonny!" she shouted.

They both appeared to want to get Sonny's attention, which seemed very strange to Luke because Sonny was a Buddhist person and did not attend church. Then, the two women did something that both startled and amazed Luke. They raise their hands inverted, and with flashes of light, swords appeared! Luke was stunned. He had never seen anything like it before, and for the first time, he felt fear. He sensed that there was something very wrong. He wanted to go and help, but instinctively, he stayed put and silent. He had no idea where these feelings were coming from. But he knew what to do!

Boo and Lorraine made their way to the sand dunes near the edge of the church's parking lot. They kept calling for Sonny, which Luke continued to think was so odd. As Lorraine began to step on one of the sand dunes, a shadow raced past her so quickly it was a blur.

"Wow!" Luke thought. "What the heck was that?"

Then, the shadow raced back again, and a second shadow came racing through! The two blurs struck the girls on the back of their legs. Their feet were knocked out from under them, and they were sent crashing down on their backs! They hit the ground so hard they actually bounced a little.

Boo yelled, "Son of a—" she stopped just short of saying a bad word and rolled over moaning, "Oh, my back!"

Lorraine also shouted, "What the bloody hell was that?"

Boo pushed herself up on her knees and moaned, "I haven't a clue!"

Lorraine also began to recover, but no sooner had the pair made it to their feet when the two blurry motion figures came flying in at them again. This time, they hit the girls' swords and sent them flying high up and away.

Stunned, the girls took one step to recover their swords when the blurry motion figures came flying in yet again! Once again the girls' legs came flying out from beneath them.

Once again Boo and Lorraine found themselves moaning on their backs.

Again, they pushed themselves up, but instead of shock on their faces, this time there was pure anger.

"All right!" Boo shouted at the top of her lungs, no longer caring she was in a churchyard or whom her language might offend.

"Someone is about to get themselves handed a can of whoop ass!"

"Right!" Lorraine shouted loudly.

Boo raised up onto her knees and found herself face-to-face with Michaleen Og. Lorraine likewise had made it to her knees but found herself face-to-face with Shamus.

Boo's look was one of total surprise. "A leprechaun!" she said.

Loraine, who was equally surprised, said, "What the hell is a leprechaun?" Shamus just smiled at her and pointed his stick but said nothing.

Luke, who was hiding behind the church steps, whispered to himself, "Leprechaun?"

"Not so tough without your sword, hey, witch?" Michaleen said defiantly.

Boo looked at him with anger and said, "Wrong!" In the same moment, Lorraine shouted, "Right!"

Simultaneously, both girls lifted one knee, and in near perfect unison, their opposite leg flew underneath and behind the legs of the leprechauns, who were taken by surprise. The girls jumped to their feet, and the swords vanished from where they had fallen and flashed back into their hands. This all happened so quickly that the leprechauns recovered only in time to see the gleaming shape of swords being raised above them into a striking position.

Boo shouted, "Say goodbye, you little green rodent!"

At the very last moment, as the two women made to strike with their swords, the leprechauns raised their sticks, and smoke shot out right into the girls' faces.

Lorraine and Boo were frozen like statues, very much resembling the Statue of Liberty, only without the book. They stood for moment and then fell over backward stuck in the same position they had frozen in.

"No!" Luke shouted in shock.

The leprechauns turned and looked at each other, and with a blur of motion in an instant, Luke found himself face-to-face with both of them.

"Good morning, Mr. Cohan," Michaleen said.

"'Tis a grand morning, Mr. Cohan," the Shamus proclaimed.

"My name isn't Cohan," Luke insisted.

"No?" Shamus said with a question in his voice.

"Suren we'll be begging your pardon if we've made a wee mistake," Michaleen announced.

Nervously, Luke responded, "Mr. Cohan is my uncle. I am Luke—Luke Carter!"

"Aye!" Michaleen said. "Well, you're the one the chancellor sent us to fetch, I'm thinking!" Michaleen had tricked Luke into telling him who he was.

"Aye, I am thinking it too," Shamus agreed.

"Chancellor?" Luke said perplexed. "What chancellor? What are you talking about?"

"Professor Phineenous Dickelbee, chancellor of the Citadel in the Great Griffin Valley behind the Adirondack Great Hole in the Wall!" Shamus announced.

"Griffin what? What's a Citadel?" Luke insisted with a mystified look on his face. He didn't have any clue what they were talking about!

The two leprechauns were wide-eyed and insulted that the boy didn't know who the chancellor was. But before they could speak their disappointment, a new voice was heard.

"It's a school—a college and university for people of the magic realm."

Luke and the leprechauns turned to their side only to find that Buddy had managed to sneak up on them. He was clever enough to sneak but not bright enough to keep his mouth shut.

"Dude—" Luke said slowly with surprise. "You know what he is talking about?"

"I've never met leprechauns before," Buddy said thinking out loud.

"He can see us, Shamus!" Michaleen said with total surprise.

"Suren he can," Shamus replied with surprise and shock.

Then, the leprechauns pointed their sticks at him, and Luke shouted, "No! Don't hurt him!"

Buddy raised his hands over his head as if he wanted to surrender. "I don't want no trouble," he insisted fearfully.

"If he can see us, he's a witch," Michaleen announced.

"Aye, and if he's a witch, he's gonna be making trouble for us!" Shamus insisted.

Both of the leprechauns gave Buddy a mean look.

"No!" Luke demanded. "He's my friend, and he won't hurt anyone! I promise! Right, Buddy?"

Buddy stood with his hands raised. He nervously nodded his head in agreement.

"Then, how is it that he knows about Citadel, and you don't?" Michaleen insisted.

"That's a good question!" Luke responded with a perplexed look on his face. "So, Buddy, tell us! How is it that you know this stuff?"

"My mom is a witch, and I am enrolled at the Citadel this year," Buddy replied, seeming very nervous about making such a revelation. In fact, he was turning pale.

"There you go," Luke insisted. "Buddy isn't going to hurt anyone! No need to hurt him the way you hurt the others." Luke was trying to sound calm.

"Hurt what others?" Michaleen said as he relaxed his stick from pointing at Buddy. "We haven't hurt no one!"

"We don't go around hurting people!" Shamus announced while keeping his eye on Buddy.

"Aye, suren and we don't!" Michaleen insisted, looking right at Luke.

"Then, well, then, ah—what did you do to Lorraine and Boo?" Luke's anger was obvious but cautious. He could still see his statue-like friends lying on the ground near the far side of the churchyard.

"They'll be fine!" Michaleen said.

Luke and the leprechauns began to take a few steps away from Buddy and toward the women who now looked like a pair of Greek statues that had been pushed over on their sides.

Luke glanced at his two friends and turned to the leprechauns and shouted, "Why did you do that to them?"

The leprechauns were surprised at the anger this boy showed them.

"No need to be worrying, Mr. Carter," Michaleen insisted. "As soon as we leave, they will begin to thaw out, and when the sun rises again, they'll be good as new!" Both of the leprechauns were staring at Luke and were nodding their heads yes and smiling at the same time. Buddy still had his hands up in the air and was watching from the other side of the churchyard.

"Then leave!" Luke demanded.

"Aye, suren we'll be doing just that right away, me lad!" Michaleen sounded cautious. Shamus kept agreeing with him, "Oh, yes, right away, Mr. Carter, before anyone else shows up!"

"Well?" Luke looked at them with a question on his face. There was a strange pause for moment while the leprechauns looked at each other.

"Oh! Right!" Michaleen said. "But first we have to give you what we came to give you!"

"Right!" Shamus agreed. Then he thought for a second, and with a dumb look on his face, he turned to Michaleen and said, "What did we come to give him?"

Michaleen looked at Shamus in frustration. "Me stick!" he said.

"Your stick?" Luke looked at him with a question on his face.

"Your stick?" Shamus said with a question in his voice and bewildered look on his face.

"Aye, yes, take me stick," Michaleen said. He looked at Luke and lifted his stick in an effort to hand him it. "I'll be leaving it with you, and Shamus and I will be on our way."

"Don't trust them, Luke!" Buddy shouted.

"Shut your mouth, you!" Shamus said, flashing him another mean look. "You'll be keeping it shut, or you'll be stuck with your hands in the air till morning, I'm thinking!"

Buddy looked back with a sufficient show of intimidation. Luke heard him, but he wanted this over with so he could help his friends. Luke reached for Michaleen's stick, and as he grabbed hold of it, his hands became stuck. He could not let go! Suddenly, a crack of thunder could be heard, and it was a bright sunny day. Out of the sky came a bright shiny light. But, no, it wasn't a light!

"It's—it's—it's a rainbow!" Luke said, thinking out loud and stunned by the site of it.

All at once, a rainbow arched out of the sky and surrounded Luke and the leprechauns. Buddy watched as the three were surrounded by it, and then they disappeared within it! As quickly as it appeared, it arched back up into the sky from where it came. They were gone!

With his hands still in the air and a frightened look on his face, Buddy stood in the churchyard just staring in shock at the place where Luke had been.

"Oh, my God! They're gone!" he yelled.

THE PEARL STREET MALL
CHAPTER 4

ON A CEMENT sidewalk, a rainbow flashed. In the next moment, Luke appeared with the two leprechauns at his side. "Where am I?" he thought. "What happened?" He was in a huge city and was surrounded by skyscrapers.

Luke had never left the Florida Keys. He had seen skyscrapers only in pictures and on television, and now they surrounded him. He was both stunned and amazed. It was hard to believe anyone could build something so large that it blocked the sun. The streets were very wide and worn. Oddly, there did not seem to be anyone around. The streets were deserted, which gave a kind of lonely look to them.

"Welcome to New York City!" Michaleen announced.

"This is New York?" Luke said with amazement in his voice. "How did we get here? Why did you bring me here?"

"We came by rainbow and the magic of my shillelagh!" Michaleen said, holding up his stick.

"Your stick brought us here?" Luke said. He wondered how stupid a kid the leprechaun thought he was to believe that.

"'Tis not just a stick," Shamus said sternly.

"Aye, no, it isn't," Michaleen agreed.

"Looks like a stick to me!" Luke said. He was having trouble believing anything they said, and now the he had been kidnapped, he didn't mind being rude about it!

"'Tis the magic of the leprechauns it carries! It's why we can't be seen by nonmagical folk. It's how we travel and share the luck and blessings of the Irish with the world!" Michaleen told him, as he and Shamus watched Luke carefully. For them, it was hard for them to believe the nephew of the great Martin Cohan, and the son of the White Robin, didn't identify with the magical realm.

"Well, I can see you, so them dopey sticks can't be working too well," Luke said, his voice soft and condescending. He didn't seem to care whether the sticks worked.

As the three talked, they also began to walk along the deserted streets.

"The reason you can see us is because you are part of the magical realm just like us," Shamus insisted.

"I don't know where you two come from! I doubt it's planet Earth," Luke said. He was making it clear that he didn't like either of them very much. He continued not believing them. Besides, he was too busy being amazed by New York City. He had never before been surrounded by buildings that stretched into the sky. He found himself continuously looking up as they moved along the sidewalk. He was in a place and he knew not where or why. "Against these buildings, I feel so small," Luke thought. "Maybe I am small!" The three walked to the corner and stopped for a moment. Luke read the street sign that said "Pearl Street."

"What am I doing here?" Luke shouted. "Why did you kidnap me?" Luke was clearly becoming frustrated.

"You're here to claim your inheritance!" Michaleen insisted.

"Aye!" Shamus agreed. "Your inheritance it 'tis!"

Luke glanced over to the opposite corner. There was a telephone booth. He looked back at the two little green-covered men, and then he began to cross the street. He announced, "I am going to call the police!"

Michaleen and Shamus looked at each other with panic. Then, they ran in front of Luke.

"Stop where you are!" Michaleen shouted at him. He raised up his stick and pointed it at Luke.

Luke had already seen what the leprechaun's stick could do. He was scared. He was more scared than he had ever been in his entire life, but he wasn't going to show them he was scared. Sam had taught him that when problems arose and emotions were strong, he would have to choose to use his head, or the emotions would make the choices for him. Until this moment, Luke had not understood what she meant. He did now. He was quiet for an instant, and he thought. He decided to forget about the phone and change the subject—something his uncle was famous for when he didn't want to talk about something.

"Where are all of the people? It's a big city, and there's no one here," Luke said. He looked at the leprechauns for an answer.

"Aye, 'tis Sunday morn," Michaleen responded as he lowered his stick. "Sunday morn in downtown New York has few if any in and around it." Once again, the three began to walk along the sidewalk. "This is the oldest part of the city, the business district, so no one is about on Sunday morning."

"Why are we here?" Luke knew he had asked that question before, but he didn't understand the first answer, so he decided to give it another try.

"We're going to buy your supplies so you can go through the Hole in the Wall and start school," Michaleen explained to him.

"Aye!" Shamans agreed. "The Hole in the Wall! Suren you'll be safe once we reach the Citadel!"

Shamus seemed a bit emotional about it. From his reaction, Luke sensed a bit of honesty. "Something is going on here," he thought. "They're up to something! If they were going to hurt me, they would have done so by now!" That didn't mean he was about to trust these two freaks! But all this talk about safety did get his attention. Luke never hurt anyone and couldn't understand why someone would want to hurt him. He was keeping his mouth shut about these things. He figured Uncle Martin would be coming after him soon, and he would get it all sorted out then.

Luke began to walk, and the two leprechauns led him toward an old wooden building. It seemed very out of place. It was the only wooden building in sight. Its size was dwarfed against a skyline that soared hundreds of feet above it. Steel and cement surrounded this wooden building in every direction. When they finally made it to the front entrance, there was a sign that read:

"The Roosters Neck Inn
George Washington slept here."

"George Washington!" Luke said out loud. He was surprised.

"Who?" Shamans said passively.

"George who?" Michaleen asked.

"Washington!" Luke looked at them as if they were complete dopes. "You guys don't know who George Washington was?"

"Well," Michaleen stated, "we're a little weak on Bennie history."

"Aye, suren that is the case," Shamus agreed.

"Duh! He was the first president of the United States!" Luke responded. He thought, "These two losers are hopeless!"

"Aye, president was he? We'll be going inside now," Michaleen insisted. "If George the president shows up, we'll be sure to shake his hand, we will!"

"Why?" Luke wanted to know.

"Well, you seem to know who he is. Don't you want to shake his hand?"

"No! He's dead!" Luke said in frustration. "Why are we going inside?"

"Because it's the only entrance to the Pearl Street Market," Michaleen told him.

Luke continued not to trust these two creatures and was feeling very uncomfortable about being led around by them. On the other hand, aside from kidnapping him and threatening him with a stick, they didn't really seem all that bad— except for the odor, of course. From the smell of them, hygiene didn't seem to be a high priority. On the other hand, taking a ride on a rainbow was both new and kewl!

Luke entered the inn. It didn't smell too good either. There seemed to be a dusty mildew odor that filled the rooms. There was smoke from tobacco and a few odors that were so terrible Luke didn't want to know what they were.

"Eeww! Yuck!" Luke said to the leprechauns. "It smells worse than the boys' locker room in here! It smells like someone's butt!"

Luke wasn't surprised to learn the leprechauns didn't smell anything. The three walked through the main entrance hall of the inn, into what looked like a sitting room that seemed to have been decorated when George Washington slept there.

"I guess they wanted the place to look the same just in case George came back for a visit," Luke thought.

Luke felt as though he were moving backward in time. There were people dressed in George and Martha's clothing too. They all had cloaks on, and the women wore long colonial dresses. The men were sitting and drinking and smoking unusually long pipes. Groups moved in and out of a bar adjacent to the sitting room. Luke didn't drink alcohol at all.

"But if I did," he thought, "first thing on a Sunday morning wouldn't appeal to me." Some of the people were quite loud. The only thing louder than the arguments was the laughter. Luke was starting to get a strong feeling of being out of place or at least in the wrong place. "Wrong! That's it," Luke thought. "This all seems so wrong and strange even for a big city like New York."

At first, no one seemed to pay much attention to them. "I guess two leprechauns and a kid from Florida come through here on a regular basis," Luke thought. The three moved closer and closer to the bar. It was a bit dark in there. The men sitting around the bar also had long pipes with smoke rising. Some among them wore large hats. It was difficult to get a good look at them. Their faces seemed distorted, which was also true of some of their bodies. Luke wasn't certain they were human. It gave him a very creepy feeling. He wasn't going in no matter what stick anyone pointed at him!

"Oh, God! What am I doing here?" Luke thought. Then, a brown-haired woman moved out of the bar and toward the three of them.

"Hello, Shamus! It's been a long time, hasn't it? What brings you to the city?" she asked.

"This woman seems happy and surprised to see the little green loser," Luke thought. Then, she turned to Michaleen, and with a distinctly not so friendly voice she said, "Oh, hello to you too, Michaleen."

Michaleen, to Luke's amazement, just looked up at her and then uncharacteristically looked away without saying anything. Luke got the distinct impression that they didn't like each other.

"And," she said, "who is this fine young lad you have with you this morning?"

"Margaret, this is himself, Master Luke Carter," Shamans replied. Michaleen turned about at his brother. He was surprised to hear Luke being introduced. He raised up his stick and knocked Shamus over the back of his head with it. Shamus turned at his brother.

"Now, what was that about?" Shamus said demandingly, raising his own stick and making as if to strike back.

"We'll not be sharing people's names today!" Michaleen seemed quite angry at Shamus. Then, Shamus just stared at him a moment. Margaret, on the other hand, was speechless and stood staring at Luke.

"You need not worry, Michaleen Og," Margaret insisted.

She continued to stare at Luke. Luke wasn't feeling too comfortable with the look she was giving him. No one had ever looked at him that way before. "She should take a picture—it would last longer!" he thought. As Luke finished that thought, the woman did the oddest thing. With a seemingly earnest demonstration of respect, she curtsied and nodded to Luke.

"This woman has spent way too much time in the bar," Luke thought. "She's bonkers!"

"Duit Duite, Your Grace!" Margaret said to Luke. "You are among friends here. You are most welcomed in this place. I am so very glad you decided to come back among us." Then she bowed slightly and nodded again.

"Well," Luke thought, "she's a lot nicer than those dopey leprechauns!" He had no clue what she was talking about. She sure wasn't threatening him with a mean stick or dragging him off where he didn't want to go. Things were looking up!

"Thank you, Miss Margaret," Luke said to be polite. "No need to be rude unless someone else tried to kidnap me today," he thought.

"Well, best be moving on," Michaleen announced while pushing and leading Luke toward the back of the inn.

"Aye, quite right," Shamus agreed but held back a moment to whisper in Margaret's ear. "Best not tell anyone he's here, lassie. His life might be in danger if the wrong sort knew he was back," Shamus explained to Margaret.

In a very proud tone of voice, Margaret responded, "Well, then, they'll have to get past me, won't they, Shamus?"

"Aye, lass, suren they would die trying, and don't I know it!" Shamus laughed.

With a smile, Shamus hurried to join his brother and Luke, who by now were making their way into a very large room at the back of the inn. The entire back wall was one whole mirror.

To Luke's total astonishment, people were moving through the mirror and not in one direction either. Some were going in. Others were coming out. They were all dressed equally as odd as everyone else. All Luke could see in the mirror was his reflection and the leprechauns. The only things that distinguished the people who were going in from those coming out were the shopping bags being carried by those who were leaving.

Luke simply had no idea how to react to all of this. He knew New York City had a reputation for the strange and the unusual, but Luke was neither, or so he thought.

"What is this place?" Luke asked to the leprechauns in a state of surprise and bewilderment.

"This is the entrance to the Pearl Street Mall," Michaleen responded.

"It's a mirror, not a door," Luke said, thinking out loud.

"Aye, a mirror it is, and it's also a door," Shamus responded. "It is like the mirror Alice walked through."

"Alice?" Luke stared at him with a question on his face.

"Aye," Shamus said. "Have you not heard of Alice in Wonderland?"

"I think," Luke said as he turned toward the mirror with amazement.

"Aye, me lad," Michaleen responded. "Beyond this mirror, suren Wonderland begins, and the Old World ends!"

"I don't understand this!" Luke figured he had entered Wonderland when he came in the front door, not out the back of a mirror. As he thought back, this was starting to seem more and more like a big mistake.

"Aye, Master Luke," Shamus said. "We know! Tis why you're here—to learn what was kept from you! About the world that you came from and the hazards you'll now face. We've been sent here to show you!" Shamus stared him in the eye with a most serious look. "You must learn if you are to survive!"

"Sent? Who sent you?" Luke insisted on knowing.

Michaleen walked up to him also with a serious look on his face. "There are people who care about you who believe differently from what your uncle thinks! They tried to reason with him. But he's an old salt of a man set in his ways. Others in your family spoke their permission to let you choose for yourself!"

"OK," Luke said cautiously and with a look of realization. "That's been the most revealing statement of the day," he thought. "Something more than what they are telling me is going on here. I knew it!"

Luke was slowly starting to realize that there was something else to his life that no one had ever bothered to share with him before. The two little green monsters were certainly right about his uncle being set in his ways. Either this was true or someone had gone to an awful lot of trouble to try and convince him there was something about his life he didn't know.

Luke thought that while these two little green things were a little vague on details, it might be worth an investigation. He had at least until near sunset to find out as much as he could. By sunset, Uncle Martin would get home and find out what had happened. Then, Luke felt certain that Uncle Martin would come and find him. These two little Irish freaks would find out just how set in his ways Uncle Martian was then! He was certain that when Uncle Martin found them, there would not be enough pieces he could tear these leprechauns into. This would certainly give him satisfaction for having kidnapped his nephew!

"Uncle Martin is going to be so mad," he thought.

"How does this work?" Luke asked, looking at the mirror.

"'Tis a simple thing," Michaleen responded. "You just say your destination—Pearl Street Mall!"

With those words, Michaleen was surrounded by a mist and sucked into the mirror. Luke was at first a little scared and then amazed.

"Wow!" Luke thought out loud.

"Aye, wow it 'tis," Shamus said, nodding his head and smiling. "Now go on with ya! 'Tis a grand place you're heading to!"

Luke turned and said with a strong voice, "The Pearl Street Mall!"

A swell of mist reached out and then surrounded him. He felt no sensation at all. There was a brief moment of white light, and then he found himself at what must have been the

Pearl Street Mall. The inn was gone, and before him stood a great marketplace of shops. It all looked like something he once saw in a history book or even in a Dickens book, except it wasn't Christmas. Everything was made of either wood or stone. There was no cement to be seen anywhere. Both the road and the sidewalk were made of different kinds of brick and stone. In every direction, there were people moving up and down the streets and in and out of the shops. There were no cars to be seen anywhere. There were carts pulled by horses, and some of the women were pushing strollers. Luke spotted a sign that Michaleen had stopped in front of. As he began to walk toward it, Shamus appeared out of the mirror and looked up with a smile still on his face. Luke said nothing; he was speechless with the wonders he was now experiencing. He walked up to the sign and read "Pearl Street ~~Market~~ Mall."

The word "market" had a line through it, and below it the word "mall" appeared. Overhead was a blue sky and perfect puffy white clouds. No sign of the city of New York could be seen. There was motion all around him, but to Luke the place seemed frozen in time, a time when George Washington must have had slept here. The way things had been going, Luke was starting to believe there might actually be an opportunity to shake hands with George after all.

"Wow," Luke thought out loud, "maybe George Washington did sleep here after all."

"Welcome home, Master Luke," Shamus said as he stepped down the steps from the looking glass mirror.

"Aye, yes!" Michaleen agreed. "'Tis a grand day, I'm thinking!"

No sooner did the leprechauns finish their welcoming greetings than shiny sparkling lights of gold and silver appeared above Luke's head. Then they dropped down on him and were absorbed. Luke felt a chill come over him, and a shiver ran up and down his spine. While looking down, he raised his hands as if to gesture for it stop. Then he spoke with the sound of panic in his voice. "What was that? What just happened?" Luke shouted.

The leprechauns looked at each other with a little concern.

"Haven't you ever cast a spell before, Master Luke?" Michaleen inquired.

"No! Well, not that I am aware of," Luke responded.

"Oh!" Shamans thought out loud.

"What? What is it?" Luke wanted to know.

"You've just had your magic centered on yourself," Michaleen responded.

"Yes!" Shamus added. "Unless you cast your first spell by 16 years since your birth, the magic is lost to the universe forever!"

"I haven't cast any spells!" Luke insisted.

"Aye, Master Luke, you did!" Shamans said.

"Aye, suren you did, indeed," Michaleen agreed. "When you moved yourself through the looking glass!"

"You mean you tricked me again?" Luke was mad.

Michaleen walked up close to him and raised his stick into Luke's face, and he shouted with determination, "It is for your own good, it was!"

"Aye," Shamus agreed.

Luke was extremely angry that someone would trick him into something he knew nothing about. He might have chosen differently if he had known what was going on.

"I may only be 12 years old," Luke shouted, "and I might have a lot to learn about everything, but I am not stupid. I know how to choose for myself when given the chance!"

Luke wondered for a moment what his Uncle Martin would do in his place. Then, he remembered something and began to look past Michaleen's stick, which was now once again pointed at him and into his eyes.

"So tell me, Michaleen Og. I've read fairytales and watched a lot of television with magic and witches in it. Tell me, if I came up with a rhyme that ends with you becoming a frog or an insect I can step on, what happens now that you have centered this magic on me?"

Michaleen lowered his stick, and he and Shamus stood silently looking at each other. Then they looked back at Luke. They said nothing. They just looked worried.

"Well, then, let's give it a try, shall we?" Luke said with an irritated tone of voice.

The two leprechauns stood shaking their heads slowly. "That would not be wise," Shamus said with a tone of caution.

"Dia Duit, young master," a young girl's voice said suddenly. "Would you care to try a fresh pastry? If you like it, maybe you'll come and visit our shop?"

Luke was distracted and looked around. He saw a pretty girl who had come up from behind them who was carrying a bit of pastry with her. "It sure smells nice," Luke thought. The girl wore a colonial-era dress and had long dark black hair and sky blue eyes and a smile. Luke liked her smile. He liked it so much so that for a moment he didn't even look at the pastry. He just kept staring, whereon Shamus took it on himself to give Luke a nudge, causing him to finally blink his eyes again.

"Dia is Muire Duit," Luke said to her.

The young Lady smiled another big smile and bowed slightly, nodding her head as Luke finally reached for the pastry and took a bite.

"Wow!" Luke thought. "This pastry is amazing!"

Michaleen and Shamus were looking at Luke. They were amazed and stunned having heard him give a proper response to the young girl's greeting. Luke glanced over at them and discovered he had two dumb stares on him. "What? Haven't you ever had a pastry before?" he asked with a sarcastic tone of voice.

"You speak the ancient Celt?" Michaleen responded.

Luke thought for a moment and then realized how he had responded to the girl's greeting.

"Well, I don't know if I do," Luke said with a tone of confusion and a mouth filled with pastry. "When I went to bed last night, I didn't, but now I don't know what you two freaks have done to me!" Luke wanted to seem upset, but the pastry was so good, and he hadn't eaten since breakfast, so he couldn't bring himself to act upset.

"Would you like to visit our shop, young master?" the young girl inquired with a smile. Luke still liked that smile! He wanted her to smile more!

With his mouth still full of pastry, Luke responded, "Quoteeeesss unt eye unt ny unie."

The girl looked at him bewildered, not having understood a word Luke said. The leprechauns looked equally mystified. Luke swallowed what pastry was left in his mouth and repeated, "Yes, but I don't have any money!"

"Suren he doesn't, sweet Cailin," Michaleen said to her. "One of the reasons we have brought him here is to claim his fortune."

Michaleen grabbed Luke by the arm and began to lead him off. "So we'll be on our way."

"I am sure if there's time to make a stop on the return, he will," Shamus added as a polite excuse to leave.

The sweet little black-haired girl just watched them walk down the street. When Luke looked back, she smiled a little and waved good-bye to him. Luke smiled and walked, tripped a little, and waved back. Then he just kept walking.

They walked a bit more, and Luke got frustrated and threw off Michaleen's arm. "Let go of me!" he demanded.

"The day is getting long," Michaleen insisted. "We haven't time for you to be playing patty fingers with every wee Cailin that passes by!"

"Suren the both of you should calm down!" Shaman insisted. "There are many eyes about, and your mouths are drawing attention to us!"

"Oh, really, Shamus?" Michaleen sounded sarcastically. "Who was it that went about introducing him to people?"

Shamus was about to answer with what sounded like an insult when two boys came flying by and nearly knocked the three of them over!

"What was that?" Luke said with amazement.

"Ah, them are those new flying boards!" Shamus told him. Then Michaleen shouted, "And they're not supposed to be using them in the marketplace!"

"Mall," Shamus quickly corrected him. "Aye, not in the mall!" Michaleen agreed, yelling at the boys flying around.

"Board?" Luke questioned.

"Yes," Michaleen responded. "'Tis a Bennie skateboard! The young folk take the wheels off and instead of bewitching a broom like any self-respecting magic folk would, they fly about on these Bennie boards!"

The boys on the boards, having overheard Michaleen's bad attitude and big mouth, came flying back again and forced the three of them to duck.

"Wow!" Luke said loudly. "That is so kewl!"

As the boys passed by, they drew Luke's attention to the building at the far end of the street. There stood and unusually narrow but very tall white building made from marble. It looked so dramatically different from every other building in the mall. Its face had several tall Greek-style columns, with a long set of stairs leading up to a pair of enormous doors. As extraordinary as the building appeared, what really got Luke's attention were the two creatures standing on either side of the building. Their size and their appearance were so shocking that Luke felt nauseous and scared. The only way they could be described was as monsters! Even though the building and its creatures were still nearly two blocks away and Luke was safe, he was completely stunned!

"Holy crap!" Luke said. He was not of the habit of using vulgarity; at home it was always discouraged by Uncle Martin back-handing him, but this time it was just a response to shock.

"What the hell are those two things next to that building down there?" Luke asked with fear in his voice.

"Those are trolls," Shamus responded with firmness in his voice.

"Aye," Michaleen agreed. "Between them is Hawthorn's Pot of Gold!"

The three of them began to walk toward this incredible site. Both of these creatures stood more than half the size of the 10-story Hawthorn's Pot of Gold, and they carried enormous hammers. Their bodies were disproportionate to their heads. Their stomachs were gigantic, as were their arms and legs. Their heads were almost normal size. But they were so ugly! Their teeth were distended, rendering them incapable of keeping their mouths shut. And they kept drooling! Yuck! Their lips and their noses bulged outward. Luke thought they were so sick looking. "If my dog looked anything like them, I would have shaved his butt and trained him to walk backward for the rest of his life!" Luke thought.

"What is Hawthorn's Pot of Gold?" Luke asked cautiously.

"'Tis the safest bank in all of the Americas," Michaleen told him.

"Aye," Shamus agreed.

"What are these creatures doing there?" Luke kept his voice low and cautious.

"They are the security guards for the bank," Shamus explained to Luke, observing that he seemed to be getting a little nervous the closer they got to the bank.

"Well, I don't imagine that security is much of a problem for that bank then!" Luke responded with a sense of resolve in his voice as they continued to walk.

"Nope! Suren no one has ever tried to rob the Hawthorn!" Michaleen confirmed openly what seemed incredibly obvious to Luke.

They kept getting closer and closer, and all of the people around them paid no attention. It was as if having trolls in the neighborhood was okie-dokie.

"Why are we heading for the bank?" Luke insisted. He spoke with a low voice and caution so as not to get the attention of the trolls. It was an incredible sight; the troll creatures cast a shadow the length of the city block!

"We are going to go and claim your fortune!" Michaleen said in a determined voice. He thought it might have been the twelfth time he had said it since he met the boy.

"Guys," Luke said, addressing both leprechauns. "I only just turned 12!" He said this in a tone of voice suggesting the two of them hadn't noticed. "I seriously doubt there is much of a fortune for a 12-year-old boy, right?" Luke didn't want to go into that bank. He wasn't all that keen on money anyway! Luke looked at them, kept walking, and looked at the bank and then back at the leprechauns again expecting an answer to this question.

"Well, not exactly," Shamus replied. They stopped briefly, and Shamus looked at Luke for moment.

"Your 12 years makes you the youngest member of one of the oldest clans in all of the magic realm!"

"Aye," Michaleen agreed. "With one of the largest fortunes in existence!"

Again Luke looked at them, then at the bank, and back at them yet again. He seemed to be considering carefully what they just said. Then he responded, "Well, I am not that busy right now, am I? It couldn't hurt to go have a brief look at the fortune, right?"

"Right!" both the leprechauns said simultaneously.

The three made their way up a long staircase under the bulging eyes of the really gross-looking trolls. Luke noticed that the street sewers were positioned in such a way that the drool from the monsters was prevented from flowing down the street! Luke made a sly comment that almost sounded like a prayer. "Oh, Lord, please don't let them drool on me!"

The enormous doors opened as they approached, and soon the three found themselves inside the lobby. They were surrounded by leprechauns! Until today, Luke had never laid an eye on a leprechaun before, but now he was surrounded by them. As a 12-year-old boy, he felt strange being the tallest person in a room full of people.

"This is so strange," Luke thought as he looked around. "I feel like I have died and gone to a little green kindergarten hell!"

"Well, there's quite a few of you in here, isn't there?" Luke made the statement with a sense of unease as the three moved toward the head desk. Behind it sat a very large and very old looking leprechaun. He wasn't tall; he just filled out the seat with his waist. You couldn't see his legs; his feet just stuck out from under his waistline. He had a long white beard, and his nose stuck out so far it drooped beneath his upper lip.

"Well, hello, Odin," Michaleen said as he stood in front of the old leprechaun. Then, with a raspy voice, Odin replied, "Well, well! Michaleen and Shamus Og! Suren my day is complete now that the chancellor's lap dogs have come for a visit!"

"Chancellor's lap dogs?" Luke thought. That's right! Luke remembered it was he who was responsible for having sent these two little green creatures after him! Luke had forgotten his name was mentioned in the churchyard this morning.

Odin didn't seem too kind toward Michaleen and Shamus. But at least now Luke remembered who it was that sent them! Michaleen and Shamus stood for moment in silence as they absorbed Odin's insult. Then they chose to ignore it, which surprised Luke.

"Odin," Michaleen said. "May I present Master Luke Carter?"

Luke was surprised because Michaleen had made such a fuss when Shamus had presumed to introduce him before. With Michaleen's statement to Odin, the smug face Odin had that was frustrating Michaleen and Shamus disappeared. Odin looked over at Luke, and with a sound of respect in his voice, he said, "Welcome to the Hawthorn, Master Luke. It has been many years since you have been among us, Your Grace." He bowed slightly, "I assure you that your fortune is safe and well accounted for."

"Thank you," Luke responded with a look of uneasy surprise. That was the second time someone had used that word "grace." Until today Luke, always regarded "grace" as something to be recited before supper.

"Not that we're not believing you, Odin," Michaleen asserted. "But Master Luke would like to have a look for himself."

"Aye, a wee look for himself is in order," Shamus agreed loudly so that all of the other leprechauns could hear. Clearly, it was a statement meant to embarrass Odin. Shamus and Michaleen seemed unusually confident once they had announced who it was they were escorting. Luke found this to be very odd.

Odin looked over at Luke very sternly. He seemed to be waiting for something. Luke looked at the lot of them. Then he thought for moment, realized what was going on, and responded, "Yes, please, Mr. Odin—if there is no problem with that."

"Aye, or even if there is," Shamus added.

Odin sat on his tall chair, nodded his head yes, and completely ignored Shamus. He said, "As you wish, Master Luke."

With that, Odin clapped his hands, and an attendant was summoned. He led the group of three back to the stairs, where they began a very long trek down 10 or more stories. It was so long Luke thought they weren't going to stop until they reached Australia! Finally, they stopped at the bedrock of the building.

"That was a long trip!" Shamus thought out loud.

"Yeah," Luke agreed, "I was about to start looking for wallabies!"

"Wallabies?"

Luke looked over at him, shook his head, and said, "Never mind!"

At the bedrock, old-style brick lined a seemingly endless tunnel. Everything was made of brick. The floor, the walls, and even the arch ceiling were all made from brick, all except one solid iron door after another, which were embedded in the walls.

These were the strangest doors Luke had ever seen. Not only were they enormous and thick, but they also had no handles and no obvious way to open them. They all seemed to have a plaque mounted on them. But Luke could not read them because the only light came from a lantern held by the attendant. It was too dark to read the inscriptions on the plaques.

Suddenly, the attendant stopped and turned to his right. In a moment more, Luke found himself standing next to him. There before him was the largest iron door they had seen so far. It stretched upward for two stories of the building. It also had a plaque with writing on it. But it could not to be read because it was covered with dirt of some kind. Luke walked over and began to clean off the plaque. The dirt smelled terrible!

"Yuck! What is this crap?" Luke said out loud.

"Aye, indeed, 'tis bat droppings," the attendant told him.

"Eeww! Yuck!" Luke thought. "This day just keeps getting better and better!"

The four corners of the plaque had mythical creatures on top of shields.

"What are these?" Luke asked Michaleen.

"They are the coat of arms of your clan," he responded.

In between the coat of arms was a message that read,

"Beware to all who call on this door,
For herein is a curse that may cause you to fall.
No one may enter; no one may leave,
Except those who are a part of the ancient tree.
On their words all will be well,
For anyone else, a curse that will cast you into hell."

"Well," Luke thought out loud. "Isn't that special?"

"Aye," Shamus agreed.

"Let's get on with it," Michaleen insisted.

"Get on with what?" Luke replied.

"Open the door!" he demanded.

"There's no handle or lock!" Luke observed.

"No, no, no!" Michaleen insisted. "You have to cast a spell to open it!"

"What spell?" Luke sounded confused.

Michaleen walked up to him and made a motion to indicate he wanted to whisper in his ear. He talked for a moment as Luke bent over and struggled to hear what he had to say. Then Luke stood upright and looked at Michaleen like he was an idiot.

"No way!" Luke said out loud and sternly.

"Aye!" Michaleen looked back at him most seriously and said, "Way!"

Luke looked at him, then at Shamus, and then over at the attendant. Then he looked up at the door and shouted, "Oscailte Cead Caite A Fhail Mo Diol!"

The plaque on the door began to glow, and a choir of sweet voices scaling notes of song in perfect harmony could be heard. Then, what sounded like latches unlocking one after the other could be heard. The enormous door began to swing open. It stopped, and all was silent. The room inside was glowing.

The attendant, who undoubtedly had witnessed the openings of many vaults, had nonetheless never seen the most important vault in the bank opened. He stood watching in amazement. Shamus and Michaleen smiled with overwhelming happiness. They looked like they wanted to do a little dance they were so happy! Then, surprisingly, with great joy in his voice, the attendant announced, "Welcome home, Your Grace!" and then he bowed to Luke.

To the attendant, the opening of the door verified who Luke was. Unfortunately, Luke didn't understand who he was, so he simply observed the attendant's behavior with a smile on his face. Then he began to walk into the vault, where he wished some supper would appear—because everyone kept using that "grace" word, and it was making him hungry!

"Come on!" Luke told them with excitement in his voice.

"Aye, suren we can't enter," Shamus said.

"Aye, only the members of your clan can enter," Michaleen announced.

Luke thought, "I have come this far, I have been kidnapped, I have watched my friends be frozen, and I have been threatened with the same stick used to freeze them. There is no way I'm not going in for a look!"

When he entered, what met Luke's eyes was beyond description. There were no words to explain his amazement. A room three times the size of his home was stacked on one side with bars of gold to the ceiling. The other side was stacked with American gold eagle coins. On the far wall, there were three enormous chests. One was filled with rubies, the other was filled with emeralds, and the last was filled with an inexplicable variety of diamonds. Luke did not know what to feel. He was not sure what to think. None of these objects were anything he had ever craved. He had grown up in America, and like all boys his age, he understood that his world ran on money. But beyond living in happiness with his family, he had no ambition for it. He did take one tiny emerald and put it in his pocket. He thought it was very attractive, and he wanted something to remind him that he had visited this place.

Believing he had to make a withdrawal to cover the costs of school supplies, he walked back to the door and inquired of the leprechauns, "How much should I take?"

"Nothing," Michaleen told him.

Luke looked at him with total bewilderment on his face.

"Nothing? Then why did you kidnap me?"

"To claim your fortune!" Michaleen told him. "There's no need to carry money around with you! Now that you and your fortune are connected, all you need to do is cast a simple spell, and whatever bill needs to be paid, the Hawthorn will just pay it! Only people without fortunes carry money around with them!"

Michaleen turned around to find the attendant standing directly behind him with a rather unfortunate look on his face. He was not happy to learn Michaleen and Shamus had kidnapped Luke.

"Kidnapped?" The attendant looked angrily at Michaleen. "Kidnapped is it?"

"Oh, no!" Michaleen and Shamus insisted. "We are here on instructions from the chancellor! You arc frcc to check with his office if you would like!" Michaleen insisted. "The boy doesn't know what he's talking about because we were instructed to tell him nothing," Shamus told the attendant.

"I see," the attendant said. He was completely satisfied with their explanation because it was impossible for one leprechaun to lie to another leprechaun.

"What if I wanted to carry a few dollars in my pocket?" Luke shouted from inside the vault.

"Then all you need to do it is cast a spell, and the Hawthorn will deliver the dollars to your pocket!" Shamus shouted back.

"Fine!" Luke had a last look around. He touched a few of the gold bars and lifted up a few of the gold coins just to see them up close. Then he left. When he reached the leprechauns again, he asked, "OK, how do we get it closed now?"

"Just tell it good-bye," Shamus answered.

Luke gazed over at the big door and said "good-bye," but nothing happened.

"No, no, no," Michaleen said with frustration. "You have to cast a spell good-bye!"

"Oh!" Luke said. "I see."

"Slain!" Luke shouted.

On Luke's good-bye, the great door slammed against the vault. It made a loud noise, followed by the sounds latches locking.

Soon Luke and his leprechaun escorts found themselves going from shop to shop. Where to go was clearly marked by a sign with a griffin on it and the word "Citadel" beneath it.

In each shop that had the official seal of the Citadel was an official list of items that all academy freshmen had to bring with them. The very first thing Luke bought was a trunk. It was quite large and impossible for any one person to carry. But it was no ordinary trunk. As Michaleen and Shamus explained, with a simple incantation, the trunk appeared and disappeared at the will of the owner. Wherever the owner went, so went the trunk. Anytime Luke needed to put something in it, he could just summon it, fill it, and then be on his way. He had to admit this was pretty nifty. He had never had one of these before. He wondered why they didn't sell these on TV. He was certain all of his friends back in Sugarloaf would love to have one.

They passed a shop called Wands and Brooms. It seemed to have the very latest in flying paraphernalia. But it had no seal out in front of it.

"That it is so kewl!" Luke said. "Wow! They even have some of those Bennie flying boards you were shouting about earlier today, Michaleen Og!"

"No, suren we'll not be going in there, I'm telling!" Michaleen said.

"Why?"

"Because there isn't anything in there that you'll be needing for school!" Michaleen told him.

"Why?"

"Will you be stopping with the, 'whys' already?" Shamus insisted.

"No! I want to know why I cannot buy something that flies and why I cannot have a wand."

Michaleen and Shamus stared at the boy for a bit. They had never had to deal with a 12-year-old before. In fact they had done more talking and explaining to Luke than they had in years. It was wearing on them, and they were certain not to accept another assignment having to deal with freshmen ever again!

"You can't fly until you have been certified," Michaleen said. "You cannot be certified until you go to school to learn how to fly. So until you are certified, you'll have to use the school's equipment."

"Aye," Shamus agreed. As they walked away from the wand shop, Shamus continued to explain, "Americans don't use wands. Long ago, when you had your revolution, American witches were cut off from their supply of wands. The making of wands requires feathers from certain mythological creatures. In America, they were true myths because in America, they truly did not exist, so American witches adopted the techniques of the Indian and African shamans—what the common folk referred to as witch doctors. These days, wands are only used in ceremonies. Wand arts were and are still a wizard's craft. There are no wizards in America. There is only witchcraft and the new techniques developed after the Revolution—a type of magic that is referred to simply as 'the method.' 'Tis mind over matter and control of the elements of the earth, like wind, fire, form, energy, and water. The magic folk with their noses in the air and a board up their backsides, they don't even call themselves witches anymore! They want to be called 'method practitioners' or 'practitioners.'"

"That was an earful," Luke thought. There was no doubt that Luke wanted a flying board. That was just too kewl to ignore! Unfortunately, the school would simply confiscate the board once he arrived. So for now, he decided to let it go. Luke also was certain he would be back to get one! Yes!

The last shop was the uniform shop. Luke needed seven complete uniforms, but Michaleen insisted that he buy extras just in case, so he bought 12. The shopkeeper had to give Luke lessons in tying the knot in his tie. "There isn't much use for ties in the Florida Keys," Luke thought.

When the uniform was finally fitted, Luke had a look at himself in the mirror. The uniform was maroon over blue with a tie that had both colors in it. It could be worn with a sweater or a double-breasted dress jacket. As Luke stood looking at himself, the shopkeeper tied a robe or cloak around his neck. "This is definitely a new and different look for me," Luke thought.

"Couldn't the Citadel have come up with a uniform that was made out of blue jeans and a T-shirt?" Luke asked.

"Aye," Michaleen responded. "Saints Preserve Us! Not all of America's bad habits have made it into the Valley of the Griffin behind the Great Hole in the Wall. Once you are there, no one is going to treat you any differently than anyone else. You'll have to pull your own weight! There will not be any uncles or aunts to run to when things get tough. There are also rules you'll have to learn to follow. One of those rules is there are no blue jeans and T-shirts behind the Great Hole in the Wall!"

"So do you kidnap everyone who goes to school there?" Luke said sharply.

"Aye," Shamus responded laughing. "Kidnapping is an up-and-coming trade, don't you know?"

"Leprechauns only do what they're told to do!" Michaleen asserted.

"And the one who tells you what to do, Michaleen Og, that would be the chancellor?" Luke was still speaking with a sharp tone to his voice.

"The only thing you need to be worrying about, Master Luke, is getting good grades if you're up to it!" Michaleen wasn't too happy with the way Luke was talking to him.

Luke glanced at himself one more time in the mirror. He looked so much older than he felt. Then he proceeded outside after having packed everything else into the trunk. He stopped at the edge of the sidewalk just outside the shop and looked at everything. He thought, "I have never dreamt this dream ever." Luke felt a conflict inside of him. He was amazed at all of the things he had seen that day, but it was all way too different from the life he had grown up in. He was now satisfied that he was in fact part of a hidden magical realm and that this realm coexisted with the world he grew up in. Uncle Martin hadn't shown up so he knew he would now have to make a choice. He was either going to have to go along with the leprechauns and walk through the Great Hole in the Wall and into the Griffin Valley or he was heading back to Sugarloaf whether the leprechauns liked it or not! Luke had to admit he felt comfortable in this new environment. It might even be a whole lot of fun! Be that as it may, the choice wasn't really a difficult one. Where he wanted to be the most was with the people he loved.

As the three of them began to make their way back to the looking glass mirror, Michaleen began to explain how to get to the Citadel. The Great Hole in the Wall was in fact a tunnel through a mountain that led into the Valley of the Griffin.

The tunnel could be found only by magical folk. None of the common people could find it. But there was no way to travel to the Valley of the Griffin by magic. Long before Europeans came to the shores of America, the Valley of the Griffin was protected by powerful magic. It was an ancient power from where no one knew it came. There were only two ways in. One could walk through the Great Hole in the Wall or attempt to transgress the Griffin Pass. No one dared to enter the Griffin Pass. It was guarded not only by powerful magic but also real griffins. These creatures were part lion and part eagle. Their talismans could crush a truck or lorry simply by grabbing it. Common folk could not find the Griffin Pass, and magical people dared not enter.

The Great Hole in the Wall lay at the end of the Chattanooga Pass. To get there from New York City, a person had to buy a ticket at Grand Central station for the Chattanooga platform. So, Michaleen, explained, the three of them would go back to the Roosters Neck Inn and get onto a subway to Grand Central station.

"First we have to stop at the pastry shop!" Luke insisted. He wanted to be smiled at again by the pretty black-haired girl with the sky blue eyes!

The two leprechauns agreed, and soon Luke found himself at the pastry shop getting a smile from the pretty black-haired girl. The pastry was still amazing to eat. The sun was moving to the west. Soon the day would be gone. The shop was crowded, so Luke moved out onto the sidewalk, where he ate and watched people moving in and out of the looking glass mirror. He observed while the leprechauns were distracted by their own pastries that not everyone who walked up to the mirror announced the Roosters Neck Inn as their destination. In fact, people were giving various parts of the country as their destinations. Luke wondered whether the trick was perhaps that they had looking glass mirrors in their homes. Luke started thinking. He was willing to bet that the great hall mirror at home was also a looking glass mirror. "There is no way the leprechauns could know that," he thought.

"OK, let's get on with it!" Michaleen announced.

The three of them walked up to the looking glass mirror. Just as before, Michaleen went first, and he shouted, "The Roosters Neck Inn!"

With that, a mist reached out from the mirror and enveloped him. Soon he was gone. Now it was Luke's turn. He stepped up to the mirror and shouted, "The home of Martin Cohan, Sugarloaf Harbor, Florida!"

Before Shamus could even utter the word "no," a mist surrounded Luke, and in the next moment, he found himself in the great hall of his uncle's home in Florida!

Everyone was gathered around the kitchen table. Luke's sudden arrival startled them. The older women gasped, and one gave a bit of a scream. They all had worried looks on their faces. The emotional look as he arrived was something that Luke had never seen from any of them before. Uncle Martin was not in the room.

One thing that startled Luke besides the scream was a person in the room shouting, "Oh, God," and others going, "It's Luke!" at the top of their lungs. There was a mixture of adult friends and Uncle Martin's workers. Sonny, Sam, Lorraine, and Boo where there, and they weren't frozen anymore! They all came forward to greet him. They grabbed him and began to hug him. The girls had tears in their eyes, and Sonny kept clearing his throat because he was unable to speak. Then it got quiet as someone walked into the room.

At first Luke could not see who it was because everyone was blocking his view. In the next moment, they parted, and there stood Aunt Claire. She took a few steps toward him. "She has the oddest look on her face," Luke thought. She put her hands on her hips and looked at Luke. Then she said, "I don't remember giving permission for any day trips!"

Luke cleared his throat and found himself wiping his eyes as he said, "No, ma'am." His voice was soft and broken.

Claire looked him over and then said, "You're rather handsome and older-looking in that uniform than I remember."

"Thank you, Aunt Claire," Luke said. His voice was still broken, and he knew she wasn't very happy with him just disappearing like that.

Claire walked up to him and wrapped her arms around Luke and hugged him as tightly as she possibly could.

"I was very worried about you, boy!" she whispered into his ear as tears filled her eyes.

"I am very sorry, Aunt Claire, but it wasn't my fault!" Luke told her as she continued to hug him tightly.

"Oh, and don't I know it!" she whispered in a broken voice, repeating herself several times, "and don't I know it!"

Claire stepped back, removed a tissue from her apron, and began to wipe her eyes. Luke looked around the room. Everyone had tears in his or her eyes. Luke took several deep breaths as he looked for something to dry his eyes.

Outside of the big house, down by where the river met the Sugarloaf Sound, near where the pearl farm began, sat two older men. Each had a long pipe in his mouth. The one sitting with his back to the house in a large rocking chair had not lit his pipe. The other man's hair from his head and face nearly reached the ground. The hair was an odd mix of black, gray, and white, and he was a dark-skinned man.

Marta made her way to the men, and on arriving announced to Martin, who turned out to be the man with his back to the house, "He's back, Martin." She spoke with a broken voice and tears in her eyes.

Martin looked up at her; he didn't seem surprised at all. "That's good, Marta. Have Luke come for a visit when he gets a chance."

"Yes, Martin," she replied as she looked over at the other man and nodded her head in a friendly gesture. The dark man with the long hair nodded back with a slight smile. Then she went off to tell Luke.

Martin turned to the other man and said, "I told you those damn leprechauns were no match for that boy!" Martin's tone of voice was one of "I told you so!"

"Yes," the man replied. "I suspected as much. But even though he's not at the Citadel, he is neither isolated nor naive anymore. Perhaps now you'll train him to protect himself a little better?" The man's voice was direct and to the point.

"He did just fine this day, I'm thinking!" Martin responded.

"That's because no one was trying to kill him, Martin!" The man seemed quite determined to make his point. "The Darksiders are coming for him, Martin! He's his father's son, not yours!"

"He's my responsibility!" There was a tone of anger in Martin's voice. "I'll be the one making the decisions as to what he should or shouldn't be doing! And another thing—I suggest you spread the word! The next person who thinks he knows better than me and tries another stunt like this one today—you'll be telling those lost souls that they will be answering to me personally!"

Martin sat back in his seat abruptly and placed the pipe back in his mouth. He used to smoke and was tempted to strike a match once again. He would have, but he knew how disappointed Luke would be if he saw smoke coming from his mouth.

The man looked at Martin, but Martin didn't look back.

"My old friend," he said, pausing for a moment to think. "We're on the same side, Martin!" His voice had both a sense of frustration and appeal to it. "Our people and I want to watch out and protect the boy from what's coming. It's just a matter of time before they make their move!"

Still not looking at him, Martin responded, "Aye, you showed what side you're on today, I'm thinking!" Martin's voice had a very strong sense of disappointment in it.

Disappointment was added to a look of frustration on the man's face also. "Martin, I sent warnings. How many letters have I written these 12 years now? You are not the White Robin, Martin! Luke represents the best hope for so many, for you, for me, for your family, and for himself! We're all on your side, man! But there's no talking to you or reasoning with you! I'm your friend, Martin!"

Then from behind Martin's chair, in walked Luke.

"I'm home, Uncle Martin!" Luke announced.

Martin looked up at the boy, who was dressed sharply in his new uniform. A very clear look of happiness and pride came on his face.

"You went off on an adventure, I hear?" Martin replied.

"Yes, sir," Luke said. "But it wasn't my fault, Uncle Martin!"

"Aye, suren it wasn't, boy! Still, before your next adventure, you'll be letting us know now. That way, your Aunt Claire will not be worrying so much about you!"

"Yes, sir," Luke replied, at which point Martin's visitor cleared his throat. Martin was so glad to see the boy he had forgotten to introduce the other man.

"Oh, yes," Martin said. "Luke, may I present the Honorable Doctor Phineenous Dickelbee, High Chancellor and principal instructor of the Citadel Academy and University."

"Ooooooooh!"' Luke thought. "Should I tell or not?"

"How do you do, sir," Luke said.

"It is a pleasure to meet you again, Mr. Carter," the chancellor responded as he stood and shook Luke's hand.

"Again, sir?" Luke said as the chancellor sat back down.

"Yes, yes," the chancellor responded. "You'll not recall our last meeting; you were far too young then. So I hear you'll be going to join us at the academy this year?" he said as he glanced over at Martin.

"I don't know, sir; my uncle has not told me yet," Luke asserted himself.

With that, Martin cleared his throat. "Well," Martin said as he sat up in his chair to change the subject, "be off with you now, Luke. Go and get your supper! Your Aunt Claire will be waiting for you!"

"Yes, Uncle Martin," Luke responded by wrapping his arms around his uncle and giving him a big hug. Then he walked off to the big house.

The chancellor watched him make his way back to the house and said, "The boy loves you very much. You're lucky man, Martin."

"Suren don't I know it, Phinie," Martin said as he turned to watch Luke walking into the house. He also turned to make sure the chancellor didn't see the tear that had come to his eye. Looking back at the house, he said, "Suren don't I know it" a few more times.

Once again the sun moved below the horizon, and another day had come to an end at Sugarloaf Sound. The clan of Cohan had faced a crisis and had won the day. Well, rather, Luke had won the day.

Soon everyone was in their beds. It was all quiet around the mini-island the Cohens called home. Then, suddenly, in the middle of the night, a rainbow appeared! It came down on the far side of the island. In a moment more, Michaleen and Shamus emerged, and the rainbow was gone. The two tiptoed around the yard and were quiet as mice. When they thought it was safe, they moved toward the main double doors of the big house. Shamus tried to turn the knob. When it wouldn't open, Shamus tried to use his shillelagh to open it with a spell. That didn't work either.

"Let's try the side door!" Michaleen said in a whisper.

They turned to tiptoe away and found themselves face-to-face with Martin. He was staring at them with an evil eye.

"We'll be begging your pardon, kind sir," Michaleen said in a nervous voice. "We just got lost and were looking for some directions."

"You got lost all right, Michaleen and Shamus Og!" Martin's voice had thunder in it. "Suren you got way off the wrong path when you came looking for my nephew today!" Martin's face was turning red. He began to walk toward them, and they began to walk backward toward the house.

"You got on the wrong path when he decided to cross swords with the House of Cohan!" There seemed to be no end to Martin's anger.

Michaleen and Shamus found themselves pinned against the wall of the house. Michaleen raised his shillelagh at Martin, and a burst of smoke came flying out, but nothing happened. Then Shamus did the same. Martin just started coughing from the smoke. The leprechauns' magic had no effect on him!

Michaleen looked at Shamus and said, "Run!"

"Aye," Shamus replied, and off the two went running toward the footbridge. They had no other way out. Their shillelaghs were not working. They couldn't even make themselves into high-speed blurs or call for a rainbow to get them out of there!

"Aye!" Martin shouted with anger. "Run, ya little turds!"

With that Martin raised his hand and pointed two fingers at the retreating leprechauns. With an amazing flash of light, bolts of power came flying from Martin's hand and right into the backs of the two leprechauns. The two hit the ground and yelled in pain. The sound woke Luke up. He went rushing to his window to see what was happening. He was stunned to see that the two leprechauns had returned. Then he heard his uncle shouting, "So? You thought you could kidnap one of my own and get away with it, did you!"

Then more energy came flying from Martin's hand, and this time Luke saw what the leprechauns were screaming about. Each time they tried to get up and running, a bolt would send them crashing down to the ground again. At one point, Martin seemed to just wrap the energy around them, lifting them high into the air, and then just turn it off, letting them come crashing to the ground! Again, they got up and tried to run. Each time, another bolt hit them. Slowly they finally made it to the bridge, but they had to toss their little green jackets into the water because they were on fire.

Luke turned from the window and sat down facing his bed. Then he thought out loud, "I am never ever going to piss off Uncle Martin!"

The First Lady of the Realm
Chapter 5

IN THE DAYS that followed Luke's first great adventure to New York City, no one said much. Luke had endless questions that he wanted answers to, but no one was forthcoming with any. Any time he raised the issue, he was given the silent treatment. He knew why. Uncle Martin had not made a decision, and no one was going to share anything with Luke until he did. Otherwise, they would risk Uncle Martin's wrath. There were late-night discussions between Claire and Martin. Sometimes they got loud enough to wake Luke out of his sleep. Everyone seemed so uncomfortable since Luke got back. Luke just kept thinking that he didn't do anything wrong.

After a few days of the silent treatment, Luke decided that he did not wish to discuss the matter with anyone. He was very sad. All of the information Luke had assembled in his mind seemed to indicate that he would be made to leave sometime soon. If Uncle Martin told him he would have to go, Luke did not believe that would be the end of it. If Luke chose to disobey his uncle, then he would have to leave the house. Luke thought that even if he left the house, he would choose to stay somewhere in the Florida Keys. He just loved living there. However, there weren't a lot of jobs around for a 12-year-old kid. Luke was a good deck hand. He had spent many summers on the ocean with his uncle, and he knew everything there was to know about being a good deck hand. "There are plenty of good captains in the fleet that would give me a job," he thought. "They won't care that I'm just 12. They might even let me live on the boat."

Aunt Claire had insisted that Luke not leave the island. After the incident with the leprechauns, Claire didn't believe that Luke's bodyguards, Boo, Lorraine, and Sonny, could protect him. The two cats and dog still stood guard in the yard. Their appearance had always been a form of camouflage against any would-be attacker. Luke, however, no longer tolerated their presence. If they got too close, he would use a slingshot on them. The three came to the table every night as always. Except now, Luke knew who they were. Luke, even if he wasn't finished with his supper, would get up and leave. Ignoring the demands of his aunt and uncle, Luke would just leave without saying a thing and go up to his room. He would talk to someone only if he had to. Otherwise, Luke pretty much kept to himself.

In their late-night arguments, Luke's aunt and uncle continued on about how best to protect him. Luke still didn't know what it was he was being protected against. He felt like an outsider in his own home. Well, Luke didn't really know what he felt. He thought perhaps his life had been a deception and he was being used. All he really knew was that he was terribly unhappy. He no longer jumped out of bed in the morning to meet the sun. He no longer rushed outside to climb up on the great rock and do the dance with Sam. He had not danced since the morning he had been kidnapped, and he no longer had an interest in it. The fun and joy he had experienced in doing the dance no longer seemed to exist. Luke felt let down. No one was rushing to explain things to him. He would walk into a room, and conversations between people would come to an abrupt end. Except for demanding that he not leave the table before his supper was done, his uncle had not spoken a word to him since the day he had returned.

Alone in his room at night, Luke would summon the trunk he had purchased at the Pearl Street Mall. He wanted to remind himself that what he went through was real. It began to almost seem like it had been a dream. He also liked to hold and look at the tiny green gem he brought back from the vault. In the morning sun, the gem sparkled like nothing he had ever seen before. Luke had no idea that the gem was in fact a flawless emerald worth more than half a million dollars. Even if he had known, it was doubtful he would have cared very much.

There was also something completely new about how he physically and mentally felt about everything in his life and around him. When Luke summoned the trunk and held the gem, he felt something new. He felt as light as a feather. He also felt unusually strong after he used magic to summon the trunk. One time, right after he summoned the trunk, he was able to lift his whole bed into the air. It scared him so much that he dropped it. Another thing about the trunk was that he had put his dirty clothing in it when he changed into his uniform. When he next opened it, the clothing was all clean and tidy. The Realm certainly was different than the real world.

On the Friday morning after he had visited New York, Luke made his way down the stairs and into the great hall. Having Uncle Harry's portrait say hello to him every morning was something he was having difficulty getting used to. The day he returned, his aunt had introduced him to Harry. He had seen a lot of strange stuff that day. None seemed more out of place than a talking picture. By week's end, the talking picture bothered him so much that usually he said nothing back. Once he asked Harry how he died. Harry would volunteer only that it had been in a battle. When he asked about his father, Harry had no answers for him. He said he was just following the rules. This was why there were no pictures of his parents in the house. Luke didn't even know what his parents looked like. Having been totally content with life in Sugarloaf Sound, Luke had never questioned why there were no portraits of his parents. He wanted to know now. He was told there were none.

Luke literally spent the last week wandering the small island this family lived on. This morning, he found himself wandering toward the pearl farm docks. He thought that these docks had been there as long as he had been, but he didn't know a thing about pearl farming. He daydreamed about the fact that the only things he knew were what he had been taught school and what his family wanted him to know. As he looked backward in time, he began to realize that information and learning had been carefully supervised by his aunt and uncle. It was as if his kidnapping had awoken a part of his brain that was just now starting to work. "Why haven't I thought of these things before?" Luke wondered.

Luke glanced out across the pearl docks, and he noticed a figure sitting on the stairs at the far end. He stood up on to the dock to see whether he could get a better look. "It's a girl," he thought with surprise. It was girl with very long blond hair, and she was just standing on the dock and looking around. "She must like the view," he thought, "or maybe she is lost." So without making very much sound, he slowly walked up behind her.

"Hello," Luke said in a friendly tone of voice. "Are you new? We get new people here every year, but it's still early for the harvest."

The girl looked over at Luke and then stood up. She was rather tall for girl, and she had a smile that was just mesmerizing. She was very pretty, with hair that was strawberry blond, just like Luke's. Luke had never met anyone with hair like his. Her hair and height, however, were not her most striking features. The way she was dressed wasn't anything Luke had ever seen in Florida. She was dressed in tight black patent leather and a belt with a big gold buckle. Outside of the movies, Luke had never seen anything like it.

"Dia duit," the girl said in a very sweet and happy voice.

Luke didn't say anything. He had never met anyone taller than Uncle Martin, and she kept smiling a big happy smile. Luke had never met a stranger who was so happy to see him before. He just kept smiling back at her, which caused her to giggle a little bit. When Luke did not respond, she said, "An bhfuit Gaelige Aget?"

Luke finally blinked a few times and then replied, "Aye, Dia is Muire duit."

The girl laughed with happiness. She had never seen a boy so mesmerized that he couldn't talk.

"You shouldn't walk around here dressed like that! People will start talking!" Luke asserted.

"Perhaps you could show me someplace where I can change clothing?" she responded with an approving tone of voice.

"Did you bring any clothing with you?" Luke asked in a friendly manner, not noticing any luggage around.

"Oh, yes, of course," she responded. "I carry my clothing in a trunk same as you."

Luke paused for a moment. "There doesn't seem to be anything dangerous about this girl," he thought." You are a practitioner?" Luke asked with surprise, as his eyes became wider.

"Yes," she said. "Can't you tell? You should be able to sense and feel when someone is a practitioner."

"Well, eerr, ah, well, I'm not really a practitioner," Luke volunteered reluctantly.

The girl looked at him with bewilderment and then asked, "Aren't you Luke Carter?"

"I don't know," he replied cautiously. "The last stranger to ask my name kidnapped me."

"Well, do I look like a kidnapper? So, no one has ever taught you how to practice the magic of the Realm?" she replied with a serious look and surprise.

"No," Luke informed her. "Until last Sunday, I didn't even know there was a Realm!"

The look of surprise on her face reminded Luke of a time at school when a girl had used that very same look. She stared at him. He had thought it was really weird until he looked down and realized he had stepped in dog poop.

"Isn't that interesting?" she said slowly with a look of bewilderment on her face. She sounded like she was asking a question instead of making a statement. "But you speak Irish."

"Aye," Luke replied as the two began to walk off of the docks and toward the house. "I didn't know that either until last Sunday—when I cast my first spell and visited the Hawthorn."

"You've been to the bank already?" the girl said. She sounded surprised.

"Yep!" Luke replied. "Was quite a ride too. Two leprechauns kidnapped me and forced me to go with them. Then they wanted to take me to a place called the Citadel in the Valley—"

At the very moment Luke was about to say the valley's name the girl joined him. "—Valley of the Griffin," they both said at the same time.

She smiled another great big smile at Luke as he said, "You know this place?" Luke was surprised.

They had stopped at the point where the dock met the sand of the island. Luke was looking at her in total amazement. "You haven't come to try and grab me off again, have you?" Luke's voice had a note of caution in it.

"Not exactly," she said still smiling. "I have come to discuss your future enrollment at the Citadel with Cohan." It sounded as though she was talking about a conversation she would rather avoid. "Where is the old fart, anyway?" she said looking around.

Luke giggled a little, and she looked down at him with a dopey smile on her face.

"He's not here," Luke reluctantly volunteered. He was laughing because he knew she was talking about Uncle Martin. "No one with half a brain would dare call him a name to his face," he warned the girl. Luke was just making sure the girl understood what she was getting into.

"I'll try to keep that in mind," she said smartly.

Then there was a new voice.

"I am afraid you will have to leave!"

Luke and the girl turned to their sides, and there stood Sonny, Boo, Sam, and Loraine. Not one of them looked very happy to see a complete stranger talking to Luke!

"I said, you'll have to leave!" Sonny repeated with an even sterner sound in his voice.

The great big smile on the girl's face was gone now. Luke had seen the face she replaced it with coming from Aunt Claire. It was the same one she showed him once when she caught him shooting seagulls with a slingshot.

The girl responded with a rather negative sound in her voice, "I'm here to see Cohan."

"He's not here!" Sonny replied. "Do you have an appointment?"

"Appointment?" Luke thought. "Since when did anyone make appointments with Uncle Martin?"

"No," the girl replied with a tone that suggested she didn't like Sonny's attitude.

"Then you're going to have to leave!" Sonny replied abruptly.

"I'll be staying 'til Cohan shows up!" the girl told him smartly. Then she folded her arms. "I go where I please, and I stay where I please!"

Sonny had a Florida tan, so it was difficult to tell when he was turning red. "He's turning red," Luke thought. He looked pissed, and then he raised his hand, and his sword appeared. When it appeared, the three women on either side of him simultaneously said, "What are you doing?"

"Sonny, what are you doing?" Sam said, repeating herself in an assertive voice.

"You can't draw down on a member of the Realm!" Boo shouted at him.

"Right!" Lorraine agreed, shouting, "Put the damn sword away!"

"Sonny, put your sword away!" Sam was pleading with him.

"I'll put it away after she leaves!" Sonny replied, raising his sword and pointing it at the tall girl, who was in fact quite a bit taller than Sonny. She seemed unmoved by Sonny's threats, and her arms remained crossed as she now leaned up against the fence in a gesture suggesting that she wasn't going anywhere.

"Fine!" he said as he began to walk toward her.

Boo stepped out in front of him and shouted into his face, "What do you think you are doing?" Boo spoke with anger, and her hands were in front of her telling him to stop.

"Sonny!" Sam asserted. "Let's get Claire and let her handle it!" Sam was still pleading with him, this time with a very loud voice.

"No way!" he shouted. "Those two bastard leprechauns were also members of the Realm, and look at what they did! It's not going to happen again because one way or another, she is leaving!"

"Oh, yes!" the girl asserted. "I heard how you handled them! If you had managed it better, I probably wouldn't even be here!"

Lorraine turned her attention away from Sonny and said to the girl, "Mind your own business!"

"I am," the girl asserted firmly. "It's what I'm doing here!"

"Look!" Sonny shouted. "Either help or get out of the way! Martin isn't here, and that means I am in charge, and I say she leaves now!"

"Let him go, ladies," the girl told them. "Shorty isn't going to be bothering anyone today!"

"Her voice is quite snobbish," Luke thought.

The three women thought that statement was rather rude also, and so they stepped out of Sonny's way. They were thinking the stranger was about to learn a new lesson the hard way.

"No, Sonny!" Luke said as he stepped into his path and held his arms up to stop him. "Let's get Aunt Claire and let her decide!"

"You should listen to the boy, shorty!" the girl said. She stood upright with her arms still crossed. "It would be a much better day for you if you did!"

Luke turned and looked at her and said, "You are not helping the situation!"

"OK, Luke, go get Claire!" Sonny said while still looking at the girl.

Luke dropped his arms and ran off to the house to get Aunt Claire. Unfortunately, as soon as he stepped out of Sonny's way, Sonny raised his sword and charged the girl on the dock. The girl did not even flinch. Sonny came running up to her, and at the last possible moment he stopped his sword pointing right at her neck.

"Leave!" Sonny shouted.

"Or what?" she asked, seemingly not perturbed by the fact that there was a sword pointing at her neck. "You're gonna stick me with your little toothpick? You'll be standing tall before the general counsel of the Realm if you do!" She didn't seem worried at all about Sonny.

Sonny drew back and swung at her. The girl ducked with an amazing display of reflexes. She was so fast that before Sonny could make a counterswing, she had already drawn her own sword. Sonny's sword went crashing up against hers and shattered into pieces. Sonny was left standing there with the sword's handle in his hand. He looked pretty stupid! The girl simply stopped, and with a flash of light, her sword was gone.

Sonny was clearly in shock, but he wasn't giving up. He flung his body into a circle, and jumping into the air while raising his foot, he tried to hit the girl in the head. With another demonstration of amazing reflexes, the girl ducked in time for Sonny to miss. He continued to move toward her as he aggressively kicked and punched at her. He was simply unable to make contact. With each move, the girl's countermove rendered Sonny ineffective.

Then Sonny stopped. He felt tired, and he wasn't getting anywhere. Putting her arms down, the girl said, "I'll give you this, shorty! You at least don't give up too easily! But is that determination you are showing me? Or are you just stupid?"

With that statement, the girl in an astonishing show of speed flung her own foot forward at Sonny and kicked him. Luke arrived back outside in time to see the end result. It was as if someone had kicked a football for a goal. Sonny went flying up into the air in an arch, and he flew over the heads of the three women who had been watching the spectacle. He came down like a sack of wet potatoes and bounced off of the sand nearly 15 yards from where he had started!

"Wow!" Luke said out loud as he and the three women looked wide-eyed back at the girl on the dock with their mouths wide open.

Sonny rolled over on the sand. He had the wind knocked out of him and was having problems breathing. He rolled back the other way and got up onto his knees. When he looked up, he was face to face with Claire.

Claire was not happy. Her face was red with anger. She looked as if she might kick Sonny herself.

"Get on your feet!" Claire said in an angry voice.

Sonny lifted himself up.

"What is going on?" she shouted.

"I was protecting Luke!" he replied.

"Protecting him, is it?" she replied, taking a step toward him. "So how is the protecting going today?" she asked in a stern voice.

Looking down at the sand, Sonny stuttered, "Not too good."

"Aye!" Claire replied. "Not too good would seem to describe the last few days, I'm thinking!" Claire was shouting at Sonny. "Where's your sword?" she insisted in a nasty tone of voice.

"My sword?" Sonny replied in an innocent voice, seeming to play dumb.

"Aye!" Claire said very loudly. "WHERE THE HELL IS YOUR BLOODY DAMN SWORD!" Claire was incensed and was screaming at Sonny as she stood face-to-face and nose-to-nose looking down at him. Like the stranger, she was also much taller than Sonny.

"She broke it," he responded, obviously intimidated. He pointed his finger at the girl on the dock.

"Broke it, did she?" Claire responded. She was turning redder than Luke had ever seen! "Will ya be telling me, Sonny, what you were doing with your sword and that girl?"

"She refused to leave," he told Claire.

"And so you drew down on her? Tell me, Sonny, do you know what a Darksider is?"

"Yes," he responded.

"Yes, what?"

"Yes, my Lady, I know what a Darksider is," Sonny replied in a voice that suggested something bad was about to happen to him.

"Is that wee girl over there, Sonny—I'm wondering—is she a Darksider? I've seen quite a few of them but never one quite like her!" Claire looked like she was about to boil over and stomp on him.

"No, my Lady," he responded in a very low voice.

"No, is it? Then, what is she?" Claire was shouting.

"She's a witch," he said in an equally low voice.

"She's a member of the Realm, you're telling me!" Sonny simply nodded his head yes. "Are you telling me you drew down on a member of the Realm?" Aunt Claire's voice could be quite penetrating.

Sonny just looked away, nodding his head yes.

"And what was that I heard about who was in charge around here? I was still in the house for that one! You'll be telling us, Sonny! Who is in charge around here?"

"You are in charge, my Lady," he replied reluctantly.

"You're bloody damned right I am!" Claire screamed right into Sonny's ear.

"So," Claire said in a calmer voice as she stepped around to make sure Sonny was looking right at her. "How do you plan on doing your job with out a sword?" she asked.

"I have another in my room," Sonny told her. "I can summon it whenever I need it!"

"You'll not be needing to summon it, Sonny," she told him. Sonny looked confused. "You need to be going and joining it, I'm thinking!" Claire asserted.

"Joining it?" Sonny asked.

"Aye," Claire said. "You go and join it in your room for the next 10 days!"

"10 days?" Sonny said with a surprised look on his face and a question in his voice.

"Aye, 10 days," Claire said in a slow, determined, and very clear voice. "If you come out anytime in the next 10 days, just keep walking right off of this island! Leave and never come back here again! Are you understanding me crystal clear, Sonny?"

"Yes, my Lady," Sonny said sadly.

Sonny walked off to his room. Claire turned and faced the other three women and shouted, "Well, I'm sure there is a day's work to be done!"

The women just looked at each other and then walked away. The girl stood at the far end of the dock where she had moved when Sonny came after her. Luke was standing on the sand next to the dock. Claire walked up to him. She looked him in the eye and bent over slightly and rubbed his hair a little bit. "Well, boy! Suren you're getting quite an education in a very short time, aren't you?" she asked Luke in a very concerned, direct voice.

Luke just looked up at her and nodded his head yes. He didn't know what to tell her anyway. It was happening around him, but he didn't have a clue why, and as usual, no one was explaining anything to him. Claire stood upright again as the girl stepped down off of the dock to greet her.

For a moment, the two just looked at each other. Then they reached out and hugged each other tightly in a very long embrace. Tears came to both of their eyes as they kissed and hugged some more. They seemed to want to say something to each other, but at first they were so choked up with emotion they couldn't. Luke was very surprised by what he observed. He recognized the two women were very happy to see each other. So while he was very confused, he was also very happy for them, and while he had only a very short conversation with the visitor, he had already decided that he liked her. But he didn't like the way she treated Sonny any more than he liked the way Sonny treated her. As far as he was concerned, they both had a rude streak in them.

"You could have handled that one a little better," Claire told the visitor. "Sonny is a very good and decent man. He is trustworthy and diligent and always tries to do a job."

"Aye, Aunt Claire," the visitor said, shaking her head in disbelief. "I am very sorry. It's just that when people are deliberately rude to me for no reason at all, I still turn into a spoiled, immature brat! It won't happen again; I promise!" The visitor then embraced and hugged Claire some more.

Luke wasn't clear on what was going on. But the visitor got his full attention when she said "Aunt Claire." So while Luke did not understand what was going on, he really, really wanted to know, and he hoped someone would finally take the time to explain it to him.

With tears in her eyes, sniffling, and still holding the hand of the visitor, Claire turned around to address Luke. "Luke, my boy," she said in a broken voice. "May I present to you the first Lady of the Realm, Lady Laura Rama Pishard Cohan Carter."

"Carter?" Luke said in a totally surprised voice.

"Aye, lad. She's your sister," Claire responded. Then she gave the biggest smile Luke had ever seen, and she turned back to address Laura.

"Lady Laura, may I present the future First Lord of the Realm, His Grace, Luke Rama Pishard Cohan Carter," Claire said while still holding her hand.

Laura released Claire's hand, and in a very precise and respectful motion, she curtsied to Luke. Luke didn't know what he was feeling. It was somewhere between total shock and total happiness. Until this moment, he never knew he had a sister.

Luke bowed slightly to Laura. He had never bowed to anyone before. His motion and voice made Luke seem very unsure of himself. He tried to speak, but emotion swelled up inside, and finally he said, "My Lady Laura! Welcome home!"

The two stepped into each other's arms. They hugged very tightly as Luke said, "I never knew I had a sister!" Laura tried to speak, but she couldn't. She had dreamed of this moment so many times, and now it was finally happening! She was tall enough and strong enough to lift the 12-year-old into the air, and so she did. She lifted him and turned him in a circle one time and put him back down again. Then she bent over slightly and looked him in the eye and said, "Hello, Luke! It's been a very long time since I last saw you!" She paused, but Luke couldn't speak, so he just nodded yes at her. "There are three things that I promised myself I wanted to say when we finally met, the three things I wanted you to know above all else. First, that our mom and dad loved us very, very much!" In that moment, Laura had to kneel down and brace herself against Luke as the pain of the past suddenly caught up to her. "That I have missed you every single day since we separated." She continued looking into his eyes and began to cry. "And more than anything else, I want to tell you that I love you very, very much!"

They embraced. Luke wanted to speak, but he couldn't. He just stood for a long time as he hugged the first Lady of the Realm.

LUKE THE ALLIGATOR ?

CHAPTER 6

THE DAY HAD only just begun for Luke and Laura. She insisted that Luke show her around Sugarloaf Sound. Claire made no fuss about it. She thought they needed time together anyway. Besides, if there were going to be trouble, the trouble-makers would have to deal with Laura—and that meant they would need an army. Anyone wanting to get to Luke would have to go through her, and clearly that just wasn't going to happen.

The two made their way off of the island and toward the docks. The day was one of many that seemed typically perfect to the village of Sugarloaf. There was only blue in the sky and not a cloud in sight. Every direction but north brought a sea breeze across the Sound. If it were out of the west or south, it tended to be a bit warmer than if it were out of the east, where the water was usually cooler. Seagulls and the sounds they made filled the air in most directions. Many of the people on the docks said hello to Luke as he passed. Some asked where his dog was and when the gray cat had shown up. Laura was impressed to see how many people knew Luke and were friendly to him. Having so many mundane friends was very uncommon in the Realm.

There were three cats following Luke around this morning. The gray cat usually stayed on the island, and Luke didn't see it much until after dark. This day, for some reason, it decided to join in. All three kept their distance. Luke didn't tolerate them anymore, and none of the cats wanted to get on Laura's bad side, so they kept back quite a distance. There were also an unusual number of bald eagles in the Florida Keys this summer. Once in a while, they would nest there because the fishing was so good, and bald eagles love fish. Now it seemed there was a whole flock of bald eagles living in Sugarloaf. Not that Luke minded; he thought they were as brilliant as the pelicans when they flew over the water.

Lucky for Luke, Laura had changed into summer shorts. Well, at first he thought it was lucky. That was before they left the island. "Now she won't stick out," he thought. He figured that would spare him the time it would have taken to explain who she was to all of the neighbors.

Like all small-towns residents, Sugarloafers were always watching and asking questions about each other. At pearl harvest time, Uncle Martin would hire some pretty odd-looking people. Luke was forever having to answer questions about them. The change in Laura's clothing, however, didn't stop the men and boys on the dock from staring at her. There were guys telling other guys to turn around and have a look at her. This was a new experience for Luke. He didn't know what the big deal was. He just kept wishing they would stop before Laura asked them what their problems were. It was so embarrassing! It was if they had never seen a girl before!

For the most part, Laura was impressed with what she saw. The place seemed carefree. The water was brilliant. She thought the church by the beach was incredibly cute and perfect. The sand dunes seemed to give a lazy feeling to the place. The lifeguards on the beach made the day seem a little warmer. Luke didn't know any of the lifeguards. They didn't live here, and most were just university students working during summer break. The lifeguards were down by the water, and Luke and Laura were walking behind against the sand dunes. The guards had to turn completely around to even notice Laura. Eventually, that's what each and every one of them did. Luke was so embarrassed. "What is wrong with everyone around here?" he thought.

Laura decided she wanted to put her feet in the water, so the two made their way down to the ocean. Laura held Luke's hand as they walked through the water. He pushed her hand off because he didn't like girls holding his hand. Laura was gleaming on the inside, so she didn't care that he didn't want to hold her hand. She was still filled with joy just being with him. Since that dark day so long ago, she had always wondered whether she would ever see him again. Now everything seemed so happy, even though in the back of her mind, she knew it wasn't so. Laura knew it was only a moment in time, and it couldn't last because of who she was. Still, for the moment, she decided to let her emotional guard down and enjoy it.

Luke was uncertain about this hand holding stuff. He had never held a girl's hand before! Girls were dopey, but Laura wasn't. "Why is that?" he wondered. He had never connected to anyone else like Laura before, and to celebrate, he pulled two red lollipops out of his pocket. Luke too was feeling happy. There was something very familiar and friendly about Laura. He just didn't understand why. The two walked with the lollipops in their mouths as the warm ocean water rolled over their feet.

"Hey, super babe!" a lifeguard shouted at them, with two others commenting on either side of him, as they blocked Laura's way. "How's about you come back around sunset and play with someone a little older, wiser, and more fun?"

Laura and Luke just stood there for a moment and stared at the three. Then Luke motioned to Laura, and she bent over as he whispered in her ear. This caused her to break out in a giggle.

"What is that all about?" the lifeguard inquired with a sense of insecurity.

"He asked me not to beat you up. It would cause him to answer way too many questions to way too many people," Laura responded as she giggled even more. She thought Luke's attitude was very cute.

Then the tallest of the three walked up to her and said, "Oh! Do you think you could beat me up, super babe?"

Laura laughed a little and then said, "You don't want me to beat you up. None of you do. All three of you want to go back to work and leave us alone."

The tall guard turned and said to the other, "OK, guys! Party's over! Back to work!"

Then the three just turned and walked away. She told them to do something, and they did it! Luke looked at them as they walked away. Then he looked up at Laura, and she looked back at him.

"Did you do that?" he demanded to know.

"Moi?" Laura responded. "All boys are bad! Bennie boys are so annoying! You just have to know how to train them properly," she said laughing. Then the two continued their walk.

Laura was really impressed with the main beach and the ocean. It seemed so much bigger than life. It was a very different world than the Griffin Valley. What she didn't know, as she watched the waves roll up onto the shore, was that there were others watching her from a distance. Along the dunes, several snakes wound their way through the tall grasses. They kept their eyes on Luke and Laura. As the two made their way down the beach, the snakes followed. They dared not to come out into the open for fear of being discovered. Besides, direct sunlight would burn them. So they just tried to stay as close as they could to Luke and Laura.

They weren't the only eyes watching. Overhead several bald eagles sat on the telephone poles and kept a close eye as well. There were also the three cats. They were on the beach between Luke, Laura, and the sand dunes. The snakes were being careful to make sure the cats didn't spot them. All in all, the beach was a lot more crowded than anyone seemed to realize. Laura and Luke had sat down on the beach so as not to get too far away from the house. The snakes carefully moved to a position opposite them.

"I keep asking questions about the Realm," Luke told Laura as he held his lollipop in one hand and moved sand back and forth with the other. "Uncle Martin will not say a word to me, and Aunt Claire keeps telling me, 'All in good time, Luke, all in good time.'"

"I know," Laura responded as she sat leaning backward against her arms. She spoke without removing her lollipop. "I am also unable to talk about it. No one is allowed to. It's possible that a child's parents could discuss the Realm outside of it in private. It might even be possible for a family group, alone in their own home; they might be able to discuss the Realm. Mostly, there's no talking about the Realm outside of it. Them are the rules."

"Why all of these rules?" Luke insisted on knowing.

"Over time, too many of us have been killed by the Bennies," Laura said, casually enjoying the sun. "When Bennies become aware of us, they get paranoid and fearful. Fear is a terrible emotion to try to control. When they get this way, they feel threatened by us, and so they attack us, call us servants of Satan, and generally say and do anything to get rid of us. It's just their ignorance, of course. All prejudice is based on ignorance."

With a confused tone of voice, Luke said, "I saw what you did to Sonny. Sonny is very strong, and only someone as good as you could have taken him on. Why worry about nonmagical people if you really have all this magical power? Do you think they would shoot us?"

"No," Laura replied as she looked around to make sure no one could hear what they were talking about. "Firearms and common explosives are useless against us most of the time."

"Most of the time?" Luke said with surprise in his voice.

"Aye," Laura said. "There are magical explosions that are far more effective than anything the Bennies might use. Against common law leaders like our family, Bennie weapons are always useless. Our titles mean we lead by consent and ordination of the mundane world. For everyone else, the Bennie weapons are useless unless they are wielded by someone ordained to have jurisdiction of the Realm, like a priest, for example."

"What?" Luke responded.

"Keep your voice down or this conversation is over!" Laura asserted.

Luke nodded his head yes. He kept thinking of the retired priest who held the service every Sunday. He thought of all of the priests who had visited over the years. These men weren't going to hurt anyone!

"I know some priests. I've never seen or heard of them hurting anyone," Luke said now in a low voice but clearly confused.

"They don't go around looking for ways to hurt people if that's what you're wondering," Laura replied. "A priest has the same flaws as any other human. When you enter the Realm, you'll learn the history. As for their abilities, if you have faith, then their authority is a leap of faith. For everyone else, like it or not, it's just the way the universe has decided to keep the balance. There are several priests and a bishop who serve the Realm and conduct services every weekend in the Griffin Valley. They are brilliant, and I like them a lot!"

"What is common law? What is mundane? What is an ordained leader?" Luke insisted.

"They sure enough have kept you totally in the dark, haven't they? A perfect target for a Darksider!" she said.

Luke stared at her, waiting. "Well?"

"Hmm. Oh, boy! You're a Cohan, alright! You don't get your way, and you get an attitude!"

"Ha!" Luke shouted. "Look who's talking about bad attitudes! You're the one who drop-kicked Sonny across the backyard!"

Laura giggled a little. "Aye! I'm a Cohan, all right! But I don't start fights! I just finish them!"

"Yeah, you almost finished Sonny!" Luke looked at her as if it were a bad thing to have done.

"Don't worry! He bounced and survived OK, didn't he? And maybe—maybe he learned a little respect along the way! Besides, I'm not the one who charged after him with a broadsword!"

"He thought you were a baddie!"

"No, he didn't, Luke! That's the whole point of what happened back there! Sonny knew I wasn't. He could feel it same as me and any other member of the Realm. Same as your girl-friends who tried to stop him. Same as you when you tried to stop him. Why do you think Aunt Claire went off on him? By marriage, she holds the rank of first witch. She also is an Alfa-Omega witch, just like Mom was. The Alfa-Omegas are the most talented and serious of the practitioners. They are the ones who enforce the laws. I don't go around deliberately hurting people, Luke. However, by accident of birth, I do instill discipline and enforce the rules from time to time. If you survive to be 22 like me, you'll have the same fun and responsibilities."

Luke just stared at her. Inside he was so happy! He was learning so much! But he kept a stern face on her as if he was waiting for something. He wanted to hear more, and if he talked too much, she might stop. Laura looked over at him. The lollipop was little more than a stick now.

"What?" Laura said to him.

"Mundane? Common law? Ordained leader?" Luke said.

"Gee, aren't you the single-minded one!"

"Come on!" he said.

"Right! But what about the rules?"

"Laura!"

She smiled a little. "Mundane means someone who is not centered, a person who by thought or will cannot command the elements of the earth. Power-lightening, for example, wind, fire, water, gravity, space, these are all of the traditional things that practitioners have command over to some extent. Not all practitioners have the same abilities. Usually, it's a matter of how strong a family line you come from and how much you practice. To outsiders, it seems like magic. So mundane means someone who has no magic, or Bennies, as they are often referred to. By the way, 'Bennie' isn't really a very nice word.

"Common law is the rules established by the original 12 civilized tribes of humans to govern society, tribal law in other words.

"The ordained leaders, in our case, the paternal or the male line, are the ones chosen and agreed to by all of the leaders of the original 12 tribes. A royal line of kings, in other words. However, members of the Realm all originated from the lowest human classes, what used to be known as peasants, commoners, or untouchables. This group has never had much use for people who are full of themselves, so no leader of the Realm has ever worn a crown. Being full of oneself in the Realm is considered very vulgar. No one would have anything to do with people who were full of themselves! Such people usually are the first ones to use their power for personal gain, which is what turns a practitioner into a Darksider!"

Luke was amazed by what he was hearing. "I have never done anything to anyone, Laura. Why do these people want to hurt me and hurt us, these Darksiders you keep talking about?" Luke seemed lost in thought as he asked this question, almost as if he was thinking out loud.

"Have you ever heard the word 'bipolar,' Luke?"

"Nope."

"It's a very difficult idea to explain," Laura began. "I'm not sure I am the one to be explaining it to you. Basically, it means two different centers of power that are opposed to each other."

Luke sat staring into his sister's eyes. No one had ever thought him mature enough or worthy enough to share so much. For the first time ever, Luke began to feel he was part of something bigger than he was. It was a level beyond just knowing something. Laura trusted him with this information when no one else would.

"At all levels of existence in this universe," she told him, "there is a positive and a negative force. This is the nature of the universe. There are positive forces like our sun, and there are the negative forces like the black hole in the center of our galaxy. There is matter, and there is antimatter. All atoms have an electron and a neutron. Even the electricity in your house has a positive and a negative part to it. These forces do just one thing to each other. They create balance. Some say even male and female represents a kind of balance. This balance is why we exist. If the universe were any different, we would not be here. It is the same for people, Luke, except we have souls, and we are conscious and self-aware. The universe is not.

"The fight we are involved in started in heaven when creation itself occurred. In order for the light of consciousness to survive, the darkness came to balance it. Selfish, self-centered, and self-serving, the Darkside wants things to be as they were before man became conscious. It wants to undo creation. There's nothing the Darkside will not do to accomplish this goal. Across time, good men and women have stood in their way. The overwhelming vast majority of these people were completely mundane. But those who had the most success defeating the Darkside were members of the Realm, and the most successful among them was the ordained line. Right now, you, Martin, and I are in the way. I cannot tell you anymore, Luke. I have told you all I can about who you are. For your success, you'll have to find out who you are on your own. You'll have to learn the hard way. I will protect you for as long as I can. Hopefully, before I am gone, you will have learned enough to survive."

"Gone?" Luke said with surprise. "You just got here! Where are you going now?"

"Luke," she said, smiling, "you, Martin, and I are the last of the naturally born leaders of the Realm. During the past 40 years, everyone else has been vanquished! Most were murdered! Daddy is lost. The Darksiders somehow captured him. No one knows where he is, only that he is still alive and has been successfully neutralized by the Darkside. Mom is gone too. I watched Darksiders vanquish her and Uncle Harry. Like Mom, Aunt Claire is a Cohan by marriage, not blood, so she is no help. Martin turned his back on the Realm a long time ago, and this created a crisis. It's why we came here to America and why Dad and not Uncle Martin is frozen in time someplace.

"The natural leadership line is paternal only, which means I cannot give birth to a naturally born leader of the future. Only you and Martin can father a new leader. Martin will not, and even if he's changed his mind, I'm not sure he's up to it anymore. He is a little too old. That leaves you, an untrained, sweet 12-year-old boy, for whom the Darkside will do anything to neutralize. Until recently, you haven't been aware of it, Luke, but next to the Bennie American president, you've been the most closely guarded person on Earth. Your biggest advantage has been the same as Martin's. The Darkside didn't have a clue where you were. Someone here tipped them off, and now for the first time in 12 years, the Darksiders are on the move again. Everyone has begged Martin to move on. He's not moving, so Darksiders are coming here. Most likely, they are already here.

"I have a plan in place that will let you get away to the Valley of the Griffin safely. I have a few friends that will help. But I have no illusions about the plan. My friends and I will stand and fight while you get away. I can't fight off an army, Luke. Aunt Claire will stand, and Martin has no place to run anymore. But there's no way we'll survive; we just don't have the numbers. What is important is that you get to where you belong, learn all you can, and find a way to free Daddy!"

"No, Laura!" Luke insisted. "There has to be another way! We need to get more help! I can't go on without Aunt Claire and Uncle Martin or you! I'm just a dopey kid. I couldn't find my way out of a paper bag if Aunt Claire wasn't holding my hand."

Tears came to Laura's eyes, which surprised Luke. She paused for a minute or two. A profound sadness came over her. Then she spoke very slowly and very softly, as if she were having problems talking at all, and she kept looking down at the sand. "There's no help, Luke!" She looked at him; inside she felt nothing but hopelessness. There was no way to explain to Luke, a 12-year-old, just how bad the situation was.

"Members of the Realm, the ones who would support us, will not expose themselves in the mundane Bennie world. The risk is too high! In this world, the Bennies have amassed enormous armies. With the right blessing and an atom bomb, the Valley of the Griffin would be obliterated in a single flash. This would be the mundane version of fighting good over evil. Even though we are the good guys, the fear our kind puts into the hearts of men wouldn't make the fact that we are good people matter very much. From the Bennie point of view, it would be just as good to get rid of all members of the Realm, good or bad. They would consider the problem solved that way. To them, life is very cheap. They don't know any better, and if someone tried to explain it to them, they wouldn't listen."

Laura continued to cry, and she felt hopeless. She didn't cry much. In fact, she had not cried like this since the Battle of the Griffin Valley. With Luke once again at her side, she had found someone she believed she could trust with her feelings. She didn't trust many people. There were insiders who helped the Darkside destroy the valley and her parents. More than a decade later, no one knew who they were. Laura didn't cry because she had deep fear, a fear that someone would think she was weak. Luke looked at her, and even though she was obviously in pain, he started to shake his head no.

"No, Laura," he told her. "You go because I am not leaving! This is my home! I don't want anything to happen to anyone!"

Laura kept crying and looked right into Luke's eyes. She whispered in a desperate, sad voice, "You have to go, Luke! There's no other way to turn this thing around! I have tried everything I could think of. The chancellor has tried everything he could think of. If you don't go and find a way to free Daddy, then they win! They will destroy us, and they will not stop until every living thing on this planet has been destroyed."

Luke looked back at her. He didn't know really what to say to make it better. "We'll find a way, Laura. I bet Aunt Claire and Uncle Martin already have a plan!"

Laura shook her head no. "They have no plan, Luke. No one will help them while they live outside the Realm, and no one will deny them the right to choose where and how they want to live."

Just then, the two heard the cats hissing. They had discovered the snakes on the sand dunes! When Laura heard the sound, she stopped crying, and all emotion left her face. She had let her guard down, but now she sensed danger. Laura seemed to be two different people: the little girl that was left behind in the valley after the great battle and the woman who grew up the hard way without the people she loved. She had always had problems balancing the two. To her surprise, Luke seemed to bring out her better side.

"Come on, Luke," Laura said calmly as if nothing were wrong. "We'd best be getting back before someone starts worrying about us."

Soon, the two were crossing the road and walking behind the convenience store and in front of the docks. Luke glanced out across the docks and said, "Oh, no!"

"What?" Laura said as she stopped walking to see what the problem was.

"That boat there," Luke pointed. "That's the Lady Sara! That's Uncle Martin's boat. It's only lunchtime; it shouldn't be here at this time of day. There's something wrong!" At which point Luke took off running toward the boat to find out what had happened.

"Luke!" Laura shouted. "Where are you going? It's not safe out here!" Laura followed, but she kept looking around in every direction.

"Oh, he's safe here!" an old man on the boat next to her said after she finished shouting. "It's not like the big city in Sugarloaf! Nope, people around here watch out for each other! We're all good neighbors! The boy's fine! Nothing to worry about."

Laura didn't say anything to the man. She just smiled at him and then walked on. "I don't recall asking for people to volunteer information," she thought.

Luke jumped down on to the deck of Uncle Martin's boat and shouted, "Uncle Martin!" He looked around and shouted some more. "Uncle Martin!"

"He's not here!" a voice from behind said, and Luke quickly turned around to find himself face-to-face with Jimmy.

"What are you doing here, Jimmy?" Luke responded.

Jimmy hesitated for a moment, smiled, and said, "Well, suren I live here now, don't I?"

There was something wrong about Jimmy, and Luke could both see and feel it. He didn't know what it was. He couldn't quite put his finger on it. Jimmy looked very different somehow. Something was wrong. The long, narrow face with the deep-seated dark green eyes and long black hair was all the same. He was wearing a torn shirt and jeans, which were stained with oil. But something about him felt different.

"Jimmy, what is the boat doing here at this time of day?" Luke asked him, wondering why he ducked the question the first time.

"We had some trouble on the port-side engine," Jimmy told him. "So we came back in and gave all of the Bennies a refund for the day!"

"Oh?" Luke said not sure whether he believed him or not. "Where's Uncle Martin?"

"He went up to the house about an hour ago." Then Jimmy put his arm around Luke and said, "Now why don't you come on down below and have a look at that engine. I'm sure a smart lad like you could figure it all out in a short time!"

Jimmy was trying to lead Luke off to the hatch that led to the bottom deck when Laura coughed and cleared her throat loudly. Jimmy turned around and saw the girl standing there.

"I'm sorry," Jimmy said politely. "No charters for today. The boat is being repaired."

Jimmy just kept looking at Laura. He looked, and he looked some more.

"Suren I'll be happy to give you a ride around the Sound if you really have your heart set on going for a wee ride!"

Laura wasn't smiling at all. She didn't think Jimmy was cute and didn't care for his obviously sexist comment either.

"I'm with Luke," she said to him.

"Oh," Jimmy was surprised. "Luke isn't allowed to hang out with strangers."

"She's no stranger," Luke told him.

"Laddy," he responded, "I'm sure if I had seen her before, I wouldn't have forgotten it."

"She's Laura, Jimmy," Luke told him. "My sister, Laura!"

"Oh!" Jimmy said with more than just surprise. He didn't know that Luke knew he had a sister. Jimmy kind of looked like the family cat that had just been caught eating the family pet bird. "Aye, well, I guess you're no stranger then, are ya?" Jimmy said looking very uncomfortable and even a little nervous.

Laura crossed her arms and walked right up to Jimmy. She got very close and looked him in the eye.

"Where's Martin?" she said.

Jimmy hesitated a little and said, "He's up at the house."

"He's what?" Laura responded with an attitude.

Jimmy stood there for a moment. He looked at her and let out a fake laugh of some kind. He put his hands on his hips and then scratched his nose a little. He looked away and then said, "Aye, he's up at the house, my Lady."

Laura held out her hand at Luke.

"Come on, Luke, let's head back."

The two were walking away when Jimmy shouted, "I suppose if I was rude or anything, you'll just give me a zap like Martin does!"

Laura let Luke's hand go and turned around and walked back and got into Jimmy's face. He had crossed his arms but dropped them when she got so close. She looked him right in the eye and said, "Do I need to?"

Jimmy looked down and away from her. Luke wasn't sure whether it was Jimmy Laura didn't like or just men in general. Since arriving, she had yet to have a pleasant encounter with any full-grown male person.

"Ah," Jimmy said as he let loose with another fake laugh, "no, my Lady. I'm not looking for any trouble. Nope."

"Good," Laura told him as she turned and took Luke's hand again. The two walked off toward the house. Laura had her reasons for this kind of behavior. Someone in Sugarloaf had told the Darkside where Luke was. That person was still there. Unless that person drew blood or used power for personal gain, it was impossible to identify a person who had turned bad. Laura was just testing each member of the realm she encountered. They might not like her very much, but being rude was the quickest way to find out who was or was not loyal.

"Oh, boy," Jimmy said to himself quietly as the two left the dock. "She's quite the looker. But I'll be so glad when this lot is gone for good!"

After a short walk, the two found themselves back on the island. Luke was about to dart into the house to look for Aunt Claire and Uncle Martin when Laura told him not to bother. "There's no one in the house," she announced.

"How do you know that?" Luke asked.

"I'm a witch—just like you," she said, smiling.

"Magic again?" Luke asked.

"Aye," she responded while walking very casually. "It's everywhere. It surrounds us and touches us in so many ways it can't be counted. Honestly, the only thing that separates us from your neighbors is the gift to be able to reach out and touch it. Anyway, the only one here is that annoying little man who attacked me. He's up in his room. Martin and Aunt Claire are not far away. Both of them are kind of hard to miss. When it comes to being centered, those two are like beacons of flashing power! The more I stay in one place, the more I can feel the environment around me."

Laura felt comfortable on the little island for some reason. She also felt others who were centered. Members of the Realm of whom she wasn't aware also lived in Sugarloaf. She didn't know whether Luke knew how many there were, so she said nothing. She was surprised but couldn't blame them, really. The place was brilliant as far as she could see.

"Show me how to touch it," Luke insisted.

"Remember the rules, Luke."

"There's no one around! I won't rat you out."

"Rat me out?" Laura laughed. "I haven't heard that in a long time! You sure do know how to make me laugh!"

Laura looked around. There really wasn't a clear view from anywhere behind the house and against the river. There was also the great big rock in the far backside. She didn't sense danger, and knowing her relations, she was willing to bet that the ground had been blessed. That meant no Darksider could walk on it, which was most likely one of the reasons she felt so comfortable on the island. Laura began to walk toward the great rock.

"This huge boulder looks out of place here," she said.

"Yep," Luke replied. "The Army Corps of Engineers never came to pick it back up, or so Uncle Martin told me."

The two walked over behind it where they were truly out of view, or so they thought. They were in clear view of the river. There were tiny sand islands covered with reefs in the river, and unknown to them, there were eyes looking at them from there. Neither could see them because they were low in the water and far away. Off in the distance, way out over the water, where neither Luke nor Laura had noticed, was an enormous black bird of some kind. It was just circling. The cats were gone. Luke had been ignoring them for so long that he and Laura never noticed they were gone. Luke's body-guards were nowhere to be seen.

The two stood behind the rock. Laura pointed at a rock to focus Luke's attention. Then it shot off and skipped across the water.

"Wow! Kewl!" Luke smiled with surprise. Laura smiled back at him. "Show me how to do that!" Luke demanded.

"All right, now! This is just between us, right?" Laura said to him.

"Right," Luke shouted back in a very happy voice.

Laura had Luke sit down next to her. There were many rocks of all different shapes and sizes.

"Pick out a rock you want to move," Laura told him. Luke pointed to a not too small rock, which surprised Laura. Usually starting out small was better.

"Great," she continued. "Focus your eyes on it. Get a good focus of the rock in your head." Luke stared closely at the rock and obeyed his sister's every word. "OK, now, close your eyes. Clear your mind of everything. Think of the rock. See it in your mind. Let your mind reach out to it. Try and feel it using only your thoughts."

After a few moments of trying really hard, Luke said, with a tone of disappointment, "I can't see it or feel it."

Laura placed her fingers between Luke's and held his hand tightly. Then she closed her eyes and began to concentrate. Luke felt what she was doing but didn't understand it. Then, in his mind, he could see the rock. He felt his mind reaching out and touching it. He could feel its textures and its warmth from being in the sun.

"This is so kewl!" Luke said.

Laura smiled. "OK, now I want you to rub the rock and keep rubbing it as I let go. Keep your concentration! Feel it! That's right. Keep it up!' Laura released her hand. "OK. Lift up the rock slowly, Luke. That's right. Good. Keep it up. OK, now, very slowly open your eyes."

Luke opened his eyes. Now he could see the rock and feel it in his mind all at the same time. There it stood suspended in the air! Rather than say something that might break his concentration, Luke stared at the rock and moved it from side to side just a little. He was amazed and stunned, but he kept his focus. He didn't let his emotions take the moment away from him. It was just like Sam's morning dance. Luke already knew how to concentrate from what Sam had been teaching him for years. He had just never realized what all of the concentrating was for! Now he understood why he had been dancing. He tapped into that part of his mind that he trained to used in the dance, and the stone went flying up into the air and clear over to the other side of the river!

Now it was Laura's turn to be totally surprised. She looked at him with wide eyes and amazement and said, "How did you do that?"

"It was the morning dance!" Luke responded slowly. "It took me a while to figure it out, but what you wanted me to do was focus the same way Sam taught me for the dance. So I did, and the rock felt so light I just tossed it!"

"That's amazing, Luke!" Laura told him with pride in her voice. "It takes years for the average witch to master that skill! Tell me more about this dancing."

Luke motioned his thumb upward and behind at the top of the rock they were sitting next to.

"Right up there, every time the sun rises, that's where you'll find Sam and the gang dancing to greet the morning."

Laura looked up and stood up. Then she bent down and leaped into the air, and with a single flip, she was on top of the great rock.

"Wow!" Luke said with shock as he now looked up at her. "How did you do that?"

"The same way you threw the rock," she told him. "Instead of pushing off of a rock, I pushed off of the ground. The ground doesn't move, so I do."

Luke looked at the ground, and he began to concentrate just like as if he were doing the dance. Keeping his concentration, he lifted off of the ground and straight up to the same level where Laura was. She was laughing at him, and he didn't understand why.

"What?" he said.

"If you're focused in one direction, how are you going to get on the rock?" she said, laughing some more. The little girl in her was out again. She was amazed at Luke's ability to amuse her.

"You mean I'm stuck?"

Laura just laughed at him, which broke his concentration. Luke went crashing down on the sand.

"That's not funny," Luke shouted as he rolled over off of his back on to his knees and back up onto his feet.

"It's OK," she said smartly. "Little boys bounce, don't you know?" She continued to laugh more and said, "I told you! You have to learn the hard way, or you'll keep making mistakes. The reason we jump and flip is to target a place where we want to land. But you have to do that and be able to concentrate on the push off at the same time. Otherwise, you'll just have to climb up here just like a Bennie would!" Laura began to laugh again. She had not laughed so much in a long time!

Luke stepped back and prepared for a running start.

"What are you doing?" Laura demanded to know, but Luke didn't respond. He began his run. "No, no, no, Luke! Don't run first!"

He didn't pay attention. He was focusing his mind for the push off. He ran, jumped, and pushed off hard. Luke flew right up and over the rock and down the other side, and he bounced onto the sand on the far side.

Now Laura was laughing so hard she couldn't stand up. Humiliated, Luke rolled over again, stood back up, and this time, he climbed up on the rock. When his head came up over the edge, Laura spotted him and broke out in a roaring laugh. She couldn't talk she was laughing so hard!

Luke stood looking at her with his hands on his hips. "She needs to shut up," he thought. She was laughing so hard he had to smile some as well. But he didn't want to! The problem was that she was laughing at him, and he didn't like that too much at all. He walked over to one of the dancing sticks that were lying on top of the great rock. He picked one up and walked over to Laura and pointing it at her, gave her a little push with it. This caused Laura to open her eyes and see what he was up to.

"What?" she said with a big smile.

"Surrender or die!" Luke said to her. To which Laura just broke out laughing even more.

"Surrender or I will have to teach you a lesson!" Luke warned her.

Still laughing, Laura looked up and finally noticed what it was he was pointing at her.

"Where did you get that tie die from?" she insisted.

"This is one of the dancing sticks we practice with," he told her.

"Someone has trained you in the use of a tie die stick," she responded with surprise in her voice.

"Yeah," Luke said smartly, "and if you don't stop laughing at me, I am going to be forced to give you a lesson!"

"You're going to give me a lesson!" Laura broke out laughing again.

"You can die lying down or standing up! The choice is yours," Luke announced.

"OK," she responded as she rolled over and began to stand up slowly. Her sides were hurting from laughing so much. "Don't I get something to defend myself with? It's only fair that I get to defend myself!"

Luke looked at her very suspiciously. He already knew how fast she was, but she had no clue what he could do with a dancing stick.

"Behind you," he responded.

Laura walked over and picked up her own stick. The two began to circle the top of the great rock.

"Are you prepared to meet your maker?" Luke announced.

"You haven't been listening, shorty!" Laura responded with a smart attitude as she played along with Luke's tough guy attitude. They were just playing the way little boys like to play, and Laura was thinking, "I'm in charge!" Laura warned him, "Haven't you noticed what happens when someone talks tough around me? Hmm? You have what we call in the Realm an `alligator' attitude!"

"'Alligator attitude'?" Luke said. "What the heck is an alligator attitude?"

"That's someone, usually a boy, who is all mouth and no ears! Like you!"

"OK, little girl!" Luke said smartly. "You talk the talk really good! I bet you don't walk the walk against a true master!"

"A master smart-ass maybe," she responded.

With that, Luke lunged forward, and Laura blocked his move. Then he went again, this time swinging a countermove to her block and forcing Laura to shift her weight to cut off his swing.

"Is that your best?" she said smartly.

Again Luke lunged, and she blocked and shifted weight to block his countermove, but Luke had only faked the move this time! His stick shifted and came down on her opposite side in the direction of the way she had shifted her weight. He stung her!

"Ouch! Ya little worm! That hurt!" Laura said as she realized that she had underestimated him somewhat. "But just how much does he know?" she wondered.

"Alligators might not listen too well, but we do bite, don't ya know! Ha!" Luke said with spite.

Now Laura lunged. Luke blocked her again and again. She tried to get him to back off or shift his weight, but she couldn't. Laura slowly realized that Luke had not only been trained to fight; he knew what he was doing and was well practiced at it! If he were to trade the sticks for a sword, he would be very dangerous! His speed was very surprising. But how much speed did this little boy have? "It's time to turn up the pressure," Laura thought. "Let's see if he really can protect himself."

On Luke's next strike, Laura spun to his opposite side. Luke was forced to step back because he wasn't ready for that move. He was surprised she knew how to do that! Maybe dancing in the morning sun was normal in the Realm and like so many other things, no one had bothered to tell him! Luke was getting mad. She was forcing him to back away instead of fight! "No!" Luke thought. "Focus, not fear. I have to think, not get mad. Remember what Sam taught me."

Laura spun at him again, and so Luke spun to block her spinning and her swing. She reversed, and he reversed. Once again they stood toe to toe, swinging, spinning, countermoving, blocking, and then they began to speed up because nothing else was working. Soon the sticks they used became blurs in the wind. Then, for just a brief momentary variation of focus, Laura shifted her weight the wrong way. Luke swung down on her sword hand and stung her very hard. The stick went flying out of her hand, and Laura went down on one knee.

"Son of a!" she screamed. "Oh, God!" She was in pain.

Luke was out of breath. He felt terrible. When jousting, one is supposed to pull one's punches. Luke became so focused on what he was doing, the speed was fast, and when her concentration broke, he wasn't ready for it. In the past, it had taken all five members of the morning dancers to do what Laura accomplished by herself. "She's incredible," he thought. What unbelievable speed she had!

They were both breathing very heavily.

"I'm sorry, Laura! You surprised me when you shifted that last time. I couldn't pull back fast enough!"

Laura looked up at him as she held her hand in pain. She said slowly, carefully, and with incredible sincerity, "Don't be sorry, Luke! No one has ever beaten me! No one! Not one other person on this planet! I am very proud of you, Luke!" Although she didn't cry, Laura's eye filled with tears, and her face was red. "Mom and Dad would be so proud of you, boy. You're no alligator either. I was just messing with ya, of course, but I was still way wrong about that. You may not be listening to me very well, or so I thought, but you've been listening very well to someone. Who the hell taught you how to fight like that?"

"I did!" a voice from below shouted.

The two turned their attention in the direction of the voice. There stood Sam, who bowed to Luke, because she was the one who had taught him, and Boo and Loraine, Martin, and Aunt Claire. They had all seen the last moment of the match. It was such an incredible sight they had been totally silent with amazement.

PARADOX OF THE HOUSE COHAN

HOUSE COHAN

CHAPTER 7

WHILE THE GROUP was surprised to see Laura and Luke matching it up on the great rock, they weren't exactly happy about it. Perhaps they were amazed and even stunned at the speed the two were able to display in their match. No one had ever seen such a display. Still, they didn't look very happy about it.

"I didn't speak my permission for Luke to leave this island," Martin announced in a not-so-happy tone of voice as Laura and Luke leaped off of the top of the rock.

Laura put her hands on her hips and was slightly bent over, still breathing a little heavily from her encounter with Luke. Although the blow from his stick was still painful, she chose to ignore the pain. She also ignored the fact that Claire had given permission for Luke to go with her and assumed full responsibility for it.

"I didn't know I needed any," Laura replied calmly without emotion.

That really was Laura's best effort at ignoring Martin's attitude problem. She was here to confront Martin. Even so, there was no reason to go at him with an audience around. She could wait for a more private moment if he let it happen. If not, she was prepared to do what had to be done, audience or not.

At that moment, a cat moved into the yard behind Laura. In a moment more, Marta appeared, and the cat was gone. Marta was as tall as Laura. She stood there silently with her arms crossed. She stared at Laura from behind. She didn't have a very friendly look on her face. Marta generally didn't like surprise visits from anyone. As far as she was concerned, Laura was there without permission.

Laura turned without moving her feet, and her arms were now crossed. She looked over at Marta. Her expression never changed. She turned back to Martin and said, "Get your lap girl off of my back, Martin, before I teach her some respect!"

Martin was about to tell Marta to move on. He wasn't too happy with the move she made either. But before he had the chance to say anything, Marta let loose with a little attitude of her own.

"I would like to see you try—"

Marta attempted to finish her sentence, but before she could finish to the word "try," she stopped breathing and began choking! She unfolded her arms and grabbed her chest as she went down on her knees. Luke watched with fear.

"Maybe you're the one who needs to learn a little respect," Martin shouted at Laura. "Let her go. Now!"

Suddenly, Marta could breathe again. Luke ran over to her to see whether she needed any help. There was silence—a very uncomfortable moment when no one said a thing. The sounds of wind and birds dominated, and everyone just stared at one another.

Martin had always been quick to settle things. He could enforce his decisions if needed. However, Martin never went around picking on anyone or starting trouble. His decisions were always about work or family. He never told people how they should, could, or would live their lives. Decisions involving the Realm were ones he made because of his position, and they were decisions that most practitioners believed he should make—he never made them because he wanted to. It was always part of a duty he never wanted. Now he was faced with someone who was intent on replacing him. Laura could take on the lot of them, and he knew it. Martin was certain she wouldn't hurt Luke or Claire. "She wouldn't hesitate to take out the rest of them," he thought. "Including me."

If he struck at her right now, he figured maybe, just maybe, with a little luck, he could bring her down. She did look ready for it, however. Martin couldn't decide, and he was more than a little nervous. He liked living, being part of life, and had avoided being part of the Realm for exactly the reason that now faced him—trouble.

Jimmy arrived to witness the standoff. Marta got back to her feet, but she was weak.

"I know it's a bit late, but I was wondering whether there was anything to eat," Jimmy asked. He knew something bad was about to happen, but he didn't know what else to say.

Claire broke her concentration by blinking and nodding her head a bit. "Aye," she said loudly. "The soup is sitting waiting for us still. No one has eaten. Let's all go have some," she insisted.

Martin also broke his concentration when the others began to walk away.

"Martin," Claire shouted. "Soup!"

He looked down at the ground as everyone but Laura headed for the house. Then he looked over at the house, and without saying a word, he headed in. As the door closed behind them, Laura headed for the river to soak her hand in it.

There was a huge kettle simmering slowly with chicken noodle soup. It was one of Claire's specialties. Everyone grabbed a large bowl and a slice of French bread. Luke filled two and grabbed two slices. He put the lot on a tray and began to leave for the yard. Martin spotted him and was about to tell him not to, but before he could make a sound, Claire put her hand on top of his. He looked over at her. Claire shook her head no without saying a word. Clearly she wanted Luke to leave. Soon he was out and gone. Everyone was silent. They sipped their soup and ate their bread and kept looking up, waiting for someone to say something.

"Laura is convinced you cannot protect Luke anymore, Martin," Claire looked at him most seriously when she spoke this.

"Who the hell cares what she thinks?" was Martin's answer.

"If you didn't care, Martin, ya thick-headed Irish oaf, you would have taken her out the moment she grabbed Marta," Claire said. She was direct, blunt, and to the point. Martin wasn't fooling anyone.

"I didn't do anything out of respect for my brother!" Martin answered.

"You didn't do anything because she was ready to cut you into little pieces if you did, damn it!" Claire said.

"How is it possible she could overwhelm Martin?" Jimmy asked.

"Without breaking a sweat!" Lorraine jumped in and told him.

"What?" Jimmy looked confused. "How?"

"She's a bloody ice woman!" Lorraine said a bit louder than normal and a little more nasty than usual. "Sonny charged her with a broadsword, and she didn't even flinch! When he took a swing at her, before he could move his arm forward, she drew down on him and shattered his sword like it was a bloody child's toy!"

"Sonny drew down on a member of the Realm?" Marta was clearly stunned by this news. "Is he gone?"

"Aye," Claire told her. "He'll spend the next 10 days in his room, or he will be leaving!"

"10 days?" Boo spoke up. "That's it? Ten days? He draws on a practitioner, and all he gets is 10 days of rest? Doesn't the General Council want to see him now?"

"You'll be minding your business!" Martin told her.

"Aye," Claire agreed. "If the council has a problem with the sentence, they can have a word with me about it!"

"Suren I wish someone would explain why Martin has to worry about this girl," Jimmy insisted.

Claire looked down at the table and said, "The chancellor told me she's a master of all of the elements. He said she is her father's daughter. Besides the White Robin himself, he says he's never seen anyone like her!"

"Still," Jimmy insisted, "Martin is a Robin! She has to obey him!"

"Martin is a Robin by birth, Jimmy," Claire explained. "He's never been consecrated. Laura is a first Lady by birth, an Alfa-Omega by trial and ordeal, and an ordained fully consecrated leader of the Realm. She doesn't take orders from anyone. If Luke completes his trials successfully and accepts ordination, he will outrank her. Until then, she is the natural and consecrated leader of the Realm."

"The boy has to go, then," Jimmy said casually.

"He goes when I say and not before!" Martin shouted as he stood up. "Does anyone here have a problem with that? Speak up now!"

Everyone else was silent, but Claire stood up. She seemed very nervous but determined and perhaps a bit scared.

"Luke has to go, Martin," she told him.

"Claire! What are you saying?" Martin was completely surprised by this.

"She's come here for her brother. She's taking him with her, and if you step in her way, she'll kill you, and you know it!"

"Over my dead body!" Marta announced.

"Aye," Claire looked at her and said with an attitude in her voice. "She bloody well almost did! What was that brilliant move of yours out there coming up from behind her? Before Martin could open his mouth, you were on your knees!"

Everyone was silent. They all looked at each other as Claire sat back down to eat her soup. Martin looked at her for a moment. Then he too sat back down.

Out by the river, near the pearl farm, Laura lay down on a rock with her right hand in the river. The coolness of the water eased the pain from the brilliant strike of her brother's stick. She lay there with her eyes closed as the flow of the water rolled over her hand slowly. Her mind was focused, and her eyes were closed, so she never noticed a long black snake moving up on her hand in the water. The sun was still bright but was getting low in the western sky.

Laura was also going over events in her mind. "The entire first encounter with Martin was all wrong," she thought. "He's Daddy's brother! I can't hurt him!" She didn't think she was very good at dealing with people from outside the Realm. Inside, she felt very very insecure around strangers. She pondered how Luke's life had been radically different than hers. She had spent the last 12 years alone, taking her parent's place as a leader, and learning everything the hard way. Luke was surrounded by people who cared about him and were willing to fight for him. Luke wasn't in charge here. He didn't have to give orders. Laura had spent the last 12 years learning how to give orders not take them. Her ways of dealing with people didn't work in Sugarloaf. They didn't work outside the Realm. Laura was with her family for the first time in 12 years and yet here again she was alone, or so she thought.

Luke showed up with a tray in his hands. He looked on the dock first and didn't see her. Then next to the water's edge, he spotted her and began to climb down. The snake spotted him and quickly swam off.

"It's time to eat," Luke announced.

Laura turned her head and looked up at him using her hand to shade her eyes. She then sat up on the rock as Luke handed her a bowl of soup, some bread, and a cold soda. Laura was impressed with the soup. She had tasted something like it long ago. Like everyone else who lived at the university, the valley's cooks prepared most of her food. The real treats came when she visited New York and Boston. Still, there was something personal about the soup. Someone had taken a great deal of care in preparing it. That care was what Laura was thinking about when she enjoyed one sip after another. It was something she had been missing and was not aware of until that moment.

The two sat for quite a while just looking out across the water while they enjoyed their bread and soup. There was something enchanting about the view. The sun was getting lower and lower, and as it did, it defused the light through the water vapor rising over the river and Sugarloaf Sound. It created a rainbow of colors as the sun sparkled in the flowing ripples of the water. Then the silence and the enchantment were broken rudely.

"I'm sorry about your hand," Luke said to her.

The sudden sound of his voice was like being woken up in the middle of a dream. She blinked a few times as the enchantment was broken and she came back to reality.

"Don't be," Laura responded. "In all competitions, there is good and bad. Sometimes you lose, and sometimes you win. I had to come all the way to Florida just to lose. I won all my matches until today. I enjoyed every single win. I suggest you do the same. You earned it!"

"But you're hurt."

"Aye, not badly. By morning it will be gone. If you want, I'll take you on again right now," she said with an alluring tone in her voice and a smile on her face.

"Ah, no," Luke told her with a big silly smile and the sound of reluctance in his voice. "I've already humiliated you. Don't want to press my luck. One can of whoop ass a day is enough."

Laura began to laugh with the spoon still in her mouth. Then she swallowed and nearly choked on the soup she was trying to eat. "Man, you are such a Cohan, aren't you?" she blurted out, followed by some coughing and tearing of her eyes as she laughed a little more.

"Nope, my name is Carter. Why is my name and your name Carter?"

"All in good time, Luke, all in good time," she explained still laughing and coughing a little.

"Laura!"

"I'm eating here!" she told him with her mouth full. "Round two is next if you don't let me eat! I have a bigger can of whoop ass over here waiting on that smart mouth of yours!"

Luke stared at her for a moment, and when she finished taking a drink of her soda, he asked the question he really had on his mind. "Are you going to hurt Uncle Martin?"

Laura didn't even look over at him. This business of going from the funny to the serious was wearing on her. Still Luke didn't know her very well, so she was trying to be tolerant. She was also hoping to change a little so she could communicate with others without them getting angry with her.

"I don't ever want to hurt anyone, Luke. It's not my choice. Something has to be done, or it's going to be just like 12 years ago all over again. Everyone has been waiting for Martin to make a move to deal with the current situation. He hasn't. He's given one bull-headed answer after another, void of logic! He's forced me into having to make decisions for him, and now, he's put me in a position of having to enforce those decisions. You'll forgive me if I am a little more than just disappointed with him."

The two didn't talk much after that. Luke had no answers for what was going on around him. His mind kept wondering about the day's events. He didn't like the welcome everyone gave his sister when they came back. She was family, and they were rude!

"Who goes around chasing strangers off with a broadsword?" Luke wondered. He thought Marta had deliberately irritated Laura by coming up from behind her. He thought his sister was scary, obviously special, and without a clear reason in his mind, he was drawn to her. He didn't believe she would hurt Uncle Martin or Aunt Claire. Luke did understand she was intent on having her way. On the other hand, it was also becoming increasingly clear that if Laura had a choice, she in fact would not be there.

What was completely unclear to Luke was the driving source of all this conflict. The dark side of something? "Was Uncle Martin on the dark side?" he wondered. The way she explained in on the beach, it now looked as if Laura intended to create some kind of balance by offing Uncle Martin. This was supposed to make sense? She had been there just a few hours and had managed to piss off everyone she came in contact with! Even the lifeguards on the beach walked away! "Maybe she's on the dark side of something. Does a secret Cohan talent of some kind possess Laura?" Luke considered. Was this perhaps another bit of information everyone figured he was too young to have explained to him?

The two spent the rest of the evening literally sitting and watching the birds fish as the sun got lower and lower. They weren't watching the river much. The sun getting low over the Gulf of Mexico was far more interesting. So as the reeds in the middle of the river filled up with more and more snakes, they didn't notice. They also didn't notice that high over the Sound where there was once just one enormous black bird now there were four.

"Luke, take the dish back into the kitchen," Claire told him as she came out to see what the two were up to. He did as she asked, and as he headed back in, he ran into Uncle Martin coming out of the house.

"We're going to have a word or two with your sister," Martin said to him. "You'll stay in the house until we're finished." Then Martin just kept walking toward the river. Luke stood there for a moment and watched him walk away. He had a very bad feeling inside.

Claire stepped down to the water level where Laura was sitting and watching the sunset. Martin came up on the other side. Laura's senses were acutely aware of both of them. She was watching the sunset, but her senses were focused on Claire and Martin. She could feel every move they made and thought things were about to go very badly.

"Is this the plan? The two of you coming at me from two different directions? It doesn't matter! You know I'll win anyway!" Laura told them both.

"I'm sorry you feel threatened by us, Laura. At least for my part, I would never try to hurt you. Hurting someone you love is the same as hurting yourself," Claire said. Her voice was soft, not at all aggressive.

Laura turned from the sunset and gazed over at Martin. She seemed very confident to Martin. "She needs a lesson or two," he thought.

"I'll go over and sit by Claire if it would make you feel safe," Martin told her. He was more bothered by the fact that he had to walk the distance than the fact that he had to deal with her. So he did and took a seat on a rock next to Claire.

Finally Laura broke her concentration on the sunset and looked over at her aunt and uncle. They were looking back at her and were waiting for her to say something.

"What?" was her response to being stared at.

"Where do we go from here?" Claire asked her.

"I'm not sure. I thought Martin and I would have a nasty fight and whoever survived would decide Luke's fate."

"You came here to kill your own uncle, did you, Laura?"

"I don't want to hurt anyone," Laura told her. "I have been forced into this!"

"So the chancellor has you out doing his dirty work now, has he?" Martin jumped in and asserted.

Laura turned and was about to say something but Claire cut her off. "Martin, you promised me you would be nice!" Claire told him.

"Aye," he responded. "It just irks me when people stick their noses into our business!"

"Luke is Laura's brother, and he is her business. We agreed on this!"

"Not her—the bloody chancellor! He's got her out here doing his dirty work!" Martin insisted.

The two looked back at Laura as she said, "I've been at the side of the chancellor for 12 years now. I have never witnessed him doing any dirty work, as you say it."

"He sent those bloody leprechauns after Luke!" Martin shouted.

"He did no such thing!" Laura told him.

There was a slight pause when a realization came over Claire's face. "You! You sent them!" Claire told her with total surprise in her voice.

"Aye," Laura responded. "They told Luke that a member of his family sent them."

"Why?" Martin insisted on knowing. "Why?"

"Because those two are master tricksters," Laura said. "Very clever they are, and I reasoned they could get Luke out without anyone getting hurt. That was the plan, anyway. Luke would make it to the valley, and I would have avoided coming here and getting him myself. I wouldn't have to lay down the law and then be made to enforce it. It didn't work out, unfortunately."

"You lay down the law?" Martin sounded as if he had been insulted.

"I was confirmed over a year ago, Martin," Laura told him. "You got invitations to come! But like everything else important to this family, you turned your back on that as well!"

"We got invitations?" Claire said, surprised. She looked right at Martin.

"Aye," Martin replied, not looking at either of them and nodding his head yes.

"Why wasn't I told?" Claire insisted.

"Because I tore them up and threw them in the bin," Martin said.

Claire looked at him in complete surprise. She was stunned by this revelation. Then she turned back to Laura. "I would have come had I known, Laura," Claire told her. She was very unhappy with this news.

"I know," Laura said. "What can you expect from a coward?"

Martin jumped to his feet and shouted, "You stand up! I'll show you what kind of coward I am!"

Laura and Claire both stood. Claire stepped between them and turned at Martin.

"Is that what you want, Martin? You want to kill your brother's daughter? It's possible, you know. You may or may not be as powerful as she is, but you know a lot more tricks than she does. You might get her, or she might get you. Whoever gets whomever will then have to face Luke. Do you want to go in and tell him you've killed his sister? Do you? What then if he learns the only father he's ever known is now dead? Is that what you want him to hear, Martin? Is it?"

Martin shook his head no.

"Then sit down now! Sit down!" Claire shouted.

Claire turned around and faced Laura.

"Sit down, Laura," she said sternly—but calmly and not rudely.

Laura sat back down without saying a word. Then Claire also sat back down. Another short moment of silence followed.

"Martin is no coward, Laura," Claire told her. "Long ago, he made a choice that no one was happy with but him, and he's been made to pay for it ever since!"

Laura looked over at Martin. He had his back to both of them now.

"What happened to you, Martin?" Laura said in a quiet voice. She made certain she would not be thought rude. She really did want to learn how not to be rude.

He didn't say anything at first. He didn't want to talk to her. He kept looking away from both of them when he finally decided to speak.

"Aye, 'twas a long time ago, lassie," Martin said. His voice had changed to a very sad tone that surprised Laura. "Seems like a long-lost dream now. My grandfather had sent my father from Ireland to the Griffin Valley so everyone there could get to know the future White Robin. Like me, my father was raised with wizard's craft. He loved it here in America. The people were so different. He spent three years learning shaman's crafts and the fighting arts. Wizards don't fight hand-to-hand, you know. His teachers were amazed at how fast he mastered the elements. My grandfather was very proud that he had made such a good impression. He died while my dad was still here. When Dad returned to bury his father, the authorities, the White Robin's caldron, insisted he marry. Without children, he was the only surviving member of the natural line.

"Dad was just 16 when he married my mom. She was just 14 years old. A year later, she had me. Life in Ireland was good for us, though not so good for the rest of the Irish. Ireland was a poor country then. Still, I went to the best schools and had really good mates. My father taught me shaman's crafts and the fighting arts. The members of his caldron didn't like that at all, mostly because they didn't think much of the American Realm. Eventually, he had to teach me in private so as to avoid dissension. My father was always a good diplomat—'twas and still is an unusual trait for a Cohan. Fighters, aye, we like to fight first and ask questions later. You'll have to grow old like me before you see a different wisdom, I'm thinking.

"To make a long story short, when it came time for me to be confirmed, the very first time when I would decide something for myself, I said no! I didn't want to be a witch or a wizard. I certainly didn't want to be in charge of anything!

"My father and his caldron spent weeks trying to change my mind. They tormented me, and when they were convinced I would never change my mind, they tried to hurt me. They wanted me fixed so I would never have children! My father stopped them, of course. He banished me from the Realm and told me never to contact him or my mother ever again.

"When she had your father, my mother was 34 years old, and she was 36 when she had Harry. This made no difference to the people of the Realm in Ireland. My refusal had started a crisis by altering the natural order of succession. Everyone blamed my parents for the way they raised me. They forced my parents out of Ireland. My father could have easily brought them all to their knees and laid down the law—the same way you are so intent on doing today! Instead, they came here to Sugarloaf. In time, they became American citizens. They changed their name to Carter so it would be difficult for them to be found. They invited the most loyal members of the Realm to come and live near them.

"The wings of the White Robin never passed to me because I was never confirmed. When my father died, your dad invited me to the funeral. All was forgiven as far as he was concerned. He was so happy I came to live with them. I was too! I had missed my mother so much that my heart was broken most of the time. I spent the last 10 years of my mother's life with her. You, lassie, you made your grandmother's face light up. She was so proud of you!"

Martin turned back to face Laura.

"I didn't come after the battle in the valley because I have never stepped back inside the Realm since that day so long ago. Although I have explained it to them many times, the Americans did not care to understand about my past. They still don't. When their entire leadership was wiped out, they turned to me for answers. I brought Luke here because I knew this place was safe. I left you there for several reasons. First, you were already of age to begin your higher education. Second, because I knew that the Darksiders had launched attacks outside the Realm, which meant the Bennie president would get involved. The chancellor would have his leadership respected if he had you at his side. I knew that as soon as someone descended, so long as you were standing next to him, no one would second-guess his decisions. I also knew that Dickelbee was the only one with the skills and connections to deal with the Bennie authorities. It was vital that he be there. You also guaranteed his respect in this area.

"Now, that is the most I have had to say to anyone in 20 years!"

"Aye, you can say that again," Claire told him.

Laura looked at him for the longest time without saying a word. Then she turned and looked out toward the setting sun again.

"I can see why the grandparents liked it here so much. This place is brilliant," Laura said to them.

She crossed her arms and sat back against the rock. She thought for a moment. She decided to be careful about what came out of her mouth next. Martin's revelations about her grandfather impressed her.

"Luke has to leave here right away, Uncle Martin," she said calling him 'uncle' for the first time ever. "One or more of your local loyal practitioners has given you and him away. The Darkside is on the move again!"

"I had hoped Luke would go past age 16 without becoming centered," he responded.

"He would have been just as dead!" Laura asserted. "He could still have children, so he would have still been a threat. They would have hunted him down anyway!"

"Aye," Martin finally agreed. He wasn't happy about it, but he finally agreed. "You can take the boy off to school," Martin told her as tears came to his eyes and his voice broke. He turned away feeling ashamed that he had failed Luke. Then Claire began to cry, and finally Laura put her face in her hands and also began to cry. She was so relieved that no one would get hurt today!

The crisis was over, or so Laura believed. Above the rocks where they all sat, Jimmy stood listening in. He had heard what was said, and as soon as he heard it, he turned and quickly walked off toward the harbor.

In the river there were now nearly a hundred snakes or more. They were swarming and watching as if they were waiting for something to happen. The sun was on the horizon's edge and was about to dip below it.

✷

THE BATTLE OF
SUGARLOAF SOUND
CHAPTER 8

✷

A DIFFUSION OF colors from the sun setting over Sugarloaf sent brilliant reds and yellows reflecting off of the boats and docks as Jimmy made his way to Lady Sara. The air was filled with wind and the noise from the seagulls swarming over the arriving fishing boats. It was almost deafening. Jimmy was not very happy. In fact he looked quite worried. He kept looking around as if he were expecting something to happen. The intense sounds of the birds seemed to disorient him.

Jimmy stepped onto the boat and walked to the aft section. His arms were crossed against himself, holding his body as if he were in pain. The hatchway behind him was open, and in it appeared a shadowy creature dressed in a blood-red cloak. The creature was so tall it had to bend over to fit in the hatchway. As soon as it appeared, Jimmy could feel it, but he did not turn around. He didn't want to look at it. He knew it wouldn't step out of the shadows while the sun remained above the horizon. Then all of the noise went away. It was as if someone had just turned off a blaring radio. In the silence, the creature's voice could be heard.

"Has the plan been successful?" Its voice was harsh and low. It was almost as if it had to exhale to speak. It was eerie to listen to and sent chills up and down Jimmy's spine.

"No," Jimmy said as if the words inflicted pain on him. He did not turn around. "The final decision was made without a fight. The boy will be on his way to the valley soon."

"Pity," the deep, dark voice said. "Now you are condemned to a life of servitude. You will live your days out surrounded by Bennies who you must serve. I would rather be dead!"

"I'll have to come up with another plan," Jimmy responded nervously.

"It's too late for that now," the creature insisted. "The membership has assembled! We will not harm you, of course. You've done us a great service. The Dark Lord thanks you. He would reward you generously if you would come among us. You would be welcomed as a hero."

"No!" Jimmy said with nervous determination. "I'll use no magic to serve my own needs! I never have, and I never will!"

"It's too late for you! You've crossed over and must learn

to be satisfied with your choices. My Lord has instructed you to make a path for us onto the island."

"I can't! The ground has been blessed!"

"You must soil the blessing with blood," the creature told him.

"I'm not killing anyone for you! Do your own dirty work!"

"You have to kill Martin anyway—before he kills you! Once he finds out you're the rat that led us here, he'll hunt you down!"

"No one knows about that!" Jimmy told it.

"If we don't get onto the island, they will, I promise you!"

"So you're gonna burn me, is it?" Jimmy told the creature as he turned pale white.

"Tonight!" the creature spoke with pride. "When the sun shines no more on the house of Milesians, the sacred Robin line, the Fomhoire peoples will rise, and there will be no more secrets!

"You have chosen to serve My Lord, and you have chosen well! Now you must finish it! You will soil the ground with the blood of your true enemy. We will take care of you. You will have peace. First, destroy the looking glass mirror. That will cut off their escape."

"Aye, I understand," Jimmy said with his back still to the creature, pale white and soaked in his own sweat. "You must have brought tens of thousands with you!"

"We don't need so many for so few!"

"You're facing two first ladies," Jimmy warned him, "who are also Alfa-Omegas, along with a naturally born Robin— all three of whom carry charmed swords. There are four centurion witches. Then there is the boy. Since we last spoke, he has become centered. If he gets a sword in his hands, he's unbeatable! I saw it for myself this afternoon. You should move on until I come up with another plan."

"Look above you, Jimmy!" the creature told him.

Jimmy looked up, and there flying above him were five black condors.

"Black condors!" Jimmy said with fear in his voice.

"Yes! My Lord has sent five of his personal minions. They fought their first battles centuries ago. They have never lost. They are here to make an end of the line of kings. The Realm will never again bow to a king! Now go and make our path clear!" Then the creature vanished.

On the island, the sunlight nearly at its end drew Luke out of the house despite his uncle's instructions. He felt ill with worry, and before the light was gone, he needed to know what had happened. He thought someone might be hurt; he thought perhaps they were all hurt. It was possible that they had hurt each other so badly that no one could call for help. There was no way to know, and Luke had to know!

He walked across the yard and looked down on the river's shore. He was stunned to see his aunt, uncle, and sister sitting comfortably just staring off into the sunset.

"Is everything OK?" Luke shouted.

Laura shook her head because her daydream had once again been interrupted by the biting sound of her brother's voice. "I am going to have to get used to having a boy around," she said out loud.

Claire smiled and giggled a bit as Martin told Luke, "I thought I said to wait in the house!"

"So is everything all right?" Luke responded with an innocent tone in his voice.

Now it was Laura's turn to giggle.

"Aye," Claire told him as she continued to watch the sunset. "'Tis a grand evening, I'm thinking!"

"It is?" Luke said with disbelief. "Why?"

"Aye," Martin told him. "Go and pack your trunk. You'll be leaving with Laura. She'll be taking you to school."

"What?" Luke shouted and then jumped down. "For real?"

"Yes," Martin said looking at the boy with a smile on his face. Luke jumped onto his uncle and gave him a huge hug. Then he jumped off and onto Claire, giving her a big a hug. He turned to Laura and said, "Is it OK to hug a first Lady?"

"You just did!" she told him.

"I did?"

"Yes! Aunt Claire is also a first Lady! Didn't you know that?"

"At this time last week, I didn't even know there was a Realm! I didn't even know there was a you either! Not until this morning anyway! I had to be kidnapped last Sunday before I knew anything! It's been a rough week!" Luke told her as he jumped up at his sister and gave her a big hug as well. When he turned and ran back to Claire and gave her a big kiss as he headed back to ready his trunk.

"You'll need your uniform and cloak on!" Laura shouted as Luke ran off toward the house.

Claire turned to watch him leave, and when she turned back, she had tears in her eyes. Laura got up and went and sat next to her. She gave her a hug and then wrapped her arm around her.

"I promise you," Laura told her, "if there were any other way, I wouldn't take him away from you."

"Aye," Claire said nodding her head. "I know. Suren don't I know it."

Laura turned and watched the last of the sun go below the horizon. Claire sat and watched with her. The shades of reds and yellows reflected in both the women's eyes.

"Martin," Laura said.

"Aye, lass."

"Do you know what Merlin's cave is?" Laura asked him without turning away from the horizon.

"Well, it's a wizard's craft, isn't it, I'm thinking? What everyone today keeps forgetting is that wizard's craft comes from many different places, and it's ancient. When you speak of Ireland, Scotland, and England, people forget there was a fight going on there long before Saint Patrick brought the light to the ancient Celts."

Laura and Claire both turned around to look at Martin.

"If this is the same type of magic that trapped Merlin," Martin continued, "then we're talking about the Fomhoire peoples. They were one of the very first groups of Darksiders to attack civilization. But they made countless mistakes. Originally they were few in numbers, so they used humans and creatures they created from humans with magic to do their dirty work."

"They created creatures?" Claire asked him.

"Aye, like fairies."

"Fairies?" Laura looked at him with bewilderment.

"Aye, your leprechaun friends come from a race of fairies," he told her.

"No way!" Laura responded.

"Aye, way!" Martin said as he broke into laughter. "But most leprechauns today aren't evil, at least not the ones here in America. Being here is one of the reasons they gave up evil. Here they don't have to worry about some fairy prince or princess trying to drag them back in. They turned along with many humans who were first taken over by the Fomhoire. One of the most famous to break their hold was Merlin.

"You see, Laura, the Darkside can grab and use a mundane human. If that human turns away from them, however, he or she does so with all of the magic the Fomhoire gave them. They are members of the Realm thereafter, and they are usually well trained in the magic arts. One of the most famous of these was Merlin. To seek his revenge, Merlin started and led new caldrons of witches and wizards across the old world. He taught them to fight the Darkside, and the story of King Author is the story of the time he tried to organize the common folk to fight the Darkside. The Fomhoire could do little to stop the damage Merlin was doing to them."

"Why?" Laura wondered.

"It's all about the greatest gift we all share, a soul," Martin continued. "The Fomhoire and all other Darksider groups cannot grasp the idea and function of God's gift. Those who are already members of the Realm have to give up their soul to join the Darkside, so they are trapped forever. Mundane people don't have a choice when they are taken. Their souls eat away at evil in all its forms. Eventually, the spells of the Darkside are broken by it.

"To deal with Merlin, the Darkside trapped, or froze, him at a point in time. How I don't know. How they managed to do it to Philo is beyond me because I thought your father was beyond anyone's magic. He was the most formidable magical entity I had ever known or heard of across all time!"

Laura stood up, crossed her arms, and began to move toward Martin a little.

"Why can the Darkside not understand the human soul?"

"Aye, that's what it's all about then, isn't it?" Martin stared into Laura's eyes. "That's what it has always been about. Right from himself to the archangel Lucifer on down! The Darkside doesn't understand love. They could not understand God's creation. They could never understand why he gave his grace to us instead of those who served him in heaven before creation. They can not understand why we protect Luke. They think it's just our tactic to carry on with Merlin's work to destroy them. They're ignorant, lassie! Ignorance is at the center of all of the evil people do everywhere no matter whether they have magic."

"How do we free Daddy, Uncle Martin?" Laura's face had a lost look on it, as if she was looking for hope.

Martin took both of her hands and folded them between his. He didn't cry, but he had tears in his eyes. "I promise you, Laura, as God is my witness, I would have defied my father and charged into the Realm like a bat out of hell itself had I one single idea how to how to find P.J." Martin was desperate that she believe him.

Laura looked into his eyes for a moment or two and then said, "I know and believe that now. I wish I had believed it sooner." Laura smiled. Then she looked over at Claire and whispered, "P.J.?"

"Aye," Claire said with a smile. "Anyone who called your dad friend or family called him P.J.—Philo John. That's his name, P.J."

Then the three heard glass breaking. They all stood up and looked in the direction of the house. In his room, Luke also heard it. He had just finished putting his uniform and cloak on. With a flash, his trunk disappeared, and he opened his bedroom door to go investigate the noise.

"What now?" Claire asked as the three prepared to head back. They had not taken two steps when all three simultaneously turned around and snapped their heads with surprise in the direction of the river.

"Did you feel that?" Laura said with alarm in her voice.

"Aye," both Claire and Martin responded.

"Let's get off these rocks!" Martin ordered.

They had not taken but a few more steps when a giant snake broke the water's surface with surprise.

"Laura, behind you!" Martin shouted as bolts of power flew from his hands. The creature roared in pain. Within an instant there were flashes of light and both the women's swords appeared. Claire pointed at the creature, and energy flew from her sword. The snake burst into dust! Then four more even larger snakes broke the surface and towered above the three. There was flash of light, and into Martin's hand appeared a long golden broadsword. All three fired power from their swords on the creatures, and they we reduced to dust.

"We have to get to Luke!" Laura demanded.

"He's fine!" Martin told her back. "Relax, this land is blessed. They cannot tread here!"

In the house, Luke had made it to the great hall. The large looking glass mirror lay broken on the floor.

"What happened?" Luke shouted, but there seemed to be no one in the house. He moved toward the next room to find out what happened from Uncle Harry's picture. But Uncle Harry wasn't in his picture! "What is going on?" Luke thought.

Luke didn't notice when Jimmy moved out of the kitchen with a sword in his hand. Jimmy moved very slowly, in silence, creeping ever closer and closer to Luke. He thought he had the chance to end it all right then and there. One quick slice, the boy loses his head, and the whole conflict was over! Luke was looking back at the mirror again, and the mess shocked him. Jimmy moved to strike. He raised his sword up, and the door opened. Jimmy quickly ducked back into the hallway.

"What happened?" Sam asked as she walked in.

Jimmy withdrew and made his way toward the door on the other side of the house.

Out by the pearl farm, Martin, Claire, and Laura had made it back to the yard. All three walked carefully and looked in all directions. They couldn't see the Darksiders, but they could feel them.

"Hit the ground!" Martin shouted. All three went crashing into the sand as an enormous black bird came swooping down on them, just missing their heads has they hit the ground.

"Black condor!" Martin said. "Wizards have come!" Martin looked back at the two women who were looking at him like he was some kind of dope. "What?" he said.

"It was just a bird, Martin," Laura insisted.

"Aye," Claire agreed in an equally negative voice. "Suren a condor is but a big flying chicken, for God's sake! You have the best sword here. Why didn't you cut the bloody thing in two instead of putting us all in the dirt?"

"Freakin' a—!" Laura shouted at him. "We could have had made more soup!"

Martin lay there with his mouth open and nodded his head in agreement.

"Aye," he said, struggling to mention while lying on his stomach. "Now that you mention it, that might have been a better idea!"

The three climbed to their feet and dusted the sand off of themselves as they went and began walking again.

"You liked the soup, dear!" Claire mentioned to Laura with a happy tone in her voice as they made their way toward the house.

"It was brilliant," Laura told her.

"You know," Martin said, casually continuing to look about for danger, "I never went through no trials! It's one of the reasons I didn't want to be in the Realm. I didn't want to go through life fighting anything! So while I may have the best sword, I haven't got your killer instincts."

"Great!" Laura says. "Now he tells us!"

"Aye," Claire agreed. "He's useless!"

"Everyone needs to get their cloaks on!" Martin said. "Wizards throw curses and spells at people! A proper cloak is all you will need to shield yourselves."

People often wondered about the clothing witches wear. Some wondered whether it's old or just the way witches dress because they are witches. The truth is that a witch's proper dress is an extension of his or her magic. Today many witches try to cut and design their clothing so that it blends in better with the latest fashion. This is why they go unnoticed in daily life. Still the clothing function has never really changed.

It adds to either their ability to project magic or protect themselves from it.

"I'll get our cloaks, Martin," Claire said as she walked past him. "Stay here and keep watch. I'll be right back!" She paused for a moment and turned back at Laura. "Where are your clothes, dear?" she asked.

As Claire and Martin watched, Laura's clothing appeared on her. She was wearing the same black leather she had arrived in, except now there was also a cloak.

"Sweet lord!" Claire said out loud as Laura's clothing finished appearing on her.

"Aye," Martin agreed, also very impressed with her magic. "That was a good one!"

"If we're still alive in the morning, dear," Claire insisted as she made her way though the door, "you'll have to teach me that one!"

"Aye," Martin said, "that was grand! Brilliant even! What the bloody hell is that you're wearing now?"

Laura stared at Martin, giving him a hairy eye, and wondered what business it was of his what she was wearing. Then she turned to see what might be happening with the Darkside and began to walk away from Martin.

Claire walked into the great hall and saw the looking glass smashed with Luke and Sam standing in front of it.

"What the hell happened?" Claire shouted.

"We don't know," Sam told her.

"I came down from upstairs, and this is how I found it!" Luke told her.

"Damn!" Claire said. "Sam, go and get the others! Sonny too! Tell them to have their cloaks on! The Darksiders are here! Go out the side entrance!"

"Yes, ma'am!" Sam said as she headed out.

"Luke, you stay in the house!" Claire told him.

Luke nodded his head yes.

"Look at me!" she shouted. "You stay in the house, you hear me, boy?"

"Yes, ma'am!" he said.

Claire ran up the stairs to get a cloak for her and Martin.

"Only a woman would have thought up super fashion magical cloths," Martin whispered to himself with a sarcastic tone as he looked around the yard for trouble and began to walk in a direction opposite Laura. Martin wasn't worried about the Darkside arriving at Sugarloaf at all!

"Bet she has a dozen matching pairs of shoes or boots for that outfit!" he whispered.

Martin wasn't worried about the Darksiders because the land was blessed. Evil couldn't walk on concencrated ground; it would destroy them. So all he had to do was wait for sunrise. Still he went to check out the edges of the island to see whether maybe they had a new idea. Martin didn't worry about the enemy, but he respected their abilities ever since they successfully invaded the Griffin Valley. Before they did that, he would have thought it impossible.

"Suren the girl has three or four different matching handbags for that ensemble, I'm thinking," Martin whispered to himself, embarrassed by what his niece was wearing. He was impressed with the magical way she got dressed but not at all with what she put on.

"I heard that!" Laura shouted.

"Ears like an owl!" Martin continued to mutter to himself as he looked around.

If worst came to worst, Martin could cover the whole area in a magical barrier that no Darksider could penetrate. After sunrise, they would all be gone, so he didn't care that the Darkside had arrived. He never concerned himself with the Darkside. They were no match for him, and he knew it! He could be in a wheelchair, and they still were no match for him!

"Darksiders think they've come to fight a big bad Alfa witch," Martin continued to mutter his objection about Laura's clothing. "When they finally show up, they'll find themselves face to face with bloody Mrs. Elvis, rock and roll super magic girl!"

"Will you put a sock in it already?" Laura shouted with frustration in her voice. "The Darkside is here! Try to focus!"

"Aye, suren they aren't here to fight, ya know!" Martin

shouted back. "They just want to be in your next music video!" The two were on either side of the main yard now.

"You let me know if you see anymore big, bad flying chickens, Martin!" Laura shouted back at him. "Try not to get too dirty this time!"

"Will you two stop it?" Claire shouted as she came out wearing her cloak and carrying Martin's. "We're all on the same side! Suren it wouldn't hurt to keep the conversation friendly!"

"Right!" Luke shouted out the window.

Claire looked up at him. "No one was asking you a thing! You'll be closing that window and staying inside like I told you!"

Martin had made his way to the far edge of the small island. There was a tool shed there, and its door had been left open. It was too dark now to see inside. The last of twilight was moving below the horizon. The lights mounted on the house were all that lit the yard now. He was about to reach for the door when Claire called to him. She came walking quickly across the yard as Luke was just finishing closing the window.

"Martin!" Claire shouted.

Martin turned.

"Hurry! Put it on before those wizards turn you into something!"

"Aye," Martin said as he completed his turn and Claire raised the cloak to help put it on him. Suddenly, out of the black shadows of the shed behind Martin stepped Jimmy. Claire looked up, and fear gripped her as she yelled, "Martin—behind you!"

But before she finished the word "Martin," Jimmy thrust his sword into Martin's back, and its tip came out the other side. Martin looked down at the sword sticking out of him, as both Claire and Luke screamed, "No!"

Laura turned and ran, and Luke came running out of the house. A flash of light occurred as Claire drew her sword. Jimmy used his boot to pull his now bloody sword from Martin, which sent the old man crashing onto the sandy dirt.

"You bloody cowardly bustard!" Claire shouted, filled with rage as she moved to cut Jimmy in two. Luke came running up to his uncle as Laura moved between him and Jimmy.

The others also came running in. Lorraine, Boo, Sam, and Sonny moved to surround Jimmy.

"Careful, ladies!" Jimmy warned them. "'Tis but a common sword in my hand! I used no magic here today! If you use those charmed swords or your magic, that's revenge, and that's personal gains! We all know what happens then, don't we?"

"You're scum, Jimmy!" Claire shouted. "Suren I knew it all along!"

"Now we know who the traitor is!" Laura said with anger in her voice.

"Aye," Claire told her. "But we'll make an end of it right now!"

"Don't do it, my ladies!" Jimmy insisted. "You have a much bigger problem than me to worry about!"

"I don't think so," Laura told him as she moved up on his side.

"Aye, you do!" Jimmy said as he turned his bloody sword down and drove it into the ground.

A flash of light from the ground and a shockwave sent the entire group crashing down and onto the sand. The wave moved out from the point of the sword and covered the entire island. Jimmy quickly recovered and ran off while the others were still making it to their feet.

"What was that?" Sonny shouted.

"He used a Robin's blood to soil and break the ground's blessing!" Claire said as she and Laura made it back to their feet.

Now hundreds of snakes made their way out of the waters and onto the island. As they came up on the ground from every direction, they began to change into dark creatures in blood-red cloaks. After their change came a flash as a sword appeared in each of their hands. Slowly they made their way off of the shore and into the yard. Large black condors landed on the rocks around the yard. There were five in all, and as they landed, they transformed into tall old men wearing black cloaks. Their teeth were red and had been sharpened into points. From their sides, each drew a wand. They pointed at Claire and Laura, and from the wand tips, balls of fire came shooting out.

Both Laura and Claire simply raised their cloaks, and the fireballs were deflected. They were scared, but they focused and ignored the fear. When one gives into fear, one loses.

"Have the centurions take Luke into the house and protect him!" Laura ordered.

The five looked over at Claire. "You heard her!" Claire shouted.

"No!" Luke shouted. "I'm staying with Uncle Martin!"

"Luke! Listen to me!" Laura said as she deflected more fireballs. "These creatures are here for you!"

"Listen to your sister, Luke!" Martin said in a weak voice.

"No!" Luke told him. "Not without you!"

"I can't move, Luke," Martin continued. "I can't feel my legs! Here, take this." He handed him his sword. Luke was stunned; he had never seen anything like his uncle's sword. It was almost too heavy for him to hold. "Remember the dance, Luke. Remember what Sam has taught you. Only now, just like this morning with Laura, don't pull your punches!"

"No, Uncle Martin, I am not leaving you!" Tears filled Luke's eyes.

"Go, boy! Remember, they murdered your mother trying to get to you! You survived then, and they lost! You survive now, and they lose again! Go! Go, I'm telling ya!"

"Come on, Luke!" Boo said as she began to pull him away.

The group began to make their way back toward the house as Claire deflected one energy strike after another. Laura picked up Martin's cloak. She brought it over to him and covered him with it. She looked into Martin's eyes with the meanest look Martin had ever seen on a girl's face, she told him in a strong, powerful voice, "I'll be back!"

"Aye," Martin said back. "Suren don't I know it!"

Laura began to make her way across the yard. She casually deflected one fireball after another, one bolt of energy after another. She wasn't even looking. She just kept getting even more and more angry. Then she began to speak seemingly to no one, and her sword began to glow.

"Ancient ones, hear my song!
 I summon now!
 The winds I call!
 From the four corners of the earth!
 To this place, begin to race!"

Where there had been clear skies and stars, now massive clouds began to form with lighting moving between them. The Darksiders and the wizards were surprised and took notice as they looked around with concern.

Laura stood opposite the back door as Claire walked up to her. The place was surrounded by hundreds of Darksiders.

"What are you doing?" Claire asked Laura.

"I will create a distraction while you get Luke out!"

"We can't," Claire explained. "The looking glass mirror has been destroyed!"

"Damn!" Laura said. "We just let them walk right in!"

"No!" Claire told her. "We just trusted the wrong person is all!"

"Can you fly him out?" Laura asked her.

Neither of the women was looking at each other. They kept their eyes on the Darksiders. Claire laughed slightly as if Laura's question had surprised her. "I haven't flown anything since I was a student! Besides, you can't fly in and out of the Griffin Valley; it's protected!"

"You haven't flown since you were a student? What's up with that?"

"Aye, I had better things to do! Like taking care of my family and the business we run!"

The wizards began to talk to the army of Darksiders in a voice Laura didn't understand.

"Do you know what those wizards are telling them?" Laura asked.

"Those aren't wizards," Claire told her. "Wizards are good people. Those are warlocks, wizards gone bad! The only ones who understand evil's words are evil people!"

"Right," Laura said. "You should give a class on this at the university! They don't like talking about Darksiders there. They just train us to fight the creatures and neglect to tell us anything about them. I guess the ball is in our court. The best defense is a great offense!"

Once again Laura's sword began to glow,

"Let the winds spread my words,
To our friends I now am heard.
Hear my plea as I call,
Evil is stalking—I send this warning to one and all!"

"Laura," Claire said.

"Yes, my Lady?"

"We have many friends here! Some are members of the Realm. Most are not!"

"Oops," Laura said slowly with concern in her voice.

"Aye, oops indeed!" Claire told her. "Brilliant spell! Why didn't I think of that one?" Claire told her sarcastically. "I have a cell phone if in case you'd like to dial 9-1-1!"

Out in the Sugarloaf Harbor, Jimmy had stolen the boat and was making his way out to sea. People started coming out of their houses that lined the docks. Others who lived in their boats stepped out onto their decks. They all stared in amazement. A storm had gathered over tiny Cohan Island. It was no place else but over the island. There was thunder as lighting reached out to the ground. No one had ever seen anything like it. Even the priest stepped out of the church to view this amazing sight. The place was surrounded by a large number of individuals wearing blood-red dresses.

Then several old people walked out from the docks. They carried swords and wore long cloaks. They were heading toward the island.

"Casey!" a man called his wife from his porch. "The Cohans are having a big-time costume party! You should see this!"

The woman walked out onto the porch in time to observe a group of old people in cloaks as they reached the island. They raised their swords and sent bolts of power flying into the Darksiders. Then they charged, and the fight was on!

"George! That's no party!" Casey shouted at her husband.

"Right!" George said with anger in his voice. "Michael! Jason!" George summoned his sons as he walked back into the house. Everywhere along the docks and on the boats, men walked back into their homes. The fighting raged on the island as one man after another, responding to the spell that had been cast, began to walk out of their boats and homes with rifles, shotguns, and pistols in their hands. While he wasn't armed, even the priest made his way out to the island!

"What is that noise?" Claire asked.

Laura closed her eyes for a moment and then said, "Strangers, members of the Realm—they've begun an attack on the other side of the house! You should go! Go around to the other side of the house! If they can punch a hole through, you can get Luke out!"

"Aye," Claire told her. "It's Martin's caldron. They are good people! Come on, then!"

"In a little bit," Laura told her.

"In a little what?"

"I'll cover your retreat!"

"You'll get your ass in gear and come with me!" Claire told her.

"I outrank you now, Aunt Claire! It's my decision."

"No one gets to decide suicide no matter their rank!"

"I have been looking for this group for 12 years! There will be no suicides here today!"

"Personal gain, Laura!" Claire told her. "Revenge is personal gain!"

"Legally, I am a princess! That makes me judge and jury! I call this justice!"

Laura's sword once again began to glow. This time it kept on glowing. Soon her eyes began to glow the same as her sword, and then her hands began to glow too. Claire couldn't go. She couldn't bring herself to leave Laura's side!

"Ionsaigh!" Laura shouted.

Eagles and falcons came racing in from many different directions. The eagles attacked the heads of the warlocks, and the falcons grabbed their wands and went flying off. Then the eagles flew down in front of Laura. As they landed, they transformed into six men dressed as Laura was dressed. They took up places on either side of her and drew their swords. Then the falcons came back, and they landed on either side of Laura. Six women transformed, and they too were dressed just like Laura. They drew their swords.

The warlocks, now disarmed, yelled, "Attack!"

The Darksiders charged by the hundreds! They drew closer and closer, and they screamed a hideous noise as they attacked. Laura's eyes and hands glowed as brightly as her sword. Then she lowered the sword at the Darksiders and slowly moved her left hand along its side. A ball of energy formed along its surface. When she reached the tip of the sword, she flung her hand at the Darksiders. A line of power and light formed a wave, a blast of energy, which went crashing into the line of charging Darksiders. As it made contact, everything was either reduced to dust or thrown up into the air and back into the river. The great rock was shattered into little stones. The little house was reduced to pieces, and most of the Darksiders were reduced to dust. No one had seen what became of the warlocks. The light that had flashed caused everyone to put their hands over their eyes. Even the people gathering on the docks were forced to close their eyes.

Claire was amazed that whatever technique Laura was using, she wasn't made weak by the discharge of power. Claire had never seen or heard of anything like it. Then Laura and her sword stopped glowing.

"Right!" Laura said. "That wasn't so bad! Let's get to the front of the house and finish this!"

"Not so bad?" Claire said thinking out loud as the group began to turn to move to the front of the house.

Laura was about to say something back, but a strange rumbling noise cut her off. Then there was another sound. It sounded like voices, only they weren't voices.

Inside the house, Luke and the others kept moving between the back and front of the house as they tried to pay attention to what was happening. In the front, there were local members of the Realm fighting with Darksiders, and the Darksiders who weren't fighting were focused on making their way around the magic barrier Claire had cast on the house. In the backyard, the yard that faced the river, it looked as if a bomb had hit. Luke kept straining to see the side of the yard where Uncle Martin was lying. He didn't know whether he had survived, and he was so worried!

Laura, Claire, and the others listened and stared into the darkness over by the river. There was an eerie chanting noise coming from it. It was pulsating and getting louder and louder. It wasn't louder because it was getting closer; it was louder because more and more Darksiders were joining in the chat. Down by the river, hundreds of snakes were swimming ashore. As they came up on the island, they transformed. As their numbers grew, so did the pulsing sound of their chat.

"I've never been in battle before. What are they doing?" Laura asked.

"Aye, suren I wouldn't be knowing that. I'm just a wee common first Lady! I leave all of the difficult thinking up to the people and the princes in charge!"

Laura turned and looked at Claire, who was leaning up against the house with her arms crossed. She didn't even have her sword out anymore.

"Aunt Claire, what are they doing?" Laura insisted.

"Oh, am I an aunt again? Thank you, your majesty!" Claire was angry. Half the island had just been flattened. As far as Claire was concerned, Laura should have asked all of these questions before she opened fire.

"Why are you giving me a hard time?"

"Aye, why indeed! Not to worry, dearie! You have the law on your side! When they come up again, you can hit them with a lawsuit. I can see it now! Step back—I got me 12 lawyers here!" Claire put her hands on her hips and moved into Laura's face. "And if that doesn't work, I'm sure another atom bomb will make them think twice! You better get your sword all hot and glowing again, your majesty, because they'll be here soon enough!"

"I can't," Laura said as she looked down at the ground and turned away from Claire.

"No?"

"No," Laura said. "The sun would have to come up and go down again before I could launch another wave charge."

"What a pity!" Claire told her. "We're bloody well fresh out of nuclear warheads. Who would have thought it?" Claire walked a little out into what use to be her backyard. There was a code of conduct that applied to all members of the Realm, and she was beginning to believe Laura hadn't been following it! The more she thought on it and looked at her yard, the angrier she got.

"Well, we have plenty of rocks! They used to be much bigger, but look, they fit in the palm of your hand now! If that's not good enough, we can go and get what's left of the little house! How will the Darksiders survive if we counterattack by throwing some wee sticks at them?"

Laura was looking down at the ground. She was realizing she didn't know as much as she thought she did. She looked up at her 12 associates and then back on the ground again. All the time the chanting of the Darksiders was getting louder and louder.

Claire walked over and stood at Laura's side.

"Who are these people? Maybe Martin was right. Is this your rock band?"

"They're my caldron," Laura told her.

"Caldron!" Claire yelled at her. "So! Your majesty is both a princess and a Robin now, is it! You are not a man, Laura! Men are Robins because that's the way the universe decided to balance power. There are rules, and it doesn't look like you've been following them!"

One of the taller men stepped forward with an angry look on his face and said, "I don't like the way you talk to the first Lady! You need to show respect!"

Laura closed her eyes with embarrassment. Claire looked over at the man with an evil smile on her face. She slapped his sword out of his hand and onto the ground. Then with the same hand she grabbed him by his neck, lifted him off of the ground, and just held him there as he began to choke.

"Claire, he's on our side!" Laura insisted.

"He has a bad attitude," Claire told her.

"Look who's talking! If you would listen to the sounds around you, you would hear clearly that he's the least of our problems!" Laura wasn't sure what to do.

"Aye!" Claire said as she tossed the man into the house, where he bounced off of the wall and hit the ground. He held his neck in pain.

Claire took a few steps back. "You two and you two!" Claire said as she pointed at a few of Laura's friends. "Boy, girl, boy, girl! You two go to the left and attack on the front end of the house. You other two go to the right and do the same! Now off with ya!"

The four looked over at Laura who ever so slightly nodded her head yes. Then they did as Claire had told them.

"So who's the one with the mouth on him?" Claire asked Laura.

"That's Randy. He's a third-year medical resident, and he's one of the good guys!"

"Oh," Claire said seemingly impressed. "Brains and a big fella. Good genes," she said as she looked over at Laura and smiled. "Randy, me boy, up now, on your feet!" Claire was tall. Randy was taller, and as she walked closer to him, he clearly was intimidated.

"Take your hand off of your throat. Go on! Let's have a look!" Claire scanned his neck. "Well, doctor, looks like you're going to live!" Then she stopped looking at his neck and instead looked into his eyes. "So, do you want to badmouth me any more?" He didn't seem as if he wanted to answer. "Well! Yes or no?"

"No," Randy said.

"No what?"

"No, my Lady, I don't have anything to say."

"Sounds like a good attitude! Now," Claire continued, "do you see the wee shed over there?"

"Yes, ma'am."

"Do you see the lump next to it?"

"Yes."

"That's a real Robin! And he's hurt! Put your sword away and go over and see how he's getting on. Help him if you can. Use your big muscles and lift him into the house!"

"Yes, ma'am! Right away!" Randy picked up his sword and ran to Martin's side.

"Sounds like the dark ones are getting back up to fighting strength!" Claire said as she looked out toward the river with her arms crossed.

"What are we doing? And don't start on me again! If we're going to argue, let's do it after the night's work is over!" Laura asked her.

Claire's hands went back onto her hips as she walked toward Laura.

"Maybe you don't know what's going on any more than I do!" Laura told her.

"Aye, maybe. Or maybe they baited you?" Claire said in a normal tone as she turned back toward the river.

"Baited me?" Laura said with surprise in her voice.

"Aye, if P.J. were here, he'd toss you around this yard like a rag doll. When you fight, you fight as a team, not as an individual! P.J. taught me that!" Claire said as if she were thinking out loud. "He would not have been too happy with you. And yes! They baited you! These Darksiders—in their current state, they are little more than zombies. They're stupid! That's why the ones around the front aren't smart enough to attack us from the rear. In their human state, you wouldn't be able to tell them from anyone else. But here they just follow orders. They're weak also. They can project power like any member of the Realm, but they weaken easy. Their strength is in their numbers. The warlocks didn't care that you wiped out so many of them. You might have just taken out a thousand of them for all I know. What I do know is that there's another thousand waiting behind them, and a thousand more behind them, and so on! They will keep coming!"

"We can't run, so we keep fighting?" Laura said to her.

"Aye, you did take out those warlocks. There must be more, or these creatures would have turned back into human form by now."

"The warlocks are the key?" Laura asked.

"Aye," Claire responded as Randy walked up with Martin in his arms.

"Well?" Claire asked with a sad tone of voice.

"I have sealed his wounds with magic. We'll have to get him to St. Richard's Hospital as soon as possible," Randy told her. "Otherwise he's not going to make it!"

"You can fly him out," Claire told him. Randy was about to say something when Laura interrupted.

"No, he can't," Laura told them both.

"Martin needs help now!" Claire told her.

"Martin is a good man, Aunt Claire. I know that now! Luke is the priority! Randy isn't here to protect Martin. Right now, if I could fly anyone out, it would be Luke!"

"Then why don't you?" Claire insisted.

Laura pointed her sword upward. She discharged a minor bolt of power. The power bolt hit what was an invisible barrier.

"That's why the lightening from the storm can't get in and we can't get out," she told Claire.

Claire was stunned by this revelation. Only someone with years of experience who had attained high ranking and become a master of the elements could have cast such a spell as the one that now surrounded them.

"He's here," Claire muttered as if thinking out loud. The look on her face was terror. There was what seemed like a long pause before Laura said, "Who's he?"

Claire turned toward her, and Laura saw the look on her face. Then she looked over at Randy and said, "Take Martin inside and put him on the couch." Claire acted as if she didn't want anyone to hear what she was about to say to Laura. Randy moved toward the house with Martin as Claire turned to Laura.

"The Dark Lord is here!" she whispered to her. "The one who started all this!"

Laura backed away from Claire and turned toward the sound of the chanting Darksiders.

"He's come to finish what he started 12 years ago!" Claire told her.

"He has nothing to lose by showing himself here," Laura insisted, still facing the direction of the chanting.

"Aye, no one in the Realm will come to help us!" Claire was certain of this.

When Martin came through the door in Randy's arms, Luke ran to help him. Martin wasn't talking. His face was a bit on the blue side, and his eyes had hints of a yellow color. Randy laid him on the couch and folded his hands on his chest. Martin, who had looked so big and strong only a short time ago, now seemed helpless. Randy patted Luke on the back and told him he had to get back outside. Luke looked at his uncle. He tried talking to him, but there was no response. Luke felt helpless and angry that someone would do this to anyone for any reason, let alone the man who had been the only father he ever knew.

Outside, things made a turn for the worse. Darksiders started feeding their front ranks. Those who had come running when the fighting started were now overwhelmed and vanquished by the Darksiders. The four friends of Laura's who Claire had sent to help were now falling back. Weakened by the long fight, these individuals showed amazing skills. They were facing dozens of swords all at once, yet their speed not only kept the dark ones at a distance but also it allowed them to vanquish anyone who came within range. But now they were weakening. Their speed was failing them, and they were moving back. All the time, there was an unending chant that was so loud it now echoed off of the house.

Claire told two of the women who had arrived at Laura's call to stay back and watch their backs. She told Laura to use only one blast from her sword and to save her strength for the main attack. The women split between either sides of the house, with the remaining members of Laura's caldron divided between them. When they moved into position, Claire ordered the ones who were still fighting to retreat behind her. As they did, the line of Darksiders advanced on her, and the same thing happened to Laura. Both of the first ladies let loose with a blast of power from their swords. Between them, their first shot vanquished more than 30 of the dark ones. Those who were not made into dust were knocked to the ground. When they got up again, they let loose with power strikes of their own, none of which could make it past Claire's and Laura's swords.

Laura and those with her charged the Darksiders. Claire was about to charge, but the Darksider charged first. She flung her hand, and the lines of Darksiders were sent crashing to the ground. Some went flying into the air, at which point Claire realized that the barrier put up to trap them didn't hold the dark ones in. They went flying right through it. On the other side were townsfolk. They leveled their guns at the dark ones and fired, but there was no effect. The Darksiders got up and let them have a blast from their swords, which sent them crashing onto the ground. They were stunned, but they were alive. The Darksiders ignored them and returned to the main fight.

With the first firing of the guns, the town priest who had just been observing from a distance came running forward in the belief that someone might need his help. He wound his way through a long line of well-armed men. When he reached the front, near where the footbridge that went onto the island, George was standing watching events unfold.

"Can't you help them?" the priest asked.

"We tried, Father," George told him. "When these terrorists come out, we shoot them, but there's no effect. Every time we try to get on to the island, we get stung by some field that we can't see."

"What field?" the priest asked him.

George took a few steps forward and reached out with his hand. The field lit up when he touched it. He had to pull back quickly because it hurt. Then the priest went up to touch the field. He reached his hand forward, and nothing happened.

"Here, Father! Take my shotgun and go bag yourself some terrorists!" George told him while trying to hand over his weapon.

The priest raised his hand as if to say no.

"Those aren't terrorists, George; they're devils!" the priest told him.

George was shocked by this news, and then the priest gave him a blessing and instructed him to move his hand forward again. This time nothing happened. George was about to rush in, but the priest stopped him.

"Hold on, George! Let me get you as much help as possible before you go charging in!"

George agreed, and the priest made his way down the line of townsfolk and gave each a blessing. But that didn't stop George from popping off any Darksider who came within range of his rifle.

On the island, the speed and power of the two first ladies and their help was too much for the Darksiders. The ones that were out front began to retreat. George and the others out front were amazed and stunned at what they were witnessing. Laura was so fast with her sword that she was almost a blur to the naked eye.

No sooner did the women finish clearing the front yard than the chant the Darksiders kept making stopped. There was complete silence. Then the dark ones started to beat their chests with the sides of their swords. Claire, Laura, and the others ran back.

The noise kept getting closer and closer. They were advancing into the yard. Suddenly the most hideous creature appeared. It stood as tall as any three men. It floated in the air in the standing position, and it moved across the length of the yard. The creature was an unholy site. Its face was blue, its catlike eyes were yellow, and its blood-red teeth were sharpened to a point.

"Oh, my God!" Claire said. The others were too stunned to speak.

Claire launched a bolt of power from her sword, but the creature was on the other side of the barrier. Luke and the others in the house saw the creature too. They were also stunned by it. Then Uncle Martin let out with a groan. He coughed, and then his hand fell lifeless on the floor. Martin was gone. The sword in Luke's hand began to glow, and then Luke began to glow, and then it stopped. Now the sword, which Luke had thought was too heavy for him, became light as a feather. Luke moved over to his uncle.

"Uncle Martin?" Luke said. "Uncle Martin!"

Outside the Darksiders moved up to the edge of the barrier. Those who were left formed two groups around Claire and Laura near to the house. They stood with swords at the ready. Then the dark ones stopped. There was an eerie silence. Both sides stood looking at each other. The hideous eyes broke through the night. The creatures looked at the members of the Realm who were ready to die in defending a house on an island in the middle of nowhere. To them it just didn't make sense. The Darksiders screamed and charged. They raced through the barrier and yelled. With their swords in their hands, they were ready to strike.

Claire and Laura launched one bolt of power after another. Dozens and dozens were reduced to dust. They kept charging, and the girls and their help kept firing. Dozens more vanished, but there were hundreds that were charging. Thousands of Darksiders had made it onto the island. They charged right past Claire and Laura and began to fight with the barrier Claire had placed around the house. Hundreds kept launching bolts of power at it. Laura and Claire began to weaken. There were too many.

The creature watching with his evil eyes, realizing the women were at an end, waved its wand, and the barrier that kept everyone on the island came down. It waved its wand up and down and created a string of power about the size of a door. The creature could control where it went with its wand. He sent it over behind where Claire was fighting. With its opposite hand, it formed a ball of energy and flung it at Claire. The ball hit her and blasted her backward and through the door of power. When she hit it, Claire disappeared into it, and the door was gone. The barrier that was around the house protecting it collapsed. The Darksiders charged the house!

Soon another door appeared behind Laura. Another ball of power hit her and forced her in, and just like Claire, she disappeared. Without the first ladies, the remaining fighters were quickly overwhelmed.

Sam, Sonny, Loraine, and Boo formed a tight circle around Luke in the great hall. The Darksiders were breaking in the windows and were trying to break down the doors. Luke and his friends stood ready for the end. Then there was an explosion, and the back wall of the house collapsed in front of them. They were all flung backward, and they crashed into the kitchen wall.

Now the only one left standing was Luke. He wasn't affected by the blast. The creature's magic had no effect on him! He stood with his sword at the ready while the others were unconscious on the floor. He focused and cleared his mind. He was ready to do his dance. When he began to focus, he realized he could feel the creature in his mind. It was like a drug trying to grab hold of him. He tried to shake it off. The creature still in the yard became overwhelmed by Luke's mind trying to shake him off. The creature yelled, "No!"

Soon a door of energy formed next to Luke. But unlike Claire and Laura, Luke knew what the creature was about to do. When he launched a ball of energy, Luke was ready for it. Like a bat hitting a ball, Luke used his sword and sent the energy ball flying right back into the face of the evil lord, which sent it flying into the river!

The Darksider who had paused to let the lord finish his work now charged Luke. Luke closed his eyes. He didn't need to see what he had to do—he could feel everything around him. As the Darksider came in at him, he spun and swung his sword so fast it was but a blur. Dozens and dozens of Darksiders were dusted. But there were hundreds coming at him. Luke had never done this before! He began to get weak quickly. He had just about had enough when the townsfolk opened fire on the Darksiders.

Some of them came through the front door. Others came running along the sides. There were dozens and dozens of them. They were firing dozens of rounds of ammunition. Unlike the first time, these bullets were hitting the mark, and the Darksiders were going down fast! The effect was dramatically different. When members of the Realm attacked the dark ones, they were either brought down or reduced to dust. When townspeople hit them with gunshots, they reverted back into their human state. The firing by the townsfolk broke the evil hold the Darkside had on them.

The dark creature raised itself up out of the water. Luke could feel it moving. He was the only one standing in what was left of the house. The Darksiders were on the run, and the townspeople were chasing them back into the river.

Standing in the river, the creature spotted the priest walking up behind the townspeople in the yard. Luke knew what the creature was about to do. He yelled, "No!" as he charged out of the house and raced as fast as he could to get to the priest.

The creature raised its hand, and in it, a ball of fire formed. He flung it at the priest. Luke jumped into the air in front of the priest to swing and deflect the ball with his sword. He missed, and the ball got past him and crashed into the priest. In an instant, the priest lit up in fire, and a moment latter he was reduced to dust.

Luke stood up enraged. He spied the creature standing in the river. He pointed his sword and a bolt of power came flying out of it as he screamed, "No!" The creature was hit but quickly recovered. Luke didn't know what he was doing, so the energy bolt had no real effect. Where the creature stood now appeared a great black bird, and the creature was gone. The bird flew off quickly and was out of sight. The remaining Darksiders stopped fighting. They transformed in to human form and collapsed where they stood.

It was over. Everywhere Luke looked, there were bodies on the ground. Most of them weren't moving. Hell had come to Sugarloaf. But just like the last attack, when it was over, Luke was still alive. If something wasn't done, this was going to happen again and again. After flash of light, the sword in Luke's hand was gone. The Battle of Sugarloaf was over, but the war was just beginning.

Out on the Gulf of Mexico, Jimmy was making his escape. He was high on the quarterdeck when Marta came walking out from down below. She came up to see what was going on and why the boat was underway. She was also quite drunk. She could barely stand. Jimmy cut the engines when he saw her and jumped down onto the main deck.

"What are ya doing, Jimmy?" she asked him, holding herself up by the rail running along the side of the boat.

"I fixed the engine, so I was testing it before tomorrow's work!" he told her.

Marta laughed. It was a stupid laugh that might be used when someone had too much to drink. "You're lying," she told him.

"Why would you say a thing like that?" Jimmy asked her as he started to move closer.

"I used to be an Alfa-Omega, Jimmy, and you know it! They stripped me of my rank and took my charmed sword, but they couldn't take my powers away. You can't lie to me!"

Jimmy pulled a knife out of his pocket and started to move toward Marta. Marta began to back up and moved across the back of the boat.

"What are you doing, Jimmy?" she said with her hands in front of her. Then she tripped and went down on the deck. Jimmy charged her. But as he was about to strike, Marta raised her hand, and he went flying up in the air and down into the water.

Marta climbed back to her feet. She looked around. Jimmy was swimming back. She wanted to leave, but she didn't know anything about running a boat. Jimmy's leg came up over the side, and soon the rest of him followed. He looked pissed! As he made it back to his feet, there was a flash of light, and where Marta stood now appeared an owl. As Jimmy rushed to grab it, the bird flew off. The first sign of twilight showed on the horizon. That gave Marta a direction to follow. Jimmy started the engines up again and kept going wherever he was off to. The night was over, and Sugarloaf Sound would never be the same.

✦

ON THE ROAD TO THE VALLEY
CHAPTER 9

THE ROOM LOOKED a little hazy as Luke woke up in his bed. He was more than surprised to find himself in his bedroom. His last memory of Sugarloaf was his home first being condemned by the town and then being demolished by bulldozers. Yet here Luke was waking up in his old room. "Someone must have cast a spell," he thought. He had been in a major fight, but he still didn't know much about how the Realm worked.

Luke quickly put on his clothes. There was something strange going on. His window was wide open as always, but there was no sound of the ocean. There were no birds. All was quiet and peaceful. It gave Luke a bad feeling inside. It was very much like the quiet that occurs before a hurricane arrives.

He opened the bedroom door and made his way into the hall and down the stairs. Here too there was something odd going on. The wood of the floors and stairs, the ones that usually made so much noise they would wake someone up, were silent. Whatever spell was cast must have fixed everything. It did now seem as if so much that was always familiar to Luke was gone.

He made his way down to the great hall. The wall that faced the river, the one the Darksiders had blown away, was repaired now. But Uncle Harry's picture was a real picture. Harry had nothing to say and stayed in one pose. The kitchen was empty and looked unused. The looking glass mirror was gone and was replaced by a solid piece of black wood. Luke called to Aunt Claire, but the only answer he got was a knock at the door. The handle on the door jiggled from side to side as if it were locked and someone was trying to get in. The door never did have a lock on it. Luke didn't understand what was going on.

Luke slowly and carefully walked over to the door, and just as carefully, he opened it. There was no one there. He stepped out onto the stairs and looked around. He stepped back in and left the door open. Everything seemed very peculiar. Luke called again to Aunt Claire, but there was only silence. Then the sun appeared in the sky through the doorway. In a moment more, the sun set, and the lights in the house came on. At one moment, it was high noon, but now it was midnight.

Luke felt ill with worry about what was happening to him. He felt a cold chill come over him. Something was near; he could feel it, but he didn't know what it was.

Luke walked past the door and headed for the great hall again. As he did, a Darksider appeared in the doorway. Its sword was drawn, but Luke didn't see it at first. It moved in behind Luke and slowly got closer and closer. Luke was in the great hall and was calling people's names when another Darksider came crashing through the window. Luke was stunned, and as he turned, he saw the other Darksider behind him. He called for his sword, but it didn't appear! He ran, first into the kitchen and then straight for the front door. He tried to open it but it would not budge, and as the Darksiders took their first swings at him, Luke ducked and made a dash for the sitting room. He slammed the doors behind him, and as he did, another Darksider came crashing through the window into that room. Luke made a dash for the living room, where yet another Darksider came in! The back door was still open, so as he ducked the swing of the new Darksider, Luke dashed for the door. Just at the moment it seemed Luke would make it out the door, the Dark Lord appeared.

At the sight of the creature that had destroyed his family, Luke came to a screeching halt. He fell backward onto his hands. He felt himself having trouble breathing. Fear struck him, which was as evil as anything else that crossed his path. The eerie blue dark creature with the yellow cat eyes and red teeth sharpened to a point stood over him, and it had his sword.

"That's my sword!" Luke shouted.

With that, the Dark Lord raised his sword and swung it at Luke's neck. Luke saw the world spinning, and then it came to a bouncing, crashing stop. He saw his own body hit the floor in front of him, headless! Then Luke woke up.

He woke up in the seat of the train he was riding in. In the distance was New York City. He could see the Empire State Building as the train prepared to makes its way across the Hudson River.

In the same car with him were Sonny, Sam, Boo, and Loraine. Marta was also there, but she was under arrest.

Sonny and Boo were under orders and carried an arrest warrant to escort Marta to the Realm Court of First Impressions. Marta was charged with dereliction of lawful duty and abandoning her post. From the talk of things, it didn't sound like it was the first time Marta had been in front of a court of law. Luke knew she drank too much, but he considered her a really good person, and he remembered that both Uncle Martin and Aunt Claire liked her a lot. Marta didn't really have much to say. She seemed as hurt and lost as everyone else. Although unlike everyone else, she wasn't covered with bruises! Everyone including Luke had black and blue marks on their face. Luke's left eye was swollen a bit. Both of Sonny's eyes were black and blue, and Boo's mouth was so swollen it looked deformed.

Luke didn't like the fact that Marta had been arrested. The one he really wanted arrested was Jimmy. He kept asking about him, but no one really had any answers. Luke was haunted by the image of his sword going through Uncle Martin and Jimmy using his boot to push it out. That evil vision of Jimmy and the nightmares he kept having all made him feel bitter and angry inside. Also occupying his mind was his home. Except for the pearl farm, there wasn't anything left standing on Cohan Island. Loraine offerred to take charge of the farm. Sonny said that as soon as they were finished with their business in the valley, Sam and he would also head back to the island and rebuild.

Luke felt numb, as though there was some part of him missing somewhere. His mind seemed to drift all the time now. He didn't really have anything to say about anything. The world seemed to be going by like it was a show on TV and he was just watching. Luke was pulling into one of the most famous train stations in the world, Grand Central Station, and he didn't really care.

The group walked off of the train and into Grand Central Station. Luke looked around; it was the biggest building he had ever been inside. They had arrived just after lunchtime. There were panhandlers asking for money. Luke summoned dollar coins into his pocket, and every time one of them asked if he could spare some change, he tossed them a dollar. Boo and Loraine suggested that that might not have been a good idea. Luke didn't really care. In a passive somewhat immature tone of voice, he told them both that he could afford it.

Outside on the street, there were vendors with carts everywhere. Luke ordered up a few hot dogs. Sonny told him that he loved dirty water dogs. That was a reference to the color of the water the dogs came out of. Luke loved them too. The group had to find a place to stay until midnight when the train left for the Griffin Valley. Everyone was too tired to do anything else.

They all got into a large taxi van and discussed where they should stay. They couldn't decide, so Luke told the driver to take them to the nicest one. A few moments later, they arrived at the Waldorf Astoria. Standing on the sidewalk outside looking up, the group wondered how many rooms they should get. Luke said one big one with lots of bedrooms. Sonny complained that that would be too expensive, at which point Luke produced from his pocket a combination ATM and MasterCard that was marked with his name and the Hawthorn Bank.

"It's only for one night," Luke told the group.

This actually turned out to be wrong—they needed it for two nights. It was explained that only Luke was leaving on the train that night. This was a surprise to Luke. He didn't like it much because he had never been anywhere alone before. Loraine explained that at midnight, Midsummer Day began, and only academy Freshers were allowed to move in and out of the valley on that day. The rest of the group would have to wait until the next day to go.

The room Luke chose was very impressive. As soon as they settled in, Sonny started looking for bedroom door keys. When Luke asked why, he was surprised to hear that Marta was to be locked into a bedroom.

"We can't do that!" Luke told him.

Sonny explained that he was just following the rules.

Luke looked at Sonny and said, "Marta is family, and we're not locking her in any room!"

Sonny just looked at Luke as Luke looked over at Marta.

"You're not going anywhere, are you, Marta?" Luke inquired.

Marta shook her head no and said, "I don't have any place to go."

"She'll stay here, Sonny," Luke said. "You guys could even go out, and she will be here when you get back!"

Reluctantly, Sonny agreed and then went over to the couch and started surfing the TV as he looked for a sports game.

Luke was so numb that he wasn't paying attention that everyone else was acutely paying attention him. Before the battle, no one really paid attention to what Luke said. He was mostly on his own except at school or when Sam was training him. He hadn't noticed that no one was arguing much with him about anything. Everything seemed so different! It wasn't just how everything looked but how everything felt as well. He was having problems reasoning things out, and having this type of problem alone was an issue he had never faced before. In the past, if he had questions or issues to work out, he would discuss it with Aunt Claire. If it wasn't a fishing day, he might even have discussed it with Uncle Martin. Now there wasn't anyone Luke could talk to. He was in a room full of friends, and yet he felt so alone he wanted to cry.

Luke stared out the window and into Central Park. Down below people were renting horse-drawn carriages to take rides through the park. Others were lying on the grass, and some were half naked soaking up the sun. Luke was amazed to see horses. There were no horses in Sugarloaf. In New York, even the police rode on top of horses. Luke thought that it was odd to see police on top of horses in such a large city. There were so many cars and people walking around, and it seemed as if every other car was painted yellow. "Yellow must be the national color of New York," Luke thought.

All those people doing all those things. "The day goes on," Luke thought. "Not one of those people down there even knew who Uncle Martin or Aunt Claire was or that I had a sister I knew for all of a single day." Luke would have given anything to have been back on Sugarloaf Beach, where he would listen to Laura sucking on her lollipop and everyone would stare at them because they were so interested in her and the way she looked. It almost seemed like a dream now. Luke wasn't even sure it had ever happened.

Luke turned around, and Sonny was watching something on TV. Everyone else had found a room and was lying down. Luke made his way through the suite. He walked around a bit and looked at objects he had never seen before. There was a golden clock that caught his eye. He wondered why someone would use gold to make a clock. He came across Marta's room. She was lying there silent. Her face was red, and she was crying. She kept rubbing her nose with a tissue. Luke went in and just lay down next to her. Marta didn't say anything, but she hardly ever did anyway.

Luke didn't want to be alone, and Sonny was no company when the TV was on. Besides, he was still tired. He leaned partly on a pillow and partly on Marta. She seemed to calm down a bit after he came in. Luke didn't know that Marta once trained under his father. Philo was her mentor. She was his star pupil, and he was her favorite teacher. Sara, Luke's mother, was the one who taught Marta the sword. Marta was never allowed to share her stories with Luke. She couldn't share all of the wonderful things she knew about his parents. Martin wouldn't permit it. She also couldn't share what the Darksiders did to her at the Battle of the Griffin Valley. She couldn't tell anyone about the scar across her abdomen, where the Darksiders took her unborn child using the sword of her husband, whom they had just finished butchering in the most hideous manner. Marta was just 19 then, and she had always kept the scar hidden. She couldn't stand it. Every time she saw it, she started to drink to numb the pain. Marta always bathed with a shirt on.

The room became silent, and Luke drifted off to sleep. In the moment between dreams and being awake, Luke could now reach out with his mind and wander the halls of the hotel. The first time he sensed his ability to do this was the day Laura arrived and taught him how to grab the rock with his mind. Then, when Martin passed away, Luke could feel everything around him. He could see everything around him in his mind. He thought he was going crazy. If Uncle Martin had this ability and passed it to him, it would explain why he always knew what was going on. Luke wished he had also passed the ability to block it. When he reached out to the Dark Lord, he almost stopped breathing. The mental encounter alone almost killed him.

Soon Luke found himself outside near where the horse-drawn carriages were parked. People were just walking by him. Luke walked up to one of the horses. He was about to pet the animal when it became spooked and backed off. This surprised Luke. It meant that the horse on some level knew he was there.

"They can't see you, but the horses can feel you," a voice from behind spoke out.

Luke turned around and found himself face-to-face with a black man dressed in old-fashioned clothing.

"Were you talking to me?" Luke replied.

"You're the only one who can see and hear me, so it must be you."

Luke didn't know what to think. "Who are you?" Luke asked.

"I am Marshal Quinn. I was hung here in Central Park shortly after the Battle of Gettysburg."

"Gettysburg?" Luke sounded surprised. "That was during the Civil War!"

"Yes," Quinn told him. "There was a riot, and white folks went around hanging blacks, and I was one of them!"

"Why?"

"Because I was black," the man explained in a calm, matter-of-fact manner.

"That's incredible!" Luke told him. "I can't imagine anyone hurting people because of their race."

"You are young still. The ways of the world haven't made their mark yet—except for that eye of yours. With whom did you get into a fight?"

"Darksiders attacked my home in Florida," Luke told him. "They killed my family and left me like this!"

"Oh," Quinn said with an interested tone of voice. "So, you're a witch."

"You know about witches?"

"Only since I was murdered," the man told him.

"If I can talk to you, do you know a way I might talk to my Uncle Martin?"

"Only if he were stuck here like I am. You would have seen him if he were still here. Most witches cannot do what you are doing now. They usually can sense me, but they can't see and talk to me."

"Why are you stuck here?" Luke wanted to know.

"I am not entirely certain why I'm here. I wasn't a good person in life. That might be why I'm stuck here. I stole and hurt many people. I even killed some. This, I think, is my hell."

"New York City is your hell? Really?" Luke said with surprise in his voice. "How many others have wound up in hell?"

"There are all kinds here from all walks of life, all races, spanning hundreds of years," Quinn responded. "I think I'm here to learn a lesson I haven't learned yet. Even though I died, I seem to be able to learn and remember and grow in spirit. I am hoping that someday, when I have learned what I need to learn, I will be given a second chance."

"Afternoon, Marshal!" another voice shouted from behind. When Luke turned, there was another black man. He was also dressed in old-fashioned clothing, not quite as old as Quinn's but still old. He was the first black man Luke had ever seen with red hair. "Maybe he's Irish," Luke thought.

"Hello, Malcolm!" Quinn responded. "This is young master—well, I don't think I got your name, did I?"

"Luke! Luke Carter!"

"Well, Luke, this is Malcolm!"

"How do you do, sir?" Luke said.

"We don't get many visitors around here like you," Malcolm responded with a big smile.

"Were you hung by white men also?" Luke asked the man.

"There were plenty around who wanted to," Malcolm said laughing just a tiny bit. "That's for sure. But no, I was shot down by black men, members of my own church, right in front of my family."

"Why?" Luke insisted.

"Ignorance!" Malcolm told Luke. "It's what we are all doing here! We were ignorant in life, and so in death, we are made to find a way to shake off our ignorance! Ignorance is at the root of most all evil! Has anyone taught you that, Luke?"

"I have been told, yes, and my family and I were also betrayed by someone we trusted," Luke responded. But just then he faded. The view of everyone and everything in his mind also faded.

"Oops!" Quinn said.

"Yes'em!" Malcolm agreed. "Looks like you're on your way out!"

"Out?" Luke asked. "You mean I am going to be stuck in New York City forever too?"

The two men laughed as Malcolm said, "No, no, you're just falling asleep wherever you are, is all. Say a prayer for us if you remember. Might help us out of here someday!"

"I will!" Luke told him as he disappeared.

Luke heard his name being called. He woke up to Marta shaking him slightly. She told him it was time to go. Luke got up and looked around. He pinched himself to make certain he was awake. "These excursions while not awake are very disorienting," Luke thought.

Luke took a quick shower and soon was saying good-bye to Sonny and Sam. Sam was certain she wouldn't hold up too well at the train station if she had to say good-bye to Luke there. She was already fairly upset saying good-bye in the hotel room. But she and Sonny gave Luke a hug, and it was Loraine, Boo, and Marta who went with Luke to the station. Sonny didn't think Marta was going anywhere. Boo and Loraine could handle any problems that might arise. Besides, there were members of the Realm all over New York on Midsummer's Eve. No one would try to make a move on Luke tonight. They would very quickly find themselves facing an army. Many practitioners showed up at the station just to watch the Freshers go off to the valley.

Luke and his friends didn't go all the way to the station. They stopped three blocks away, partly because Luke wanted to walk the streets a little bit and partly because there was a sub shop and Luke was hungry. He ordered up a roast beef sub with mayonnaise and just a touch of salt. Marta produced something from her pocket, and when she unfolded it, a small cloth carry bag revealed itself. It was something the tourists would buy back in Florida. On the side it read "Sugarloaf Sound."

Luke laughed a little bit as he put a sub and soda into the bag. He slung the bag over his shoulder, and the group began to make their way to the train station. Luke realized that was the first laugh he had since the trouble in Sugarloaf. It made him feel just a little less numb. They all walked together along the sidewalk and headed for the station. There were people dressed in cloaks in the middle of a summer night in New York City. No one seemed to think much of it. It seemed fairly odd to Luke. A lot of these people looked like some of the ones he had seen at the inn when the leprechauns had grabbed him, only the clothing they had on this time was modern and formal. "Perhaps they're on their way to a Broadway show or something," Luke thought. When he would pass these people, they would bow slightly. The girls would nod their heads and Luke would give a friendly smile. He didn't like smiling that night. It made his black and blue eye hurt.

Soon the group arrived at the station. As they made their way across the long station floor, the girls just stopped. Luke kept walking until he realized they had stopped. He walked back to them and asked, "What's up?"

"This is as far as we can go, Luke," Loraine told him.

"Why?"

"Those are the rules. Freshers, parents, and siblings only allowed on the platform tonight."

"Where do I go?" Luke asked.

This time Marta replied, "There's the ticket counter behind you. You'll buy your ticket, and the platform is listed there."

"So I just go up to the counter and ask for a ticket to the valley?" Luke asked.

All three of the girls smiled for the first time in a long time. Marta and Loraine even giggled a little.

"No," Marta told him.

"The Bennies don't have any idea about the valley," Loraine added.

"You ask for a ticket to the Chattanooga Pass," Marta told him as she reached out her with arms to give him a hug good-bye.

Each of the girls gave Luke a hug, and he walked off toward the ticket counter. He got in line, and when he looked back, the girls were gone. He looked around, but Luke was all alone, and it wasn't a great feeling being all alone.

There seemed to be quite a few others his age in line. By the time he had reached the front of the line, he had heard the name Chattanooga Pass seven times. He watched the others as they went off, and when he had his ticket, he followed.

It was amazing how much more he paid attention to Grand Central Station now that he was alone. He went through several doors, and with each one he went through, the space inside got smaller and smaller until he arrived at a very old stairwell. He could hear others in the distance echoing up and down a solid brass staircase. So down he went, stepping very slowly, listening to others making their steps in front of him and still others now behind him. Some students passed him, girls and boys, and they all seemed to be about the same age. Finally the stairs came to an end at a large sign with a pointing arrow that read "Track 49."

"Oh," Luke said out loud as he wondered why there were so many rail tracks coming in and out of one station?

The sign really wasn't the whole problem. The real issue was that both sides of the corridor were made of cement block. So if he followed the arrow, he would walk into the wall. He stood there looking at the solid wall to his left when two girls just walked past him and disappeared right into it.

Luke reached forward and watched his hand disappear through the wall and out again. With one big step forward, Luke found himself on platform 49. It was amazing! Once again he seemed to have stepped backward in time, just like the first time he entered the Realm at the inn on Pearl Street. Nearly everyone except the Freshers who had just arrived was dressed in colonial style. The train was very old. It had a steam engine, every car was blue and white, and it was all wooden except for the undercarriage. On the side of the train was a sign that read "Hole in the Wall."

Then Luke did something unexpected. He turned around and stepped back out into the corridor. He stood at the base of the brass stairwell as others passed by. He looked around, and then he sat down on one of the stairs. His heart was racing, and he was sweating for no apparent reason. He thought he might be scared. It was very much like the feeling when he arrived in New York the first time. He wanted to make a phone call and go home. Luke didn't know what he wanted to do. If he went forward, there was no going back. If he didn't go, he didn't know what would become of him. If he headed back to Sugarloaf, and that was what he really wanted to do, he thought he would just be a target for the bad guys. He understood now what had kept Martin safe. Martin had found a place to hide that no one knew about. That's how he made it all the way to his seventy-first birthday. Luke closed his eyes with all his thoughts and put his head into his hands. He didn't know what he wanted! Yes, he knew. He wanted to talk to Aunt Claire and ask her what she thought! He needed some help.

"Dia Duit, Your Grace," a man's voice said. "'Tis a fine Midsummer's Eve, isn't it?"

Luke looked up with teary eyes. There stood a man of about 40 in an old-style train conductor's uniform.

"Dia Is Muire Duit. Yes, I suppose it is for some," Luke said with sadness in his voice.

The man took off his conductor's hat and held it to his chest.

"I am Master First Conductor David Killen, sir. I only just heard word of an old and very dear friend of mine. Her name was Claire Monaghan, well, until she married another very good friend of mine, Harry Cohan. Although we are strangers to each other, Lord Carter, I do hope you will accept my most sincere condolences in the matter of her and your sister's and Lord Cohan's passing."

Luke nodded his head and began to cry a bit. "That is very kind of you, sir. Thank you! I am sorry you lost a good friend, and I am sorry she is not here to help me now." Luke placed his arms on his knees and laid his head down on his lap sideways.

"My Lord Carter, she may not be here, but you should understand that you are among friends! I would have done anything to have been at her side when the dark ones came for her. I didn't know where she was. After the last great battle, she went into hiding. We all knew it was because of you, but we all thought that when the going became difficult, she would have called for help! She never did."

Luke nodded his head while still lying on his arms. "Yes," he told the conductor. "Aunt Claire could be very stubborn about things."

"Aye," David said as he sat down next to Luke. "Suren you'll be speaking the truth. Your Uncle Harry was the same. Those two were a perfect match. Did anyone ever tell you that the night they decided to get married was proceeded by a day-long argument about what each other's role would be in the marriage if they ever did decide they wanted to be married?" The man laughed out loud. "They were shouting at each other for hours! The entire campus was going on and on about it! Everyone was waiting for them to draw swords!" The man laughed some more. "First, your mom showed up and told them to put a sock in it, and when that didn't work, your dad showed up. That was a big deal, you know! If you drew the attention of the Lord White Robin, it had better be for a good reason, and everyone knew it. All we knew was that as soon as he walked in the room, it went quiet. When he walked out, he slammed the door, and there was no more shouting. That night, at dinner, their engagement was announced!" The man looked at Luke with a big smile.

Luke was also smiling as he slowly sat back up again. The tears were no longer coming down.

"No," Luke said, "no one had ever told me that story. Thank you, Master First Conductor, for sharing that with me."

"Now, if you like, Your Grace, I would be happy to take your bag and show you to the train."

Luke smiled at the man. "No need to take the bag," he told

him, and as he held it out, there was a flash of light, and the bag was gone. Luke could call it back anytime he wanted.

"My name is Luke, Master First Conductor. I am new to the Realm and its ways. I prefer to be called Luke if you don't mind."

"Aye," the man said as he spit in one hand and rubbed both together and then reached out with his right hand to shake Luke's.

"Me friends call me David, Master Luke."

"It's very nice to meet you, David. I bet you know a good seat on the train. Would you mind showing me the way?"

The two stood up and walked through the wall together. Luke had decided to go into the Realm. He was no less scared than he was the first time he walked into it, but at least this time he had made the choice to do it.

MR. AMADE
CHAPTER 10

THE MASTER FIRST conductor had instructed Luke where to go. He didn't think it would be wise if he led Luke around. It might make him stick out. Luke was directed to a center car on which the conductor knew the smoke from the engine hardly ever fell. Most everyone else seemed to know one another, and no one knew him, or so he thought. When Luke sat down in the car, he watched for a long time the goings-on in and out of the train. There were many families on the platform. Moms and dads and brothers and sisters were allowed on the platform. They seemed to be divided between groups dressed in modern and old-style clothing. Slowly, all of the groups were breaking up, and the students made their way onto the train.

No one was coming in Luke's car. Individuals would come through, have a peek in, and then move on. There was a girl who came by with others who peeked in, and she was surprised by Luke's presence. Luke was looking out of the window, so he never really noticed. She also kept going. Then the conductor shouted, "All aboard!"

When the clock chimed midnight, the train moved out. Luke was alone until the girl came back and sat down. In her hands, she had two large books. One was a book of "Translated Ancient Celtic Spells," and the other was entitled "The Life and Times of Wolfgang Amadeus Mozart." There was a noise in the hall that drew Luke's attention, and when he turned, he saw her. It was the girl from the Pearl Street Mall, from the pastry shop! Luke just looked at her. His mouth hung open, and his eyes were full with surprise. It was as if he were suddenly caught in a daydream. When last he saw her, he had been kidnapped and felt nothing but fear until they met. Luke didn't understand these feelings very well. Girls were something he was used to ignoring. Still, the train car suddenly seemed more comfortable. Just like when they had met at the mall, the fear of being alone in a strange place seemed to relax a bit. Once again, like in the mall, Luke was able to think clearly again. This clearness was what let him focus and get away from the leprechauns. Luke could only wonder what magic this girl had to have such an effect on him.

"Dia Duit, Your Grace," the girl said.

"Dia Is Muire Duit," Luke said back, followed by a long pause when each stared at the other and said nothing. Then Luke blinked and shook his head a little. "You know who I am?"

The girl just nodded her head yes.

"How?"

There was another pause, and then the girl said slowly, "That day at the mall, everyone was going on about a very young Robin who had just become centered. A member of the House of Cohan whose name was Carter, a boy who was the son of the Great White Robin. I just figured it was you," she told him.

"They let you work at age 12 in the mall? If I fail at school, do you think they would give me a job there? I could have worked the boats in Sugarloaf. No one would have cared about my age, but that place isn't safe for me anymore."

"Yes, well, I kinda work there, but not exactly. My parents own the shop. I like to help out and meet people."

"So people talk about me now that I visited the mall?"

"Of course, I overheard my mom and dad talking about you. They went on for an hour trying to decide whether you were a natural-born leader. My dad told my mom you were maybe the last one. Everyone has heard what happened to your family. It was in the Realm paper, you know. I am very sorry! I could not imagine life without my mom and dad. If I could be of some help, you can ask."

"Thank you," Luke said slowly and with a question in his voice. "Natural-born leader?" he said shaking his head and looking out the window. "I couldn't lead a one-man band out of a paper bag," Luke was talking low and to himself. Then he asked the girl, "What is your name?"

"Abi. My name is Abi, Abi Bishop."

"Abi? Is that short for Abigail or another name?"

"Nope, it's just my name."

"I'm Luke, Luke Carter."

The girl started laughing. "Yes, you are, aren't you?"

Then Luke started to laugh also. "Yes," he said to her, "I guess everyone is going to know that now—now that it's been all over the newspaper," he thought. Luke laughed a little more, and then he realized that his name was going to be a big problem. Whatever magic Abi had brought into the room with her to let Luke focus was working for sure. Everyone would be calling him Lord or Grace and treating him differently, and that realization was because Abi had walked in. "Imagine what would happen when I face the whole school!" Luke thought as his heart began to sink a little when he thought about it. His smile went away as he looked out into the darkness of the night. He thought he would have no friends.

"Did I say something wrong?" Abi asked him.

Luke shook his head no and then glanced over at the books Abi had.

"The book there on the musician looks rather thick."

"Yes, well," Abi said, "I have finished my grade four in piano, and I am moving onto grade five, and I have chosen some of Mozart for my exam. He was one of several options, and I was going to read about him on the way to the valley."

"Piano? Wow, I don't play music at all. You must be good to be able to do Mozart!"

"Thank you."

"The other book—where did you get that?"

"The spell book? It's the translated abridged book of Celtic Shadows. You've never heard of it?"

"Except for the last two weeks, no one has told me anything about anything. The first time you saw me was the first time I had heard anything at all about the Realm. I am really useless at this Realm stuff. No one knows me, but they know my name and who I am, and I think soon things are not going to be so great." Luke sounded tired, disappointed, and frustrated.

Abi thought Luke seemed very sad. Of course, all of the news of what happened at Sugarloaf had spread through the entire Realm. Luke's family story was on the front page of the Pearl Street Observer for three days last week. Abi doubted he even knew what the Observer was, and he was right— everyone had to know he was coming. She also understood about how his name was going to cause him problems.

There weren't a lot of well-known famous people in the Realm. There was no family more famous than the House of Cohan, and as far as she knew, he was the last one, and the newspaper made sure the name Carter was all over the Realm.

"Why not change your name?" Abi asked.

"Change it? How do I do that?"

"Well, you could use a spell, couldn't you?"

"I wouldn't know," Luke told her. "Besides knowing how to fight, no one has taught me anything. I told you, as a witch, I am useless."

"Well, you're going to need something in your possession that has a strong magical connection to the Realm, an instrument of some kind. I would suggest a cloak, but yours hasn't been worn much. The strength grows the more it is worn. Yours would be a very weak connection."

"Why do we need something connected to the Realm?" Luke asked.

"My father explained to me that humans were created outside of the Realm. They aren't a natural part of it. They only connected with it when its forces were used against us by the Darkside. So we have always needed a device to connect with. In the beginning, we borrowed from creatures that were created inside of the Realm, like a unicorn or a phoenix feather, which are used by Europeans to make wands."

"Wow," Luke said, "no one has ever explained this to me. My sister was able to command the wind and storms with just her mind."

"Really?" Abi said with surprise in her voice. "That is amazing! She might have been a master of the elements!"

"What does that mean?"

"Usually, they are individuals who have a strong family connection with the Realm. They are almost always men, and they are very rare. Women masters are very unique. Their connection allows them to command magic using only their mind. I think I would have loved to have met your sister."

"Think again," Luke told her. "I liked her a lot. I knew her for single day; she seemed a bit full of herself. You might not have liked her much. I say this because in just one day, she successfully managed to piss off every single person she met."

"Really! Maybe I still would have like to have met her," Abi assured him with a smile on her face. "Sounds like my kinda witch," she said with a laugh.

"My Uncle Martin, he must have been a master. Remember those leprechauns that took me to the mall?" Abi nodded her head yes. "They didn't have permission. When they came back the second time, I watched my uncle throw energy from his hands at them. It was the scariest thing I had ever seen."

"That is so kewl!" Abi told him with a little excitement in her voice. "I have heard of such people, but I have never met one before! Wow!"

"Well, you won't be able to meet my Uncle Martin. He's gone now. I watched him go. I just want to find the person responsible and hurt him!"

"If you ever do, don't use magic! If you use magic for personal gain, then you lose your soul, and you go to the Darkside!"

"How is that personal gain?"

"It's revenge," Abi told him. "Revenge is a sin, and any magic used to commit a sin turns you!"

"Glad you told me that!" Luke said with surprise in his voice. "I would have cut that bustard in two if I found him."

"Cut him in two?" Abi said with surprise. "With what?"

"My sword!" he said with a question in his voice. "Doesn't everyone have a sword?"

Abi looked at him with little surprise and fear.

"I think I had better be going," she told him as she started to gather her things to leave.

"Wait, Abi! Why? I thought everyone carried a magical sword." Abi kept gathering her things and was about to walk out when Luke stepped in front of her.

"What are you not telling me? I told you I know nothing about the Realm! What you have told me here tonight, this is the first time I am hearing all of this. I swear it's true!"

Abi looked into his eyes and saw that Luke was quite upset. He was scared too. Luke didn't know what was going on. But just like in the pastry shop, Abi's eyes had an unusual effect on him. Luke didn't understand what it was about her, but it was clear to him that he liked being around Abi. She felt like someone he could trust.

Abi put her things down and walked up to Luke. Her face was up against his when she told him, "No, Luke! Freshers don't carry weapons! Duh! Students only carry weapons inside the valley and then only for training. Carrying a sword around with you is the same as someone walking around with a rifle on their shoulder and a six-shooter on their belt. We haven't been trained to use weapons, and for anyone who hasn't, it's just like playing with fire! People get hurt, and they get hurt badly!"

Luke turned and went and sat down again by the window.

"I'm sorry, Abi. I didn't know. I understand if you want to go."

"Why not just get rid of it then?"

"I tried," Luke told her. "I tried to give it to one of the people who worked for my uncle. I tried to give it to each in fact. None of them could lift it. To make things worse, I couldn't leave it anywhere. Every time I left the room, the sword automatically recalled itself back into the holding space and waited for me to call it again. I can't get rid of it! It's stuck to me!"

Abi was more than just a little surprised by his revelation—she was in shock. She was also frightened because she was traveling in the same car with an armed 12-year-old boy. If that alone wasn't bad enough, the type of sword Luke was describing, a charmed sword, was in the hands of a boy, and this information made her ill. It was as if someone had walked in with a loaded gun and sat down beside her!

"You are describing a charmed sword," Abi said with fear in her voice. "I have never heard of one that others couldn't pick up, but a sword that automatically follows its master, that's a charmed sword!"

"I wouldn't know. I told you; as a witch, I am useless."

Abi once again turned to leave.

"I will tell you this," Luke said in a last effort to get her to stay. "The sword was given to me by my uncle just before he died. If I didn't have it, I would be dead too. The sword is what forced the Dark Lord to retreat. Otherwise he would have murdered me like the others!"

"Dark Lord?" Abi said with more surprise as she once again put her things down. "You've seen it? The Dark Lord? Is that how you got those bruises and that black eye? There was nothing in the paper about the Dark Lord! No one is aware of this!"

"Yes, a warlock with a wand. Rather gross looking it was! I feel sick even talking about it, and yes, the fighting that went on is why I am black and blue. You should see my back! It's much worse than my face."

"It attacked you?"

"It's why I'm here and my family isn't!"

"Luke, you must not tell this to anyone ever again, at least not to any student! If anyone finds out you've had contact with the Dark Lord, you will be an outcast! They will be so afraid of you! You will not survive in the Griffin Valley. You will not even make it past first trial. People will try to kill you if they think you've been near that thing!"

"Right, well, I think I am going to have a rough time of it no matter what choice I make. Besides, my name is going to make me an outcast anyway. I should have done what Uncle Martin did and find a nice quiet place to hide."

"You're a natural-born member and leader of the Realm. No matter where you went, in time, the Darkside would find you. Here at least, among us, there is strength in numbers. As for your name, the spell book has a translated name change in it. So long as you cast no spell to lie or to hide from wrongful acts, you can call yourself by any name, and it's no one's business. If you really do have this sword with you, if it is at your command, you need only draw it and cast the spell. There is no stronger connection to the magical plane than a magical sword—particularly a charmed one."

"What name should I use?" Luke said.

"Hmm. Well there are all kinds of names. How about Pierce? Yeah, Luke Pierce."

"Nope, not a Pierce," Luke responded.

"Lee? Luke Lee?"

"Nope," he said as he shook his head.

"Bourne?"

"Nope."

"Juan? Luke Juan? That sounds kinda cute!"

"No!"

"Hanks? Luke Hanks?"

Luke kept shaking his head.

"How about Otter? Luke Otter!"

"No, I am definitely not Otter!"

"Mozart?" Abi said as she began to laugh. Luke smiled a bit also.

"No!"

"Wolfgang! Yes! Luke Wolfgang," Abi shouted as she broke into even more laughter.

"No, I don't want a name that will attract attention, but I don't want to repel people either!"

"Amadeus! Luke Amadeus!" Abi laughed, but Luke didn't.

"Hmm," Luke sounded.

"No, no, no! I was just messing!" Abi insisted. "Your mom wouldn't have named you Amadeus! Duh!"

"Not Amadeus," Luke hinted he had an idea as Abi looked at him oddly.

"What?" Abi asked.

"Not Amadeus but Amade? Luke Amade? I have never heard such a name before, but it sounds very neutral. It doesn't draw attention, but it's not repelling either." Luke put both his hands behind his head and sounded as if he were thinking out loud.

"Luke Amade?" Abi said out loud as she sat back and thought for a bit. "Well, it's not bad, and we could spend the whole five-hour trip trying to think up another one." She smiled and then she looked over at the hall doorway. "If you're going to summon your sword, we'll have to cover that window with something."

Luke snapped his finger, and with a flash of light, his Sugarloaf dinner bag appeared. As Abi looked up the spell they would use, Luke removed the contents of the bag and used it to cover the window. Then he pushed the locking latch on the door and sat down by Abi.

"Here it is," she showed him. "I have cast very few spells, only with my parents looking over me, and never anything as complicated. In theory, this will do what you want."

Luke nodded his head yes as he stood up with the book in his hand. He laid it down on the opposite seat and stared at it the whole time. He raised his right hand, and with a flash, his sword appeared. Abi was both scared and truly amazed! She had seen charmed swords before but only very rarely and never anything like this. The golden glow from Luke's sword was so dense that it nearly hid the blade. The sword also had something else Abi had never experienced before, a hum. Luke's sword seemed to be humming, and when he moved the sword, there was a shifting noise it made.

Luke grabbed his sword with both hands and raised it in from of him. As he was about to recite it, he turned to Abi and asked, "Do I need to read it in the Irish?"

"Nope, only when you are projecting magic, not when you are internalizing it."

So Luke began the spell and substituted his old and new names.

Ancient ones from distant lands,
I call to you for a helping hand.
In this time things cannot remain the same,
So it is my choice to now change my name.
Let those who know me not forget,
But those who now meet me must relent.
Where the name Carter was written, let it now be changed.
Where it was known to strangers, let it not remain,
And for all those now who come my way,
Let them not know Carter but Luke Amade.
This spell is cast.

There was some kind of flash or light shift or something weird the moment Luke finished his spell. He and Abi both saw and felt it. It went away quickly, and Luke just as quickly sent his sword away. He sat down and looked at Abi, who was staring at him grimly.

"What?" Luke asked.

"That was really scary!" she told him.

"Did it work?" he wondered.

"I don't know. We'll have to wait 'til someone comes in or we go."

Luke just looked at Abi and said, "Oh," at which point he took half his sub and one of his sodas and handed them over to her. No sooner did the two bite into their sandwiches than there was a tremendous knock at the door. Well, it was more like a tremendous bashing at the door with a loud male voice demanding to know why the door was locked.

Abi got up and unlocked the door. A teenager sharply dressed in some kind of school uniform came stomping in.

"Why was this door locked?" the boy shouted. "Why was there a cover over that door? Get on your feet, boy! When an upperclassman walks into a room, you will assume the position of attention! Do you understand what the position of attention is?"

"No," Luke said with a broken voice.

"No? No what?"

"No, I don't know what you mean!"

"You! Was that a "you"? A "you" is a female sheep! School recruits do not call upperclassmen names!" The boy stood in Luke's face. "Do you hear me?"

"Yes," Luke said with a touch of fear in his voice. He hoped this boy, who was easily twice his size, would shut up.

"Until you have earned the title of academy student, when you address an upperclassman, you will address us as sir or ma'am. Is that clear?"

"Yes, sir," Luke told him.

"That's outstanding, school recruit! What the flip is your name?"

"Luke."

The upperclassman looked over toward the door where a female upperclassman stood with a list in her hand. When he looked at her, she simply responded, "Amade! Luke Amade! That's the one who we were missing, and this must be the other one, Abi Bishop!"

"Are you Miss Bishop?" the large boy shouted at her.

"Don't yell at her!" Luke insisted.

The room went silent. It was a cold silence too, kind of like the silence just before the executioner tells the firing squad to shoot. There were several upperclassmen at the door who were now watching. The older boy in the room turned at Luke and walked right up into his face.

"You are not at the position of attention! Do you know why?"

"No, sir," Luke said, believing now that opening his mouth about Abi being shouted at was maybe not such a brilliant decision.

"That's because you didn't attend first muster like the rest of the Fresher recruits! Because you were here instead of at the back of the train where you belonged!"

The older boy's verbal assault was unrelenting.

"The definition of attention is at the standing position. Your feet are at a 45-degree angle with heels together. Your thumbs are at your side and are resting on the seam of your trousers. Your eyes are front and locked. And let's not forget the most important part. Your mouth is shut! No one cares what a recruit says or thinks or why he or she does either! Do you hear me, recruit?"

"Yes, sir!" Luke responded.

"When an upperclassman enters the room you are in, you will assume the position of attention right away. Do you understand recruit?"

"Yes, sir!"

"I can't hear you!"

"Yes, sir!"

The older boy quickly swung around again and looked Abi in the eye.

"Are you Bishop?"

"Yes, sir," Abi responded already at the position of attention, having learned by way of Luke being screamed at.

"When I say go, you two pukes will gather your crap very quickly, and you will proceed at a very quick pace, making certain that you don't run into people, and you will proceed to the back of the train and join the rest of the puke recruits! Do you understand me?"

"Yes, sir!" Luke and Abi shouted.

"Go!"

Luke and Abi grabbed their stuff and made their way out into the hallway. All along the way, there were upperclassmen shouting at them. Some would call them pukes, others yelled for them to hurry up, and still others demanded to know what they were doing outside the back of the train. The two moved along as quickly as possible, but the train's corridors and connecting doors between the cars were narrow. To make things worse, the upperclassmen lined the halls and made it even more difficult to pass. All of these upperclassmen had gray uniforms with black trim. They bore various types of rank insignia and all seemed to have well-trimmed hair. Luke really had no idea what was going on. These weren't the clothes he bought at Pearl Street Mall.

Finally they made it to the back of the train. There were students their own ages in all of the cars. They weren't talking much. Some had laid their heads up against the wall and had fallen asleep. Near at the end of the train, Abi and Luke found cars that had empty seats. It seemed odd because everyone else was crowded together. So they sat down and were just silent for a moment.

"I bet if you hadn't changed your name, that wouldn't have happened," Abi said out loud not really looking at Luke and not sounding too happy.

"Well, at least I know the name change worked!" Luke told her. "Who are these people?"

"My mom and dad told me they would be here. No one is supposed to discuss first trial with Freshers. Not even parents are supposed to discuss it because it's kind of a test. Those upperclassmen are part of the Cadet Corps. They are individuals who are candidates to become centurions. Most hope to become Alfa-Omegas."

"Are they going to be in our classes at school?" Luke wondered.

"We aren't going to school. Well, not yet, not unless we pass first trial."

Luke just looked at Abi kind of dopey for a bit and said, "We're not going to school?"

Abi shook her head slowly and then said, "Nope."

"I thought we were on our way to the Griffin Valley."

"We are," she said, "but we're going to the first trial."

"First trial?" Luke responded with a sinking feeling in his heart and surprise in his voice. "I think I have been abandoned," he said thinking out loud. As his eyes became teary, he looked out into the dark night. On the edge of the horizon, the tops of mountains could be seen against the moonlight, and his swollen black and blue eye and cut face reflected in the window. "What am I doing here?" he thought.

Just then, more upperclassmen walked in. This time there were three, but only the lead one was shouting.

"Who the hell told you pukes you could have a car to yourselves?"

Abi had already jumped to the position of attention, but Luke kept looking out the window, and although he could see all three of the boys' reflections in window, he ignored them.

"When an upperclassman walks into the room, you will assume the position of attention! Get on your feet, boy!"

Luke turned and looked at all three of the boys. His sadness turned to anger, and these three boys just happened to walk in at the wrong moment. Luke was mad about not being told of the Realm and who he was. He was mad about being left alone to fend for himself. He was enraged that his family was taken from him, and now he was pissed because strangers, who had no good reason to, kept screaming at him! For whatever reason, at this moment, Luke wanted to lash out at someone.

"Did you hear me? Get on your feet!"

"Right!" Luke said. He focused his pain on the three boys, which, given the anger he was feeling, wasn't much of an effort, and all three of the boys—each of whom were easily twice Luke's size—went flying into the air backward and out the car door, where they crashed into the hallway wall. Luke stared at them for a moment and watched as they shrugged to get back to their feet. Each of the boys had the wind knocked out of him but was getting up, and once Luke was sure they were all OK, the door on the car slammed closed, and the lock engaged. Then Luke's bag went flying up onto the window and hung there.

Abi was just standing there, stunned and surprised, wondering what she had managed to get herself in the middle of.

"Maybe I should go," she said cautiously.

"Nah, let's just finish our soda and subs and try not worry about anything. At least now we can eat in peace." Luke's tone of voice had no sound of urgency. He seemed so confident that Abi did as he suggested. After all, even if they didn't know who he was, she did. But it wasn't confidence driving Luke's attitude; it was a lost feeling of hopelessness and a strong sense of giving up.

"They are going to be really mad at us!"

"Right, and then they are going to scream some more," he told her. "It doesn't matter if it's now or when the train stops or when we get off. They are going to do nothing but scream at us! So we might as well wait until we get to where we're going so we can get all the screaming done at once."

Luke took a bite out of his sub sandwich and stared out the window. Slowly, Abi sat back down. There was some odd logic to what Luke had just said. She took a sip of her soda, and then she too started to enjoy the other half of Luke's sub sandwich.

"Did you ever cross paths with any of these upperclassmen in the mall or at your shop?" he asked.

"Yes," Abi replied, "almost everyday."

"Did they tell you much about this first trial thing?"

"Yes, they thought it was fun to scare Freshers into worrying about going to school alone."

"So they enjoy this stuff?"

"Well, they certainly were looking forward to it, that's for sure. I imagine it will be our turn to be in charge someday."

"Hmm, I didn't think about that," Luke considered. The idea was that this was all a process and that everyone was on line to the next level, that each level had to be completed before a person could become a part of the higher level. Luke had never thought about these things before. He wasn't emtional anymore like he was when they came into the car. Now—a bit late—Luke regretted tossing those boys into the hallway. "Sam was right, emotions will make decisions for you," he thought.

Still, Luke was so unsure about what was going on around him and his position in all of these events, and the best he could do was try to protect himself by changing his name.

It was hard for him to feel too guilty about tossing out a few boys he felt threatened by. "If I were indeed on a line to get somewhere else," he thought, "I should stay put and wait for my turn. It would be helpful if people would explain things a bit better, like what was going on and why."

"I think I made a mistake dealing with those last three. I do not understand all this very well. I have to remember what Sam taught me. Focus with your head, not your emotions," Luke said.

"Who's Sam?"

"She's one of the women in charge of my uncle's pearl farm."

"Pearl farm? You have a real pearl farm?"

"Yes," Luke told her. "There are several different sections. There are these really big ones from Australia. Loraine is in charge of those. The ones from Japan, China, and Tahiti— Sam is in charge of those. The Tahiti ones are black." Luke looked out the window again. "Not all of the sections are harvested every year. Some are harvested once a year. Others are harvested every two years. Once every three years, we have to hire so many people my uncle would have to rent tents to hold all of the workers. Every three years, all of the shells get harvested. Uncle Martin would even bring his boat into the river so there would be another platform to work from. The boat is gone now," he suddenly remembered.

"I guess the pearl farm belongs to you now?"

Luke looked back at her and then looked down. That was yet something else he had not considered. "Yeah, I guess you're right. I don't know really."

"Kewl! Think you could show me this farm and maybe some of the pearls someday?"

"Sure," Luke told her, "but if we go, you better have a sword by then, and you better know how to use it. Sugarloaf is a brilliant place, and I am sure you'll love it, but it's no place for practitioners after sunset."

Abi just looked at him while chewing her sub.

"Abi, you have been in the Realm your whole life?"

Her mouth was full, so Abi just nodded her head yes.

"You went to school inside the Realm?"

Abi again nodded yes.

"So, many of the other Freshers on this train, you know them?"
Abi kept nodding.

"Then if you had the choice to go and sit with all of your friends, why did you come into the car with me?"

In between bites Abi said, "If I had done that, you would still be Luke Carter!"

Luke laughed a little at that and then replied with a slight smile on his face, "Yes, I know, and thank you. Are you messing with me again?"

"I dunno," Abi said sharply. "Maybe I should have gone with the others. At least I wouldn't be sitting with an armed 12-year-old who just tossed three upperclassmen out of the car and most likely has got us both in deep trouble. Maybe I remembered you from the mall. Maybe I've kept thinking about you and wanted to get to know you better."

Luke just looked at her for a moment. She had gotten a bit superior in answering his question. It was as if she had taken offense at his asking something personal, or maybe he just wasn't used to being around girls who grew up inside the Realm. Luke didn't know what to think. He always considered talking with girls to be a major waste of time. Yet here he was, with the one person he could call a friend, and his friend was a girl.

Luke nodded his head slightly at her and said, "OK, maybe all your maybes are possible. What happens next? I have made so many mistakes already. A little help, if I can ask you for help, would be very nice."

"It's a test!" she told him. "It's the first trial. The first trial is to put pressure on new people to see whether they can handle the stresses of going to school in the valley. It's also a kind of training camp. They will go through the basic training in shaman's craft. They will test to see how much natural ability you have and teach you in the areas where you are weakest. It's not so much if you pass or fail. It's more like if you survive, you get to have a chance at going to school."

"What happens to those who don't survive?"

"They go home. Some can have another go around before classes start, but most go home."

"Maybe I'll just get to go home after all," Luke said thinking out loud."

"I doubt that."

"Why?"

"Most 12-year-olds are lucky if they can lift a pebble or a pencil. Most are considered gifted if they can lift a glass of water. You just tossed three 150-pound boys out a door and slammed and locked the door, and you didn't even break a sweat! So long as you control that temper of yours, I doubt you're going to have much problem at first trial!"

"Oh," Luke said as he once again turned toward the window. He was feeling very alone again. Maybe it was just fear setting in, or maybe he was tired. The darkness out the window seemed endless to him. He needed to feel some sunshine on his face. Although it was very dark out, Luke knew the sun was going to come up again. He was remembering more of Sam's lessons. When she was teaching him what he considered to be weird stuff, Luke didn't really know what she was talking about. She told him once, "Every day you look for the next, and when things get bad, just remember the next day is still coming."

Until now, Luke's first reaction to stuff like that was "Duh!" He didn't really get it at all. Now things were not so good. Everywhere he looked, he saw the darkness—in the events that brought him to this train, in what happened to his family, in his future. Luke saw only the night. He had to believe that the sun was going to come up again and that he would be there to see it! That's what Sam was trying to tell him! He had to believe, at least for now, that no one was out to try to hurt him. He thought he had to calm down and let things in his mind settle. Reminding him to focus is what Sam was trying to tell him and that he should put his mind over his emotions. None of this way of thinking was helping Luke feel something other than very lonely, and it just kept him wondering whether he was doing the right thing.

Luke thought about the fact that his uncle did give his permission for him to go to the valley. Uncle Martin had to know what was going to happen and what Luke would be going through. He must have thought it was right. Luke had to keep Sam's lessons in his mind. "That's all I have to do," Luke thought but wondered, "or is it all I have left?"

The Griffin Valley was only two hours away now. Luke had no idea what was going to happen next.

THROUGH THE GREAT HOLE
IN THE WALL
CHAPTER 11

A SPARKLE OF brilliant colorful light shined through stained-glass windows as Luke found himself walking through a hallway made from massive blocks of ancient granite stone. The walls were ornately decorated in early American colonial style; a pattern of decoration Luke had noticed the last time he had stepped inside the Realm at the Mall. There were various different types of portraits of the American founding fathers everywhere. In fact, there were all kinds of portraits. The ones that were painted were huge and did not move. The rest were all animated, and as Luke passed them, they bowed and curtsied to him. Luke didn't know who they were, but he assumed they were all past members of the Realm. Their portraits moved just like Uncle Harry's did after he had become centered.

Luke continued to walk the hall. Every so often he would come to a stairwell that seemed to spiral upward forever. He passed through a pair of great doors and into a breezeway that overlooked an enormous valley. The sun shined on a breathtaking and seemingly perfect scene of green trees, meadows, rivers, and snow-covered mountain peaks. Luke had never seen anything like it. As he turned around, he realized that he was inside a great castle. He had never seen anything like it either. Luke didn't understand where he was he kept walking. He passed through more doors and found himself in yet another great hall like the last. This one had a sign at its entrance that read "Family Tower #5."

Like the last hall, this one was also lined with animated portraits. As he approached the center of the hall, the point at which a large corridor went off in another direction, he found what seemed to be the largest of all of the animated portraits. Its size was what first got Luke's attention. But then the man in the portrait seemed familiar. He sat on a great golden chair that glowed slightly. He was finely dressed in an elegant colonial costume, and unlike everyone else, he only nodded his head at Luke—he didn't bow. There was a caption on the wall that read,

First Lord and White Robin of the Realm
Lord, Sir Arthur Rama-Pershard Cohan Carter

Luke had a sinking feeling in his heart and stomach. He backed away from the portrait. He looked at the man, and the man looked back at him. This was the person who had been the subject of so many late-night heated discussions. Luke had never participated in those discussions. But like any child who lay in bed at night as parents discussed things much too loud to ignore, Luke knew who this man was, and while he might be family, Luke didn't think he was a friend. In the days after Luke became a centered practitioner, those late-night loud discussions between Aunt Claire and Uncle Martin turned to the reasons why Uncle Martin refused to re-enter the Realm. Aunt Claire never was able to get an answer out of Uncle Martin, but she kept insisting he was afraid of something. Uncle Martin never admitted anything.

"This is why Uncle Martin wouldn't enter the Realm? He knew you were here?" Luke said to the portrait.

"Aye," the old lord said, "most likely so. But just like you if he had not said a word to me, then I would not have spoken to him."

"I doubt that would have mattered," Luke replied abruptly. "Just seeing you again would have been bad enough. He was scared of you, and he hated you! I'm not certain why, but it had something to do with being kept away from his mother."

"Aye, I banished the boy from the Realm. I wanted to bind his powers, but just like me, and now just like you, he was a natural-born leader of the Realm, and no one could bind his powers. Nature cannot be undone except by an act of God or death, and I could not bring myself to kill my own son."

"Well, he's dead now!" Luke said spitefully and with a deep anger in his voice. "You and the others who hurt him should be proud and happy!"

The man bowed his head and wiped his eyes with just one hand. Without looking up, he said, "Martin was a good boy, an honest man, but he couldn't handle responsibility, and he was forever dreaming." Then he looked up at Luke. "Even when his brothers were lost, even when he was the First Lord by default, still he wouldn't come to accept his responsibilities.

So no matter how good of an uncle he was to you, he was always a big disappointment to me."

"Well, guess what grandfather?" Luke said in a rude tone of voice. "I don't know dick about the Realm! So I suggest you prepare yourself for a whole lot more disappointment! And just in case you haven't heard, Laura and Aunt Claire are gone too!"

The man in the portrait again bowed his head again and wiped his face with his hands very slowly. "You cannot hurt me, boy. I am but a shadow of a person who once lived. It is only your magic that allows you to experience what I once was, what I knew, and how I managed to survive. If a mundane person stood where you are now, they would see but a picture. You're wasting your anger on me. I am long gone, and I will never be back again."

"Where is my father?"

"Aye, I don't know, and neither does anyone else."

"Where can I look for clues?"

"Laura looked for many years. Everything she learned must be somewhere inside your home. She kept a diary, I think."

"My home?"

"Aye, at the end of that corridor behind you. The barrier that was there the day your father was lost still stands. No one but a Cohan can enter. Unless, of course, you let someone pass with a spell."

Luke looked down the long corridor, and as he did, he began to fade in and out a bit.

"What is happening to you?" his grandfather asked.

"I must be waking up again."

"You're not here?"

"No," Luke told him. "I'm on a train approaching the Great Hole in the Wall, whatever that is."

"It's the entrance to this valley," the portrait told him. "You can reach out with your mind such a long distance?"

"Only recently. When Laura came, she put me through an exercise to teach me to move things with my mind. She wanted me to experience my own magic. When I had trouble with it, she grabbed my arm and hand, and she was able to teach me with her thoughts. I moved a huge rock then. Later, during the battle, when Uncle Martin died, I was holding his sword, and there was a brilliant flash of light in my mind. Right away, I could see everything, even though my eyes were closed. I could see through walls, and I could see the Dark Lord, and I knew what he was up to. I could even feel things if I wanted to. Since then, I have been experiencing these walk-arounds every time I go to sleep. I can't tell whether they are real."

"Oh, they're real all right," the portrait told him. "Luke, you are the First Lord of the Realm now. It's a fact you will have to learn to live with. You can't change it. It can never be undone. Except for God's grace, it is one of the greatest gifts ever given to man. We are part of a family line that cannot be corrupted by the Darkside. That is why everyone will want to listen to you. They will heed your decisions because they know that the Darkside cannot blind you they way it does common folk."

"Well, they aren't going to know who I am!"

"They aren't going to know?" the portrait responded. "Why?"

Just then Luke faded in and out once more.

"I cast a spell and changed my identity!" He continued to fade. "Unless you are someone who knew me before I changed my identity, you will not know that I am the First Lord of the Realm, grandfather, and that's the way I want it!"

With that, Luke disappeared. The man in the portrait looked surprised and concerned about this revelation. He could never tell anyone. Except with members of his family, the old First Lord could only answer specific questions of passersby and only if he was sure that it would do no harm, and he could never share any secrets. The nature of a secret makes it impossible to know whether sharing it will do any harm.

Slowly, Luke began to wake up. The sound of the train breaking made a screeching noise that was impossible to sleep through. Abi stretched as Luke glanced over at the door. With a snap of his finger, the bag that hung on the window disappeared, the door unlocked, and he and Abi slowly made it to their feet. Luke moved to have a look around. Still a bit nervous about what had gone on so far, Luke was hoping for a little information about what he was certain was going to be an endless about of surprise events. He peered out from the rear of the train and watched as upperclassmen screamed at the Freshers to get on line, to stand at attention, and to "dress right dress," which involved lifting one's right arm — pointing one's fingers at the shoulder of the person to your right — while staring in that person's ear. The point of this was to make a straight line with equal distance between students standing in formation. Then the upperclassmen shouted, "Front!" Everyone stood with his or her arms down and eyes front. "They must have been practicing that all night," Luke thought. They all had their cloaks on as well. Not their school uniforms but their cloaks, and with good reason, they were high on a mountainside. Summer was about to arrive, but Luke could see his breath with every exhale. It was cold!

Luke walked back inside the train car and informed Abi what was happening. Both summoned their trunks and put their cloaks on. Slowly they made their way out to where the rest of the students had lined up. They arrived at the rear of the line without the upperclassmen noticing. Luke did the dress-right-dress thing to get the spacing right, and Abi just followed his lead.

In the cold of the morning, there was a colorless light noticeable in the sky above. The sun was making its way to the horizon, but the eastern horizon was on the other side of the mountain from where they stood. The landscape was heavy with old trees, and as the light grew stronger, Luke became aware of a cliff opposite them in the direction of where the train had parked. There was a valley below, and in the far distance, a grand river was emerging as the light continued to brighten. The ground seemed frozen, and the air was crisp and cold. There had been so little sleep through this night that was near gone now, everyone should have been too tired to do anything, but the crisp cold mountain air that filled their lungs was enough to wake them all.

The countryside seemed brilliant to the eye but harsh compared to the warm, soft sunrises of Sugarloaf. The one familiar sound that Luke took delight in was the sound of the birds rising for the day. Their songs were far different than those of the seagulls he had grown up with. Still, there was something welcoming about them. All of this was in sharp contrast to the sounds of upperclassmen shouting out directions that were now echoing off of the long stonewalls of the mountain.

Luke was not sure what to make of the events that were unraveling before him. It seemed a silly human folly of errors. A Fresher would be told to do something, and no matter how he or she did it, right or wrong, it was always wrong. A loud and continuous chastising followed from the upperclassmen. Sometimes two or three would join in and harass the poor Fresher who had caught their attention. This went on for some time when a curious thing happened. Several people wearing backpacks passed by. A group of teenagers, who, to Luke, seemed to be on their way somewhere, just walked on by. They glanced at the scene of students gathering on the same trail they were walking, but they didn't seem to pay much attention. Luke continued to watch them trek their way out of sight when Abi volunteered, "They are trailblazers."

Luke looked over at her with a question on his face.

"They follow the Appalachian Trail. Some start all the way down in Georgia and walk all the way to Maine."

Again Luke said nothing but had a curious wide-eyed look on his face as he mouthed the word "oh" and nodded his head yes.

"Why the heck would someone want to do a dopey thing like that?" Luke whispered to Abi.

Abi said nothing but raised her shoulders and shook her head.

Luke stared over in the directions where the trailblazers had gone and said as if thinking out loud in a whisper, "Isn't that what they invented cars for? To go from Georgia to Maine without having to take long walks?"

"Who the hell is talking?" a loud, stern voice shouted from the head of the line of students. "I know I heard someone talking! Speak up or I'll have this whole group do 10 laps around the damn train!"

The person doing the shouting was the same upperclassman that had banged his way into the first train car compartment that Luke and Abi had sat in. He continued to make his way down the line of Freshers and demanded to know who it was that had dared to open their mouths. He came to the end and spotted Luke and Abi.

"Well, well, well! If it isn't Mr. Amade and his girlfriend, Miss Bishop!" Luke and Abi just continued to stand at attention and faced forward, saying nothing. "We are honored you two came out of your hole to join the rest of us underlings. I heard you tossed several upperclassmen out using magic. School children like you two aren't allowed to practice magic outside of the Realm. When the First Centurion reads our report, you will have your powers bound, and you'll be sent home. Honestly, I can't wait to see it!"

"Mr. Finch!" a new strong female voice shouted. Finch, the upperclassman who had been chastising Luke, turned abruptly. Behind him stood a female student officer. Her uniform was quite different from the rest of the upperclassmen's. She stood in formal ropes and a cloak and wore a proper white and blue uniform hat. She also wore trousers and boots, but they were nearly hidden behind her draped robes. Her hair was brown and properly wound and dressed on her head. Mr. Finch snapped to attention and rendered a salute to the new-comer. On return of his salute the girl ordered, "Role call and then report, Mr. Finch!"

Mr. Finch rendered another salute and then responded, "Aye, ma'am!"

Finch turned and looked at Luke and Abi meanly as he moved out in front of the student formation to take the role. The arrival of the student officer made everyone realize that Finch, the person who had been screaming at them all night, wasn't the person in charge. He didn't seem to like the fact that everyone had realized that he wasn't the person in charge.

In a few short moments Finch began to take the role of students. When students' names were called, they had been instructed to answer with the word "Yo!" Well, it really wasn't a word—it was just the sound one made when called. Luke and Abi didn't know this because while the others had been harassed and tormented with instruction all night, they had been sleeping. So when their names were called, they simply did as the other students had.

"Luke Amade!"

"Yo!"

"Abi Bishop!"

"Yo!"

Listening to the role call, Luke closed his eyes and tried to keep himself from laughing. To him, it sounded like a really bad rap song. Finch took notice of Luke's smile. He finished the role and smartly walked up to the student officer, saluted some more, and reported the role. When he was done, he hurried back into Luke's face and shouted and demanded to know why he was laughing, Luke stood there and said nothing.

Before long, the student officer had returned. She instructed that any more discipline training would have to wait until after the first light ceremonies and the Fresher group had finished making their way to their training barracks. Soon all of the students were moving north along the Chattanooga Pass. Every so often, some trail blazers would walk by. Some were heading north, and others were heading south. None of these people seemed to pay much attention to the three or four hundred Freshers walking along side of them.

As they walked, in the distance, the face of the stone mountain appeared as well as what looked at first to be a cave. On closer inspection, the cave seemed as if it had been carved into the mountain by hand. Someone had tunneled a hole in the mountain. To Luke, it appeared rather odd at first. Equally odd were the various types of mundane people walking by it as if it didn't exist. The hole was long, but a small measure of light could be seen coming from the other side. Clearly, the tunnel was pointing east, and the sun was preparing to rise on the other side. However, the movement of people was breaking what little light there was making it through. The Freshers had stopped right in front of the hole, and quite a few people seemed to be on the way out.

In a short time, men and women wearing all sorts of costumes began to emerge. Well, at least to Luke they seemed like costumes. The more he was in contact with the Realm, the more it appeared that one person's costume was another person's uniform. Certainly, there wasn't great demand for cloaks anywhere else in America.

The largest assortment of individuals came out of the hole. Nearly every race of human was represented, and the clothing they wore was as different as Luke had ever seen. The men who did not wear uniforms had hair that was as long as the women's. They wore hats, some of which had rims and a point, and others just had points, and still others looked formal and might have been something that George Washington would have worn. As they moved out of the hole, they parted and gathered on either side of it. They faced the newly arrived Freshers. Everything and everyone was new to Luke except the last person. The tall dark-skinned man with the long multishaded hair was the man Uncle Martin had introduced as Doctor Phineenous Dickelbee, High Chancellor and principal instructor of the Citadel Academy and University, the man Luke almost accused of sending those two leprechauns after him.

Dickelbee stood on a short rock above the crowd and was careful not to block the view of the hole in the wall as he spoke. "Good morning, boys and girls."

The crowd of students enthusiastically responded with, "Good morning!"

"I am sure you are all tired from what was a long, and likely a loud and unfriendly, journey. But for a few moments, let us put your training aside as we all gather to welcome you to the Valley of the Griffin.

"This is an important day, not just for us here in the valley but for all of the members of the Realm. Today is the summer solstice. Today the light will be the strongest, and the darkness will be the weakest. The days that follow will hold many celebrations, for many important reasons, and it has been this way since man first walked here. In this place, we celebrate in two very distinctive ways. First, we welcome to the active society of the Realm its newest trainees. That would be all of you young and eager Freshers. Second, we stand here on the west side of the Great Hole in the Wall and watch for the sun to rise. For on this morning and only on this morning, the sun will shine between the Realm and the mundane world. This is the only moment every year that a mundane person can see the Great Hole in the Wall because today, at sunrise, is the only day the sun will shine right through it. Tradition says that any person who is not more than 16 years of age can walk through the Great Hole while the sun shines through it and into the Realm. That person has earned the right to try to become a member of it. As all of you are about to, such a person could join the first trial and earn a place among us. In the past, such people have even become centered with magic.

"Most important, today marks a new beginning for all of you. Today, your childhood will end, and your adult life will begin. Walking through the Great Hole is, for you, a right of passage and a moment of permanent change. Inside you will see for yourselves one of the Realm's great prizes. The Valley of the Griffin is a place that has not been changed by time. Creatures that have existed throughout time are still alive and well in this place. There are other places like this throughout the world, but none has remained as isolated and untouched as the Griffin Valley.

"Boys and girls, over the next four years, as you complete your academy studies and prepare for university, you will experience the greatest amount of change in your entire lives. Never again will you grow so much physically, socially, and intellectually. In four years, you will look back and remark with pride how far you have come in such a short period of time. You will be a very different person, and you and your families will be so proud.

"There is, however, no substitute for hard work. You are about to enter your first trial. It is a very difficult test to discover whether you have the focus and the discipline to join the student body of the Griffin Valley. Some of you will not make it. There may be any number of reasons why, but it usually means that you are not yet ready to join us. Do not fear failure; you are entitled to try three times, and for most of you, this will be your first attempt. The Board of Trustees and

I, along with the entire staff of instructors who stand before you right now, wish you the very best of luck!"

With that speech, all eyes turned to the Great Hole in the Wall as the first of the day's sunlight began to shine through. The sun broke over another mountain on the far side of the valley. The light reflected off of the walls of the Hole in the Wall and delivered a rainbow of shining colors to welcome the new Freshers. As amazing as this scene was, it was nowhere near as amazing as what was overhead. Outside the Realm the sky was cloudy, but inside there were blue skies and sunshine.

"Very well," the chancellor announced. "Let us begin!"

What happened next surprised everyone. No sooner had Dickelbee finished his sentence than a young redheaded girl, wearing a backpack, jeans, and a sweatshirt, came dashing out from behind a tree, behind all of the teachers, and dashed at a full sprint into the Hole in the Wall. Some of the upper-classmen were about to run in and pull her out, but Dickelbee stopped them. Once the light had touched her and she was inside the hole, she couldn't be stopped.

"Very well, Freshers. Lead the way!" Dickelbee shouted.

Soon, everyone was piling into the Great Hole in the Wall. The rainbow of light continued to shine around them on the walls as they made their way through. As they left the hole behind, they moved into a brilliant sea of green. Every one of the Freshers was stunned and silent by what met their eyes. The hills wound their way off of the valley and even higher across the countryside until they became mountains with brilliant white snowcaps on top. There was a loud roar of water crashing down on rocks. To the north was a brilliant crystal blue waterfall whose vapors filled the air and created an astounding shimmering glow and a rainbow of colors that floated down the river and into the valley. A person was literally drawn into the valley by following the colors of the rainbow. The students pursued the path the rainbow made down into the valley. Where the path split in two, the Freshers were directed toward the river and to a small armada of boats waiting to take them into the valley.

Only as they approached the river did the sound of the crashing water subside enough so that people could talk to one another.

"Luke, have you ever seen anything like this?" Abi asked.

Luke had never been so impressed. He looked at Abi and shook his head no.

"My home was brilliant," he told her. "This is even more so!"

INTO THE VALLEY
CHAPTER 12

EVERYONE WAS TAKING their time walking down to the boats and the river. While endlessly looking around, Luke and Abi found themselves ahead of the crowd. Others were stopping to talk and to point things out to one another, but Luke and Abi wanted to keep their distance from the mean upperclassmen, so they kept moving until they reached the boats. There they found the redheaded girl who had made the brave dash into the Hole in the Wall.

The closer Luke got to her, the more familiar she seemed. He had seen her before, but he couldn't remember where. As he approached her, she bowed to him, which sent a chill up Luke's spin.

"Dia Duit, Your Grace," the girl said.

Abi had been looking around, but when the redheaded girl said her greeting, she turned abruptly and stared at her.

"I guess you two have met before?" Abi said.

"I guess we have," Luke responded. "But I can't remember where."

"On your family boat," the girl responded. "Two summers ago. My dad and your uncle were longtime friends. Your uncle told my dad all about the Realm, and he told me. This is why I wanted to come here! I have been dreaming about this day ever since!"

"Well, don't let anyone else know who he is!" Abi insisted, a statement that drew a surprised look from the girl.

"Right," Luke agreed. "I have changed my identity. Just call me Luke. My last name is Amade, and if anyone asks, that's what you tell them." Her statement left Luke wondering why his uncle would teach others about the Realm but not him.

The girl had a confused look on her face. "I'm Kaitlin. My friends call me Katie, or K-T. Gardener is my last name. I like your new name. I think I'll ask you more after we survive the trials—if we survive the trials!" Katie spoke with the sound of prayer and hope in her voice.

"Fine," Luke told her with a small smile on his face. "That was quite a dash you made to get in here!"

"You can say that again," Abi agreed.

"I knew I would have only one chance, so I took it. I had camped out near the train station. When the Hole in the Wall showed itself, that was the one and only moment I had, so I took it!"

"You certainly managed to surprise everyone," Abi said. Her voice had a touch of sarcasm and spite, which surprised Luke. He looked at her and said, "What's wrong with you?"

"She doesn't belong here!" Abi told him.

"Why?"

"She wasn't born into our society, and we know nothing of her background. She could be a Darksider for all we know! She has never been to the market, so she can't possibly have what she needs to go to school!"

"Dickelbee said she got in fair and square. Do the rules allow her to be here or not?" Luke insisted.

"Yes, technically, but she's not going to be well treated!"

"Why?"

"I told you! She's an outsider!"

"It's OK, Luke," Katie insisted. "I knew I would be in for a rough time when I came here. Many people tried to warn me off, but I came anyway!"

Once again Luke said, "Why?"

"I'm just a thick-headed Irish girl, I suppose," Katie said with a smile.

"Well, well, Amade! Already making friends with the wrong sort," Mr. Finch announced himself.

"Hello," Katie said innocently. "I'm Katie Gardner."

"You do not talk to upperclassmen unless they give you permission or talk to you first! Is that clear, little girl?"

"Yes," Katie responded, surprised by the boy's verbal attack.

"Mr. Finch!" a man dressed in robes asserted.

Finch turned about and said, "Yes, professor!"

"That can wait 'til you're in barracks."

"Yes, professor!" Finch responded as he turned around and gave an evil look to all three of the new arrivals. Then he walked off.

"Well, wasn't that interesting and different?" Katie wondered.

"It's only going to get worse, you know," Abi told her.

"Yeah, for all of us it looks like," Katie agreed.

This statement reminded both Abi and Luke that they were still in trouble as well and caused both to glance at each other sadly.

Up at the entrance to the valley, a tan-skinned university student who was clearly from the land of India kept staring at a long list of students who had arrived. He looked concerned as he walked along the path and checked and rechecked the lists.

"Good morning to you, Mr. Pershard."

The student turned and found Professor Dickelbee addressing him.

"Good morning, sir!"

"You have a look of concern on your face. It's much too early in the morning for such looks. What is bothering you?" the chancellor inquired.

"He's not on the role, sir."

"He? Who is 'he,' Mr. Pershard?"

"Carter, sir. He's on none of the lists!"

"He didn't show up, or he didn't make it onto the lists of new students?" The chancellor was concerned but not overly worried, and if he was, he wasn't showing it.

"I put him on the lists myself," Pershard insisted. "But he's not there now, and all of the students have been accounted for. Looks like he must have gone into hiding like his uncle."

"We don't know that, Mr. Pershard, and I don't want rumors going around, so you will keep these details to yourself, understood?"

"Yes, sir, but what if a member of the board asks me?"

"You can't lie to them, but don't volunteer information. Wait until you are asked."

"Very well, sir!"

By now, all of the students had gathered in the boats and had begun their trip downstream toward the Citadel. Although the water moved swiftly, it wasn't going to be a short trip. The valley was nearly 90 miles long and more than 60 miles wide. On its northern edge, it climbed up onto a plateau, which was nearly as wide and as long as the valley. To its south was the famous Griffin Pass. No one knew much about the pass because most who entered were never seen again.

It was difficult for all of the newcomers to grasp where they had arrived. They moved along the river in awe, and while there were short bursts of conversation, most kept quite and just stared. Even the upperclassmen who had been away from the valley for session break were quiet, and they stared too. Luke had never seen a greener place or one filled with so many amazing and wonderful creatures! It seemed to be a kind of magic all of its own.

The newcomers had not been on the river but a half-hour when suddenly everyone started to feel and hear low-pitched tremors. It was as if someone was hammering the ground with a tree, and it kept getting closer and closer—so close in fact that tremors were creating ripples on the water. The newcomers started getting nervous as the upperclassmen just smiled at them.

There ahead on the river's bend stood a creature as tall as a tree with the head and body of a lion and wings and claws of an eagle. It let out a noise that sent shivers up and down Luke's spine. The girls screamed as all of the students raised their hands to their ears to protect themselves from the griffin's roar. As they got closer and closer, two more griffins came flying in and stood next to the one that was already staring at the approaching boats.

A man in robes at the rear of the boat stood up and announced, "Stay calm, everyone! As some of you might have already guessed, those are griffins, and this is their valley. Now, those of you who have hats on will want to remove them so the griffins don't think you're trying to hide something. As we pass in front of them, we are all going to stand and bow with respect. They just want to have a smell and a look at you. These great and powerful beasts are looking for Darksiders! If any of you happen to be one, this would be a good time to jump boat and head for the tree line. Griffins can't maneuver very well in heavy woodland. Of course, once the timber wolves get upwind from you, it's not going to make much difference. When they and various other creatures in that forest smell fresh meat, they generally don't give up until they find what they're hunting."

As it turned out, no one jumped out of any of the boats. They passed under the griffins, and everyone stood and did a polite bow to them. The huge creatures made a slight rumbling noise as the Freshers passed, and they sniffed at each boat. It wasn't clear whether the griffins could in fact smell a Darksider. There was a time, back before the Battle of the Griffin Valley, when they didn't care who came and went. Now, they made every effort to be certain that whoever arrived should understand whose valley this was. In this way, any potential troublemaker would know what they were up against. Their impression wasn't lost on either Luke or Abi or Katie. The enormous creatures properly intimidated each of them. None of them had ever seen anything like the griffin. For Luke, it was the beginning of an understanding that he really had in fact stepped into another world—one that was radically different than the one he grew up in.

What impressed Luke the most on his boat ride was the quietness of his fellow students and the hush of the countryside, broken only by the sounds of the many rambling creeks that fed into the main river. The fields were filled with cows, sheep, horses, kangaroos, wallabies, and others creatures that Luke couldn't even begin to guess what they were. The air was filled with many birds, some of which he doubted anyone had ever seen before. The river was filled with fish that had duckbills. The vastness of the valley and all its creatures seemed to be welcoming the new students.

There was a sudden outburst of talking from the students sitting up front. Luke turned to see what they were going on about. They had spotted the Citadel! Its great stonewalls dominated the countryside. There was a town next to it with an equally impressive cathedral in its center. A man standing on the dock raised a horn to his mouth and sounded the alert that the new students were approaching.

As they began to arrive, the people of the town came out to greet them. A spontaneous band of music formed, made up of individuals carrying various types of flutes, handheld drums with double-sided drum sticks, and several people playing mandolins. As the first students stepped off of the boat, people applauded and moved quickly to shake their hands. Townsfolk clapped in time with the music and shouted words of welcome to the Freshers. They all moved to the town square, where breakfast was waiting.

In the friendlier atmosphere of the town, the students began to introduce one another. On the train, it had been impossible, so everywhere names were being shared, and there were finally some smiles and laughter. The food was good, and Luke was enjoying himself, as were Abi and Katie. A boy came up to sit down next to Luke. He was a very thin boy, tall for a Fresher, and his complexion was dark, but his voice had an accent that sounded as if he might be from England.

"Hello, I'm Selwyn. Selwyn Kidney," the boy told him.

"Hello, I'm Luke. Luke Amade."

"Interesting. I was wondering why everyone was ignoring you. You've changed yourself?"

"You know who I am?"

"Yes, of course," Selwyn told him. "My father is an investor from the island of Trinidad. He knew your father, and for many years, he had done business with your uncle. He was one of your uncle's top agents for the sale of pearls. I've been to your home several times, but you were there only once. My father pointed you out to me. In fact, he asked me to ask you, that is if and when we met again, whether there was going to be a pearl harvest next year."

Luke just glanced at the boy for a moment and thought a bit. His identity was more known than he had thought possible. There might be any number of individuals who had visited Sugarloaf while he was growing up. They knew who he was then, but he didn't know who he was, and now the possibility of crossing paths with all of these strangers was at best troublesome.

"Let's keep who I am to ourselves, OK, Selwyn?"

"Of course, if that is what you want. We can be friends if you like. I have been through this once before. I failed out last year, and now I am on my second turn."

"Failed!" Luke responded with surprise. "Why did you fail?"

"My family line isn't a strong one. I am good at academics, but in field competition, I have very little to offer. I am not very good with a sword, and when it came to flying, I always had to get someone else to enchant a broom or a board for me. My magic was not strong enough. Everything you're about to go through over the next seven weeks will test your ability to be competitive. I am only competitive from the neck up. In the Realm, that doesn't seem to be enough."

"Well, you can't be much worse of than Katie here, right?"

"No one is worse off than Katie."

That was the second person who didn't want to give Katie a chance. Luke found this to be very odd.

"Why does everyone dislike Katie so much? They don't even know her."

"She's not centered," Selwyn responded. "She's looked on as a weak outsider, and the upperclassmen are going to trash her anyway. No one is going to stop them, which means she is not going to be around very long. I give her 24 hours to leave or be killed!"

"Be killed?" Luke nearly choked on his food at this revelation. "Why would anyone want to kill someone they don't know?"

"Because they believe she is weak and can be turned by the Darkside, and they will kill her before she gets a chance at any of them."

"Have you seen people killed here, Selwyn?

"Not firsthand. But people disappeared, and it was obvious why."

"Great," Luke said, looking really upset and really unhappy with the way things were working out.

"If we're going to be friends, I should tell you something else, Luke. You're right. I have not come across one person who seems to know who you are. But they know you started trouble on the train, and everyone has noticed your bruised face. You are already being targeted as a troublemaker. Here, troublemakers are thought of in the same light as Katie."

Luke peered over at Katie, who was across the way enjoying pancakes and a conversation with a rather round boy. He wasn't responding much, but she did seem desperate to make friends. Luke was aware that he was being pointed out among the new students. People were staring at him and were using not very friendly expressions. Luke had a feeling he wasn't going to like it there too much. He also knew he didn't really have any other place to go.

"I'll have to get back to you about the harvest thing. I won't know what we'll do until I talk with the Sugarloaf people again. That might be a while."

It was not long before the Freshers were on the move again. They were not taken into the fortress of the Citadel. Instead, they were taken off to the campus training grounds. This place was partly on the woodland and partly in the open fields. The Training Grounds was the valley's sporting complex. There was a large stadium and several practice fields. There was a building with a dome that seemed to have a great deal of activity around it. There was also a residential area simply referred to as the barracks. Selwyn explained to Luke that there were times during the year that sport competitions would draw large crowds, and they would run out of space to keep everyone inside the Citadel. So the barracks gave people a place to sleep during the season, and in the summer, it held the Freshers who wanted to become students.

"Why don't they just use the looking glass and magic to come and go home from competitions?" Luke asked Selwyn.

"You're forgetting, Luke. You can use magic inside the valley or outside the valley, but you can't use it to move between the valley and the outside."

"Do you know why?" Luke asked with wonder in his voice.

"No one knows why," Selwyn reminded him.

Luke walked along side Selwyn as they talked, and Katie walked directly behind the two. Abi walked alone at a distance. She wanted to walk with Luke but not if he kept hooking up with the low end of the student population. She didn't understand what was going on! Abi knew she was in trouble because she was with Luke on the train, and she knew he was in trouble because he kept making friends with losers. She wanted to warn him of these people but doubted he would listen. Abi also wondered what would happen if someone found out Luke was armed. She was scared that that might start a serious fight and people would get hurt. So Abi's first day in the valley wasn't working out the way she had dreamt about since her parents told her she was a witch. Things were not about to get better anytime soon, and Abi had no clue just how bad they could become. But she was very worried about it.

She had a very sad look on her face when an upperclassman stood on a tree stump and shouted out, "OK! Listen up! This is really simple! You walk up to the quartermaster," he pointed at a student dressed in blue robes. "He will give you your barrack assignments. When the trumpet sounds, you will all go to your assigned areas, wherein, marked on the racks, or beds as you Freshers might still call them, you will locate your name and you will stand in front of that rack until you are given instructions. Now this sounds simple, but someone always screws this up! So the ones that do will stand the first night watch!"

It wasn't long before everyone had his or her assignment. Selwyn had walked off and was talking with a group he seemed to know. Abi was talking with girls she knew, and Katie was made to stand alone where the quartermaster was standing. She had no rack assignment, and some of the boys talking among themselves seemed to think that she would be made to sleep outside on her own. Luke looked around the green-covered landscape and noticed, off behind a large wide oak tree, there seemed to be smoke rising. He slowly walked over to investigate. As he maneuvered to the far side of the tree, there sitting on a stump was the High Chancellor himself.

"This is a dangerous game you are playing, Luke," the chancellor told him without even looking at him. He just puffed on his pipe and looked out into the distance.

"I have played no games with anyone, professor—not that I am aware of, anyway." Luke didn't seem too happy to see this man who held the highest office in the valley.

"Why did you cast a spell to change your identity?"

As far as Luke was aware, this was the man who sent the leprechauns after him. Luke was not interested in having a friendly conversation. He was inclined to draw his sword and cut the man in two. Luke didn't really have anyone else he could point his finger at that he could identify as the cause of all his problems—no one except Dickelbee.

"I really don't see that as being any of your business," Luke said. His attitude was spiteful. He was getting angry and wanted to lash out.

The chancellor did finally look over at Luke. To his surprise, he realized right away that he was not on friendly ground. The boy wasn't just angry. With his bruised face and eyes that were locked on him, he seemed ready to attack. It was as if he had been waiting for this moment.

"Your grandfather told me you weren't too happy about being here."

"Did he, now? It's going to be a real shame having to take a match to that portrait!"

The chancellor was clearly not prepared for Luke's surprising attitude. At first it confused him, as if he were being accused of having done something wrong to the boy, and from the chancellor's point of view, Luke seemed very arrogant for a 12-year-old.

"I have served the House of Cohan and Carter honorably and faithfully my entire life. I have done you no wrong!"

"Well, as the last surviving Cohan and Carter, I might be satisfied if you would faithfully find a very high, very short cliff and take a very long walk off of it!"

There was a pause for a moment as the two looked at each other. The chancellor's surprised expression was face-to-face with Luke's anger.

"Before I go off and meet this untimely fait," the chancellor said as he rose to his feet, careful to make sure that no one on the other side of the tree noticed him, "before I am to fall on my sword for my prince, might I at least know why I have been sentenced?"

"I'm here, aren't I? My family is dead, aren't they? That's enough for me!"

"And you blame me for those things?" the chancellor responded with a true sound of surprise in his voice.

"This whole mess started when those leprechauns showed up, and they made it very clear who it was they worked for!"

The chancellor stared into Luke's eyes sadly for a moment. Then he looked down to the ground, shook his head slightly, and looked back up.

"Leprechauns, Luke," he said clearly and carefully, "are by their nature liars and tricksters. The only ones they cannot lie to are each other and the master they serve. The Og brothers are outcasts among their own kind, and the only master they serve is the head of the House of Cohan and Carter—and now as I understand it, the House of Amade? As God as my witness, Luke, I could not even order lunch from the Og brothers. I could certainly never order them to go on an assignment."

A chill came over Luke as he decided he believed the man. This led to a new realization that in turn made him feel ill. "You're telling me Laura sent those freaks after me?"

"Yes, and I fully supported her decision."

"Why?"

"Luke, you were a sitting duck! The Darkside was on the move! They were coming after you, and no matter what anyone said to Martin, he refused to do anything about it! What you have got to understand, what you must accept for all our sakes, is that you are it! There is no one else! There is no one else walking on this earth but a 12-year-old boy who has any hope of turning the situation around! So out of desperation, Laura sent the Og brothers."

"Why didn't she just come herself?"

"Laura was convinced that if she went after you, she would have needed to kill Martin to get you out!"

Luke was silent for a moment. The chancellor was right about Uncle Martin—that was for sure.

"Laura is dead!"

"I know, Luke," the chancellor responded in a broken voice. "I am very, very sorry about that. Laura was the closest thing I had to a daughter. I loved her very much!"

"Really?" The sound of spite had returned to Luke's voice again. "Well, you certainly came flying to your daughter's rescue in her greatest hour of need, didn't you?"

The chancellor sat back down again and looking at the ground in frustration said very slowly, "Luke, I understand that you are something of a history buff."

"I like history."

"Then you're familiar with the American Civil War?"

"Yes, of course," Luke answered.

"Are you aware that most of the military engagements were won by the South, not the North."

"I suppose that is true," Luke said in a questioning tone of voice.

"Most of the battles were won by the South, but the North won the war. Is there not a very important lesson to be learned from the South's experience?"

"Maybe, but I am too tired right now to think about what it might be."

"It's a simple lesson, Luke. One can win all of the battles but still lose the war!"

"You're telling me Laura knew she was going to lose?"

"Yes, we both did," the chancellor insisted. "But Laura's goal was to win the war, and the only way any such plan would work was if you were brought into the safety of this valley and if you were properly trained and, with some hope, were able to locate and free your father."

"Laura tried to tell me the same thing, but I wouldn't listen!"

"Well, you are the First Lord of the Realm," the chancellor responded with the distinct sound of disappointment in his voice. "What do we do now, Your Grace?"

"We start by not calling me lord or Grace," Luke insisted. "Those titles are embarrassing!"

"That's certainly original thinking, I must say," the chancellor replied.

Then Luke just started to blurt out the things that were on his mind. "What happened to Buddy Sanders? He was supposed to meet me here."

"Buddy's mother was a member of your uncle's caldron. When the battle began, she rushed in to fight along with the rest of the members. She didn't survive, which left Buddy's father in charge of Buddy. He has decided not to allow Buddy to come."

This news surprised Luke. He would have gone to be with his friend if he had known his mother was gone. Luke knew Mrs. Sanders well and thought she was brilliant. "I guess Mr.s Sanders hasn't much use for the Realm. Can't say I blame him much," Luke thought outloud. He turned around and looked back at the Freshers. He was looking right at Katie standing alone with no one going near her and not being allowed to move. "I can't help Buddy, but let's see whether I can help Katie," he thought.

"Do you see that girl over there, chancellor?"

Dickelbee, careful not to be seen, glanced around the tree at Katie.

"Oh, yes, the girl who dashed through the Hole in the Wall. She's a clever one, she is," he said with a slight smile on his face.

"She has no place to stay," Luke told him. "I want her to stay, and I want her to be given a bed to sleep in."

"Well, I am not the board member in charge of admissions," he responded with apprehension. "It would be very politically incorrect for me to stick my nose into another board member's jurisdiction."

"Do you know where the Og brothers are?"

"No, not really."

"I want to talk to them," Luke told the chancellor. "As far as Katie goes, if anyone asks, just tell them the First Lord insisted she stay and be given a bed."

"Maybe he is a Cohan after all," the chancellor thought. "If Luke really is going to start accepting responsibility, then perhaps there is hope."

"OK, Luke, I'll see what I can do," the chancellor said, his face filled with agreement.

GET ON LINE!

CHAPTER 14

IT WASN'T LONG before a trumpet sounded and the students assembled into their new barracks. It was a rather odd-looking place. There were double racks of beds on either side of a very long room. The room was a dingy blue gray with hanging lights in its center that ran its length. Luke was not impressed. There were yellow lines that separated either side of the barrack. On one side were all boys, and on the other side were all girls. There were several levels to the building with nearly 60 students on each level.

"There must be more here than were on the train," Luke thought. He counted the different levels and concluded that the new class of Freshers was more than 1,000 students. There was a great deal of talking going on until three upperclassmen walked in with a tall officer. He was dressed in what looked to be the most perfectly pressed uniform ever and wearing what was commonly known as a "Smokey the Bear" hat. He was also the meanest looking white man Luke had ever laid his eyes on. Luke wasn't certain what a Darksider would look like without its cloak, but he imagined, based only on appearance, that this guy might qualify.

"Get on line!" the upperclassman with the most stripes on his sleeve shouted.

With that, all three of the upperclassmen, one girl and two boys, charged forward and shouted at students to stand at attention on the yellow line. They tormented the Freshers and demanded to know why they couldn't carry out simple instructions. Soon, the entire barracks went silent, and all of the Freshers were standing on line. The only thing that could be heard was the steps of the tall, mean-looking officer in the middle, who then began to speak in a loud single-toned voice.

"My name is First Centurion Crinshaw! I am the supervising centurion for training series 2084! From here on out, the first and last words out of your mouth will be 'sir'! Do you hear me?"

The room responded, "Yes, sir!"

"I can't hear you!"

"Yes, sir!"

"I still can't hear you!'

"Sir, yes, Sir!"

"That's right, 2084! The first and last words out of your worthless mouths are always 'sir'!

"I am here to test you. You are here to be tested. These upperclassmen are here to assist me. The drill is simple. Do as you are told, try as hard as you can, or go home! If you cannot perform what we teach, live by our rules, and in every minute of every day strive to be the best you can be, then you do not belong here! You are weak! That means you're most likely to be the one who uses magic for personal gain! Such people are no longer tolerated in this Realm! We are here to test and see who you really are. Your mommy isn't here to hold your hand, and she's not going to show up, either! So, from this point forward, all decisions are yours and yours alone! You want your mommy? Then go home and don't come back! Good decisions have rewards, and bad decisions have consequences. Make bad decisions and your butt will be in my back pocket! Do not make the mistake of testing my resolve. You will do what you are told, when you are told, and how you are told to do it.

"The next reason you are here is to be sorted into your Baile. That means you are here to show us what you can do, what we can teach you, and how much you can learn over the next six to seven weeks. Then, based on your performances, you will be assigned to one of 12 Bailes for the rest of your academic career. While you are here, your Baile and the people in it are your home and family!

"Finally, you will decide on a service track. This is the service you will do for the community of which you have chosen to become a part. I am a First Centurion! I command 60 other centurions! We are the keepers of security and peace! We are trained to fight Darksiders. All of you will be trained at some level to fight Darksiders! Those who show the most talent for this task will be offered the chance to join us. The very best of those who join us might be offered the chance to become an Alfa-Omega. The Alfa-Omegas are the most talented of all the practitioners in the Realm! They are masters of the natural forces. They are the keepers of the law and its leadership. Those of you who have the highest dedication and focus of mind may be offered the opportunity to join the best of the best! Do you hear me 2084?"

"Sir, yes, sir!"

"There are many other careers and challenges you might be interested in choosing. Each has its place and contributes to the strengths of our society. I am here to see whether you rate the opportunity to find out. You may find I am hard and rude to you. You may not like me. You may want to give up. But even if you may want to give up on yourself, I will not give up on you! So you may hate me more! Do you hear me?"

"Sir, yes, sir!"

"These upperclassmen and I are not your friends, and we are not interested in being your friends. We are here to see to it that you train properly! I promise each and every one of you that as God as my witness, you will learn what you need to learn, or you will hate me like no other you have ever crossed paths with. Do you hear me?"

"Sir, yes, sir!"

"2084, when things get hard—and they will be getting very hard—when you lay down at night, there are two things to remember. No matter how hurt and frustrated you may be, and you will be hurting quite a bit, no matter what you think or for what reasons you may think it, in the eastern sky on the next day's morn, the sun will rise, and you will be here to see it. That is our promise to you. As a practitioner who has been a member of this Realm for well past 50 years, I will also tell you this: you have made the right choice. You are in the right place, you are doing the right thing, and you are doing it for all the right reasons! Does anyone not understand that?"

For a moment, the room was perfectly quiet, and then the First Centurion turned to the upperclassmen and ordered them to carry on. Salutes were exchanged, and then the real firestorm began.

The upperclassmen let loose a rage of shouting, the likes of which Luke had never heard before. They tormented anyone who moved slowly and usually made the Fresher start the task all over again until he or she did it faster. With the slightest error, a Fresher could find himself or herself surrounded by all three upperclassmen screaming! Luke was able to anticipate their actions. He made certain they didn't find the slightest excuse to target him. He just seemed to be able to sense what was going to happen next.

Those upperclassmen in charge wanted to target him. By now everyone knew what Luke had done on the train. They were searching for an excuse to go after him. Abi too was on the receiving end of their scorn. Every mistake she made found her surrounded by at least two upperclassmen. They shouted her down again and again. To her credit, she never gave in. She stood there and took every shot they could toss at her. Luke could not help but feel guilty. He knew things would not have been so bad for her had she never walked into the train car and sat with him. As bad a time as Abi was having, it was Katie and Selwyn who were having the most terrible day of their lives.

At one point, all of the students had to summon their trunks, called footlockers in the Realm, for inspection. Everything was dumped on the floor. The upperclassmen went through a list of items everyone was required to bring. When Freshers were unable to produce the required item, they were shouted down brutally. Katie had no locker at all. All she had was the rucksack she came with. So for every missing item, she found herself surrounded by all three upperclassmen.

They were relentless in their harassment. They kept reminding her she wasn't invited and was free to leave at any time. Time and again, they demanded she get out. Katie stood her ground. They called her names and placed her parentage into question; they did everything but beat her. When that failed, they began to exercise her, ordering her to do push-ups and sit-ups and bending and thrusting her legs in and out. If she stopped, they threatened to put her in jail for disobeying an order. Soon, Abi found herself right next to Katie, and they were doing the same thing. Then Selwyn joined them.

As far as the upperclassmen were concerned, Selwyn was already a loser. They didn't understand why someone who had already failed would be back for a second go around. His experience made Selwyn ready for most of the tricks they used on Freshers. Unfortunately, they seemed to have new tricks designed especially for anyone who failed and returned. At one point, nearly half the barracks were on the deck and were doing exercises of one type or another.

On the levels above, Luke could hear that the other Freshers were in the middle of the same situation. He could also reach out with his mind and see what was going on. "It's a nightmare," he thought. "And nighttime is still a long way off!"

Although Crinshaw was in command, the other levels of barracks had three upperclassmen supervising about 60 Freshers. At least one in every three upperclassmen was a girl. In some cases, there were two girls and one boy. The senior ones wore black hats, and various types of colored hat rims represented their rank. They were addressed as prefects. Each prefect had two lieutenants, who wore gray hats with different colored rims, and again, the color represented their rank. They were addressed as training instructors. A conversation with any went something like "Yes, training instructor, no, training instructor" or "Yes, prefect, no, prefect!" God help the one who used the words "I," "me," or "you"! When asking or responding in the first person, the answers went something like "Sir, the Fresher doesn't know, Sir" or "Sir, the Fresher would like to go to the bathroom, sir!" Either way, the entire experience was rather unpleasant, and it was obviously meant to be. In this way, anyone who was not tough enough to handle becoming part of the academy's fall semester would be weeded out.

Outside in the open yard, members of the Board of Trustees and other Alfa-Omegas, known as the First Caldron, gathered. This was the leadership of the valley, and by default, without a First Lord, the leadership of the Realm. Out into this group walked First Centurion Crinshaw. He had a very stiff walk, and he almost always had his arms behind his back.

"Well, have you found him yet?" a voice that was low and demanding addressed Crinshaw. It belonged to Mr. Pershard, the student who was so concerned when he discovered Luke wasn't in the valley.

"No," Crinshaw answered. "I have gone though each barracks and looked each Fresher in the eye, and I'll be damned if I can tell whether he's here!"

"This is ridiculous," Pershard insisted in an annoyed tone of voice. "Our people on the outside insist that he is here, and no one here can find him!"

Just then one of the board members walked up. "Good morning to you, First Centurion!"

Crinshaw nodded his head with great respect. "Good morning, Chancellor Cole."

"And to you, Mr. Pershard."

"Chancellor, good morning," Pershard responded.

Chancellor Cole was an older woman. She did not stand as tall as Crinshaw but was slightly taller than Pershard. She kept her hat on, which like her robes was a mark of her office, so her dark black hair could barely be seen. Unlike most women, her voice had a strong base tone to it. Often her questions sounded overbearing, even the simple ones. But it was mostly her voice, which often left people thinking she was being rude when she wasn't.

"So, First Centurion, how goes the first day for the Freshers?"

"Well, ma'am, not quite what we were expecting," he told her.

"Why do you say that?" the chancellor responded with surprise in her voice.

"Well, our new First Lord was to show up today, but he's not here. If he is, no one seems able to locate him. I have this boy inside named Amade—he's on all of the lists, but no one has ever heard of him before. We don't know where he came from or how he got here. We don't even know who his parents are. To make matters worse, he and this girl, Bishop, tossed three upperclassmen out of their train car. And I have a Bennie in my barracks!"

"A Bennie, you say? How is that possible?"

"That little Gardner girl, the one who dashed through the Hole in the Wall this morning, the High Chancellor ordered the quartermaster to give her a bunk in my barracks!"

"Really? That is astonishing! I promise you, First Centurion, that I shall complain to the other board members. Admissions are within my brief, not his! If he has done as you say, he has exceeded his brief, and the board shall have to consider it most seriously! As for the other boy and girl, just make certain you follow the rules in dealing with them. In an hour or so, we'll gather in the mess hall and deal with the matter!"

"Yes, ma'am. Thank you, ma'am," the First Centurion responded with a slightly better tone of voice. "The sooner that Bennie and those two troublemakers are gone, the safer we'll all be!"

"Thank you, First Centurion, for calling these matters to my attention! I will have a look around now," she said as she moved off. The two men bowed to her slightly as she left.

"Well?" the First Centurion said with frustration to Mr. Pershard.

"Well, what?"

"What do we do now?"

"The only thing we can do is wait," Pershard asserted with equal frustration.

"Martin managed to evade everyone and stay in hiding for over 50 years! What if he taught the boy how to do the same?"

"I don't know," Pershard insisted. "All we can do now is wait! If he's here, we'll find him! He's a complete amateur! He knows nothing of our ways. If he did, they would never have sent those two stupid leprechauns after him!"

Luke had no idea what was going on outside. Inside the shouting continued for hours until a complete inventory of clothing, books, and other articles was accounted for and everyone's lockers were in good order—everyone except Katie, of course. The upperclassmen were having a conversation at the far end of the barracks. It gave Luke the chance to look around while they weren't watching. Selwyn was holding up OK. He had obviously expected all of this. Abi's hair was a bit of a disaster area, but so was everyone else's. Abi seemed to be holding up well. Katie, well, Katie was not holding up well at all, but she was holding. She was traumatized by the shouting and exhausted by all of the forced exercise.

She must have done 200 push-ups in four hours, but she was still there. Luke felt sick to his stomach. He believed for certain that the upperclassmen were far from finished with her.

Sitting on top of all of the racks was a copy of the Uniform Code of the Realm. It was the magical world's basic law book. The upperclassmen finally relaxed their grip by ordering everyone to rest. Lunchtime was approaching, and Luke thought perhaps that they were organizing to head out to eat. There was no talking allowed, so he didn't try walking up to any of the others. He picked up the Uniform Code and started thumbing through it. Abi sat on her trunk and rested her head on her arms. Katie sat on the floor alone in the corner, and Selwyn just leaned up against the wall. The code was more than just a curiosity to Luke. Each of the rules and regulations wasn't just written down—along the side of the words were windows that were fully animated. The characters in the book were arguing the case law of each regulation. All of the pages had a court scene with a judge in it. Points and issues surrounding the regulations, or legal argument, went back and forth depending on what the holder of the book was looking at. But only the person holding the book could see and hear what was going on. It was very much like the picture of his grandfather and the way he had explained about the other pictures on the wall. Only someone who was part of the Realm and who had the natural magic to enchant an object could hear and see what was going on. This gave Luke an idea.

He put his copy of the Uniform Code back on his rack. Then, moving behind the racks and against the widows, he made his way to where Katie was sitting.

As he walked up to her, she glanced at him and then went back to looking at the floor. Luke bent over and whispered into her ear. "Go pick up the book on your rack and open it."

She looked at him and responded by mouthing "Why?" Luke said no more and just pulled on her hand to get her to start moving. Abi had noticed what was going on. She turned to watch while keeping her head lying on her arms. Selwyn also turned to watch as Katie made her way to the book. She looked at it and then back at Luke, who mouthed "Open it."

Slowly Katie opened the book and became wide-eyed and amazed as the pictures inside came alive. She could hear the arguments and was so surprised she forgot for a moment where she was. Luke looked up and over at Selwyn with a smile on his face.

"You can see and hear those pictures, Katie?" Luke asked her in a whisper to be certain of her response to the book.

"Yeah!" Katie nodded her head in amazement.

"What the hell is going on in here?" The First Centurion announced his presence with his usual charm.

"Who the hell gave you two the permission to talk? Mr. Amade, do you often interact with Bennies?"

Luke was about to answer, but he was cut off.

"I thought Miss Bishop was your girlfriend! Aren't you worried that she is going to dump you now that you prefer the company of Darksiders?"

"Sir—" Luke tried to answer the man, but he was cut off.

The First Centurion stepped right up into Luke's face. His nose was nearly touching Luke's.

"You shut your yap, boy. No one gave you permission to do anything! Certainly no one wants to hear your yap running! OK. You two follow me."

By now, Abi had her face lying directly in her arms, and her hair covered everything as she pretended not to know what was going on. The First Centurion passed on by.

"You too, Bishop. Get your butt up and in gear! Let's go!"

The group made their way across the commons to what was called the chow hall or mess hall. This was the kitchen or place where people ate. As they walked in, there was a very large room filled with tables and chairs. On the far side stood a group dressed in formal robes. Both the Board of Trustees and the First Caldron had gathered to make decisions about Luke, Abi, and Katie.

"Good morning, practitioners," the First Centurion announced as they stood before the group. They returned his greeting with a simple "Good morning."

"Members of the Board and the First, these are the two Freshers who caused the problems on the train earlier this morning. This girl, who has identified herself as Katie Gardner, is the mundane who ran through the Hole in the Wall at first light. I have complained to Chancellor Cole that she has been given a rack in our barracks without my consent."

Chancellor Cole was the first to speak. "Miss Gardner, we certainly admire your passion and willingness to take risks, but I am afraid that given the hazard that mundane people have for being seduced by the Darkside of magic, we are going to have to ask you to leave."

The High Chancellor was sitting all the way to Luke's left. He had his pipe in his mouth, but it wasn't lit. He waited to see who would speak up first before he announced, "I am sorry to say we cannot do that, Chancellor Cole. We would be breaking our own rules, not to mention the uniform code. The girl got in fair and right, and now she is entitled to have a chance to prove herself."

"I must say, High Chancellor," Cole reasoned, "I am surprised to hear a member of the board defending a Bennie!"

"She's not a Bennie!" Luke said loud and sternly.

"No one was talking to you, boy," the First Centurion was angered by Luke.

"I am defending only our bylaws, Madame Chancellor."

"Is that why you exceeded your brief by ordering a Bennie be given a bunk in our barracks?"

"I am High Chancellor here," Dickelbee responded. "I am the chief executive officer of the Realm, appointed by the First Lord. Everything that goes on here falls within my brief!" The High Chancellor sat back and relaxed a little. "However, in this case, I wasn't giving an order. I was just delivering one."

"From whom?" one of the other chancellors asked with surprise.

"From the First Lord of the Realm."

"He's here!" another of the chancellors said with surprise.

"Yes, he's here."

"Where is he?" Cole demanded.

"You're looking at him. He's the boy our First Centurion just shouted at rudely."

There was a gasp of surprise as both the members of the board and First Caldron looked at Luke.

Luke looked over at the High Chancellor with anger on his face.

"I knew I shouldn't have trusted you," Luke announced with deep irritation in his voice.

"Not to worry, Luke," the High Chancellor told him. "Once you leave the room, they will not remember, and if I remind them, they will not believe me!"

"What?" Everyone in the room echoed Luke's reaction.

"Yes," the High Chancellor continued, "I have no idea of the identity spell you cast. In fact I have never known or ever heard of anything like it. But it's true. No one will believe me when I tell them you are the First Lord."

No one in the room was more surprised by the revelation than the First Centurion. He glanced over to the far side of the room where Mr. Pershard stood looking very nervous. Luke turned to Abi to seek some sign that this was all possible. Abi just raised her shoulders slightly and shook her head, indicating that she really didn't know herself.

"Are you Lord Carter?" Chancellor Cole asked Luke.

"I am Luke Carter, yes. I cast a spell to change my identity in hope that I might fit in better with my new school mates."

"I just can't believe this," Chancellor Cole insisted. "This is the heir of the House of Cohan?"

There were others in the group who also expressed disbelief. Some accused the High Chancellor of creating a hoax so he could hold onto his job. Luke was very confused by everyone's reactions. He understood none of it. The forces that supervised the Realm were not in harmony. Their discord since the last attack of the Darkside had been competitive. It didn't help that Martin refused to resolve disputes. Now Luke was faced with a group of people who were self absorbed, had command of their own little hills, and were unwilling to cooperate with one another. They were not a team. They were individualists protecting their own turfs— just like Bennie politicians.

Luke observed each of the people in the ruling councils. He looked into their eyes as they argued with one another. The First Centurion stood with his hands on his hips and watched everything that was going on. The High Chancellor sat calmly in a chair and watched all that was happening. He seemed to have been through all of this before; he didn't seem overly concerned and looked to be a little amused by it. Luke turned and looked at Abi and Katie.

"What do we do?" he asked.

"I don't know," Katie told him. "It seems that even if we tell the truth, no one will believe us about you."

"What if I reversed the spell?" he asked Abi.

"One," Abi, said, "I don't have the spell book with me, and two, if you reverse it, the reasons you cast it in the first place haven't changed. What was it that you said to me about what that woman told you? Sam, was that her name? All about using your emotions or your head to make decisions?"

"I cannot think of an unemotional answer to this situation, can you?"

"You still have your sword."

"You're armed!" Katie said with surprise.

"Yes," Luke responded. "I have Uncle Martin's sword. I can't get rid of the damn thing!"

"Draw it," Abi told him. "They will believe you then!"

"Oh, my God!" Katie said out loud in a tone of shock, fear, and worry. She even stepped backward away from Luke.

Luke turned and stared at the group of leaders once more. He remembered back to Sugarloaf and old Mrs. Willerbee, who kept a flock of chickens in her backyard. They all used to stand close to each other and make noises at each other. That was how this honorable group of fearless leaders seemed to Luke right now, like a flock of noisy birds.

With a flash of light, the powerful charmed sword appeared in Luke's hands. There were sounds of shock and amazement. The High Chancellor jumped to his feet. The First Centurion stood with his arms out to his sides and a stunned look on his face. Everyone was silent and stared for a moment.

"I want that sword, boy!" the First Centurion demanded. "You are going to put the sword down at your feet, and then you are going to walk away from it!"

Luke turned his head toward Abi with a look of "What do I do now?" on his face.

Abi lifted her shoulders, tilted her head slightly, and said, "If he wants it, give it to him."

Luke put down the sword and stepped away. The First Centurion kept staring at him as if he thought it was all a trick of some kind. He walked over to the sword, wrapped his hands around it, and began to pull. Nothing happened! He couldn't lift it. Then he put all his weight behind it, and using all his strength, he lifted one end of the sword but an inch off of the ground when a tremendous surge of power sent him flying into the air and across the room.

Luke grabbed his head and eyes in pain. There was a tremendous flash of light in his head, and it was as if he couldn't see! Then the flash cleared, and he could see everyone in the room while his eyes were closed. It was happening again—the same sight he first experienced in the Battle of Sugarloaf. Everyone looked OK except the First Centurion. It was the same uniform, but his face and hands they had become black as coal, and his face was distorted. Luke opened his eyes long enough to shout, "He's a Darksider!"

All of the leaders drew their swords, but the First Centurion threw a ball of energy from his hand, and when it exploded, they found themselves trapped behind what looked like a big spider web of energy. One of the chancellors launched a bolt of power at the First Centurion, but it bounced off of the web and nearly hit him on the rebound. Another tried to cut through the web but was thrown back against the wall.

Now the only ones on the same side of the web with the First Centurion were Abi, Katie, and Luke. The First Centurion's eyes turned blood red as he gazed over at the Freshers. He smiled an evil smile, and his teeth now revealed were sharpened to a point. The girls screamed and ran for the door, but Luke didn't move. His eyes were closed, but he could see the Darksider in every detail as it began to come at him. Everyone in the room screamed at him to run, but Luke didn't move. The two girls stopped at the door, looked back, and just screamed. The Darksider reached for Luke, but just before he touched him, Luke opened his eyes, and the creature was thrown back high into the air and crashed hard against the far wall and then to the floor. The room fell silent with stunned amazement.

Finally, Luke blinked. He looked over at the girls who stood staring back at him. They had never seen such a display either from a Darksider or a 12 year-old boy. He looked back in the other direction, and all of the fearless leaders stood silent with their swords drawn, as they glared at Luke. The High Chancellor placed his pipe back in his mouth with a dumbfounded look on his face. He just didn't understand how a boy could center so much power so quickly. Then one of the chairs on the far side of the room moved and fell over. A black hand reached up as the Darksider crawled slowly to his feet.

"Run!" everyone shouted at Luke. It's not that Luke wasn't scared or didn't feel the need to run—he was scared and wanted to run, but with a Darksider so close, all Luke could see in his mind was Jimmy's sword cutting into Uncle Martin from behind and with it sticking out the front of him, Jimmy violently removing the sword using his boot. Luke wanted revenge on Jimmy, but it was every Darksider he crossed paths with that would feel the sting. So Luke felt no need to run anywhere, even though he did want to. He was numb with hate, and he would stay that way until someone paid for what the Darkside did to his aunt and uncle.

The First Centurion began waving his left hand counterclockwise until a vortex of energy began to circle in front of him. Then he drew his sword and began to make his way toward Luke again. Luke was attempting to grab and throw him again, but he couldn't. This energy vortex was blocking him! The Darksider got closer and closer, and girls kept screaming for Luke to run. Luke wasn't running. He looked over at his sword on the floor and raised his hand and summoned it to him.

The leaders of the Realm began to panic. Despite the danger, they fired at the barrier again and again. There was no effect on it, and several members were hurt by the discharge of power bouncing off. Others tried to cut their way through but found themselves repelled and lay injured on the floor.

Luke stood his ground. He took the first position of the dance. He closed his eyes and focused on the Darksider and stood ready to strike. The Darksider hesitated for a moment, surprised that a boy would dare to stand against him! Then using only his mind, he began to pick up chairs and sent them crashing into Luke, who was completely unprepared for it. He was hit again and again, but once he realized what was happening, he used his sword to block the chairs. But he hesitated, and that was enough for the Darksider to send an entire table crashing down on his head.

Crinshaw moved in for the kill. Luke was helpless as the Darksider kicked the table off of him. He drew back his sword and was about to strike when Abi jumped onto his back and screamed as she dug her teeth into his neck and shoved her fingernails into his blood-red eyes. The creature screamed in pain as Katie grabbed hold of his left leg and dug her teeth into his Achilles tendon directly behind his ankle. The creature dropped his shield, grabbed Abi by her hair, and flung her across the room like a rag doll. Abi went down hard, and she wasn't getting up. He raised his sword high above Katie, still screaming in pain, and as he was about to cut her in two, Luke's sword came flying in and sliced his sword hand right off of his arm! He screamed as Luke drew back and sliced his other hand off. Luke shoved the point of his sword under the creature's throat and held it there as he yelled, "Katie, run!"

Katie let go and took off as the creature, still in tremendous pain, spoke in a scratchy, hissing evil voice. "You cannot win, Your Grace! In the end, you and the others will lose. It's just a matter of time!"

"Maybe," Luke responded, "but not today!"

With that, Luke spun his body so fast he was but a blur to anyone watching. Like a golf ball being launched off of a tee, the creature's head bolted off of its body and across the room. What was left behind exploded into dust and dissolved onto the floor. The head collided with the far wall, and then it too exploded into dust. It was over.

Luke let his sword fall to his side out of exhaustion. He slowly began to look around the room. Katie picked herself up off of the floor and gazed at Luke for a moment. Then she glanced over at Abi. She realized what had happened and quickly ran to help Abi. Luke glared at the leaders of the Realm. They still looked like chickens to him, only now they were caught in a chicken coop. Once again he raised his sword and let loose with a bolt of power. It hit the web barrier and instantly dissolved it. The leaders were free, as Luke now used his glowing gold humming charmed sword as a walking cane and moved over to a chair to sit down. At this point, he put the sword away.

Several of the board members went over to see about Abi. The rest gathered around Luke. He just sat, bent over, looking at the floor and wondering when the pain in his head was going to go away.

"Well, Elizabeth, do you believe me now?" the High Chancellor asked Chancellor Cole.

"No, Phinie. No, I do not believe you, but Mr. Amade has certainly convinced me! For some reason, I still don't believe it, but what you said before about forgetting once he leaves the room, that I do believe."

With that, Chancellor Cole, without Luke paying attention, kneeled down on one knee and bowed her head to Luke and said, "Welcome home, Lord Cohan!"

Then the others did the same except for the High Chancellor, who waited until Luke looked up again. Luke raised his head and found all of the elders on one knee bowing to him.

"What are you people doing?" Luke was not a happy Griffin Valley camper! "Get up! That is so embarrassing!"

The group all stood back up again.

"I am not your Lord or Your Grace. I am Luke! If you absolutely find it necessary, you can call me mister!" Luke stood up and faced them with anger. "I don't want to be here! I am here because dirt bags like your First Centurion butchered my family and blew up my home! If I had a choice of someplace to be, this place would not be it!"

Luke became quiet and sat back down, once again looking at the floor and holding his very sore head. He continued in this manner until Abi came up and sat down next to him.

"Hi," she said.

Luke turned and saw it was her, and he reached out with a hug and said, "Thanks for saving my ass!"

Abi hugged him back and said, "I think you saved all of ours. He would have just finished me off after he was done with you!"

"Right," Luke replied with a smile on his face. "I knew that," he continued as he laughed slightly.

Katie stood in front of them. Although Abi didn't really want to, they both stood a turn giving her a hug also.

"Thank you, Katie," Luke told her.

"Abi is right," she replied. "He would have whacked the lot of us if he got you."

Abi rubbed her head. "I have a huge lump!"

"I have two," Luke told her. "I had one from last week's fight on the right side of my head. Now I have one on my left. So at least the pain is balanced now! The good news is I think the left side of my face is going to be the same black and blue color as my right."

"You'll be setting a trend," Katie told him.

"That's not funny," Abi said in a friendly tone—the first friendly tone Katie had heard that day and the first time Abi addressed her in the first person since they met that morning.

"Nope," Luke agreed, "not funny."

"I think we need to find some place to go lay down," Abi insisted.

"There's a big oak tree out back with grass underneath," Katie told them.

"Right, let's go have a nap," Luke said as the three started to walk out.

"Where do you think you are going?" Chancellor Cole announced.

The three turned around and looked back.

"We are off to have a nap under a tree," Luke responded.

"The issues that brought you here have not been resolved," she insisted.

"They haven't?" the High Chancellor said with surprise and a question in his voice.

"No," Cole responded. "We must decide their status!"

"Right," Dickelbee said. "All those in favor of them staying please, say 'aye.'"

Everyone but Cole raised his or her hand and said "Aye!"

"All opposed," Dickelbee said as everyone stared at Cole, expecting to hear a descent.

Chancellor Cole glared at all of the board members that were giving her a negative look and instead of a descent she said, "I'll give the Gardner girl until Monday to have a proper kit and locker."

"OK," Dickelbee told her. "That's fair!"

Everyone agreed, and as Luke and the two girls turned to leave, all of the kitchen workers, who had been watching from a safe distance, now started coming out to greet them. People reached out their hands and shook theirs. They thanked Luke and the girls for what they had done. They congratulated them and patted them on their backs, which to Luke meant more pain because his back was still hurting as much as his head. As they continued to walk out, the workers handed the three sandwiches and cans of soda.

Katie and Abi tried to eat a little under the big oak tree, but they were too tired. Soon they fell asleep on the grass next to Luke. He finished his sandwich and was about to doze off himself when two blurry objects came racing in and stopped right in front of him. It was the Og brothers.

"Oh, great!" Luke said with a drowsy disappointment. "Just when I thought the day couldn't possibly get any more special!"

"Good afternoon, My Lord," Michaleen said as he dropped to one knee and bowed his head to Luke.

"Don't call me that!"

"Yes, Your Grace!" Shamus said as he dropped to his knee and bowed his head to Luke.

"Don't call me that either!"

"Master Luke," Michaleen said, "we were told you wanted to speak to us?"

"Yes, but at the time I asked, I had it in my head to take a sword to both of you for spite!"

"Aye, we were only doing what your sister ordered us to do, Master Luke," Shamus told him.

"Yes, so I now understand," Luke responded. "Do you see the girl without the cloak over yonder?"

The two brothers looked over at Katie, who was sleeping on the grass, and Michaleen responded, "Aye."

"I want you two to go up to my barracks. Her rack is the last one on the right. It's the only one with a rucksack instead of a trunk locker in front of it. I want you to open it, use her clothing to get her measurements, go to the mall, and get her all of the supplies and clothing she needs for school and a trunk of her own. Have her named carved into it!"

"Aye, My Lord—Your Grace—I mean, Master Luke. How are we to pay for all that?" Michaleen asked him.

"You know, you are a really an annoying creature, Michaleen!" Luke's tone was slow and very sarcastic. "Tell Odin to put it on my account. If he needs confirmation, bring me something to sign!"

"Aye, Master Luke," Shamus responded. "Are you sure that's a wise thing to do?"

"Why, Shamus? Do you think there's any chance that I will be able to spend all my money in this lifetime, or the next, or the one after that?"

"No, Master Luke. What I meant was, is it wise to be helping a Bennie?"

"She's not a Bennie! She just doesn't have money of her own!"

"Aye, Master Luke," Shamus told him.

"If you'll be needing us again," Michaleen volunteered, "just call to us in the ancient words, and we'll come running!"

"Aye, we will," Shamus agreed.

"Good! Go!" Luke said as the two disappeared with a blur. He lay down under the tree and slipped off into a nap.

IS MY FRIEND EVIL?
CHAPTER 15

LUKE HAD NEVER been to a church service outside of Sugarloaf before. He certainly had never been near a cathedral. Because of the church's size, he found the experience impressing. "That place is huge," he thought. After five days in the valley, here was the first and only connection he shared with home. He took notice that half of everyone there didn't attended service. He wondered about this. Until now, he thought everyone went to church on Sunday. He was there for two reasons. First, this is what he had done every Sunday for all of his life, and he would have felt uncomfortable having missed it. Second, he was feeling a lot of pain, both emotional and physical, and he thought doing something familiar would help make it better.

The priest talked about challenges. He was urging all of the students to stand fast and have a strong belief that they would pass their training. It sounded more like a prayer than a sermon to Luke. It did not do much to ease the pain he felt. The pain wasn't just from all of the fighting of the past 10 days; this new training at the valley was inflicting its own kind of discomfort. The big reason he was hurting was for all of the people who were gone now. Unfortunately, thinking about it made him feel sad, not better. It was bit of a puzzle, really. "If more pain is the result of Sunday church," he thought, "perhaps I might skip it next week." On the other hand, still being alive was amazing. "Someone is looking out for me," Luke thought. "I should be dead by now!" So maybe Sunday church wasn't so bad. "I wish Aunt Claire was here so I could have someone I could talk to!" he thought.

On Sundays, even Freshers were allowed to do what they wanted. They were warned not to go to certain places in the valley. Like many places, with or without Darksiders, the valley had never been ideally safe. Its heavily wooded areas were a little hazardous. They were more than 200 million years old. All of the types of creatures that had existed for that span of time were thriving from the valley's isolation. Exploring them without someone who was experienced was considered very foolish if not outright hazardous. The far north end of the valley bordered a plateau. It was a high plane beginning atop a cliff that was as tall as the mountain peaks, totally inaccessible and heavily forested. Luke had heard some of the upperclassmen describe it as the griffin hunting grounds. So unless someone wanted to become part of the low end of the food chain, he or she stayed away! The catch was this: all members of the Realm could go where they wanted in the valley so long as they didn't invade someone's privacy. This held true even if that meant doing something completely stupid.

Hell week was over. The orders and the discipline were not over, but the eternal shouting and harassment had passed. Now, so long as one did what one was told, there would be no problems—in theory anyway. Quite a few people had not survived hell week. They were sent home. They had until age 16 to past first trial, or they would have their powers forever bound. Luke now knew that the class had started with 1,451 students. After the first week, only 1,211 were left. It wasn't easy. Luke had never run so much in his life. His legs were sore from it, and the running had included an obstacle course. One section of the course had a 10-foot drop where, unless one could levitate, there was no way to avoid getting hurt. The obstacle course was a fast way for the training instructors to find out who had developed what kind of skills. Luke did well; he just followed what Laura had taught him. Abi had some difficulty overcoming her fear, but she did make it. Neither Selwyn nor Katie could make it over the top. It was a wonder how they would survive the rest of the summer.

The four of them stuck together most of the time. Abi still didn't talk to Katie and only occasionally to Selwyn. For Abi, it was embarrassing to have had Katie come to her aid during the fight with Crinshaw. But she had to admit that Katie was the only one who did. So while Abi avoided all conversation with her and did not like even being in the same room with her, she now tolerated her presence. Still, she couldn't bring herself to trust Katie.

When not training, the three basically just followed Luke around. They did it in a kind of order. Abi was first up next to Luke, followed by Selwyn, and then Katie. When Luke went off wandering, he never said what he was up to.

The others just got up and followed him, which on Sunday morning meant going to church.

The group was returning to their barracks. They wanted to change into something they could explore in rather than their church clothes. On entering the barracks, they noticed right away a new trunk in front of Katie's rack. The group made their way toward it and discovered Katie's name on the trunk.

"Oh, my God!" Katie shouted with surprise.

They all watched as Katie opened her trunk. Inside were the nicest uniforms and supplies money could buy. Luke was smiling a big smile until a sword inside was uncovered.

"Oh, no!" Katie said.

"Yeah," Abi agreed. "How did you manage that?"

"She didn't," Luke volunteered. "I did, but I didn't order up a brand new sword, that's for sure. I told those two just to get her what she needed for school!"

"What two?" Abi asked.

"The two you saw when we first met."

"Not those two stupid leprechauns!"

"Aye," Luke said with a smile. "Suren they were the only ones I could think of that would help her."

Katie came over and hugged Luke. "I hope I am worth it," she told him.

"Me too," Abi added in a sarcastic tone.

"Abi, at least make an effort to be nice!" Luke said.

"Yeah, right! We have another sword in the barracks! What are we going to do about it?"

"Right," Selwyn agreed. "Not to mention that when people find out you did this for her, Luke, you're gonna be on the receiving end of a lot of bad attitudes."

"Nothing new there," Luke responded as if he was just thinking out loud.

Luke first encouraged Katie to try to call up the sword. But she couldn't call it up, and she couldn't put the trunk away like everyone else either. Luke reached for the Uniform Code book, and when Katie opened it, the pictures did not move. Katie began to get a sinking feeling inside. Something was terribly wrong!

"What is going on?" she shouted.

The group looked at her in an odd way, not really able to make sense of it either.

"Her powers have been bound!" a new and foreign voice announced.

The group turned around, and there stood a uniformed black woman. She stood tall with a narrow face and nose. Her eyes were an unusual shade of light blue that made them very noticeable. Her hair, what they could see of it tucked under a Smokey the Bear hat bearing the rank of First Centurion, was a natural auburn with natural light highlights. Her bodylines were well defined like that of an athlete. She wore a perfectly pressed uniform, and she mostly kept her arms folded behind her.

The woman spoke with a very different kind of English accent. Luke didn't know what it was but felt he had heard it before. Also, there was something familiar about her, but he wasn't certain what it was. The group just looked at the woman in stunned silence. The last First Centurion tried to kill them. Luke was already feeling defensive and careful. Katie's locker was wide open with the sword on top. The woman walked over to the trunk, looked at it, and then shouted, "Cadet Morris!"

Very quickly, an upperclassman appeared and rendered a salute.

"Cadet Morris reporting to the First Centurion as ordered, ma'am!"

"Mr. Morris, take this sword over to the arms inventory. Check it in under Miss Gardner's name. Sometime after dinner tonight, come back and do a proper inventory of Miss Gardner's locker."

"Aye, ma'am!"

The upperclassman picked up the sword and rendered another salute as he went off and out of the barracks. The First Centurion stood watching until she was certain they were all alone. The four, who had not said a word or taken their eyes off of her, just stood there waiting and wondering what would happen next. Katie leaned over to Abi and whispered, "Is she evil?"

Abi just elbowed Katie away from her and gave her a look whose message was unmistakable: "Shut up!"

Katie stood rubbing where Abi's elbow had met her side when the First Centurion first spoke and then turned around, slowly saying, "No, Miss Gardener, I am not a Darksider."

"Kewl," Katie responded, which caused Abi to turn with her hand raised, threatening to belt her over the head if she didn't keep her mouth shut. Katie took a few steps back and away from Abi.

"Who are you?" Selwyn asked.

"Mr. Kidney, hell week is over, but when addressing an officer, you will continue to stand at attention, and the first and last word out of your mouth is still 'sir' or 'ma'am.' Is that clear?"

"Yes, ma'am. Ma'am, who are you, ma'am?"

The First Centurion was not shouting, nor was there a condescending tone to her voice. This was a clear and remarkable change from the last First Centurion. She spoke very professionally. It let everyone in the room understand who was in charge, but she was not aggressive.

"Who am I, Mr. Kidney? I am First Centurion Thronbasa. I am the new commanding officer of training series 2084." Then she turned to Luke, Abi, and Katie and said, "I understand you three whacked the last commander?"

"He started it!" Katie asserted drawing yet another evil eye from Abi and a smile from Selwyn.

"I also understand that this group knows who the First Lord of the Realm is?"

Everyone looked at Thronbasa and waited for something to happen as she circled and walked around them.

"So, Mr. Kidney, who is the First Lord?"

Selwyn hesitated for a moment and said, "I don't know, ma'am."

"Miss Bishop, I know you know who he is, don't you?"

"No, ma'am," Abi responded.

"And you, Miss Gardener, you wouldn't still be here if you didn't know who he was."

"No, ma'am," Katie told her.

Then the woman walked up from behind Luke and bent over, more or less talking into his ear, saying, "What I really want to know is who thought up a dopey name like Amade?"

"It's short for Amadeus," Abi blurted out, covering her mouth with a surprised look on her face as she was smacked on the back of her head by Selwyn and Katie shoved her! She couldn't believe she had said that!

Thronbasa, still staring at the back of Luke's head, began to laugh.

"Amadeus?" She laughed some more.

Luke turned around and looked at Thronbasa. She remained bent over, so he was looking into her eyes.

"Who are you?"

"Did you forget to say 'ma'am'? I know who I am, My Lord Rama Pershard, Cohan, Carter, and Amade!" She laughed some more as she began to walk out in front of the group, and then she turned to them again. "I know who you are, but what I do not understand is why everyone else, with the exception of the Lord High Chancellor and these three, doesn't recognize you. What do these three very new yet very loyal friends of yours have in common with the High Chancellor?"

"They all knew me before I came here," Luke told her calmly. "How do you know me?"

"For the same reason," she said with a pause and an amazed look on her face. "It would seem we all have something in common, yes?"

"How?" Luke insisted.

"I am Elizabeth Monaghan Thronbasa. My sister was Claire Monaghan Cohan. Same father, different mother."

Luke stood stunned.

"Who's Claire?" Katie said with bewilderment.

Abi looked at her. Frustrated, she said, "Katie, shut up!"

"Look who's talking!" she said right back at Abi.

"She was my aunt," Luke responded while keeping his eye on Thronbasa. "She was killed in the fight that brought me here."

Nothing about Thronbasa was a surprise to Luke except her showing up. Luke now completely understood that his aunt and uncle had strictly controlled all information coming to him. If Uncle Martin and Aunt Claire were able to keep his own sister a secret for all of his life, Luke wondered, how many other relatives did he have that he knew nothing about? For Luke, however, such revelations were not grounds for either celebration or trust. This was the lesson the 12-year-old Luke had learned. Every time he trusted an adult, some kind of crap started happening. Someone tried to kill him or managed to kill someone he cared about. "No more!" Luke thought. "From now on, if some adult makes a move on me, the sword is coming out! I don't care who they are!" So there was just no way he was going to trust Thronbasa. He proceeded carefully, with anger in his heart and more than a touch of his usual sarcasm.

"Did you love your sister, Aunt Elizabeth?" Luke's tone of voice was spiteful. "Where were all of these newfound friends and relatives when my family needed them the most?" he wondered.

Thronbasa stood and stared at the boy for a moment. She could hear and even feel Luke's hostile attitude. "Yes, she was very special to me."

"So, where were you when she needed you the most?" Luke wondered in a continued rude tone.

"I was where she wanted me to be, doing exactly what she would have wanted me to be doing. But that would not have stopped her from calling for help if she needed me. I can only guess the attack was a surprise. She wasn't ready, or the Darkside blocked her from calling for help."

Luke relaxed his stare at Thronbasa. The anger he was feeling went away. He blinked a few times as he thought and wondered, and he looked at the ground and scratched his head a little. Feeling angry was getting to be a habit he neither liked nor had ever been accustomed to.

"It was a little of both, I think," he responded. "I still don't understand how you know me enough to break the spell I cast."

"We were together until you were four years old. My husband and I were replaced by Sonny and Sam."

"Replaced?" Luke was surprised by her use of the word "replaced." "Why?"

"There wasn't just one reason," she continued with her hands still resting behind her back. "Martin and I never really got along. That was most likely the biggest reason. Another was that I got pregnant with my first child. Martin wasn't too happy when he found out. He thought guarding you should have been my highest calling. So when Sonny and Sam showed up, we went home to South Africa."

"South Africa?"

"Yes, my husband, Marcus, and I were born and raised there. We have three children. You should come and visit sometime."

"Aunt Claire was all Irish."

"So am I," she told him with a bit of a smile on her face. "When I get pissed off, anyway. Although I think I would have loved being raised in Ireland with Claire, it never worked out. Our mothers never really liked each other. Claire and I always got along, and we loved each other. She was my big sister, and it didn't bother her that I was black. I thought she was brilliant—something our mothers never approved of because they were jealous of each other. Claire's mother could never come to grips with the fact that the man she loved had been with a black woman. She hated him for it. Our father was a very odd, and even eccentric, Irish wizard, but he was a powerful one. He preferred to live away from practitioners. He earned an engineering degree and lived in the Bennie world. I don't think he ever liked being a practitioner."

"I know exactly how he feels," Luke told her.

"Felt," Thronbasa corrected him. "The Darkside got him many years ago. Although to me, it still seems just like yesterday."

"You just left your children behind and came here?" Katie said in a surprised tone of voice.

"Katie," Selwyn responded. "Will you stay out of it?"

"How many times does someone have to say something to you before it sinks in?" Abi demanded.

Luke had turned slightly, looking at Katie and the other two. A question came over his face as he turned back to Thronbasa and asked, "What did you mean that Katie's powers have been bound?"

"Yes, Chancellor Cole has been in charge of her since you offed Crinshaw. She came in one night and bound her powers while she was sleeping."

"What?" Katie shouted.

"You have a bad attitude there, Miss Gardner!" Thronbasa said. She would not tolerate students raising their voices at her. "Don't force me to discipline you. I will not hesitate if you don't change it, and I do mean now!"

Katie stood there looking very angry. Her feelings were hurt, but she kept her mouth shut.

"How do you know this?" Luke wondered.

"Chancellor Cole," she said, "not Dickelbee, is the one who called me in. She trusts me, so she told me everything she knows. Then the High Chancellor filled me in on the rest, and, as for my children—not that it's anyone's business—they are over with my husband in our quarters here."

Luke stared for a moment. He didn't sense any dishonesty at all. "Why would Cole bind the powers of someone who had already proven herself in a fight with a Darksider?"

"She is the executive office in charge of the admissions. She believed it was her decision to make. She doesn't trust Ms. Gardner. She believes she's just a Bennie who knew the rules and became centered without being an original part of the Realm."

"And the High Chancellor went along with it?"

"He doesn't know, and I do not share with other members of the board what they share with me. They are very political, so I keep everything shared with me in confidence."

"But you are telling me?"

"The First Lord of the Realm is the exception to everything. Oh, and by the way, Cole wants me to take your sword away. She has forgotten who you are but remembers you have a weapon."

Everyone's expression changed, and Thronbasa noticed the change. The last person to demand Luke's sword was a Darksider.

"What?" Thronbasa said with bewilderment. "I have to have the sword, Luke. Twelve-year-olds cannot walk around with swords. They aren't trained. It's too dangerous."

"You want my sword? Fine!"

Luke summoned his sword. Thronbasa had seen it before. It was Martin's sword. She was stunned to see it in Luke's hands. Luke moved toward her. He was standing sharp and ready. He didn't sense danger, but he wasn't sure whom to trust anymore. He spun his body and swung the sword at her. With a brilliant reflex, Thronbasa summoned her sword and blocked Luke. Her sword didn't shatter. It stood strong! It glowed like Luke's, and it made a sound of its own.

"No, Luke!" Selwyn shouted.

"She has a charmed sword, Luke!" Abi shouted. "She can't be a Darksider! They can't hold and operate a charmed sword!"

Luke stopped and backed away from Thronbasa, still holding his sword at the ready.

"She's not evil," Selwyn said in a calmer tone of voice. "She's an Alfa-Omega."

"You're very fast Luke," Thronbasa said. "If you hadn't telegraphed your move or had your body been just a hair bit looser, you would have had me!" In truth, Thronbasa was totally stunned. She had never seen such speed and coordination in a 12-year-old. In addition, without warming up and practicing, she knew she had no chance of matching it. She would have been happy not to cross swords anymore.

Luke just stared at her for a moment.

"I wasn't aware that Alfa-Omegas were also centurions."

"Centurions aren't necessarily Alfa-Omegas, but if they hold leadership roles, they can be," Thronbasa explained.

"Put your sword away," Luke insisted. "I will not strike again."

"I am not so sure I can trust you now."

"No, you can," he responded. "Now do it because I said to," Luke said with arrogance. "I believe Abi and Selwyn. Do it because I am sorry! The last First Centurion tried to take my head off, and I think your uniform is making me nervous." Luke didn't bother to tell her that once he crossed swords with her, he could feel whether she was evil or not.

Thronbasa looked at him for a moment and then relaxed her stance and put her sword away. Luke also relaxed his stance and turned to Abi and said, "Go get your book of spells and find me one that I can center Katie with."

Abi was surprised by Luke's request. She looked over at Katie, who looked back at her, and then Abi looked back at Luke. With an obviously reluctant image on her face, she went off to find her book of spells.

"What are you going to do?" Thronbasa said with a tone of concern.

"I am going to give Katie her magic back."

"That is not a good idea, Luke," Thronbasa told him.

"I think it is!"

"Luke, there is a political structure here that you know nothing about and that you have no hope of understanding even if you spent the next four years trying."

"Well, everyone keeps shoving this Lord of the Realm crap down my throat, so let's find out if I am or not!"

Thronbasa stared at him for a moment as she crossed her arms and replied, sternly shaking her head, "You're not there yet, Luke. You are arrogant—and for no reason! I hear Crinshaw took you down on his second charge! I would be willing to bet that Sam never taught you a thing about four-dimensional fighting. That's when a person uses the power of his or her mind to attack. That's how all of the furniture came flying at you after you crossed swords with Crinshaw."

Luke stared at her for a moment and said calmly, "The only thing Sam ever taught me was how to dance, how to pretend to be something you aren't, and how to lie."

"But you know now that her dance instructions were really training, right?"

"I said she was good at lying and pretending to be something else. They all were: Aunt Claire and Uncle Martin too. They all lied to me and put me into situations I didn't want to be in! They pretended that I was someone else, and they never cared what I thought or bothered to explain one thing to me! Laura was the only one who never lied to me, and I got to know her for all of one day! I hadn't made a single choice of my own since the day those two stupid leprechauns grabbed me! I don't know what anyone has told you about Crinshaw, but I did not choose to be shoved into that position either. I am choosing to fully center Katie and Abi and Selwyn. I am going to center them, and then I am going to find Chancellor Cole and see how she likes having her powers bound!"

"So, instead of fighting the fight, you're going to go looking for one?" Thronbasa was not happy about Luke's revaluations. But in the end, if he wanted to go out and get himself killed, there was little she could do about it.

"You think that old fart is going to want to fight?"

"Martin was 70-something years old," Thronbasa said to him. "How well do you think he could have fought if he had the chance to? Despite her appearance, Cole is only in her late 40s, and she is a fully trained Alfa-Omega. She knows how to fight and fight very well, Luke. You have no idea what you are doing!"

Luke just stared at her in silence for a moment. He knew she was right but wasn't going to let her know what he was thinking.

"Luke," Abi said. "I found it."

Luke and Thronbasa went to see what Abi had found. There between the pages they both read the Center of Powers spell. Luke stood there with sword in hand as he read. Thronbasa became alarmed and told Luke that he could not use the spell. It was the spell used to center Alfa-Omegas after they had finished their trials. She complained that none of them had been properly trained to be masters of the elements and that because of their ages, anyone of them, except Luke, could still be turned to the Darkside. If other students realized how the three of them had been centered, they would fear them, and they would be outcasts.

Luke insisted that his friends would keep their mouths shut. They had proven themselves when Crinshaw attacked. Thronbasa insisted that Luke was in the valley to make things better, not worse. Then Luke insisted that either she give him a good centering spell that wouldn't be so overwhelming or he would use this one!

Thronbasa was in a terrible position. Luke had a birthright to do as he was suggesting, but his decisions and lack of experience could alert the very people who would want to hurt him the most.

"Luke," she asked him politely, "can we talk for a few minutes before you cast these spells?"

Luke put his sword away, crossed his arms, and looked at the tall, beautiful woman.

"Do you know what you are facing here? Do you know who and what is stalking you and why?"

"Laura explained about the Darkside. The universe is polarized between positive and negative. These forces seek balance, but the Darkside wants to pull it all to their side and will do whatever it takes to get the job done."

"That is a very basic view," Thronbasa replied. "You are describing the natural world, and before you go off guessing what it's all about, you need a much better understanding. You don't have that understanding, and Martin did you a great disservice by not training you sooner. That's why he and I never got along. I kept insisting that by age five, you should be told who you were and kept in a regiment of discipline so you could learn as much as possible as soon as possible."

"What is it that you want me to know?"

"That is going to take years to explain, Luke. It's not my fault, but if you give me the chance, I will teach you. What you have to understand for now is the basic nature of the conflict that faces you. To do so as best as you can at such a young age, you need to look at the most honest, fundamental essence of it. In South Africa, for example, there is eternal conflict in nature. At the top of it and the food chain are the lions. They are the kings of the jungle. When they work as a team, they can kill almost anything, including an elephant. When they don't act as a team, they are lucky if they can catch a rabbit. As powerful as they are, there are creatures that can push them out. When a herd of elephants comes, they move! But their greatest rivals are hyenas. Hyenas are the only things lions kill but don't eat. When they work as a team, hyenas can take on an entire pride of lions and win—when they don't, they get killed. That is the nature of the conflict here, and you just don't have enough facts to make even the most basic of informed judgments, and you have no team."

Luke sensed the same kind of honesty coming from Thronbasa as he had from Laura. She was starting to make him feel comfortable again. He had forgotten what it was like to be at ease and not have to keep looking over his back to see what might be coming.

"I have the makings of a team here," Luke responded in a relaxed tone. "These three know me, and as you have seen for yourself, they can be trusted."

Katie, Selwyn, and Abi just looked on and paid attention to every word in silence. They smiled when Luke suggested they could be part of his team.

"Yes, Luke," Thronbasa agreed. "You have managed to draw in three good individuals you can trust. But they can't help you."

"Why?"

"The most obvious reason is that they cannot defend you. They haven't been trained to fight. And although they have a center, they are most likely very far from being perfectly centered. There are many degrees of magical centers, and it takes years of training to find out all that is possible for a new student. Mr. Kidney is here for the second time. He was originally rejected because his power is weak, which means he's far off center. Ms. Bishop's is a little better, and we know that because she can run the obstacle course without assistance. She is considered more centered. I have no idea how centered Ms. Gardner might have become if given the chance. The point is they can't help you. They have neither the magic nor the skills to get the job done."

"Then who?" Luke insisted.

"There were several very powerful Alfa-Omegas that came to watch over you when you first left here."

"When I first left? Why?"

"They thought the Darkside would hunt you down in Florida. They waited for the battle, but after two years, it became obvious that the Darkside had no idea where you were, so most went back to their jobs because they weren't needed. They could be summoned, and they would answer the call because they believe in the cause. Some might already have been here if it weren't for this spell you cast."

"If they knew me, then the spell shouldn't have affected them."

"Right, but, Luke, you did not consider the end result of your spell beyond hiding behind it. Everyone here who is responsible for sharing information outside of the valley had no idea who you had become. No one knew where you were or what had happened to you. So the followers of the Cohan haven't a clue what was or is going on! When we tell someone here, a follower and supporter of your clan, for example, they don't believe us!"

"Oops," was Luke's response.

"Yeah, 'oops' is right! Luke, you have to learn! You have to listen! You have to keep your mouth shut to figure out what the rules of the game are and who the players are. Most important, you have to grow up! There is no one who likes being in the middle of this mess. We all have to live with the current situation. Given what happened to your father, I have to tell you that everyone who supports you thinks the current situation stinks. They don't like who is in charge here. They don't like the way things are run, and they all believed you were the best hope for change. But there is nothing to be done about it except to make as few mistakes as possible, and casting spells on yourself, and your friends, is a big mistake! We all live by our choices. That is what makes who we are and separates us from the Darkside."

"OK, then unbind her powers," Luke agreed calmly.

Thronbasa looked at him. She was surprised and glanced over at Katie. Then she said, "I can't. I can't break Cole's spell. She ranks me both laterally and magically."

"Then give me the spell."

"If you break her spell, she'll go berserk! She will be infuriated!"

"What happens if I use the spell in Abi's book?

Again, Thronbasa hesitated and just glanced at Luke. She did notice he was now asking, not acting, so at least he had started listening.

"Your friends will be in as much control over their magic as you obviously are not. I am starting believe Martin centered all his powers on you, Luke. Do you have any idea what you are doing? That's what will happen to your friends if you cast that spell."

Luke was sure she had a good point there, but he didn't say so. He was certain he that he didn't have a clue about what he was doing. There was a kind of a stand off going on between Thronbasa and Luke. Both were determined to have their way. Luke had the upper hand, but Thronbasa wasn't letting on that he did, and Luke didn't know. Thronbasa was starting to remind him a lot of Laura, so he was a little happy with that. Luke glanced over at Abi. "Forget the centering spell. Look for binding and unbinding magic," he instructed.

Thronbasa exhaled with frustration. Luke noticed and glanced over at her.

"There is no way anyone is going to get away with hurting Katie!" he told her.

"What if she's a Darksider? She wouldn't know it if she was! What if she's like the person who shoved his sword through Martin?"

"How do you know about that?"

"Marta told me."

"Marta wasn't there!"

"That's right. She wasn't, which is why they put her on trial and convicted her, by the way! Sonny and Sam explained to her what happened, and she told me."

"Where is she?"

"In jail where she belongs!"

"For how long?"

"Three years, and that's a light sentence for someone who has now been convicted twice for desertion."

"Three years! I never heard of a trial so fast. It's been all of six days since I last saw her!"

"There's no way to hide the truth in magic, Luke," she told him. "In an enchanted trial, there's no way to lie or deceive or to get away with anything. It's not like in the Bennie world where lawyers try to win the case for their clients. Everything surrounding the events of a person's arrest is known; the facts are never in dispute. Not even the accused has any cause to dispute the facts. Even for the worst of crimes, trials are short."

"But three years!"

"Right," Thronbasa continued. "Last time she lost her charmed sword; this time she's been stripped of her powers. Most people in the Realm don't get second chances. She got one because Martin agreed to it. If she had been doing her job, there's no way anyone would have surprised Martin. He might still be alive! He had the power to defeat the warlocks. You might still have a home, and your family, if Marta had been doing her job!"

Luke looked at her in silence and sadness. Marta was his friend, and learning she was in jail made him hurt inside. Then he looked over at Katie.

"OK, we'll give Katie her powers back, and then I will test her," he said.

"Test her? How?" Thronbasa insisted.

"The same way I just tested you. I'll use my sword."

"Your sword?"

"Yeah, my sword doesn't react well to anyone who has been touched by evil!"

"You can say that again," Abi added.

"That's how Crinshaw was discovered. He tried to take my sword."

"I found it!" Abi shouted as the both Thronbasa and Luke turned their attention to her.

The two read the spell, and Luke translated it into Celt. Once again he drew his sword, pointed at Katie, and said the spell. Brilliant lights swirled around her as Katie's magic was returned to her. Then Luke turned to Thronbasa and said, "Let her have your sword for a moment. Please?"

"My sword?" Thronbasa said with surprise. She had never given up her sword since the day she had earned it.

"It's charmed, and if she a Darksider, then she couldn't hold it."

"Why not your sword?"

"No one can hold my sword," Luke told her. "I have been trying to give it up since I got it. Crinshaw wrapped both his hands and pushed with his feet, and he couldn't lift it."

Thronbasa looked at him wide-eyed as she summoned her sword. Abi put her hands over her eyes and peered through her fingers. She couldn't believe this was happening. Selwyn stepped back and looked very nervous as Thronbasa slowly and carefully put her sword into Katie's shaking hands.

"Don't worry. Don't be nervous," Thronbasa told her. "If you're not evil, it will not hurt you."

Katie stood holding the sword very nervously. Luke drew his sword and was about to strike hers when Thronbasa started shouting, "Woah! What are you doing?"

"If I strike her sword against mine," Luke said with a very confused look on his face, "if she has been touched by evil, I will get a flash in my head. I'll be able to see even if my eyes are closed."

Thronbasa stood there with her mouth open. Luke had just described one of the highest magical powers possible. She was stunned to hear it.

"You have mind sight?" she questioned slowly.

"I guess that's what you could call it," he told her.

There was a very sad look on her face. "If you cross swords with her, you will flash her. She might not wake up for a week, if not longer."

"Why?"

"That's what charmed swords do. They channel power and magic. With a normal sword, the holder channels his or her own magic. If the holder does it too much, he or she grows weak and passes out. A charmed sword channels the power of nature itself. That's why it takes years to become an Alfa-Omega. A practitioner has to train for hours every day to control the flow."

"It didn't hurt you when we crossed swords."

"Yes!" Thronbasa said forcefully. "I have been training with a charmed sword for more than half my life, so I was able to block your flash. For me, it's a reflex."

"Is she going to die if we do this?" Luke asked.

"No, I don't think so, but it's going to hurt!"

Luke turned to Katie, looked her in the eye, and said, "It's going to hurt."

Katie nervously nodded her head and responded, "Yeah, OK, let's get it over with then!"

Luke drew back. He had no real force behind his swing, but as soon as his sword crashed into hers, Katie went flying up into the air and across the length of the barracks, and she crashed into the door on the far side. The force of bouncing off of the doors was so hard it sent her sword flying out of her hands and sliding back down the floor and right up to Luke.

Abi removed her hands from her eyes and like everyone else gazed with her mouth open and a stunned look on her face. She looked at Luke with shock on her face.

"Well, she's not a Darksider," Luke responded to the look she was giving him. "I told you so!"

Everyone but Luke walked down to Katie to see how she was. Abi rolled her over on her back and called her name a few times. Katie opened her eyes and said as she wrapped her hands around her head, "That hurt! That hurt a whole lot! Please tell me I passed the test."

Katie lifted up with her arms and inched her way backward until she was sitting upright against the door. Selwyn walked away and toward Luke. He picked up the charmed sword and walked behind Luke. Luke wondered what the heck he was up to. Luke turned to face him.

Selwyn struck a defensive pose with the sword and said, "OK, do me now!"

"What?" Luke said in stunned amazement. "What do you mean?"

"If I have been touched by evil, I might not know it—that's what the First Centurion said!"

"Yeah, so?"

"So I want to know!"

"Have you gone bonkers or something?"

"Go for it, Selwyn!" Katie shouted like a cheerleader. She even managed to raise one arm into the air to cheer him on.

Luke refused to swing, so Selwyn swung at him instead. Their swords crossed, and Selwyn went flying up into the air and crashed into the doors on the opposite side of the barracks. Just like Katie, he bounced, and the sword went sliding across the floor and right back to where Luke was standing.

He glanced at the sword and then looked at Thronbasa and said, "Why does that sword keep doing that?"

"You won; the sword is yours—particularly when it's a charmed sword."

"For real?"

"Yep."

Now Abi came walking toward Luke. She had a really odd look on her face. She stopped in front of Luke and briefly smiled a dopey smile at him. Then she reached down and picked up the charmed sword.

"Abi, no! There's no way you could have been touched by evil. Your magic is well centered, and you come from a strong magical family. You would have to be turned to become evil!"

Abi said nothing, and she smiled and swung the sword at him. Luke had no choice but to block the swing. She went flying up into the air and right at Katie, who had cover both arms over her head in expectation of Abi crashing down on her. But Abi hit the door next to Katie and came crashing down right next to her. Once again the sword went sliding back to Luke. This time, he picked it up before someone else had a go at him. He put his sword away and walked over to Thronbasa. He handed her sword back to her and said, "I think everyone needs lunch. They've all gone weird on me. Maybe their sugar is dropping or something. Low sugar, that's what Mr. Henry, the guy in charge of the beach back home, used to say was wrong with all of the lifeguards—low sugar. They did plenty of weird stuff too. Not with swords— just weird. Just in case someone asks, there's nobody evil here, especially Katie. If they start going on about Katie or the others, just tell them the First Lord says 'duh!'"

Then Luke went over and tried to help his friends back onto their feet.

THE BOOK OF BLACK SHADOWS
CHAPTER 16

IN THE DAYS that followed the return of Katie's magic, Luke and his friends began to explore for the first time their many abilities. Instead of a fear that once plagued their every waking moment on their arrival, now each new lesson and instruction of the summer session became an exciting adventure. Although painful, both Abi and Selwyn benefited from their encounters with Luke's sword. To everyone's amazement, Selwyn demonstrated abilities he never had before. His encounter with Luke's sword, although it was three days before he could walk without getting dizzy, had centered his powers more than they had ever been before. It was as if he had been given a new chance to prove himself. Each time he succeeded in a lesson, he could barely contain his happiness. For him, it was nothing like the summer before when in the end he was asked to leave. Selwyn was so proud now that he would not have to return home a failure.

The joy of exercising new abilities was also a great experience for Katie. Within a week, Katie had moved to the top of the admissions list. She had become nearly as centered as Abi, who now ranked second only to Luke. Given Abi's attitude toward Katie, one might have wondered whether she would have continued to reject her for not being a naturally born member of the Realm. But Abi's encounter with Luke's sword had done more than just improve her magic. Abi seemed more self-secure than ever. She no longer felt threatened by Katie. In fact, her entire attitude toward the summer had relaxed. Somehow the sword had put her at ease, and everyone had noticed the change.

It wasn't just their newfound skills that were driving Luke's and his friends' success. Luke had returned to the dance. Each morning, hours before wake-up call, just as he did in Sugarloaf, Luke rose with the first light of the day. He climbed a hill next to the barracks. When he started, he did it alone. Sitting with his legs crossed in the cold morning mountain summer air, he could see his breath as he sat and said his morning prayers. He focused and concentrated the way Sam had always taught him. His encounter with Thronbasa had renewed hope in Luke. He did have family left, and they did care about him. This simple thought was enough to renew his spirit. Although Thronbasa's accent was radically different from Aunt Claire's, within it contained familiar sounds of the only mother he had ever known. There were even several familiar attitudes that matched. He had given up all hope of ever hearing them again.

It was not long before Luke's friends realized that he was out of his rack already before first call. Within days, Luke had been joined on top of the hill. While facing the rising sun, he began to instruct his friends as Sam had once instructed him. They brought sticks from the woodland that could be left on top of the hill. For two hours every morning, the four slowly learned the steps of the ancient dance. Luke also taught them as much as he knew of fighting. They had nowhere near his speed and abilities, but they learned well and quickly. Within two weeks, they could follow Luke in the dance in near silence. Abi had even begun to follow Luke with her eyes closed. In four weeks, they could match nearly 12 different jousting moves with the sticks, and every morning Luke taught them a new move to practice.

When they were in formal school training sessions, the other Freshers could not defend against them or match their moves. After a few weeks, Luke and his friends held the top four positions of the 2084 training series. Never before had two girls held such high Fresher rankings. Never before had a student who had been first rejected like Selwyn returned to claim any rank in the top 10. It was a year of firsts, and many in the Realm were starting to take notice. There were others who didn't like what was happening.

Chancellor Cole made her way out of the university commons and toward the Fresher training area. Since Thronbasa's arrival, she had spent little time supervising any of the happenings in the training sessions. In fact, she had been gone for two weeks. Cole had known Elizabeth Thronbasa since she had attended university. As a graduate student, Cole had been her advanced botany instructor for two semesters. So she had every confidence in her former student and in her experience to get the job done that needed doing. She was very happy with her decision to appoint Thronbasa to command the 2084 training series, or so she thought.

Cole walked along the path and soon came to Thronbasa. She was standing facing east with her arms crossed. She was leaning against a tree and just staring off into the distance.

"Good morning, First Centurion," Cole announced herself with a glad tone of voice.

"And to you, chancellor," Thronbasa said as she glanced at the woman and bowed slightly. "I hope your vacation has made you well rested and ready for the coming semester."

"Oh, yes. Harold and I went near your neck of the woods, Elizabeth. A safari in northern South Africa! It was brilliant! Wish you were there—we could have come and visited with you. Instead, you are burdened with this rat race. I am sorry we had to call you in to handle all of this for us."

"That's quite all right," Thronbasa replied, keeping her eye on the far hill. "Marcus and I haven't been in the valley for many years. Our children are enjoying the experience."

Cole notice Thronbasa was distracted and glared off into the distance. On top of the hill opposite the training ground were four students.

"What they up to up there?"

"They are dancing the ancient chouline," Thronbasa replied. "Mr. Amade would seem to be a master of the technique and has been teaching the others. In a just few weeks, they have mastered the basic steps, and as you can see, they have become quite coordinated for a group of 12-year-olds."

"Amade is still here?" she said with disappointment.

"Yes, and he is now ranked number one in overall standing."

"What?"

"Yes! His friends up there are ranked second, third, and fourth. Two girls in the top 10—first time ever."

"How is that possible?"

"You can see for yourself, chancellor. Mr. Amade has been training them outside of their lessons. It's quite a little team he has assembled."

"Did you get his sword?"

"I tried," Thronbasa explained, "but I could not lift it, and neither could anyone else. The moment the boy left the room, the sword was recalled to him. There's nothing more I could do."

"What?" Cole responded with outrage. "We cannot have a 12-year-old boy running around with a sword he knows nothing about!"

"The First Lord has given him permission to do just that!"

"Where is our First Lord? I want to have a few words with him!"

"That would not be wise, chancellor."

"Why?"

"He unbound Miss Gardner's powers, and he knows you're the one who bound them."

"That Bennie is still here?"

"Yes, look! She's right up there with the rest, dancing. She is ranked third in overall standing."

"What? That is outrageous! This is a scandal! How dare he interfere with my spell!"

"He did more than interfere, chancellor. His unbinding of her powers leaves no one else who could ever bind them again except himself. I am not certain he grasps the full impact of his decision, but he did add a very important reminder to anyone who dared hurt one of his friends again. He intends to bind the powers of the responsible party."

"What? A 12-year-old boy making threats against the leadership of the Realm? Where is he? He needs to be taught a lesson or two! Have you reported this to the members of the board?"

"Yes," Thronbasa responded.

"And?"

"And they say you broke regulations by binding the girl's powers in the first place. They maybe more inclined to review your conduct than his. But none of them seemed overly fussed by it all. The decision of the First Lord is final, and they have all accepted that."

Cole was made silent by this news. She realized her position had been greatly diminished by the arrival of someone whose orders she had little choice but to follow.

"I wish to speak to the First Lord, Elizabeth," she insisted.

"He doesn't wish to speak to you, chancellor. Even if he did, it would be problematic at best. The identity spell he cast was executed using one of the swords of the 12 original princes. He has no idea of the sword or its power. But it does mean that anyone who even entertains the thought of crossing him is in for a rude awakening."

Cole looked at Thronbasa with bewilderment and said, "Only a sanctified member of the White Robin's Caldron could carry a Sword of Princes."

"Right," Thronbasa agreed, "which means Martin was a fully consecrated member of his brother's caldron. No one here ever knew that, and Martin never told anyone. I don't think that Claire even knew. But before he died, he absorbed Luke into the caldron."

"The board knows all this?"

"Yes, I told them."

"A 12-year-old carrying a sword of power is a bomb waiting to go off!"

"Perhaps, if he's not trained properly." Thronbasa gazed sideways at Cole, who wasn't looking at her. Cole was gazing at the ground with a worried look on her face. "As things have turned out, he is listening and is accepting training. Short of another major attack of the Darkside, I think he'll do fine."

"Yes," Cole responded still staring at the ground. "If they don't get to him first and turn him!"

"He cannot be turned, chancellor. It's why his family line exists. They cannot be corrupted."

"Ha!" Cole turned to her briefly, took a few steps, and then looked outward across the valley. "It's all ancient tales, fairy tales, a propaganda instilled into the Realm to give its people a false sense of security!" Then she turned back to Thronbasa and told her, "The only thing keeping this Realm safe is the commitment of its leadership! We've developed a system of checks and balances to weed out the weak, train the strong, and to prepare for the next attack of the Darkside! Girls like Gardner have no place in it, and neither does a rouge boy with a sword!"

Stunned by this revelation, Thronbasa showed no emotion at all. "What do you suggest we do about it?" she asked with agreement in her voice.

"Leave it to me, Elizabeth," Cole insisted. You have your hands full with the summer session. I'll find a way of dealing with the situation!"

Cole was soon walking back the way she came. As she headed off toward the university, Thronbasa stared at her for a while. She was intent on making trouble—that much was sure. On the other hand, she was technically in charge of the admission process. She had the right to make her own decisions. All Thronbasa could do was wait for her to cross a line that would cause the rest of the board to lose confidence in her and remove her. It wouldn't hurt if Luke was ready for her. She couldn't tell anyone about the conversation without betraying a confidence. But she could give Luke a lesson or two, maybe bring him a little up to speed on the real world of hand-to-hand combat.

Soon Thronbasa was making her way up the hill where Luke and his friends were jousting. In a moment of fun, Luke had taken on all three of his friends. While they were not much of a challenge to him, he was enjoying himself. He did like showing off a bit—just in fun, of course. His moves were so quick in blocking every move his friends made it encouraged them to look for new ways to get at him. At times, their frustration was something Luke found very funny. Still, even for Abi, Katie, and Selwyn, it was all in fun.

There were many small sticks and branches lying around on the ground in all directions at the top of the hill. Thronbasa reached out with her mind and grabbed one. She sent it flying into Luke's head. It distracted him long enough for Selwyn to get a sting in on his leg. Suddenly, Luke found himself in pain, and things were not so funny anymore.

"What was that all about?" Luke shouted.

The three looked at Luke, but past him, staring in silence. Realizing they weren't looking at him, he turned around, and there was Thronbasa with a long strong narrow stick in her hand—only hers had a rather sharp point on it. She was swinging it like a sword and with great speed. In fact, she seemed be warming up for something. Then she stopped and walked very abruptly and in a not so friendly way right at Luke.

Katie, Abi, and Selwyn began to back away, but Luke struck a defensive pose with his stick.

"Good morning, First Centurion," Luke announced.

Thronbasa said nothing. Instead she began to lift up sticks of wood with her mind and throw them at Luke. She waited until he was fully distracted before she struck at him. Luke turned on the speed and was able to block her, but she kicked his legs out from under him! Luke went crashing down to the ground. Abi covered her eyes. Katie and Selwyn looked away. Luke rolled over in pain, moaning.

"What's the matter, Mr. Amade?" Thronbasa inquired. "Not so funny anymore, is it?"

Luke kicked out and leaped to his feet. He turned and spun at Thronbasa, striking her stick again and again. Because of his speed, it took all of Thronbasa's concentration to block him. When that didn't seem to work well, she refocused on the objects around her, and once again sticks came flying at Luke. Luke put on even more speed and blocked her and the sticks again and again. But the sticks kept getting larger and larger, until full-size pieces of wood started showing up, flying right at his head! In another moment, Thronbasa managed to distract him, and once again Luke found himself flying up and into the air, his legs kicked out underneath him. This time, as he came crashing down on his back, Thronbasa swung at his sword hand, hitting it hard enough to knock his stick right out of it. Everyone could hear Luke's hand getting whacked. It sounded so painful!

Luke lay on the ground in pain. Thronbasa was bent over slightly and was out of breath after having to deal with the boy's speed.

"What's the matter, boy?" Thronbasa wondered. "Can't handle it?"

Luke rolled over and looked at her. His hand was in major pain along with other parts of his body. None of which mattered—Luke didn't much like being called "boy."

"So, Luke," Thronbasa continued. "The High Chancellor tells me you threatened to take a match to your grandfather's portrait?"

Luke said nothing. He grabbed his stick and went right at her. Again and again various sizes of wood came flying and crashing into him. The more he fought, the larger the wood became until finally, and once again, his legs came crashing out from under him. This time, however, Thronbasa's stick was pointed right at his throat. Luke was pinned beneath it. He couldn't move a muscle without sticking himself.

"But what I really want to know," Thronbasa said with the point of her stick at his throat, "is how you knew that portrait even existed!"

Luke focused his mind on Thronbasa, and she went flying up and into the air. She crashed down backward and rolled down the hill. There was a pause of silence when Luke got up, and Abi, Katie, and Selwyn stared in shock, waiting to see whether the First Centurion would also get up.

They didn't have to wait long. Thronbasa came right back up the hill. But this time, she had no stick. She was rubbing her hands together and brushing the dirt off of herself. She was laughing a little when she announced, "Well, it took you long enough!" Thronbasa glared at Luke. "Next time use your mind first, not last. Your mind is your best defense and offense. The sword can't even come close. Do you understand?" she said staring into Luke's eyes.

Luke was breathing heavily and nodded his head as he responded, "Yes, ma'am."

"How did you know about your grandfather's portrait, Luke?"

"On the train in," he told her, "I fell asleep and found myself wondering in a hall when I crossed paths with it."

"That's called 'soul walking.' I have never heard of a boy soul walker. If you can soul walk, why didn't you know that Chancellor Cole had come in at night and bound Miss Gardner's magic?"

"I have been forcing myself to stop," he told her. "I find the experience a bit scary, and I've focused on staying together when I sleep. I can usually control it unless I am too tired to focus."

"Don't focus on stopping anymore, Luke."

"Why?"

"Because soul walking is for learning. You'll cross paths with other souls, and you will learn from them, and they will learn from you. That's the point of it, understand?"

"Yes, ma'am," he told her.

"I require your pledge and promise that you will not do any harm to the portrait. The old lord is very special to many people here. His knowledge and experience teaches many students across many generations. By threatening it, you've made many people begin to panic."

"Well, then, he had better keep his nose out of my business!"

"Unless you address him first, he'll have nothing to say."

"Then he better not go around talking about me to others!"

"I will tell him that all information about you is a secret. He cannot talk about secrets; it's forbidden to him."

"OK," Luke responded favorably. "Then I will promise not to trash him."

"Good," Thronbasa said with an odd look on her face. "Go on now. Get a shower in before breakfast!"

"Yes, ma'am," Luke told her.

Thronbasa looked up at the other three and told them to do the same. The four walked off, and when Thronbasa was certain they weren't looking, she reached around, grabbed her back in pain, and limped off of the other side of the hill.

Chancellor Cole made her way through the great halls of the university. The rooms and walls, the classrooms and the people, were radically different from the time Claire Cohan had walked them in a pointless search for her husband. Everything that had been burned and destroyed was all repaired. There was no sign of the evil that once stalked in search of victims here, or so everyone believed—blindly perhaps. In their determination to make things right, the leaders of the Realm were willing to overlook certain irregularities. In time, they had done so much overlooking that a strange kind of blindness had overtaken what was once one of the great education centers in the world. Soon Cole found herself walking through a door marked

"Graduate Assistance Offices."

Through another hall and up to an office door she went. She opened it and walked in. Sitting behind his desk was Mr. Pershard, and in the desk next to him was a girl who, like Pershard, was from India. In fact, the two looked a great deal alike. They both stood up as the chancellor entered.

"Good morning, chancellor," Pershard greeted her as both he and the girl bowed slightly with respect.

"It's not such a good morning, is it, Mr. Pershard? And you, Miss Pershard," she said addressing the girl, "shouldn't you be out helping with the morning lessons or something?"

"Yes, ma'am," the girl responded as she looked over at her brother, gathered her things, and then left.

"Chancellor, what has made the morning so bad for you?"

"That Bennie girl is not only still part of the training series but also she is now ranked in the top 10!"

"Yes," he responded with confidence. "Quite an accomplishment for a girl. Girls don't usually start doing well physically here until their third year, so she and the other one, Bishop, are very impressive!"

"And that boy, Amade—he's still armed!"

"Yes, the board is well aware of these things, chancellor. They have done nothing!"

"Well," Cole said slowly, "you aren't going to do anything, are you, Mr. Pershard?"

"Me, chancellor? What makes you think I can do anything?" Pershard was concerned with what the chancellor might think she knew, and it showed on his face.

"Do you think we are ignorant, Mr. Pershard? Do you think we didn't notice when you dropped out of the trials to earn a charmed sword? You, who have sat at the top of his class since he arrived here—refusing a charmed sword? Don't think we didn't notice what friends you were with Crinshaw. Birds of a feather fly together, Mr. Pershard."

"I'm sure I have no idea what you are talking about, chancellor, and I still don't understand what you want."

"Our First Lord, Mr. Pershard—I just learned he carries a Sword of Princes! One of the 12 original princely swords!"

"You must have been misinformed, chancellor. A 12-year-old boy cannot carry such a sword! He could never pick it up; only a Robin could pick it up."

"You're wrong. Apparently, he used it to cast an identity spell, and that's why no one can understand who he really is. I want you to flush him out! I want you to get that sword away from him!"

"I cannot match magic with someone who carries a Sword of Power, chancellor, and neither can you or the other members of the board. What is it you want done?" Pershard seemed lost for ideas.

"These four that he calls friends, Amade and his groupies—I want you to turn up the pressure on them."

"The pressure?" Pershard had a question in his voice and bewilderment on his mind, all of which was demonstrated by a confused look on his face.

"Yes, Mr. Pershard, the old fashioned kind: peer pressure. I want you to send those senior academy students that follow you around every afternoon. Have them turn up the pressure. Have them make certain that Amade and his friends feel very unwelcome here or—even better—get badly hurt 'accidentally' on purpose!"

"Hell week is long over, chancellor. They would be hard pressed to explain themselves if something went wrong."

"I don't care, Mr. Pershard. They can always come running to me, and I will pass a light sentence on their misconduct. Their efforts will force the First Lord to come to his friends' defense and show himself. Then I want you to figure out a way to get the Prince Sword away from him."

"Chancellor," Pershard responded with confidence because he now understood where the conversation was going. "The only thing that can deal with the First Lord's sword, or take it away from him as you would want, is the Calibur. This is at best is problematic because no one knows where it is."

"Yes, of that you are certain," she told him, "because you've been searching for it ever since you got here." Pershard seemed unnerved by this statement. "Yes, we know, Mr. Pershard. No one cares because there is always a fool's treasure to be found with some dreamer searching for it. Everyone just figured you were another one. Still, by now, I do believe you have an idea or two as to how to find it."

"If it's not in the White Robin's House, then the information as to where it can be found certainly is. The problem, however, is that the place is protected by a very powerful charm. No one can get in, except Laura, and she's dead."

"There were powerful magics long before the original 12 civilized tribes formed the Realm, Mr. Pershard. In the security section of our library is the Osiris Book of Black Shadows. The ancient Egyptians knew all about powerful magic. I am sure there's something there to open the White Robin's door with."

"I cannot get into the security section of the library; no student can, chancellor. It's restricted to established scholars only."

"I can get in and get the book out. You will have until the end of the summer session to break the charm protecting the White Robin's door. Each night between midnight and sunrise, you'll have the book. You and your associates can work on it then. No one will know."

"My associates?"

"Yes, Mr. Pershard," Cole told him in a commanding voice. "I know all about you and your friends, and I don't care! You're insignificant compared to the work that needs to be done, and no 12-year-old boy is going to ruin a decade's worth of hard work! The days of princes and kings are gone forever! We govern ourselves now, and no one is going to change that! Understand?"

"I understand, chancellor."

"Good! Now collect your associates, and they will have a go at the door tonight. It might take a while to find the right countercharm. Make sure they understand their services will be required until the White Robin's door is open. Tell them it is in their best interest to get the door open. Make sure they

understand that unless they succeed, the whole lot of them—
and you—will be exposed and dealt with! Very harshly dealt
with!"

"I am certain you can count on their cooperation, chancellor."

TIME TO FLASH
CHAPTER 17

LUKE AND HIS friends were walking out of breakfast when they heard their old friend Mr. Finch calling. They didn't have to jump to attention anymore, but they did have to follow directions and show respect at all times to upperclassmen and instructors. So they turned and paid close attention to what Finch had to say.

Monday, Wednesday, and Friday during first trials were assigned to two primary training courses: flying and fighting. They were known simply as the "F" days. The two disciplines were kept together because one of the primary skills, levitation, was linked to both functions. Levitation was a mind skill that among other things prevented practitioners on broomsticks from flying into very hard objects, like the ground, for example. It wasn't just for lifting objects. Levitation was now considered a fighting art, something that had never been true in the Realm until the Battle of the Griffin Valley.

In that battle, for the first time in history, the Darkside used levitation as a weapon. Research completed afterward indicated that the new use of levitation for fighting was the primary cause for Darksider success. Had the Griffins not intervened, the valley would have been lost. Now all practitioners had to learn the discipline of tactical levitation techniques, or TLT. TLT was also known by its professional term, "fourth-dimensional combat." This term came from the fact that the human mind did not exist within the normal three dimensions of time and space.

Mr. Finch had news for the top 250 ranked Freshers. They were being separated from the rest and were moving on to higher, more difficult skills. The reason given was that the Fresher class now stood at slightly over 1,000 students. It had been a very long time since the valley had had such a large Fresher class, so the best students were being moved off of the basic training fields and out onto the competition fields. Mr. Finch even managed to say "Congratulations," and he shook hands with Luke, Abi, Katie, and Selwyn. The four looked at each other in amazement as he walked off. Luke and his friends were now to report to the main flight-training course.

The flight-training course, which during a normal school semester was a sports competition field, was a very curious-looking place. It was 100 yards wide and 260 yards long. What made it odd looking was that the sides, stretching across its length, had groups of erected cut pieces of granite. The rocks were on the sideline, and each faced an identical group of rocks on the other side of the field. Each group was a set of six rocks, cut flat facing the field, with each rock progressively taller than the one in front of it. In each group, the rock farthest from the center was a monolith that stood 150 feet. It was an imposing site to see an entire field lined with these rocks. It almost looked like an outdoor cathedral. In each group, the progression of rocks moving from beginning to end was 5, 15, 25, 50, 100, and finally 150 feet high. All were 3 yards wide. As a unit, the groups of rocks were called competition rock formations, or comp-rocks for short. Lengthwise, there were stacks of comp-rocks facing each other on either side of the field every 20 yards, and a large number marked each. Each comp-group also had sensors. If anyone touched any of the rocks in the group, a different-colored light would come on depending on what level rock was touched.

Waiting at the field was a group of students no Fresher had ever met before. They wore single-colored athletic clothing, and they weren't just upperclassmen. There was a combination of senior academy and university students. Not all wore the same color. The colors were broken into groups of 20 or so individuals.

"Oh, my God," Abi said as the group of four walked toward the field with brooms in hand.

"What?" Luke responded.

"These are the academy and university teams. These people are famous!"

"Freshers, line up over here," shouted a tall girl with a whistle around her neck and a note pad in her hand.

They all lined up and gave their names, which the girl looked up on a list. Each had a score that had been earned during the basic training classes. Based on that score, each student was assigned to a team for training. Each team had been assigned different skills to focus on based on the level each Fresher had demonstrated in class. Luke, Abi, Selwyn, and Katie were all assigned together because they had the top four scores of the class. They and 21 others went with the House of Cameron team, a group generally referred to as the blue and white team, which were their colors.

The players of the blue and white team stood behind a tall, well-built dark-haired student who introduced himself as Jason. He announced that he was a graduate student, that he had played many sports for his house over his many years at the academy and university, and that he now served as assistant coach for the fly football team.

"Today, we are going to start off with some drills," Jason announced.

The drills he was referring to were simple ball drills: lift the ball, or positive levitation; bring the ball to you, or negative levitation; send the ball to another player, more positive levitation.

They broke up into groups based on rank: four students in each group and one player to supervise. Luke and friends were assigned to Joe, a fly ball player. This was Joe's first time teaching, so Jason came along to supervise. Katie was up first. All she had to do was lift a ball that was about 20 yards away, bring it to her without touching it, and after levitating in front of her, send it off to Joe. Joe was standing about 20 yards off to Katie's left, trying to give instructions. He didn't seem too good at it.

"Focus," Joe said in an encouraging tone of voice. "Look at the ball, feel it touching you, and then lift it up."

Katie proceeded to do just that. With her hands outreached as if she were about to catch it, the ball came to her, hovered for a moment, and then went flying off to Joe, who caught it.

"No, Joe," Jason said. "You can't catch it. You have to grab it so the students can experience a counterforce. Give them some resistance to work against so they get used to it."

"Right, OK," Joe responded in a very accommodating manner.

Jason looked down at Katie and said, "You did that really well for a Fresher." That was no understatement. All one had to do was look around at the groups to see how much the other students were struggling. "Where did you learn to focus like that?"

"Luke taught us," she replied. "Every morning before breakfast, he teaches us how to focus the same way his family taught him."

"Really? Which one is Luke?"

Luke raised his hand but didn't say anything. Jason had noticed him before, but now he was close enough to look him in the eye.

"Well done," Jason said. Then for no apparent reason, he went silent and stared at Luke oddly. He stood there in silence for a moment before Katie said, "Are you all right, sir?"

"Yes," Jason said as he blinked his eyes and put a fake smile on his face. Luke and his friends just looked at one another and wondered why this guy was acting so oddly.

"Well, who's next?" Jason asked.

Selwyn stepped up, and so did Katie. Abi was next, and she not only demonstrated great focus but also she put some speed on the ball. Jason was really impressed. Fresher girls normally weren't able to do this very well. Usually it wasn't until their third year, when they had gained some body size that they could perform well. There was a direct connection between body size and how much a person could levitate. For the first time, as far as Jason knew, here were two Fresher girls who were outperforming the boys. It had never happened before.

Now came Luke's turn. Luke raised only his right hand, and the ball came flying up to him so fast that it was almost a blur. This was nothing new to Luke—not since he had come to the valley anyway. Anytime he was bored, he would focus on an object and levitate it to amuse himself, as he had been trained since age four to focus his mind. This was all second nature to him now. He didn't even have to keep his eye on the ball. He looked over at Joe and sent the ball flying to him. Joe tried to put some counterforce on it but was unprepared for the level Luke was projecting. Joe caught the ball and went flying backward and crashing to the ground. He rolled over three times before stopping flat on his back!

"You OK there, Joe?" Jason shouted with surprise and concern in his voice.

Joe put his hand in the air and stuck his thumb up, shouting back, "OK!" But he wasn't getting up so quickly.

Jason looked down at Luke and then back at Joe. He rubbed his chin and looked at the ground as he took a few steps closer. Then, after a moment of careful thinking, he glanced at Luke and said, "I think we're going to have to work on your control technique there, Luke."

Luke nodded his head several times in agreement and then said, "Yes, sir!"

"OK, Joe!" Jason shouted. "Take this group over by the edge of the woodland. Work on control exercises. But do it away from anyone else in case one gets past ya! That way it will hit wood instead of somebody else!"

Right away Luke and friends were on their way. Jason watched closely as the group moved off. He seemed to want to get the four Freshers away from everyone else. Maybe it was for safety reasons, but Luke wasn't sure. The look on his face was rather peculiar. Joe was limping quite a bit. Soon the group stood alone near the woods and far away from any of the other groups. Jason was still watching but then closed his eyes as if he were concentrating. When he opened them, he turned and looked at the red and yellow team. He seemed to be searching for someone. They were nearly a hundred yards away, and he focused on one female instructor. Her height, blond hair, and athletic build made her easy to spot even at such a distance. But for some reason, Jason didn't want to be seen getting her attention. He closed his eyes again, and everything went silent. The loud sounds of the groups, the birds, the lawn being mowed all went silent. When he opened his eyes, he said one word: "Lisa!"

The female instructor he focused on was the only one who could hear him. She started to look around to see where he was. When their eyes met, all of the sound around her went silent as well. She did not speak but just nodded her head at him once.

"Do you see the group of four with Joe over by the woodland to my right?"

Lisa glanced over and then back, nodding her head one time.

"Go over and relieve Joe. The blond boy is surprisingly strong. The others are also big surprises. They need to work on control, and I think they're too much for Joe."

Lisa nodded her head several times in agreement. Then all of the sound came back. She told the other instructors that she was leaving. Lisa jumped onto what looked like a snowboard. It quickly levitated, and she went flying off, making a surprise landing in front of Luke and his friends. They were all really impressed because that board looked like a whole lot of fun! Then Joe jumped onto her board and left. The four turned and watched him fly across the field with amazement on their faces.

"OK," Lisa announced with a smile on her face and great deal of enthusiasm. "Let's just focus using one ball, OK? We're going to pop this ball back and forth to me."

The four stood in a half-circle and faced her. Katie was all the way to her right and Luke all the way to her left. She would move the ball at them, and they would stop it and move it back to her.

"Wow!" Lisa said. "You guys are really good at this! I am so impressed!"

Then she came to Luke. She had been warned about him, so she was ready when he rebounded.

"Wow, dude! You're a bit on the strong side," Lisa said with a big smile on her face and a great attitude in her voice. "Concentrate on what I'm saying. Close your eyes. I want you to think about moving your hand in a tub of water. Go on! Close your eyes! Go ahead!" Luke complied. "OK," she continued, "remember what it's like. You're moving your hand back and forth. The more you push the water, the more resistance there is. Now I want you to imagine you're the water, not the hand. Think of yourself as controlling the hand's movement through you. So when you open your eyes, I want you to think of the ball as the hand and as yourself as the water. Do you understand?"

Luke nodded his head yes, and Lisa said, "Open your eyes!"

Luke complied, but when he did, Lisa's eyes met his, and

she hesitated and then popped the ball at Luke. This time, Luke had more control and so she popped back at him several times to see whether he had truly understood her. It seemed as if he did, but Lisa was silent now. The smile had gone from her face along with any sign of her enthusiasm. At first she seemed intimidated or maybe hurt. When she was sure Luke had understood, she started popping at the others as well. Everyone noticed the change she was going through. What they hadn't noticed was that Jason was now closing in from behind. Each time Lisa popped the ball at Luke, she got slower and slower, and Jason got closer and closer until he was almost at Luke's back.

Lisa stopped, her face turned red, and tears came to her eyes. She looked like she was getting ill, and she went down on one knee. Abi and Katie went up to her to see what was wrong. Luke knew Jason was behind him. He had no weapon, so Luke wasn't worried. At this point, Luke had been practicing so much that he could summon his sword and swing faster than Jason could blink his eyes. Luke took a few steps toward Lisa. When she saw his shoe, Lisa looked up and said with tears in her eyes, "Duit Duite, Your Grace!"

"Oh, no!" Abi said with a tone of shock and surprise in her voice.

"Oh, my God!" Katie cringed.

"Freakin' unbelievable!" Selwyn added.

Luke just looked at the woman and said nothing at first. She had taken him completely by surprise.

"Cad é an saghas atá aige Tarlaigh Ró Tú?" Lisa said to Luke.

(What happened to you?)

"Tá triú díobh ann Cath Amhlaidh Cinneadh Tu Seithe," Luke responded.

(There was a battle, so I decided to hide.)

"When Laura didn't return, we became sick with worry," Jason said.

Luke looked up at him.

"Then there were the stories in the newspapers." Lisa said. She spoke with a broken voice, and Luke turned back to her.

"The First Lord of the Realm was dead. At first no one understood you were with Martin. So at first there was no mention of you in the papers, just the details of the level of destruction to your home in Florida. Then it was revieled you had been with your uncle all this time. But that was it. No other news was repoprted on you."

"The High Chancellor refused to discuss the matter!" Jason added.

"A bunch of us wanted to go looking for you in Florida, but we had no idea where to begin," Lisa told him. "Poor Laura!" she cried. "We all wanted to go with her, but she refused anyone but the cauldron she had formed!"

"Luke, why couldn't anybody find you?" Jason asked.

"I cast an identity spell using my Uncle Martin's sword. No one should know who I am. How do you know who I am?"

"I'm Lisa Barns," she told him. "This is my husband, Jason Fesserack. We were the two students that came during the battle. We came with Lady Claire to rescue you! We fought a battle right outside your door. I stood guard over you for three days and nights until you left. But you were just a baby then. When you opened your eyes just now and I realized who you were, I almost fainted. I thought you were lost! Can I give you a hug, Lord Carter?"

"Oh, boy!" Luke thought. "Why do all of these girls here keep wanting to hug me? This is ridiculous! If I say no, their feelings might get hurt, and that could be bad!'

"Yes," Luke smiled, "if you promise to just call me Luke and don't try telling anyone who I am. They will not believe you anyway. Aunt Elizabeth has tried, and everyone thinks she's gone nutty!"

"I promise," she told him as she reached out and wrapped her arms around him.

"Aunt Elizabeth?" Jason said with a big question in his voice.

"Yeah," Abi told him. "First Centurion Thronbasa."

"Thronbasa? Isn't Thronbasa black?"

"Yeah, we noticed that too," Selwyn told him.

"Well, at least they're not evil and didn't try to kill us," Katie said.

"It's only morning," Selwyn added. "We have to get through the rest of the day yet!"

"Yep," Abi agreed. "By nightfall, a herd of dinosaurs could be chasing us down."

"No, that's not possible," Jason told them. "They are up on top of the high plain north of the valley. It's too high for them to climb down."

The three just stared at him in amazed silence. Luke was too busy talking to Lisa. After a moment or two Abi said, "I was just kidding!"

Jason laughed at first, and then a blank expression came over his face as he replied, "I wasn't. Some of them used to be down in the valley, but we had to put them up there with the rest because they were causing too many problems."

"Is that what the griffins hunt, dinosaurs?" Luke asked.

"Kind of," Jason replied. "They hunt the smaller ones. They have to be able to fly off with whatever they kill. They can't stay on the ground up there too long. Some of the larger Rex dinosaurs might try to take a bite out of them."

"How big are these Rex animals?" Katie asked.

"Do you see that grasshopper at your feet?"

"Yeah."

"That's about what you would look like to a Rex."

"Safety tip of the day," Selwyn said abruptly. "Let's all agree to stay the heck away from a Rex!"

"Good safety tip," Luke said.

"OK!" Jason announced. "You all obviously have control over your levitation techniques, so I think we can move onto the flash field and do some flying! Grab your brooms, and let's go!"

Luke and his group went off happily with Jason and Lisa. They had met two honest and real friends. It was a rather refreshing experience from being the four outcasts of the Fresher class. Now they were going to have their first real competition training flight!

"As a training ground, the objective of the flash field is fairly simple to understand," as Jason said as began to explain to Luke and his friends. At least from Jason's point of view it was simple.

For the purpose of learning how to fly it, students would mount their brooms and move out across the field as fast as possible. They would come as close to the first set of rocks as they could without touching them and then reverse their direction. This would lead them to moving off to the next set of rocks on the opposite side of the field. All of the Freshers had to do was learn to move back and forth across the field. This required using magic to accelerate the broom and then bring it to a halt without hitting the ground or the set of rocks they were targeting. As they got better practiced at the maneuver, students were allowed to go progressively higher and faster, zigzagging their way up the length of the course and then back again. Each day, students were graded on how fast and how high they covered the course. Simple, right? Not quite!

There was a big catch to this kind of training, and it wasn't something the instructors, which Jason headed, wanted to share right away. The reason for deliberately avoiding the topic was because they wanted to see which Freshers could figure it out for themselves. So they practiced levitation with balls and not brooms. It was a very important skill, and those who mastered it on their own were considered highly competitive.

The catch was this: using just magic to accelerate and slow the broom wasn't very fast. The method was OK for traveling long distances between cities, but for competition, it wasn't impressive. It was similar to the differences between driving a car on a highway or a racetrack. In fact, after two weeks, most of the Freshers who had survived really found this easy because flying was their favorite thing to do. So everyone learned the basics fast.

To pick up speed, a student needed to use positive and negative levitation. They used positive levitation to push off from the rocks, negative levitation to pull themselves quickly to the next set, and then positive again. They came to a stop or reversed direction. The more abruptly a player could make the maneuver, the faster that person went. But there was still another catch. A player had to constantly remember that levitation was a mind and body power, not a magic power. If players didn't pace themselves, they could get worn down quickly. It was very much like jogging or running. The longer and faster people ran, the quicker they wore themselves down. Doing it consistently would increase strength and build up endurance. However, when starting out, a runner would wear down quickly. The same was true of speed broom flying, or flash competition, as it was known in the Realm.

Surrounding the flash field were bleachers or stadium seats. At either end of the field was seating that climbed 150 feet into the air, matching the height of the tallest comp-rocks. Encircling the field were various flags that identified the different Bailes, or Houses of the Griffin Valley. During the fall semester, the Bailes held the women's flash competitions and in the spring, the men's competitions.

Each Baile had a team of 15 players. Each game had three legs of competition, and five players from each team were randomly picked to fly each leg. No one on the competing teams knew for sure which players they would be flying with or against until the names were announced. Unlike Fresher training, it was not a simple matter of flying up and down the field. The first half of each leg was individual competition. Each of the five players would take turns flying one-on-one against a player from the opposing team. The judges randomly picked the pattern they flew on the field just before they began. The numbers on the rocks lit up to identify the pattern, and the players were allowed one practice run. Then they would move off of the field, behind the rocks, and at the sound of the bell, they would reenter the field at a point of their own choosing.

The bell started the clock running. Each player carried a football bearing the same number and color they were wearing. If the ball hit the ground, they had to start the pattern over again. Each of the comp-rock sections had a white box painted on the ground. In order to reverse direction, players had to be inside the box. If they didn't turn inside the box, they had to start over. If they so much as touched one of the rocks, a buzzer would sound, and they would have to start over. The clock stopped when players tossed the ball they started with into a net at the end of the run. The nets for each team were on opposite sides of the field. So players had to figure a way to fly the pattern so that they ended at their team's net. Each second on the clock equaled one point, and whomever had the least amount of points won the match.

Each pattern was run twice, and the shortest run time was added to the team's score. The ball couldn't hit the ground, but that didn't mean it couldn't hit the other player, and often it did. It was also the practice to try to grab the ball away from the other player. The players who lost their balls had to retrieve them by the end of the pattern, or they had to wait until the other players tossed it at the end of their run. It really got interesting during the second half of each leg because that's when the patterns were run in team formations. All of the players, five from each side, would be on the field at the same time, and they raced off against each other for the fastest time. Team formations were the best of three runs. The patterns of each leg of the competition were progressively more difficult. Every player wanted to be in the first leg and not the last. For people who liked racecar competitions, this was the sport for them.

When Luke and his friends got to the flash field, many of the other Freshers were already on brooms and were making their way across the field, so they had to wait their turn.

Luke asked Jason, "Is this the sport you coach?"

"No," Jason replied. "I used to compete in flash when I was your age. When I was an undergrad at university, I coached then. Now I coach fly ball."

"What is fly ball?"

"Fly ball is American football played on boards like the one you saw Lisa on before."

"Wow!" Luke told him.

"Yeah, it can get real wild. There's a fly field on the other side of the sports complex. When you get a chance, you should have a look. You can't miss it. It's the field surrounded by nets on all sides."

"Why do you use nets?" Katie wondered.

"When they first started the game, they didn't use nets. Unfortunately, even though every play starts at almost ground level, the body hits can get really nasty, and players were getting shot off into the woodland. Sometimes it took hours if we ever found them, assuming something didn't try to eat them. That's one of the reasons all of the dinosaurs are up on the high plain now. Every time a game started, they would gather at the edge of the woods and wait for a player to be tossed out. The teams started losing some of their best players, and that would change the outcome of the game. The nets are there for safety and to mark the end zone."

On the flash field, students were making their way up and down. The faster they went, the sooner they wore out and came back down to the ground. Some just went and lay down on the grass they were so worn out. Others went off with medics because they went too fast into the rocks.

Luke and his friend were watching the spectacle when Jason said as if he were just thinking out loud, "This is good. All of the weak ones are getting weeded out fast."

Luke thought that was a very ruthless and unkind comment and way of thinking.

"Are there any competitions that are a bit safer?" Abi asked.

"There are cross-country competitions. They aren't so bad," Lisa told her.

"Cross-country?"

"Yep, there's one for girls and one for boys. They are broken down into air board or broom events. Essentially it's a race around the valley. It's very popular, and hardly anyone gets killed anymore."

"Are there any safe competitions?" Katie asked.

"No competition or sporting event is completely safe," Jason told her. "What would be the point of having them?"

"Right," Lisa agreed. "I suppose you could join the chess club. But that's not a sport."

Soon it was Selwyn's turn to step onto the flash field. Selwyn focused. He was feeling very competitive. He had no problems getting through the first level and onto the next.

The same was true for Katie. They both made it through the third level before they wore out. Most of the Freshers weren't making it past the second level. Abi made it halfway through the forth level. Then it was Luke's turn. He was the last Fresher, so everyone was watching.

The instructor told him to go, and Luke started shooting back and forth across the field and between the rocks. He was almost a blur. Everyone, instructors and students alike, just watched in amazement. He zigzagged down one level, up to the next level, and zigzagged down again. He completed 260 yards five times in less than five minutes. Then he landed right down next to Jason and Lisa. He was ready to go again if he had to, but he just said, "Time for lunch, right?"

Lisa and Jason looked at each other. They seemed stunned, but the only response Jason could muster was a very slow, "Yeah, sure, let's do lunch."

The good news was that all of the students had brooms, and instructors had boards, so no one had to walk all the way back to the mess hall. They could all ride. During lunch, Mr. Finch got up and announced that the 250 students assigned to the flash field that morning would muster on the south side of the mess hall, without brooms, after lunch.

The afternoons were dedicated to hand-to-hand combat training. This day's lesson would not be quite like any the Freshers had experienced. Today their lesson began inside the main athletic training center. For nearly four weeks, students had spent four hours a day, three days a week, learning martial arts. For these 250 students who had mastered basic levitation, the martial arts had new meaning. When combining the ancient Asian fighting arts with a Fresher who could also use mind over matter techniques, like levitation, all students quickly learned to protect themselves. They could even take on an adult.

The inside of the building was enormous. A very large gym whose walls, floor and ceiling were all padded distinguished its main training area. The Freshers moved onto the training floor and separated themselves in the way they always did for class. The routine was the same. First came the kicking exercising.

Normally they did 200 kicks in one hour and then 200 punches in the next hour. Then the third hour was split between blocking and body throwing, but not today. They had gone through all of 10 minutes of kicks before they were told to switch to punching. In 10 minutes more, they had moved onto blocking and body throwing. Then it was over, and the students were all warmed up.

Now the lead instructor came into the room. He was a not very tall Japanese man. He instructed all but the top 10 rated students to leave the floor. So 240 stood against the walls as 10 remained in the center of the room. Then 20 instructors dressed in martial arts clothing walked in. Two instructors squared off on opposite sides of each student remaining on the floor.

Luke sensed danger but no weapons. While the other students stood nervously watching what they thought were instructors warming up in front of and behind them, Luke waved in his three friends for a brief conference. They huddled up as Luke told them to do as they had done that morning and use levitation technique to control their opponent's attack as if someone were popping a ball at them. Luke said he thought that the test that morning and the one they were about to face were the same thing. They wanted to see whether they could adapt levitation for fighting the same way they did for flying.

While this huddle was going on, the head instructor had been distracted by a brief conversation. When he turned around and saw the huddle, he shouted in broken English to break it up and to get back on line. Luke and his friends complied right away. But as the two instructors he faced off with finished their warm up, Luke struck the first position of the dance. The other three saw what he was doing, and in turn each closed their eyes, focused, and likewise struck the first dance position. The instructors on the floor looked over at the head instructor and wondered what was going on. The headman nodded his head one time, indicating he wanted the contest to begin.

The instructor opposite Luke struck an attacking pose, and Luke, still with his eyes closed, turned to a defensive pose.

Then the one behind Luke also struck an attack pose, and Luke spun around and defended again. Luke's three friends did the same, except they had to open their eyes to do it. The rest of the Freshers also stood to defend. The head instructor made a sound, and the contest was on. The first ones off of their feet and on their backs were the losers.

Both of the instructors facing Luke came at him. He leaped backward into the air and landed behind one instructor. Then kicked him so hard in the back that he went flying into the other, and both went crashing to the mat. Abi, Katie, and Selwyn didn't have Luke's speed. They had to block several punches from men and women who were all bigger than they were. In the end, they used the instructors' height against them by ducking low, out of the instructors' reach, and sweeping their legs out from underneath them. Luke and his friends stood victorious. Everyone was staring at them. The room was quiet. No one had ever seen anything like this before. The head instructor simply said, "Next!"

Freshers rose to replace the ones who lost, and instructors squared off against Luke and his friends. All Luke could say to his friends was a warning not to do the same thing twice. That should not have been too much of a problem. They were more worried about the size of the instructors than whether they could perform the moves. Over the past four weeks, Luke had taught them more than 24 different offensive and defensive moves.

Through 12, 14, and 16 matches, Selwyn, Katie, and Abi successfully defended themselves. By the time they fell to the mat, they were just too tired to defend themselves anymore. Luke stood through more than a dozen matches, and he hadn't even broken a sweat. Finally all of the instructors surrounded him. Luke thought that was a bit unfair, but he didn't care. They were going to come at him if he wanted them to or not. To his happy surprise, they didn't come at him. They all bowed to him. Luke bowed back. The head instructor stepped forward. He also bowed to Luke and then handed him a red armband. After reaching out and shaking Luke's hand, he proceeded to call forward 59 more students. Of the

250 Freshers, 60 got the new armbands. The rest were dismissed for the day. The ones with the armbands were led out of the building. Luke turned to Selwyn and asked where they were heading. He told him they looked to be heading for the weapons range.

"Weapons range?" Luke responded with a question in his voice and surprise on his face.

THE DARKSIDE MAKES A MOVE
CHAPTER 18

WHEN THEY ARRIVED outdoors, it was indeed a weapons range. The place had a long target range and an equally large sand trap area. It was into the sand trap that the 60 Freshers walked. As they entered, they picked up one tie die and one pugle stick out of a barrel. The tie die was used to simulate sword fighting. The pugle stick was just a long shaft, held in the center, with its ends used to strike at an opponent. Luke had known the tie die almost all of his life. Like everyone else, he had trained nearly four weeks with the pugle stick.

With the pugle stick on the ground, the students squared off with each other using their tie dies. Focused precision was what was required to spar with a tie die. Knowledge of many moves and countermoves was equally important, but most of the Freshers did not have these qualities yet. It took time and focus to master them, and that was why Luke's family started him on the ancient dance when he was very young. The students stepped back and forth and made the moves they knew the best. They did the same with the pugle stick. Then, just as they had done inside the training center, the instructors squared off with the students.

Luke was worried about his friends now. This type of fighting required a great deal of speed. He didn't think Abi, Selwyn, and Katie had it. Even without his levitation techniques, Luke knew he had the speed. "If the others could just remember the lessons of the day," he thought, "they could use levitation to joust with their opponents and perhaps slow them down." All four closed their eyes and focused, waiting for the head instructor to call the start.

The call was given, and with almost uniform movement, Luke, Abi, Katie, and Selwyn made the same block and counter move and disarmed their instructors. The four stood with their tie dies sticking in the throat of their adversaries. They dared them to move and waited for the all done call. The head instructor was watching, and he began to laugh with joy. He had never seen four of his instructors so embarrassed before. He had quite a good laugh before he called, "Next!"

Each time "next" was called, Luke and friends found themselves facing a new instructor. Each time, the students made different moves, and each time, they stood victorious. When all 60 were finished, the head instructor stepped up on a stool, and in his hand he held what looked like a handle. It was only slightly wider than his hand. He gripped it and held out his arm, and with a flash of movement, the handle transformed into a tie die stick, except this was made out of light metal. Then with another quick movement, the same handle became a pugle stick, and then it was just a handle again. The head instructor demonstrated this device several times, and then he began to speak in English as best he could.

"You 60 Freshers here today have passed the first two and most difficult tests of your first trails." Everyone began to smile with surprise. "You were not told this because those of us who lead the training grounds wished to see who among you was the most competitive. There was no intent to deceive anyone. The device in my hand is called a fighting pike. Today each of you has earned the right to carry it. As you leave, you shall be given one. I and the other instructors here wish to offer our congratulations to each and every one of you. Well done!"

The man bowed one time to the students, and then Mr. Finch stood up on the stool.

"OK, listen up! I am going to call 10 names. Those 10 stay here. Everyone else will move off onto the obstacle course. You will run the course one time and then a one-time run through on the cross-country track on your way back to the barracks. Does anyone not understand? Fine!"

Luke and his friends stood together with six other Freshers whose names had been called. They waited for all of the other Freshers to leave, and when they did, the head instructor walked over to a closed rack just outside the sand trap and motioned for all of the students to follow him. When they all gathered together, he unlocked and opened the rack. To all of the students' surprise, there were brand new swords inside. The students stood wide-eyed as the head instructor explained that each year they were a part of the academy class, they would be given a different style of sword with which to train. This would allow them to get a feel for each sword and to decide which one they would choose as their own once they left the academy. That year's sword was the Japanese Samurai. The head instructor warned everyone not to touch the blade of the sword. The slightest pressure could cut.

Soon, the group of 10 Freshers found themselves standing in front of tightly wound stalks of bamboo sticks. The head instructor demonstrated the 12 basic sword strikes, which everyone already knew, and he swung his sword against the bamboo stalk as he shouted a noise that no one understood. Each strike made a clear cut right through the stalk, and by the time he had finished, the bamboo stalk had been cut to the ground. The final 10 students took turns showing their ability to do the same thing. Once they were finished, they moved out onto the live fire range.

Now the time had come for the Freshers to discharge their very first bolt of magical power. It was explained to them very carefully that this was both magic and mind control and that when they let loose with their first discharge, they would likely feel very tired. Anyone who felt the need to lie down would be allowed to do so. For their very first effort, one of the instructors held the sword. The blast of power would fly down 100 yards to a target. Once the students understood how the method was used, they were allowed to send a blast down the range on their own.

Everyone except Luke had made his or her first try. The instructor held the sword with him. He instructed Luke how to focus and how to imagine the sword was just an extension of his arm. He wanted him to feel the magic gathering around him and direct it to the sword. When Luke felt he was ready, he was given the OK, and a bolt shot from his sword and missed the target.

"That's OK," the instructor told him. "You'll be able to learn better when you do it on your own."

Luke began to concentrate and focus. It had been a long day, and he was feeling a little tired, so he wasn't concentrating as well as he should have been. He let loose a bolt of energy that flew down range, hit the target, and sent it flying straight up about 100 feet. Everyone on the range just watched the thing as it went up high into the air and then crashed back down again. "Oops," Luke thought. The target was in tiny pieces. "Guess I'll have to pay for that one," he said as he looked over at everyone else. They were looking at him with blank expressions on their faces. The headmaster came down. He stared at Luke for a moment and then downrange at his target in a billion pieces and said, "You must learn control!"

"Yes, sir," Luke replied.

"Come, let us concentrate together."

The man wrapped his hand around Luke's left hand. Luke focused the sword using his right hand. The head instructor focused with Luke in very much the same way Laura did the first time Luke lifted a rock.

While this was going on, the other students were leaving. They walked up to the exit and then demonstrated their ability to put their sword away with magic. They had to show they could do it four times. Each was handed a fighting pike, which they could put in their pocket. To their armband was pinned a small golden badge. It was the seal of the First Lord of the Realm. The seal signified they had the right to bare arms even through they weren't 16 yet. Several of the instructors went out of their way to shake the hands of the remaining 10 students. After that, like all of the Freshers who had gone, they were to run the obstacle course one time and then the cross-country course, and then they were done for the day—except now they wore the seal of the First Lord.

Katie went to the head of the line, and she turned and watched Luke's next discharge. He hit the target dead center and didn't blow it up this time. She was satisfied. Katie demonstrated to the instructors her ability to put her sword away, was given her badge and pike and several handshakes, and then left.

Abi watched Luke's next discharge, and again he hit dead center. "He's getting good," she thought. "He's been carrying a sword going on four weeks, and no one here knows." Abi was also impressed that he wasn't getting weak from the weapons fire. Then she too showed the instructors how she could put her sword away, got her badge and pike, and then ran off onto the obstacle course.

Selwyn was next. He wasn't sure he should leave Luke alone. It didn't feel right to him. But everything seemed all right. Luke let loose with another power bolt, and Selwyn put his sword away and got his badge and pike. With one last look back at Luke, he ran off onto the obstacle course.

"What is your name?" the headmaster asked Luke.

"Umm, I am Luke, Luke Amade."

"Well, Master Luke, I am Zen Master Sha Ono." The man bowed to Luke, and Luke bowed back. "I have rarely seen a student with so much talent, and I have never met a freshman with such abilities. I am very impressed, and it has been a pleasure to have you here today."

The man reached out and shook Luke's hand. He seemed very pleased. Luke thanked the Zen master. Then like everyone else, Luke demonstrated his ability to put his sword away, shook the hands of many instructors, and was handed his badge and pike. Luke felt a strong sense of pride as he moved off to the obstacle course. He also felt as tired as he did on the day he first showed up in the valley!

As Luke was just about to begin his run, Katie was nearing the end of the cross-country course. Cross-country was a path through the woods between the training grounds and the barracks. It was slightly over a mile long, and every Fresher ran it once a day. It had many natural obstacles that they needed to get over or go around. The last turn before the barracks was around a hill. Katie entered this turn in a slow jog. When she got to the end of the turn, out of sight, there were two senior academy girls blocking her way. They wore uniforms and carried pugle sticks. Katie had never seen either of them before.

"Well, well," the girl with the long hair said. "What have we got here?"

"Looks like a Darksider," the girl with short hair said.

As the two got closer, the girl with long hair sniffed the air and said, "It smells like a Darksider!"

Both of these girls were much bigger than Katie. Fear and surprise were all over Katie's face. She started to back up and go back the way she came. She took but a few steps when she ran into something. She turned in surprise and was visibly shaken to find a senior boy standing there. He also wore a uniform and carried a pugle stick. He was so tall that Katie's head was barely above his belt buckle.

The boy shoved Katie back in the direction of the two girls and said, "We need to deal with these Darksiders now before they burn this place down again!"

"I'm not a Darksider!" Katie shouted.

The girl with short hair shouted at her, "No one gave you permission to talk, bitch!"

They started asking Katie questions about what she was doing there and how she got there. They wanted her out of the valley by sunset. Each time they asked Katie a question, they would poke her with a stick. Katie wasn't answering, but she did start to cry. They were about to hit her when Abi shouted, "Leave her alone!"

Abi walked right past the tall boy, and as she did, she kicked him so hard in the shin he dropped his stick and started shouting lots of bad words. She walked up to Katie, took her by the hand, and told her, "Come on!" Abi began to walk off with Katie in the opposite direction only to discover her path blocked by three senior boys she had never seen before, also wearing uniforms and carrying pugle sticks.

The boy closest to Abi shoved his stick into her stomach. She went flying backward and down onto the ground. Katie screamed, only to have the short-haired girl hit her in the face with a pugle stick.

"Time to clean up the valley!" the boy in the center of the three new arrivals said.

Selwyn had been jogging at the beginning of the cross-country path when he heard Katie's scream. Then he went into a full sprint! He was still running when he came up behind the three senior boys. The three turned around just in time to see Selwyn jump into the air. Flying feet first, he crashed into the center boy while grabbing the ears of the other two. The whole group went onto the ground, and Selwyn rolled one time. After gaining his balance, he kicked the legs out from under the two senior girls and yelled, "Run!"

Abi and Katie jumped to their feet in time to see the fourth boy, the one Abi had kicked, shove his stick first into Selwyn's stomach and then up under his chin. Selwyn hit the ground and rolled over in pain. These seniors were just too big and experienced for the three Freshers to deal with.

Selwyn looked up at the two girls and said in pain, "Don't draw weapons on them! That's what they want you to do! You draw weapons on them, and you get expelled from the Realm!"

The long-haired girl walked up to Selwyn and kicked him in his side for speaking without permission. "Let's finish it!" she announced.

Right after she finished speaking, there was the unmistakable sound of wood breaking under someone's foot. They all turned toward the sound, and there standing with a surprised look on his face was Luke.

"Well, well," the leader of the group said. He was the boy who originally was standing in the center until Selwyn shoved his foot in his face. "It's the leader of the Darksiders himself!"

Luke gazed at his friends and felt shock. Abi had tears running down her face, and she was in pain. Katie had blood running from her nose, her eye was swelling, and she also had tears on her face. Selwyn was bent over in pain on his side. Luke stayed calm. He sensed serious danger, and he found himself once again deciding between what his heart was telling him to do—which was to draw his sword and kick ass—and his head—which was telling him this was the wrong time and the wrong place to pick a fight.

"You guys!" Luke said to his friends, "Come on! Get up and let's get out of here!"

Once again the lead boy spoke. "The only place you're going is out of this valley, Darksider!"

Luke glared at the four senior boys and two girls. They were all way bigger than he was. The one boy Katie had kicked was big enough to play basketball. There was another problem. Luke was very tired. He had used a great deal of magic that day and wasn't really up to taking on a crowd. However, Luke and his friends weren't as alone as they might have thought. Selwyn wasn't the only one who heard Katie's scream.

To the front but behind the senior students, a pair of eyes was watching from behind a bush. Behind those eyes were several other eyes. There, slightly stooped over, Crystal Tamcke was watching. Behind her were about 20 other Freshers all wearing red armbands like hers. They were among the last 60 students who had finished their trials that day.

Crystal was a rather different girl from the rest of her class. It wasn't her light brown hair or hazel eyes or even her pretty face and smile that separated her. Most everyone who talked to her agreed that she was thee most polite 12-year-old they had ever crossed paths with. She spoke with a Southern accent because she was from the Carolinas. She never raised her voice or lowered it. She spoke evenly all of the time, and so sweet was her voice and general demeanor that if she had called someone a terrible thing, it would have been impossible for the person to take offense. Even if she wasn't being nice, she always sounded as if she were.

"What do we do now?" a boy standing behind Crystal asked in a whisper.

"I'm going to go out this way, and all you strong boys can go around that way, and I will create a distraction!" Crystal replied.

"Then what?" another boy asked.

"Then you come up from behind them, open up a can of whoop ass, and hand it to them!"

"Are you crazy?" the first boy insisted. "Those are six senior students out there! They outrank all of us!"

"Anyone who would attack another member of the Realm has turned to the Darkside! Anyone who would wear that red arm band like you and do nothing is a poon dog!"

With that, Crystal got up and began to move into position. The boy who was complaining got tapped on the shoulder and told by another boy from behind, "Come on, poon dog, time to open the whoop ass!"

"Come on, poon dog," another boy said, and then another, and then a girl. Finally, the boy turned to join his classmates and said as he walked with them, "I don't even know what a poon dog is!"

A boy walking next to him suggested, as if he knew what he was talking about, "I think it's something they fought for in the Vietnam War, maybe. I'm not sure."

Three of the senior boys began to make their way toward Luke. The tall boy was behind them with the two senior girls, watching. Luke, tired, closed his eyes and focused. When he opened them again, he attempted to grab the three coming at him and throw them backward with his mind. But they raised their hands together and blocked his move.

"Oh, no, Amade! We know all about you and what happened on the train. We are ready for you, boy!"

Luke really hated being called "boy" in a nasty tone of voice. He was about to make his next move when he spotted Crystal walking up behind the tall boy. "Oh, no!" he thought. Abi and Katie spotted her too with expressions of silent amazement on their faces.

"Excuse me," Crystal said to the tall senior boy, which compelled him to turn around with surprise on his face. When he finished turning, Crystal reached out and used her mind in a surprise move by grabbing his stick and pulling it away from him and into her hands.

"You little runt!" the boy shouted. He walked toward her quickly and in a stern manner. He was shouting all kinds of bad words. Crystal stood there, looking sweet and innocent, until he moved within range of the stick she was holding. Then, with a little help from levitation, and to the complete surprise of the mean senior boy, she sent the bottom of the stick flying up between the boy's legs as hard as she could! The senior boy stopped in his tracks. His face turned red, and his eyes filled with tears as he grabbed himself with both hands at the point where Crystal had found her target. He crashed to the ground and moaned in pain.

"My big brother used to be as rude with words as you are," Crystal told him in her typically sweet and very calm voice. "But after I hit him a few times like that, he didn't use bad words around me anymore."

The two senior girls were about to go after Crystal when they heard several Fresher boys say hello from behind them.

"Hello! Hello! Hello! Hello!"

The girls turned, but the boys were already very close to them. They grabbed their pugle sticks away from them and charged the two, kicking their legs out from underneath them and whacking them fairly hard quite a few times.

Over by Luke, the three senior boys had turned to look at what was happening. Several Fresher boys and girls had climbed up on top of the hill behind Luke without them noticing. They made running jumps using levitation and shouted, "Look out!"

Two of them turned just in time to have several feet hit them in the head. The lead boy was still standing. Luke reached out with his mind and pulled his pugle stick out of his hand and into his. The rest of the Freshers charged down the hill, but the leader boy pulled out his sword. They all stopped in their tracks. They all had shock and fear come over their faces. Luke stared at the boy. The other Freshers were too frightened to make a move. The lead boy had drawn on other members of the Realm. It was one of the greatest offenses one could commit!

He charged Luke and screamed an angry noise. Luke closed his eyes and reached for the last bit of his strength. When he opened them, the boy swung his sword at Luke. Luke ducked the swing with an amazing display of speed and coordination. He ducked the next swing and the one after that and again and again! Luke didn't run. He kept ducking until the lead boy had worn himself out. Then Luke took his pugle stick and swung. He knocked the boy's sword right out of his hand. The next swing found its target in the middle of the lead boy's chest and the one after that at the bottom of his chin. Then a reverse swing went flying between the boy's legs. He turned red and went crashing to the ground in serious pain.

Dragging the stick because he was too tired to lift it, Luke headed for his friends. As the rest of the Freshers passed the lead boy, each took a turn kicking him and calling him a bad word. The one that Crystal had picked on called him a Poon Dog!

The tall boy who had been on the receiving end of Crystal's wrath was still in pain but managed to get to his feet. Crystal wasn't watching. Her attention had been drawn away by Luke's fight with the lead boy. The boy reached out with his mind and grabbed the stick away from Crystal. She turned in complete surprise to see the tall boy holding the stick like a bat and getting ready to knock her head right off of her shoulders! As he swung, a hand reached out from behind and grabbed the stick. The tall boy turned around to see what had happened and found himself face-to-face with Thronbasa!

His hands were still on the stick as she used the top of it to bash him in the head, which sent the tall boy crashing to the ground.

Crystal yelled, "Attention on deck!"

Everyone froze and assumed the position of attention—everyone except the lead boy, of course. He was still down on the ground where everyone had been kicking him.

"My, my, my! Look at this mess!" Thronbasa said loud and clear.

"Miss Harten," Thronbasa said, as she walked in front of the short-haired senior girl, "you're a long way from the castle today. What are you and these other seniors doing out here?"

One of the senior boys now standing behind Thronbasa spoke up when Miss Harten remained silent.

"We came out to help with Fresher training," the boy volunteered.

Thronbasa turned around with a look on her face that seemed like she was ready to kill someone. She hit the senior boy so hard he went flying straight up into the air, went feet over head, and came crashing down on his back—bouncing at least one time! Thronbasa walked right over to him.

"Was anyone talking to you, boy?" she shouted as she grabbed him by the neck, lifted him off of the ground with one hand, and held him there as he choked while she yelled again. "Did anyone give you permission to speak?" Then she dropped him on the ground like a wet sack of potatoes.

"You Freshers listen up! When I say 'go,' you will run; you will not walk to the barracks! You will shower, and you will get to the mess hall for supper! Do you hear me?"

"Ma'am, yes, ma'am!" they shouted in response.

"Go!" Thronbasa shouted and the Freshers took off, but almost right away, she shouted again. "Not you four!"

Luke, Abi, Katie, and Selwyn knew whom she was talking to and stopped in their tracks and stood next to one another.

When the Freshers were all gone, Thronbasa turned around and picked up a sword off of the ground.

"Who does this belong to?"

Luke and his friends pointed at the lead boy who had not yet picked himself off of the ground. Thronbasa walked over to him.

"Mr. Masters!" Thronbasa grabbed him by the neck and lifted him off of the ground. She held him in the air with one hand. "What is this sword doing here?"

Mr. Masters choked and struggled to say, "I was defending myself!"

Thronbasa threw the boy into the air, and he came crashing down again about 5 yards away. Then she walked over to the first two boys she decked and shouted, "Get on your feet, or the pain you're feeling will be the least of your problems."

The boys struggled to their feet and tried to stand at attention.

"You seniors, listen up! When I say 'go,' you will run, not walk! You will go back to your quarters, you will clean up, you will put on a dress uniform, and you will report to me for inspection at sunset in front of the barracks! You and your uniforms will be in good order or you will go to jail! You will walk a perfect military line until the sun comes up again! If you break protocol just once, you will spend the next three months in a prison cell! Do you hear me?"

"Ma'am, yes, ma'am!"

"I can't hear you!"

"Ma'am, yes, ma'am!"

"Go!"

The senior students ran off—all except Mr. Masters. He didn't look like he was in any shape to be going anywhere anytime soon. Thronbasa walked over and surveyed Luke and his friends. She still had the sword in her hand but was holding it behind her back. She walked up to Katie, and Thronbasa reached out with her hand and held Katie by her chin. With a caring look on her face, she examined Katie's bloody nose and swollen eye. Then in a soft voice she said, "Are you OK, Katie?"

"Yes, ma'am," she responded as a tear fell from her eye.

"When I get back, I'll send a medic to come have a look at you."

"Yes, ma'am."

Thronbasa gazed over at Abi. "Are you OK, Abi?"

"I think so," Abi said. "My ribs are in pain!"

"Selwyn," Thronbasa continued. "Are you alright?"

"I will be," he responded.

Then Thronbasa turned her gaze to Luke. Her friendly face went away, and her nasty face came back.

"Luke! What the hell was going on out at the flash field today?"

"They put us through first trails," he responded with an innocent voice.

"You were showing off!" Thronbasa shouted at him.

"No!" Luke responded.

"You were showing off at the flash field, and when you finished there, you went over to the firing range and showed of some more! And now you have that stupid armband on with that stupid badge! After having gone to an extraordinary effort to hide who you are, now you stick out like a sore thumb!"

"I was just doing what I was told."

"You were showing off! Now, if the bad guys want to whack the First Lord, all they have to do is off anyone with an armband! What the hell do they care? If they get all of the armband wearers, they have the First Lord and still over 900 Freshers for the new academy class! They can't lose now because you woke up this morning and took a stupid pill!"

She paused for a moment and then shouted, "Right?" into Luke's face.

Luke was silent for a moment. He never thought that doing the best on the tests would cause him to be identified or that the rest of the Freshers with armbands would now be at risk of attack. In a sad, reluctant tone Luke said, "Yes, ma'am."

Thronbasa stood up and spoke to all four of them in a much more kind tone of voice. "I promise that the ones who caused all of these problems here today will be punished." Then she walked back to Luke and bent over him, and with her mouth close to his ear, she whispered, "I am quite disappointed in you today. Do you understand me?"

"Yes, ma'am," Luke whispered back to her.

"It's not enough to be better than the bad guys. You have to be smarter than they are. Understand?"

"Yes, ma'am."

"Tomorrow is going to be a better day, right?"

"Yes, ma'am."

"Tomorrow you're going to show me that you're not just better than the bad guys—you are smarter than they are too, right?"

"Yes, ma'am."

Thronbasa stood back up and told all four, "OK! Hit the showers and then get some dinner."

"Yes, ma'am," all four said.

"Dismissed," Thronbasa told them. Luke and his friends headed off to a hot shower and supper. Now Thronbasa turned her attention to Mr. Masters, who was still lying on the ground.

She walked over to him, tossed him into the air, and dropped-kicked him into the side of a big tree.

"The only piece of crap that would draw down on another member of the Realm is a Darksider!"

She picked him up and kicked him down the trail heading off to the barracks.

TOO MUCH DUST!
CHAPTER 19

THERE WAS A new feeling in the barracks on the night after the great woodland Fresher event. There was no doubt that the Freshers' first act of teamwork would be spoken about for a very long time to come. Certainly all of the returning students would want to know the details.

After supper that night, the barracks were all abuzz about the day's events. Stories were being told and retold. It was well known that 10 of their own now carried swords. It was equally well known that many of the Freshers had passed the two most difficult of the first trials, and those who had triumphed now wore armbands. They were the heroes of the day, and many Freshers exchanged handshakes with those who wore the bands. It was quite an accomplishment, and everyone looked forward to wearing his or her own armband.

As Luke, Abi, Selwyn, and Katie entered the barracks after supper, it was hard not to notice that everyone was staring and talking about them. The fact that they had removed their armbands was a focus of many of the conversations. Katie had been treated for her injuries but was too worn out for conversation. She made all preparations for crawling into her rack for a well-needed sleep. Generally, Freshers wore athletic clothing to bed. They would change in the bathrooms, which had individual compartments for privacy. Katie emerged from the girls' room wearing sweats and walked across the barracks in silence. Normally she never had anything to say to anyone except Luke and her friends. She was just about to jump into bed when she suddenly stopped, thought for a moment, turned around, and walked to the opposite end of the room. Both Abi and Luke were watching with amazement. Selwyn, who was reading a book on his rack, put the book down to watch. Katie didn't go near anyone alone.

Sitting on her trunk at the opposite side of the room as she read and gossiped with other girls was Crystal Tamcke. After the way she had been treated when she arrived in the valley, Katie had avoided all conversation with most of the Freshers. She didn't trust them any more than they trusted her. For the first time since she arrived, Katie had something to say to one of them.

"Hi, Crystal," Katie said bringing an end to the gossiping.

Crystal and her friends looked up with a slight expression of surprise on their faces.

"Hi, Katie," Crystal responded in a friendly voice.

"About today," Katie continued. "What you did and the way you did it—thank you! Thank you very much!"

A slight smile with more surprise came over Crystal's face as she responded, "You're welcome."

Katie turned to walk away when Crystal stopped her by saying, "You're allowed to wear your armbands to bed, you know—particularly if you earned a badge with it."

Like many of the Freshers who earned armbands, Crystal felt their achievements of the day deserved a little showing off, even while sleeping. She was also trying to pull Katie into their conversation. Crystal felt she and the others wearing bands were the heads of a class. They were 60 special students out of 1,000. She wanted everyone to know who the leaders were, if for no other reason than to make certain they could rub it in! Katie stopped and turned around. She realized Crystal felt like talking, but the day had been too long, and she was hurting.

"I know what you mean," Katie agreed a little. She felt proud also. "But the Darksiders are still searching for the First Lord. They can't find him. There's no way he could perform badly on first trials. So if they can't find him, they just might vanquish everyone who performs well to make sure they get him one way or another. The easiest way to off someone is in their sleep. Goodnight, Crystal."

Katie walked away nearly too tired to do the walking. The smile on the faces of Crystal and her girlfriends went away. They looked at each other, and the girl sitting next to Crystal said, "We're girls! If they were after the First Lord, there would be no reason to come after a girl, right? The First Lord can't be a girl!"

Crystal looked at her with a kind of flat, near emotionless expression. She understood her reasoning and even agreed with it, but she took off her armband anyway. Before bedtime everyone had removed his or her armband.

The night had come, and a full moon had risen over the valley. It was a warm summer's night, so all of the barracks windows were open. There was but a dim night light reflecting from one end of the barracks. Everywhere, students slept in their racks. Luke stood gazing at himself sleeping in bed. Usually he just sat around waiting to wake up again. It was a good way of keeping watch. He often wondered whether this was the way Uncle Martin had managed things, doing a task at night while he slept, things that time might not have otherwise allowed in his life. Luke was finally getting used to the fact that his mind remained awake as his body slept. After a while, he used the time to read and do things he otherwise might have been too tired to do. He couldn't physically lift anything. So long as no one was watching, he could move objects with his mind. People couldn't see him, but they might see something move. The people who walked the fire watch couldn't see him. He was kind of scared to go out and cross paths with someone who might be able to see him. Luke was afraid he would run into others like he did in New York.

The day's events had made this night different than others. This was the first night when he didn't feel completely alone. This was a night when he could finally look at the other Freshers with less fear. Tonight was the first time he felt hope and believed in it. The sight of all those Freshers running to his aid in the woodland continued to flash in his mind. If people had suggested it could happen before yesterday, Luke would have considered them nuts. Now the faces lying around the barracks were not to be feared. Things had changed.

The open windows brought sound in from the outside. Except for wolves howling at the moon, there usually wasn't much noise. Tonight there were voices. Luke moved over to one of the windows to observe the senior students being punished outside. Walking the line was a tedious thing to do. Essentially, pairs of students would walk in a straight line for about 25 yards in opposite directions and then reverse. When they met, they had to meet in perfect time or else they had to start over again. So the pace had to be constant. They would salute one another, do a perfect military about-face, and then begin again. It was boring and annoying, and it was made even worse by the fact that it was after 10:00 at night, and they still had until sunrise before they were finished.

Luke made his way out the front door. Sitting on the steps was Thronbasa watching the students going through their drill. Sitting along the edge of the building in both directions, parallel but on opposite sides of the stairs, were what at first appeared to be quite a few members of the Realm in uniform robes. Some even had their pointy hats on. Luke thought punishment must be a spectator sport in the valley.

Thronbasa couldn't see Luke as he walked past her and moved out a little toward the ones who had attacked him that day. He looked at them closely. He was searching for something that would show there was something wrong with them—something the Darkside could take control over and make evil. He couldn't see anything. When he turned around, everyone but Thronbasa was standing. As Luke glanced at them, they all bowed to him. Some went down on one knee and bowed. Luke said nothing because he was stunned that they could all see him and they obviously knew who he was. They weren't current members of the Realm after all. They were all former and now passed members of the Realm— passed as in passed out of this life and into the next and "I am a ghost now!" Luke bowed back, and as he finished, they all stood upright. Luke made his way back to the stairs, but no one was looking at him directly, so he turned around and sat down on the stairs, and when he did, everyone on either side also sat down.

"Oh, boy," Luke thought. "If I get through one day without a surprise, I am going to die from shock!"

Luke sat on the middle stair. He leaned backward in a relaxed position and watched the students going back and forth. Suddenly, an older-looking former member of the Realm, a thin man with long gray hair, kneeled down right in front of him. He didn't look up; he just kept his head down at the ground. "This is something new," Luke thought. "Now what?" Luke said nothing because in many ways he was still sleeping and these events often seemed like a dream—particularly when the events required a great deal of thinking. When he was sleeping, Luke's thinking ability was very much like a computer without enough RAM to run the software. Another man came up to the kneeling one and said, "No, no, Lucas! You cannot bother the First Lord! You cannot approach without permission! You cannot go around breaking the rules!"

The man grabbed Lucas by the arm and tried to get him to stand up, but Lucas pushed him away. Then he signaled two others to come and help, and together they lifted him.

"Lucas, you must stop this, or you will never leave this place!" the first man insisted.

Luke didn't want to say anything. Every part of his body and mind was telling him to keep his mouth shut. He had no doubt that he didn't want to know what this man had to say. Every time a new adult came into his life, bad things started happening! Still, Aunt Elizabeth told him that the reason he had this ability to walk around in his sleep was because it was something from which he could learn. He regretted his words almost as soon as he said them, but he did finally give in and asked the question, "What does he want?"

The man that had been insisting he not bother Luke said, "He wishes to complain to you, My Lord."

"Complain?" Luke replied with a question and confusion in his voice.

"Yes, Your Grace."

"About what?"

The man went down on both of his knees and did not raise his head as he said with alarm in his voice, "The Book of Black Shadows has been removed from the library, My Lord!"

"The Book of who?" Luke seemed bewildered.

"The Book of Black Shadows, Your Grace," one of the other men repeated.

Luke thought for a moment. He wasn't sure how to react. These men were obviously distressed and were looking to him for help. He wasn't sure what to say. What came out didn't feel right, but he had no idea how to react.

"Why did that happen?" Luke felt he was reaching for something to say, but he didn't know what to say. He had no idea what they were talking about, and these events were occurring on the edge of his sleep. While in this slightly altered state, each time something drew his attention, his ability to stay focused was limited. While these events where happening, from Luke's point of view, he was dreaming.

The three men standing looked at him. They seemed to have little expression on their faces. That didn't mean there was no expression. It meant Luke was having trouble paying attention to their expressions. He was running low on RAM! As a result, Luke's mind kept drifting. The man on his knees said nothing. "That obviously didn't work," Luke thought. "I need to say something else!"

"Do you know who took it?"

"Yes!" the man on his knees shouted.

The man who originally intervened spoke with fear and anger in his voice. "We cannot disclose secrets! We cannot interfere in the lives of the living!"

"Why?" Luke asked.

"We had our chances to make a difference in this world, Your Grace. Our days are over, and we are in our penance now. We must not break our vows, or we shall be rotted until the end of all time!"

"She is approaching, Your Grace!" the man on his knees shouted. "She has turned from the light for personal gain!"

The man on his knees burst into flames and in but a flash of a moment was gone from view. Luke felt terrified. He had no idea what to make of these things. He had seen so many strange events since he was told who he was, and because everything he experienced while he was sleeping didn't always seem real, he didn't really feel the terror. He just knew something terrible had happened, and as usual, he had no idea what was going on. On the other hand, he had no problem identifying the person he saw approaching along the path from the Citadel. It was Chancellor Cole! Luke didn't even need to see her face anymore; he could tell by her walk it was her.

Luke seemed to be trying to understand what was happening in front of his eyes. In many ways, he wasn't himself. In his altered sleepy state of mind, every new event was a distraction. The last event became unimportant. The new event grabbed his full attention. It was almost like a movie was being run in front of him and he was just another spectator. The only difference was that he could communicate with some of the actors.

As Chancellor Cole approached, Thronbasa stood up. There was something different about the look on Cole's face. Luke had never seen her there after dark before. It was a general understanding that wandering around the valley at night wasn't a wise thing to do.

"Good evening, First Centurion!" Cole greeted Thronbasa, who nodded slightly to her and replied, "You are out late tonight, chancellor."

"Yes, we have a student in medical care tonight, and I was told you put him there."

"That is not entirely accurate. I mean, I wasn't the first one to hit him; I was just the last."

"I think there will be a full inquiry into your conduct today, First Centurion."

"Really?" Thronbasa replied, holding down any show of emotion. "I cannot think of a reason that would cause anyone to question my conduct."

"You think a student in the hospital isn't a reason?"

"I could have put him in a grave if I had wanted to, but I took pity on him. I bound his powers and let him live."

"I am not so sure that a formal inquiry will agree, and I don't see where your authority to bind his magic came from either!"

Thronbasa was having trouble believing her ears. An Alfa-Omega doesn't need permission to defend against the Darkside. She could have killed the person, and had he not been a teenager, she might have. Thronbasa stared at Cole for a moment, crossed her arms, and took several steps toward her to keep her eyes locked on her.

"I do not require nor would I be interested in anyone's opinion when defending the Realm against a Darksider, chancellor. As for the boy, the moment he leaves the hospital, he leaves the valley forever. If I cross paths with him again, I will do my duty. When I am done, he will never hurt anyone ever again!"

Cole looked at her most seriously. She didn't think the conversation was going anywhere. When Crinshaw had been vanquished, she had thought it was a brilliant idea to summon her old student to replace him. Now she was really regretting it.

"I must say, First Centurion, I am very disappointed in your attitude. What are these upperclassmen doing here so late?"

"They are the ones who helped the Darksider attack a group of Freshers. Unlike him, they didn't draw down on anyone, so they are walking lines until sunrise."

"Until sunrise?"

"Yes, that is their punishment."

"I am sorry, First Centurion. I cannot agree!"

"I have made my decision, chancellor, and I am standing by it," Thronbasa responded.

"And I have made mine, First Centurion. You will release them at midnight."

"Chancellor!"

"That is an order, First Centurion!"

Cole turned and walked away very abruptly. Thronbasa stood with her arms crossed and watched her walk away. Luke stood up, and the whole lot of former members of the Realm who had been sitting and watching the whole event stood up. Luke glanced at them for a moment but then ignored them. He walked out, peering at Thronbasa as he passed her, and began to follow Cole.

The path to the Citadel seemed a lot longer and lonelier at night than during the day. The woodland on either side of the path was dark and deep. The sounds of the creatures inside made it eerie. There were also some rather large bats flying around. Luke was glad he wasn't really there, or he might be worried about getting his blood sucked by one of them. Cole didn't seem to pay much attention. She had this rather odd, very brisk walk. She didn't make a sound but kept moving her arms. From a distance or behind she looked as if she were talking to someone. In reality when she passed someone, she didn't seem to be paying much attention.

One person who was paying attention was Mr. Pershard. He was standing on top of one of the Citadel's ramparts. The path from the training area had a night light once every 20 yards or so. So distinctive was Chancellor Cole's walk that looking out across the valley, Pershard could identify her motion down the path in the middle of the night. He observed her as the door behind him opened and in stepped a shadowy figure. The area by the door had no light, but the full moon's light cast a shadow on the wall from this person. The individual did not approach but instead chose to stand opposite Pershard on the rampart.

"I hear a few of your lapdogs didn't do so well today, Rajay," the stranger told Pershard.

"News travels fast here, doesn't it?"

"I also hear you may have found a way inside the White Robin's nest."

"Maybe."

"I already told you there's nothing in there."

"If the Calibur isn't in there, then information as to where it could be found must be there!" Pershard insisted.

"Well, I never saw it, and if it were there, don't you think Laura would have done something about it?"

"Laura was an arrogant girl," Pershard told him. "She thought her feminist attitudes could change her into a Robin." He laughed a little. "She thought she could form a caldron of her own and make all of the rules, but women cannot rule here. No matter how many bras they burn, they cannot undo the acts of God. The information could be there, and unless you knew how to access it, you wouldn't know it was there. There are some messages that can only be read in magic if the person doing the reading is male. There are other messages that only a Robin could read. Laura was never any of these things, and she never let anyone who was into the White Robin's home. In the end women are always just women, and that's because God made them that way."

"But you can access this information?"

"Maybe, or at least I should be able to. In the end, I am only trying to undo a terrible mistake. So, yes, I will succeed! There are no alternatives!"

"You thinking hanging out with the Darkside will undo history?"

"I think," Pershard said as he turned around, "that I do not understand all of your interest in these matters. If you believe I have been compromised, then why don't you go and 'rat me out,' as you Americans say?"

"I'm just trying to judge which way the wind is blowing. Let's just say that I think you have some legitimate issues to deal with. Let's also remember that I was here during the last attack and would like to avoid having to deal with it again. If you were so interested in the Calibur, why didn't you ask Laura about it?"

"She and I never spoke. My sister Magda was in one of the classes she taught last year. She found her difficult to get along with."

"Laura was difficult to relate to; that's for sure. She wasn't hard to look at, however."

"Yes," Pershard agreed. "Pity she had to be dealt with. She might have made a good wife."

"Now you're dreaming."

"The only dream I have is to restore balance, to return things to the way they should be before a coward chose himself over the rest of us!"

"And you think making friends with the Darkside is going to do that?"

"The only thing members of the Realm have ever done to the Darkside, as you and they call it, has been to attack it." Pershard sounded sure of himself. "No one has ever tried to negotiate with it. No one has ever tried to strike a deal that would keep everyone safe."

"What about the boy prince who showed up? Doesn't he drop some dirt into the fan of your plan?"

"A 12-year-old boy? He is but an insect I need to swat to move on!"

"I watched that insect today. He outflew every flash Fresher in history on his first pass. He brought combat instructors to their knees. He's very talented, and word has it he carries a charmed sword. Do you have a charmed sword, Rajay? Oh, no, that's right! You declined to qualify for one, didn't you? Why is that?"

"Every step I take is for a larger cause. I have a goal of bringing balance back to the Realm. Every decision I make is in an effort to achieve that goal. It would be in your best interest to aid and assist me rather than playing these word games."

"I am not your enemy, Rajay. I have no issues with you. But I have no idea what it is I could do, if anything, that would be of help to you."

"You could deal with this 12-year-old for me," Pershard insisted.

"Deal with? I have already tried to point him out to some of your more benevolent followers. It did no good. They refused to believe me, and later they had forgotten the entire conversation. That is some kind of magic that boy cast to make that happen. This morning, I walked up behind him. I could feel him reaching out with his mind. He wasn't even looking at me! If I had so much as twitched the wrong way, he would have lopped my head off like he did your buddy Crinshaw's. The first rule of sport is never to underestimate the other team. If this boy is your opposition, you have greatly underestimated him."

Pershard could hear the sincerity in the man's voice and believed him. "At the right moment, you could take him yourself."

"Yeah, and lose my soul in the process. I will never use my magic or my sword for personal gain, Rajay! I will use it to serve the Realm if you win this—whatever it is you are up to. I serve the First Lord of the Realm, whoever he is."

Pershard began to walk toward the doorway. He was about to go through when he turned back and said, "You say telling me who the First Lord is will do no good? That I will not believe you, and then I will forget? But could you tell me where he is right now?"

The man stepped forward as Pershard opened the door slightly. The light shined from within on the shadow man's face. The man was Jason Fesserack.

"Yes," Jason responded. "Building one, barracks one."

"I seem to believe you, so I guess I will remember it," Pershard said. "Thank you, Jason. I will not forget you or your lovely wife."

Pershard left, leaving Jason outside wondering whether he had just made a pact with the devil.

Luke was now making his way through the Citadel directly behind Chancellor Cole. The pictures on the walls were all bowing to him. Cole thought they were bowing to her, and she tried to acknowledge their bows. Luke had walked these halls before, and he was still mesmerized by the size of it all. He kept glancing at different things while keeping up with Cole. He followed her down several corridors and through several doors until they reached the library.

The library amazed Luke. It was three stories high, and there were endless racks of books in every direction. He was so surprised by this sight that he stopped in the doorway and let Cole move on without him. This turned out to be a mistake because now the enormous wooden doors came flying in at him. When he realized what was happening, he yelled with surprise and crossed his arms in front of his face, but then nothing happened. They passed right through him and closed behind him. Luke slowly lowered his arms and looked around. Realizing what had happened, he looked down at himself and said, "That was interesting! Guess I don't have to wait to open a door after all!"

Luke was about to move into the library when Cole came around the corner at him as she carried two large ragged circular things under her arms. She went back out into the hall, and Luke followed. He followed her through several stairwells, large doors, and corridors until the place they wound up in started to look familiar. Luke knew where he was as soon as he spotted his grandfather's portrait on the wall.

Cole went right up to the portrait of the old First Lord and said, "We are conducting secret research." Then she moved down the hall toward the White Robin's home where Pershard and several others were waiting. Luke glanced up at his grandfather but chose to follow Cole so as to hear what was going on.

"Good evening, Mr. Pershard," Cole announced herself. "I see you are ready to begin. Do these friends of yours understand the assignment?"

"Yes, chancellor," he replied. "But I will explain it to them again before we begin."

"Good! I will be back just before first light. If we don't get results tonight, then we'll have a go every night until we do, understand?"

"Yes, chancellor."

"Good," she told him as she turned and left, walking right past Luke.

There were three boys and two girls with Pershard. They began to unroll the two ragged things Cole had given them.

"Oh, my God!" one girl said with shock. "This is the Egyptian Book of Shadows!"

"Right," Pershard replied. "Except this isn't a textbook copy—this is the real thing, and it's very dangerous! You've all studied this in class. You know how to search the text and have practiced the spells. This time you're doing it for real. The one you are holding is the script version. I have the graphic one, and I am taking it with me. It's too dangerous for you to try your hand at anyway. Every graphic is a charm that can leap off of the pages at you! So use the script version and get us into the White Robin's Nest!"

"What do we do if we make it in?" one of the boys asked.

"Nothing," Pershard replied. "I will be back in an hour. Wait for me! I am taking this book with me to deal with another problem. When I get back, I want the door open, and we're going to be looking for the Calibur!"

"The Calibur?" one of the girls responded. "There's very little chance that it's in there or anywhere in the Citadel."

"Chancellor Cole disagrees, and so do I. If it's not in there, then information as to where it is has to be. Either way, we're going in!"

Pershard turned around, and with one of the books under his arm, he moved off past Luke. Luke began to follow. As they turned the corner, Luke again glanced up at his grandfather on the wall. The old man had a very serious look of concern on his face, but unless Luke spoke to him first, he could say nothing, and Luke had nothing to say to him.

Through seemingly endless hallways, Luke followed Pershard on his way out. But as they approached the final exit, Luke started hearing voices. Pershard walked out, and Luke stopped in the hall. He was being drawn toward a large door to his right. It was almost pulling at him, and he could hear voices, familiar voices, coming from the other side.

Luke turned and began to walk toward the door. He didn't have to open it. He learned he could just walk past it, and so he did. Luke found himself at the entrance to the hospital wing of the Citadel. There was ward after ward, most of which were empty. Here and there were portraits on the walls that bowed to Luke as he passed by. There were medical personnel walking around, but Luke was being drawn to a door at the end of the hallway.

When he walked in, he realized that all of the doors had heavy bolts on them. There were bars that separated the center of the hall, and as he walked past them, one of the men at the end of the hall began to look familiar. It was High Chancellor Dickelbee. He was talking to a man dressed in a doctor's uniform. They kept gazing through a glass at something. Luke approached the glass, and as he looked in, he could see Marta. She was in a terrible state. She was on her knees with tears running down her face, and she was talking to a doll. In the room with her were three others dressed as medical people.

"Why is this going on so late at night?" Dickelbee asked the doctor standing next to him.

"We think these attacks occur now because this is the time of day that the battle she was in began. She sleeps during the day only, and before her magic was bound, she would transform into a cat to sleep. We give her the doll as an instrument to represent her lost baby. It gives her a target for her feelings. We are trying to work on the source of her pain this way."

"Is it not unusual for this amount of trauma to be affecting someone after so many years? Should she not have healed some by now?"

"Not really, emotionally, because all of this pain has never come out; it has remained unchanged. Remember that the Darkside basically dissected her and tortured her husband to death right in front of her. With all of her training and magical abilities, she could do nothing to stop them. They broke her, ripped her child out of her, tortured the man she loved to death right in front of her, and then left her for dead. We cannot undo the damage. The best we can hope for is some healing that will help her deal with her drinking problem."

"She has been twice convicted of crimes. Doctor, does this have anything to do with those convictions?"

"This psychological state is almost certainly the central reason for those convictions. Her so-called lack of responsibility is just symptomatic of her condition."

"You believe that this should be brought before the board and her case reconsidered?"

"Yes."

"Thank you, doctor," Dickelbee responded. He took once last look inside at Marta, who began to lie down on a couch, and the people inside with her began to leave the room. Luke watched Dickelbee walked past him and the others walked out. They all walked down the hallway and kept discussing Marta until Luke could hear them no more.

Luke turned and stared at Marta lying on the couch. He couldn't believe his ears when the doctor had shared the revelations about what had happened to her. Luke had no idea just how evil the acts of the Darkside could be. He walked right through the wall and stood looking at her. Her long red hair was a mess, and she was very thin. She looked so sad and hurt. Up on the wall were a grease marker and a white board. Luke lifted the marker with his mind and suspended it in front of Marta. When she didn't open her eyes, he let it drop on her hands once and lifted it up again.

Marta opened her eyes and sat right up with surprise all over her face. She stared at the marker as it made its way up to the writing board. Then it wrote out:

"There's no way Uncle Martin would have blamed you for what happened, and neither do I!"

Marta began to smile in amazement and said, "Luke?"

"Aye, suren it be! Did you miss me?"

"Oh, God! I think about you all the time! I say prayers for you every day! Where the hell are you?"

"I'm sleeping right now. If I knew where you were, I would have come sooner. I only just found you tonight."

"Sleeping? You can soul walk? At 12 years, you can soul walk?"

"Yep, that's what Aunt Elizabeth said too."

"Aunt Elizabeth?"

"*Thronbasa.*"

"Elizabeth? You mean Claire's sister is here?"

"*Yep.*"

"You know she and Martin didn't get along?"

"*Yep, too much like Aunt Claire when she gets her Irish up, and she's just as mean too!*"

"My God, you really have met her!"

"*Yep, she didn't know there was trouble but as soon as she found out, she came. No doubt whose side she's on!*"

"So, you're learning about whose side everyone is on then?"

"*Yep, been following a few of the darker ones tonight, which is how I found you.*"

A look of serious concern came over Marta's face.

"Luke, you don't have the experience and training to deal with those people. You need to tell those who do and let them deal with it."

"*I am! I'm telling you!*"

"I am nobody, Luke. If I was worth anything, Martin would still be here!" Marta's eyes filled with tears as her voice became strained by emotion.

"*Not true! No one could have guessed what did happen! Uncle Martin, Aunt Claire, Sam—no one saw it coming, and neither did you!*"

"I am useless, Luke. I have no magic and can't help you."

"*Not for long! Start working out! Get your speed up! Stuff is happening, and I need you!*"

"I would be in the way, Luke. My powers have been bound!"

"*They will be unbound soon enough, so start working out!*"

"Who's going to unbind my powers?"

"*Me!*"

"No, no, no!" Marta said shaking her head. "You can't break the law!"

Luke's writing became very fast. The more emotion he felt about something, the faster his writing became. It got to the point that Luke was able to write faster with levitation than he could if he were using his own hand.

"*I've been forced to grow up a lot over the last few weeks, and I have finally learned a lot too. I am not asking.*"

There are bad people here, and I need help, so I am telling you to be ready when I come for you!"

Marta stared for a moment, amazed at the words she was reading. She couldn't believe it. After a pause, she responded, "Very well, Lord Carter. When you need me, you know where to find me!"

"Marta, do you know what the Calibur is?"

"You mean thee Calibur?"

"I guess."

"Of course, and so do you."

"I do?"

"Yes, certainly! But most likely, you know it by its story name: Excalibur."

"Excalibur?"

"Aye, it's the Sword of Kings! It's older than the Realm. It was reforged by Merlin himself and given to a mortal king to fight the Darkside. Good King Arthur led an army of mortals against the darkness. His powerful sword laid waste to any Darksider who crossed its path! It's the thing Darksiders fear the most. But mundane people, no matter how noble, can be corrupted. Arthur could defeat the demons of this world, but he never ruled the ones inside of himself. So the sword was impaled on a charmed stone that only a Robin could free it from. Even free, only a member of the line of kings could make it work."

"Are there any members of the line left?"

"Aye," Marta paused for a moment and took a breath. "It's you, Luke. Arthur's blood still runs inside of you!"

Luke was stunned by this revelation. How could this be possible? Just then, Luke faded in and out. It surprised him! It was very late at night, and there was no way he could be waking up at this hour!

"I'm fading, Marta. That usually means I'm starting to wake up. I will see you soon!"

Then the marker fell to the ground, and Luke was gone. He thought he might wake up in his rack, but instead he found himself right outside his barracks. When he appeared, all of the former members of Realm were still there, and they bowed to him. Thronbasa was gone and so were the upper-classmen who were being punished. Kneeling on the stairs with his ragged book unfurled was Mr. Pershard. He seemed to be looking for something, but he kept turning around and looking at the distant horizon for some reason.

Luke approached him as the former members looked on. Again he looked backward. Luke gazed at the open pages at Pershard's knee. They seemed to be endless rows of pictures. As Luke stood there, Pershard once again turned and looked at the horizon.

"Does anyone know why he keeps doing that?" Luke said to those present in a sound of frustration.

"He's waiting for the moon to set, My Lord Robin," an old woman responded. "The moon's light is a natural light of this universe. Contrary to popular belief, it weakens dark magic!"

The woman burst into flames and in a flash was completely gone. Luke was stunned, but he didn't understand why that kept happening. Pershard stood up and looked at the horizon as the moon went below it. He walked up the stairs, and Luke followed. They walked past two members of the fire watch who lay on the floor unconscious. Someone had hurt them and knocked them out! Pershard entered Luke's barracks and began to read from the Book of Shadows. Luke walked over to himself sleeping. He used his mind to start shaking himself, but it wasn't working. He started lifting his rack up and down and shaking it. Pershard saw it moving and was surprised by it, but he kept reading.

Luke was concentrating so much that all of the boys' racks started shaking and making noises. Then the boy who slept on the top section of Luke's bed fell off and made a terrible noise when he hit the cement floor. For the first time since returning to the barracks, Luke began to fade in and out.

He was starting to wake up! But he wasn't the only one waking up. Half the barracks had been startled by the sound the boy made when he hit the floor.

Finally Luke faded out. His eyes opened just as Pershard finished his incantation and ran before anyone saw him. Luke jumped to his feet at the sound of screams. With few exceptions, everyone was screaming. There, blocking the way out, was an enormous cobra snake. It made a hissing noise so loud it could be heard over the screaming. The cobra's head stood as big as a man. Its neck was flat and wide. Its very long and large forked tongue darted in and out between fangs that were as long, sharp, and pointed as any sword could ever hope to be.

The creature began slithering its way out toward the Freshers. It used its tongue to sniff the air. It darted its head in the direction of one Fresher after another and caused the girls to scream and run. When they finally gained some composure, the Freshers began to throw anything they could get their hands on at the snake.

The upperclassman Mr. Finch, responding to the screams, ran in behind the snake. He was stunned and terrified by the sight. He drew his sword, but before he struck, he dashed to the far side of the hall and hit the fire alarm. The alarm rang throughout the buildings and all the way to the halls of the Citadel. Dozens and dozens of members ran from their homes. As they exited the buildings, there were racks of brooms waiting. With but a flick of their hands, each member made the brooms fly off of the rack, and they jumped onto the brooms. They all took off like rockets and then landed at the barracks a few seconds later. They dropped their brooms as they landed, and they ran toward the barracks.

Mr. Finch sent his sword crashing into the snake's tail. The creature screamed with pain. As it turned around, the snake slammed against the sleeping racks, which dropped like dominos and trapped Luke and several other Freshers beneath them. The girls on the other side dashed to aid the boys, as Mr. Finch sent a bolt of energy from his sword flying into the snake. The snake turned and lunged at Finch. It swallowed half his body and began to try to eat him! With quick help from the girls, Selwyn was freed from the rack. He stood up and summoned his sword. Concentrating as hard as he could, he launched a bolt of power at the snake. The snake dropped Finch, and as it turned its attention to Selwyn, more energy bolts came flying in from the doorway. The members who had arrived when the alarm was sounded now launched a stupendous attack on the creature. The snake felt the pain of their energy bolts but seemed unstoppable even after dozens of strikes. Finally, it stood high, and then fire flew from its mouth and out the doorway, into the crowd of members who had gathered. The force of the fire blast discharge sent individuals flying into the air in all directions, and the ones closest to the snake were reduced to dust!

The snake turned back toward the Freshers. Those with swords drew them. They jumped out at the snake and swung at it as best they could. The snake was too fast for them. It was so fast that it was able to grab away one sword after another and crush them in its mouth. For those who got too close, the snake used its head to swing into them and send them flying across the room!

Katie, Abi, and Selwyn opened fire on the snake. It began to rise up again. It looked ready to launch its fire on the students! Then, Luke, now freed from beneath his sleeping rack, launched an enormous bolt of power from his samurai sword. The discharge hit the creature so hard it went flying backward to the far end of the barracks. The other Freshers were stunned by Luke's firepower. They couldn't believe a student could make such a display!

Stunned, the snake regained its composure, and when it turned around at Luke, its eyes were glowing! It raised its head, and its fangs stuck out at Luke as venom flew at him from the creature's mouth. The venom took on a life of its own! It immobilized and wrapped itself around Luke. It began to squeeze him! Luke was having trouble breathing. He fell to the floor and gasped for air.

Thronbasa came in behind the snake. Her sword was drawn as she leaped on the creature's neck and wrapped her legs around it. She drove her charmed sword into the skull of the creature and tried to hold on. But the snake, still with the sword in its skull, flung itself backward. Thronbasa went crashing into the cement floor three times before she was knocked unconscious.

Luke lay struggling to get free. The venom he was wrapped in repelled everything his friends tried to do to help. Now, most of the members of the Realm board, lead by Dickelbee, began their attack. Their discharges of power, one after another, had little effect. Thronbasa's charmed sword was still in the creature's skull, and slowly it seemed to be having an effect. But the snake was still repelling one attack after another! Luke lay on the floor, and his body began to turn blue.

Katie screamed at the members of the board, "Luke is dying! Help him!"

But no matter their best effort, their ways were blocked. Luke's skin was blue, and the life in his face was beginning to fade. Then he began to whisper with nearly the last air in his lungs the Celtic words, "To the winds I send my call and summon now the brothers Og!"

The window facing south began to glow, and then it shattered in a spray of glass. It shined the brilliant light of a rainbow! In a moment more, the light was gone, and there stood Michaleen and Shamus Og.

"Help him!" Abi shouted at the brothers.

With but a blur of motion, the two brothers stood in front of Luke as the members of the board battled the snake from behind.

"Suren that's a bad color for him to be!" Shamus said to Michaleen.

"Aye, better drop some pixie dust!"

"Aye!" Shamus agreed. "Pixie dust it 'tis!"

The two leprechauns reached into their pockets and then tossed a sparkling dust into the air around and onto Luke. Then they spoke in the ancient Celt together:

"Ancient ones of distant lands,
We summon you to lend a hand.
Aid us against this creature from hell.
Center your powers and break this spell!"

Golden sparkling lights began to circle around Luke. Then there was a brilliant flash of light, and Luke was free!

Luke took several deep breaths as he lifted himself up. He sat there for a moment as the creature continued to fight with members of the realm.

"Are you OK, Master Luke?" Shamus asked.

"Aye, Shamus," Luke responded. "I just feel like someone tossed me in a press and tried to make orange juice out of me is all." Luke began to stand up. "What took you so long?"

"Aye, we're sorry, Master Luke," Michaleen responded. "We were sleeping."

"Aye," Shamus agreed. "For sure we were counting the sheep in County Cork."

Just then, the snake flew out of the window the brothers Og had come in. With a look of extreme concern, Luke said, "You two are now officially forgiven for kidnapping me!"

The brothers Og produced some smiles, which quickly turned to confusion as Luke climbed up and out the window in pursuit of the snake. They looked at each other in confusion as Selwyn, Katie, and Abi did the same.

"Suren these boys and girls have some strange habits, Michaleen!"

"Aye, Shamus, they do!"

Outside members of the Realm sent bolts of power one after another into the snake. The creature let loose its fire again and again, but it was weak now, and unless someone was close, the snake couldn't burn anyone.

"It's time to end this!" Luke said as he summoned his charmed sword. The Sword of Princes shined so brightly it nearly turned night into day. Everyone was amazed when Luke drew his sword. They were even more amazed when Luke sent a bolt of energy into the creature that lifted the snake's whole body into the air! For a moment, the creature stood as tall as the trees, and then it exploded into a thousand pieces! Everyone was covered with snake guts!

"Eww! Yuck!" Abi shouted. "Luke!"

"Sorry, Abi!" Luke told her. "I didn't know that was going to happen! But I should have done this right away. I was just too scared to draw the charmed sword with everyone watching!

"No!" Abi said.

"No!" Selwyn agreed.

"No!" Katie said.

"No?" Luke asked.

Abi told him, "If you had done that inside, you would have brought down the building, and a whole lot more people would have been hurt!"

"Good safety tip!" Luke said as he put his sword away.

Then Luke thought for a second and said, "Aunt Elizabeth!" He ran back inside and found the Freshers had put a pillow under her head.

With all of the Freshers around, Luke knelt down next to her and said, "First Centurion!"

There was no response. He took her hand. It was cold so he wrapped both hands around hers and ignored where he was and who was listening.

"Elizabeth!"

Thronbasa opened her eyes and saw Luke there. She smiled a little and said, "Did we win?"

"Aye!" Luke said with a smile. "We kicked its bloody ass! That's where all the snake blood on me came from!"

Thronbasa looked at him for a moment and then said, "Finch! He was hurt badly when I came in."

Thronbasa was about to raise herself up when all of the Freshers around her started saying, "No, no, no!"

"No!" Luke told her. You have a crack or two in your head maybe. You can't get up! I will go and see about Finch!"

Luke walked to the far end of the barracks and was followed by Abi, Katie, and Selwyn. There in the corner also surrounded by Freshers was Mr. Finch. The Freshers were staring at Luke as he approached, and they quickly got out of his way. It was a reaction that Luke found surprising. There on the floor lay Finch. Luke approached him. He was obviously in very bad condition. The snake's fangs had pierced his body. He was bleeding and coughing up blood. He looked up at Luke and said, "I am sorry, Lord Carter! I came as fast as I could! I am sorry!"

"You know who I am?"

"I do now, yes. I am sorry for the way I treated you and your friends when you first came. I just believed I was doing my job!"

"Easy, Finch!" Luke told him in a calm voice. "I don't blame you for anything, and neither does Abi, Katie, or

Selwyn. You were brilliant tonight! You were braver than me! If I had acted faster, this wouldn't have happened to you! I am the one who is sorry!"

"Thank you, Your Grace!"

"Hold on, Mr. Finch!" Dickelbee announced. "The medics are on their way!"

"Aye, sir," Finch said.

It was obvious to everyone that no medic would get there quickly enough. Luke stood up and turned around. Everyone bowed slightly to him. "Oh, boy!" he thought. "This is going to get really old really fast!"

"Michaleen! Shamus!" Luke shouted.

The brothers moved in via their normal speed and blurred motion.

"Yes, Master Luke!" they responded.

"You used too much dust!"

"Too much dust?" Shamus responded.

"Right, everyone knows who I am!"

"Suren we be sorry, Master Luke!" Michaleen told him. "We've never used pixie dust on venom from an Egyptian snake god before!"

"Aye!" Shamus agreed. "Snake gods are so rare that we've never had one to practice on before! We'll do better next time!"

"Aye, we will," Michaleen agreed.

Luke was convinced that an intelligent conversation with these two was almost certainly impossible.

"Do you see Mr. Finch over there?" Luke pointed.

"Aye," Michaleen said. "Poor boy is in a terrible way!"

"Aye," Shamus agreed, "a terrible way he is for sure!"

Luke glared into Michaleen's eye and said, "I want you to freeze him!"

The two brothers looked at each other, and Shamus said, "Freeze him, Master Luke?"

"Right, like you did down in Sugarloaf the first time we met."

"Are you sure, Master Luke?" Michaleen said.

"Now, Michaleen!"

"Aye, Master Luke. As you say, sir."

Michaleen walked over to Mr. Finch and said, "I'll be begging your pardon, Master Finch, sir! I have to do as his lordship tells me!"

With that, the leprechaun summoned his stick, and with a flash of smoke from it, Mr. Finch was frozen!

The two leprechauns glanced back at Luke as if to ask, "What now?"

"Pick him up," Luke told the two brothers.

"Pick him up?" Shamus asked.

"Right, use your speed and take him to the trauma center! They can give him a proper look-over like this, and when he starts to melt, they will be able to fix him up."

"Aye," Michaleen said scratching his head. "That is really clever thinking, Master Luke! Come on, Shamus! Take his legs!"

The two lifted up Mr. Finch, and Shamus said, "Oh! Suren he's a properly fed boy, isn't he, Michaleen?"

"Maybe a little overfed, Shamus! Good night, Master Luke! Give us a call if you need us again," Michaleen said as the two left the room in a blur of speed with Mr. Finch in their arms.

Luke turned around with Abi, Katie, and Selwyn at his side. The entire room bowed to him. Thronbasa wanted to laugh, but she was hurting too much!

"Oh, boy," Luke said out loud.

"You can say that again," Katie told him.

"Aye," Abi said in a vague attempt to sound like one of the Og brothers. "Suren we've stepped out of frying pan and into the fire!"

"Right," Selwyn agreed. "I can feel my feet getting toasted already!"

SIRE OF THE WHITE ROBIN

CHAPTER 20

A WEEK HAD gone by, and a week was left in the first trials, so Luke and friends were trying to enjoy their last weekend together in the summer barracks. Their month and a half of training had changed their lives forever. Luke couldn't believe what a different person he was now. He had arrived in the valley full of fear and apprehension. He remembered being so scared that the conductor had to talk him onto the train. He remembered being too afraid to get off of the train when it arrived. He remembered hell week and how little sleep he had been able to get. Now it all seemed like a nightmare that had ended, hopefully. Yesterday they had all scored well on their first aid trial. Luke could now apply a battle dressing with the best of the Realm's warriors. First aid was the last of the seven trials, and now Luke, Abi, Selwyn, and Katie needed only to wait for everyone else to pass or be asked to leave.

The four were sitting outside after lunch and were enjoying some ice cream. They watched workmen decide where to place a plaque marking the spot where the First Lord vanquished the deadly Egyptian snake god. All of the names of those who died fighting the snake would be embossed on it. It was sure to be a major tourist attraction as soon as the fall sport competitions got underway. The barracks had been repaired and made normal by an incantation the same night of the snake fight. It took the High Chancellor all of 30 seconds to repair the barracks.

Luke and friends sat on top of a garden wall. Everyone walking by would bow to Luke. It was impossible for him to acknowledge everyone. In fact some people got so carried away with it that they fell on their faces. This made Luke feel even more embarrassed.

"Should we all bow to you now, Luke?" Katie asked.

Luke glanced at her, never removing the ice cream cone from his face while rolling his eyes in his head. Katie thought he might have said "duh," but she couldn't tell what noise it was that came from behind the ice cream. Now Dickelbee and a few members of the board and a few of the First Caldron were approaching. Luke wasn't paying attention, so Abi gave him a little nudge with her elbow, which caused him to look up. His eyes shifted at Abi for a moment and then back to the approaching leadership, but the ice cream cone stayed in place.

"Good afternoon," several of the approaching leaders said as they all bowed to Luke.

"Are you enjoying all this attention?" one of the chancellors asked in a sincere, friendly tone of voice.

Luke finally did lower the ice cream long enough to say, "I feel like a fish in a bowl and everyone going by is bending over for a look."

The leaders looked at one another and then laughed a little at Luke's description of the conduct of the people around him.

"You must know that everyone's conduct is an act of affection, Your Grace," one of the female chancellors remarked. "Everyone here at one time or another believed that the natural leadership of the Realm was gone forever. They all believed that the darkness had won. The arrival of the snake god seemed to confirm their worst fears. Then you launched your attack on the creature. In doing so, you brought the light back into this valley. It's been gone so long that some had given up hope. Now everyone has real hope that it has returned. I have not seen such joy in this valley for more than a decade!"

Luke thought for a moment. "At least when I'm awake, I can stay focused." Once again, he lowered his ice cream and responded, "Chancellor, it was all of the members who brought the fight to the snake. They are the ones who stood against the evil. Some of them are gone now because of it! I was just the last one to attack it, not the first. They are the ones who deserve to be praised!"

"True," Dickelbee spoke up. "But all of us, myself included, we hit that creature with our best shots, and it stood. It wasn't until you drew the sword we gave you that it was first brought down. Not even Thronbasa's charmed sword driven into its skull could bring it down! But you in your first shot, using a common magical sword, brought the creature to its knees! None of us ever came close. Then, later when you drew the Sword of Princes and launched your second attack, the evil couldn't survive against your magic, Your Grace."

"Fine!" Luke said with a slight hint of frustration. "You've made your point, but we have to do something about these titles and this bowing, or I am going to go crazy! We're mostly Americans here! Americans don't go around doing this stuff and calling people by title. John Adams would be hurling all over me if he saw this!"

"John Adams?" one of the chancellors asked.

"An American founding father and one of the first American presidents," Dickelbee told him. This drew an "oh" from some of the chancellors.

"Hurling?" another one of the leadership asked.

"A slang word for 'vomit,'" Dickelbee told her. Again the revelation drew another "oh."

Then one of the tallest of the leaders commented, "Hurling doesn't sound vulgar at all, does it?" He began laughing, and then so did the others. Luke and his friends just looked at one another, wondering what planet these people grew up on.

Dickelbee began to explain: "All of these titles and expressions are terms of endearment for many of these people here, even the students your own age. Your word is law here. If you end it, it's going to hurt a lot of feelings, and the hope you've lit up inside of them might turned to doubt."

Luke turned to Abi with a question on his face. Abi hated it when he did that! She squinted her eyes at him, and he made puppy dog eyes at her in a sign language that was asking for help. She hated when he did that too! She stared at him some more, not wanting to say anything, but she finally did.

"Couldn't we just tone it down a little?" Abi asked.

"Tone it down? How?" Dickelbee wondered.

Abi looked at Luke, but it was Katie who spoke up and said, "Couldn't they just nod their heads instead of bowing all the time?"

"Yeah," Selwyn added, "and the Og brothers call him Master Luke rather than 'Lord' or 'Grace.'"

"Would that be satisfactory, Master Luke?" Dickelbee asked.

"I thought 'Master' when out with slavery, didn't it?" Luke wondered out loud in between ice cream licks.

"In this context, it would mean a boy who is too young to be addressed as 'Mister,'" one of the female leaders added. "It's Old English and a little informal, but if you are truly uncomfortable with the way people address you, then it's better than nothing. If you agree, your decision will be announced formally."

"What about Cole?" Luke asked.

"We can't find her," Dickelbee responded.

"Pershard?"

"He's gone as well as the ones that you said were helping him in the Citadel hall outside your father's home and the Book of Shadows. They cannot be found."

"Jimmy?"

"We can't find him either, although every Bennie police officer on all of the continents has his picture and a murder warrant for his arrest."

"Marta?"

All of the leaders looked at one another when Luke mentioned Marta. Luke wasn't looking at them. He wasn't trying to be arrogant; in fact, when these leaders turned to him for answers, he was more than just a little embarrassed about it. Not looking at them meant he wished they would just go away!

"She has been convicted," the tall man said. "She had a no defense for what she did."

"If Uncle Martin shows up," Luke replied, "like so many other former members of the Realm seem to do around here, he's going to be so angry if he finds out Marta is in a jail cell!"

The tall chancellor was about to argue with Luke, but Dickelbee looked at him and shook his head very slowly. They all understood they were dealing with a boy of 12 and that emotional reactions were to be expected.

"What would you suggest, Luke?" Dickelbee wondered.

"Let her out!"

"Well, you could order her release, that is true, but people might lose confidence in you if you did. Maybe you might like to consider commuting her sentence?"

Luke glanced over at Dickelbee. He wasn't sure what he meant. He was aware that the leadership was a kind of audience and they were expecting him to put on a performance. He just hated being in the situation. He wanted it to all go away!

"What do you think, High Chancellor?" Luke wondered while trying to be diplomatic—his very first effort at being diplomatic.

"Time served and continued rehabilitation. She is still quite ill and needs help."

"But she's free inside the valley!"

Dickelbee looked over at the other members of the leadership, and they nodded in agreement. "OK, Luke, that sounds good to us."

"And on holidays and weekends, she can go with me anywhere I go."

Once again Dickelbee looked over at the others, and they very reluctantly nodded their heads. "OK, that's fine with us, Luke."

"There was one other matter we wanted to take up with you, My Lord," one of the female chancellors asked. Luke glanced at her with an evil eye for having called him "Lord." She then corrected herself, "I mean, Master Luke! Yes, please forgive me, Master Luke. It's going to take time for some of us to get used to that title."

"You had something you wanted to ask?" Luke responded as he went back to his ice cream.

"We lost two members of the board while fighting with that snake god, and now that Cole has been expelled, we were wondering about your thoughts on replacements," the woman continued.

"Thronbasa," Luke replied.

The board members looked at one another and seemed rather impressed with that choice. They even wondered why none of them had thought about it.

"And the other two?" the woman continued.

"I would prefer Chancellor Thronbasa decide the rest. She knows more about these things than I do."

Again the group was impressed with the 12-year-old's decision.

"Before we go, Luke," Dickelbee began, "there was one question we all had about your report that Cole and Pershard were after the sword in your father's home. Those two had no reason to believe that sword would be there and every reason to believe otherwise. On this we all agreed. Also, if they had turned to the Darkside, they both would have understood that going near the sword would have been fatal for them. We wondered whether there was something else you remembered about your encounter with them. Laura lived there until she was 12 and then again starting from age 16. She often had friends join her. If there was anything there, she or one of her friends would have mentioned it."

Luke shook his head and then said, "It's hard for me to remember. I wasn't exactly awake. Information I had when I woke up faded quickly. I do remember Pershard thinking there was information inside he could make use of. But really, that's all I remember."

The leadership group thanked him, nodded their heads to him, and then moved off. Luke watched the group moving away and talking to one another. He breathed a sigh of relief when they finally left. He just felt so wound up and tight inside when they got close to him. Not long after, Crystal Tamcke and some of her girlfriends walked up to Luke with a camera. They asked to take pictures with him and then to have him autograph the pictures. The girls wanted to send them home to their parents. Luke didn't like the idea much but said nothing. He certainly owed Crystal a favor or two—or 10 perhaps.

When they had finished with the pictures, Luke turned around to find Abi, Selwyn, and Katie making jokes and laughing at him. He just looked at them with an evil eye, and when they realized he was paying attention, they stood upright as if nothing had happened. Luke took a few steps toward them and said, "Bet you think you're funny!"

Abi looked back, bowed, and said, "No, Your Grace!"

Katie and Selwyn did the same but said, "Yes, My Lord!" Then all three broke up laughing.

"My good friends," Luke said sarcastically. Then he started to think. He seemed to zone out for a moment in thought. Katie, Selwyn, and Abi noticed.

"We're just messing with you, Luke," Selwyn told him.

Luke glanced over at him and replied, "I know, but what about what Dickelbee said?"

"Dickelbee?" Abi said with a question in her voice and bewilderment on her face.

In fact the whole group looked bewildered including Luke until he started to walk away. He walked out onto the main path and started heading for the Citadel. The other three looked at one another and then dashed to catch up to him.

"Luke!" Katie insisted. "Where are we going?"

"Didn't you hear Dickelbee? The barrier that protects my parents' home doesn't keep out family and friends. My grandfather had told me the same thing when I arrived. But I have so much trouble remembering everything that happens when I am sleeping. I forgot!"

"We're not allowed in the Citadel until after we graduate first trials!" Selwyn insisted.

"Right!" Luke agreed. "You guys stay here!"

All three responded, "No!"

"What? Disobey the First Lord of the Realm? Off with your heads!" Luke was just being sarcastic again. "What? I don't hear any laughing now!"

"Luke," Katie questioned while taking large steps to keep up with him, "are you sure you know what you are doing?"

Luke stopped in his tracks and turned around, and all three abruptly stopped in front of him.

"Katie," he said, "the one thing that I am completely certain of is that from the moment I discovered this Realm, I haven't once had a clue what I was doing! All I know is that some really bad people want that sword. I am certain that they want it so they can hurt others with it. I don't know what I am doing. What I am going to do is find that sword and keep the bad people away from it!"

Luke turned around and started walking again.

"It was just a question," Katie pleaded as she dashed to catch up, thinking his reaction was way too serious.

The group made their way up and into the entrance of the Citadel. It was for Abi, Selwyn, and Katie as if they had climbed a great mountain and now beheld a new world. Luke had been walking these halls and looking around in his sleep all week. He didn't know the castle very well, but he knew how to find his family's home. As always, the portraits on the walls noticed him, but because of his decision with the leadership, now they simply nodded their heads to him. News traveled by magic in the Realm, so they all knew that only nodding was the rule now.

Abi, Selwyn, and Katie were having trouble keeping up with Luke. This was their first time inside. Their senses were overwhelmed by what they saw. The place was so different than anything they had ever experienced. Adults who spotted the group might have had something to say about them being there, but as soon as they noticed Luke, they backed away. Luke wished all adults would do that. He still didn't trust them and doubted he ever would.

It took 15 minutes of nonstop walking from the time they entered the castle to when they entered the hall where Luke's grandfather's portrait was hanging. This was the first time Luke was approaching the portrait while he was awake. He and his grandfather had never met face-to-face before. He stopped in front of the old lord of the Realm. His three friends read the title of the portrait, and they each looked up at Luke a little surprised.

"Is he?" Katie asked.

"Yep," Luke replied.

"Do you talk to him?" Abi wondered.

"Once. I usually try to avoid all conversation."

"Why?" Selwyn wondered.

"Because he chose the Realm over his eldest son, and my uncle, who raised me. Because he hurt my uncle. Because my uncle feared and hated him and now so do I. So long as you don't ask any questions, he's not allowed to start any conversations."

"But he's your grandfather, Luke!" Katie asserted.

"Yeah, I know. Come on. Let's see if we can have a visit in the family home."

Luke and his friends left the old lord behind as they made their way down the hallway. They were approaching the home of the White Robin. The four of them could feel they were approaching the barrier. The veil everyone believed the White Robin had left to protect his family if something happened to him had proven itself impenetrable to all who had challenged it. Now, Luke, feeling he had reached its invisible horizon, reached out with his hand. Where he touched the barrier, white energy sparks surrounded his hand but did not stop it from going through. His friends looked both amazed and a bit fearful. When Luke turned around, he could see the apprehension on their faces.

Luke reached out with his other hand taking Abi's. Holding hers, he told everyone to hold hands. Abi held Selwyn's hand and he held Katie's as the group made their way through the barrier. When they were on the other side, they had to smile at each other in amazement. Then they approached the main door that was locked.

"Do you have a key?" Abi asked Luke.

Luke shook his head no and smiled at Abi. Then he said, "Oscailte Cead Caite A Fhail Mo Diol !"

The enormous door opened.

"What did you just say?" Abi asked him.

"Oscailte Cead Caite A Fhail Mo Diol."

"Yes."

"It's 'open says me' in ancient Irish," Luke smiled.

"No way!" Abi insisted.

Luke laughed and told her that was his very same reaction the first time he heard it and then laughed some more. Now the group slowly made their way into Luke's family home. The first and most obvious thing was how high the ceilings were—more than twice as normal and all made from various colors of carved marble. The picture graphics carved into the walls were depictions of various events in Realm history.

The main living room was a great hall with an enormous fireplace at one end. There was a balcony above it, and stacks of books surrounded the main room above the balcony. There were portraits on the walls, but none of them moved. The room was furnished in a medieval style that truly made it seem that it was part of a castle. They moved into the next room, a sitting room, filled with family pictures from long ago. There were also pictures of Luke from when he was one year old until just last year. Aunt Claire must have sent them, and Laura must have kept them. Everyone was looking around. The rooms were beautiful, and everything was well kept. Then Luke began to move toward a table filled with pictures. There, for the first time, he laid his eyes on his parents.

His mother was tall and beautiful. It was clear that Luke had gotten his hair from his mother. Next to her was his dad. He was also a tall person with auburn hair and strong looks. He looked like a young Uncle Martin. Luke stared at them both. He searched his mind for some reflection of a memory of them, but he couldn't feel or see either of them in the past. Then he gazed over to another table, and there was his father holding a baby in his arms. The picture was part of a dual frame, and on the other side of the frame was some writing. Luke walked closer to see what it said. Abi and Katie were now on either side of him. They seemed to look at whatever Luke was paying attention to. The writing next to the picture of Luke's father holding a baby was a poem.

"On first autumn's day of this year,
My life was changed so listen clear.
A touch of love I dare to share,
A gift from God and an answer to a prayer.

Once before I was blessed with a child,
A beautiful girl of whom I am so proud.
A special day when she arrived,
My life before I wondered how I survived.

She is my life, my love, my most precious one.
She celebrates with me, a gift from God, I now have a son.
His mother's hair, his sister's eyes,
He brings a new fire to the meaning of my life.

I want my boy to know this day,
I hope my coming age does not let it stray.
My life is tempered by the birth of this soul,
The love of my son has made me whole."

Philo John, on the occasion of the birth of Luke.

There were tears in Abi's and Katie's eyes as they finished reading the poem.

"Your father was a very sweet person, Luke," Abi said.

Luke replied with a very soft voice, "I don't know if he was. I never knew him. I know what Laura told me. It was the first thing she said after I found out who she was, and she was crying. She wanted to make sure I understood how much our parents felt for us. I have never felt their loss. Aunt Claire and Uncle Martin were always there. Up until the day those two leprechauns showed up, I never even thought about Mom and Dad. I've wondered about that after having been in this Realm for a several weeks and seeing how things work and how people here think. I've wondered about the possibility that a spell might have made sure I didn't think about them. When I became centered, I think the spell was broken and I started to remember and question everything around me. I learned that there were really bad people who were looking for me. I have just never known why. "

"Then, today, when the leadership walked up to us and asked me for decisions— me, Luke Carter from Sugarloaf, Florida, being asked to make decisions for everyone else. I got scared! I was ready to hurl my ice cream and lunch. Lying on the floor having the life crushed out of me by snake venom was not as scary as that moment. Now I know why Uncle Martin walked away. I'm not like my dad; I'm like my uncle."

"No, you're not, Luke," Abi told him as Katie listened carefully. "I saw how you reacted to Crinshaw and that snake god. All of us wanted to run! You just got angry! You faced the evil, and you didn't run! Even when that snake tried to run away, you just went after it!"

"That's because of Jimmy," Luke told her.

"Jimmy?"

"Yes, every time the darkness comes near, all I can see and feel is Jimmy! All I can dream about is ramming my sword through his heart! All I can think of is his sword sticking out of Uncle Martin's chest! That's what you see on my face."

"You have to let that go, Luke!" Katie insisted.

"I've tried! I can't!"

"Katie is right, Luke. You cannot act for revenge. That's personal gain! You do that, and then the Darkside wins!"

"Laura seemed to think that a prince was both judge and jury and that rule didn't apply."

"Don't find out if she's right!" Katie insisted. "That kind of force can only be used out of desperation. To protect yourself and your family and friends, my dad told me that justice is a matter for a community, not an individual."

Luke was amazed at his friends' reactions. He wondered how different it would be if someone had murdered their parents. He didn't get a chance to argue the point because just then Selwyn walked in and announced, "Luke, you should come and see this!"

Selwyn, who had continued to look around the home as Luke glanced at his family pictures, led all of them into a room that struck everyone silent. They couldn't believe their eyes! They had walked into a room that was part armory and part museum, and it glowed and had a slight hum to it. The hum sounded a little like singing.

At its opening was a rack of properly mounted swords with the same gold plate that charmed swords had. But they didn't glow or make a noise. Everyone watched as Luke picked one up. Right away it glowed and hummed. When he put it down, the glow and sound went away.

"Those are whole racks of charmed swords," Abi spoke as if she were just thinking out loud.

Then they walked up to a sword mounted on fine dark cloth and sitting on a short pedestal. The sword was stunning to look at. It gleamed beautifully in the room light. Its handle was carved ivory and gold. It had many symbols on it. It almost seemed alive it was so stunning. A gold seal next to it read:

The Durandal
Holy Sword of Roland

There was another sword also mounted on fine cloth atop a short pedestal. This one was metal, and it shimmered as one approached it. It was also marked with many fine carved symbols. Luke and his friends' eyes were so wide! They were amazed beyond description as they read its seal.

The Arondight
Sword of Sir Lancelot
A Noble Knight and Defender of the Faith

There was still another sword. The closer Luke got to it, the more it glowed and hummed. It was as if it knew he was there. It glowed white instead of gold like the other swords. It was not only carved in ivory and gold, but it also had brilliant jewels mounted on it. They shined like stars in a rainbow of colors. Its seal read:

The Pellinor
A Sword of King
The Sword That Shattered the Caliburn
And Caused It to Be Reforged into
Excalibur
The Sword of Kings

There were many other swords that were amazing to behold. As they continued in the gallery, they came to a group of wands. Luke was surprised to see them. He thought wands had no place here and that they were associated with the Darkside.

"What are these doing here?" Luke said out loud.

"Why wouldn't they be?" Selwyn replied.

"They are wands! Only Darksider wizards carry them!"

"Where did you get that idea, Luke?" Abi asked.

"Because the ones who attacked me carried them!"

"My dad has carried a wand all his life! Wands are not evil, Luke," Selwyn insisted. "People are evil, not wands!"

"I am all confused again! Damn it!" Luke was not happy to hear this information. He thought wand-carrying anythings were something to be vanquished right away.

"If I had not met you, Luke, if you had not helped me the way you have, I would have become a wizard," Selwyn explain. "Because I am not an American, I would have been accepted in Europe. I would have been trained in wizard's craft, and I wouldn't have had my powers bound for life because I failed here. My father wanted me to understand what I was getting into by coming here. The American Realm is survival of the fittest. He thought because I was so weak with magic I would just get hurt.

"Americans were denied access to magic devices like wands for centuries. My father made sure I knew and understood this. Humans are mortal, and originally they had no connection to magic and no defense against dark magic. So they used devices that were forged from creatures born inside the Realm. This is the Realm, and we are inside of it. We are not a natural part of it. Many of us need devices to command magic—like me, until I met you and we did that thing with your sword. Americans are practitioners and masters of the old shaman's craft. No one knows where it came from! There is a theory my father explained to me once that it might have come from the tribes that first formed in Africa. But for real, no one really knows.

"After the revolution here, a new group of magical people took over in North America, a people who didn't need devices. Your grandfather out there on the wall, he is a legend! I read about him as soon as I could read! A man born and raised as a wizard, who was the White Robin of the Realm, who became a practitioner! Next time you pass him, show some respect!" Selwyn waved his finger in the air.

"Until your grandfather did it, there had never been a White Robin who was a practitioner of shaman's craft! My dad told me about your's. No one had ever seen or heard of anyone or anything like your dad. A Darksider couldn't even survive after looking at him, let alone picking a fight! That's why they had to get him out of the way. There's no way they could have attacked this valley with your dad in it."

"Why did you wait six weeks to tell me this?" Luke demanded.

"The truth? I didn't believe in you, Luke," Selwyn told him as he shook his head. "I thought in six weeks or less, you and Katie would be dead, and I would be kicked out again."

"Then why did you come back?" Abi asked. It was a question she had been dying to ask all summer!

"Because everyone believed that the First Lord of the Realm would return this summer, and I wanted to meet him! Even when my father first pointed him out to me in Florida, I never got to meet him."

Luke had his arms behind his back like his Aunt Elizabeth. He stared into Selwyn's eyes without blinking as he walked up to him and sternly said, "Howdy!" He reached out with his right hand and continued. "Nice to meet ya!"

Luke broke into a big smile, and so did Selwyn as he reached to shake Luke's hand. They were still shaking when Katie leaped onto Luke's back. She wrapped her legs and arms around him as she spoke to Selwyn.

"I never doubted him! Duh!"

"Katie!" Luke shouted. "Get down!"

Katie did, and Luke, in a very poor attempt to sound like Selwyn's Trinidad accent, and waving his finger like Selwyn, announced, "Katie you're in the House of the White Robin! Show some respect!"

"That stank!" Abi told him.

"Show some respect!" Abi shouted, trying to sound like Selwyn. Then Katie did it, and the three of them kept trying while Selwyn watched with his face turning red.

"Very funny," Selwyn told them.

"OK," Luke said. "Wands are not evil, and they do not do evil things; only people do evil things. Maybe demons do too. That's today's lesson! It's a good thing you explained that, or I might have fried the first person I saw carrying a wand!"

Luke made his way into the Hall of Wands. He had to admit he was impressed. Most of them were phoenix wands that ranged in age from 300 to 3,500 years old. Typically, a wand was made with a feather from a magical creature inside of it. There was a Garuda wand from the third century B.C. A Garuda bird was from India. It was a creature that was half man. There was an American Chippewa wand. It was made from a thunder bird that had gone extinct 10 centuries ago.

There was one from Egypt that was at least 3,500 years old, made from the feather of an Egyptian Benu bird. There was a Tibetan Khyung and a Mayan Camulatz. There was even one from China called "Yu-qiang."

There was a brilliant perfectly white wand at the end. The closer Luke got to it, the whiter and brighter it became. It was very difficult to read its seal. Luke had to block the light the way he would block the sun outside. When he finally got close enough the seal, it read,

The Pegasus
Made from the Feather of the Greek Equestrian God Pegasus

"Wow!" Luke spoke in amazement. Each of his friends reacted in much the same way. They didn't know what to make of all of these things they were seeing. It was now clear, however, why no one was allowed inside the White Robin's home. There was so much here that could do so much damage in the wrong hands. Unlike a charmed sword, magical wands couldn't tell the difference between good and evil, and these wands were among the most powerful in existence. Still, there was no sign of the Sword of Kings. Clearly, had Pershard made his way in here, he would have found much of what his followers might have needed. Luke understood that now, but he also remembered clearly what their main objective was, and none of this was it.

The next room the group walked into was quite a mystery. It was as large as the main room at the entrance. Its walls had carvings of many different kinds of symbols, none of which they could read. Abi asked Luke whether any of it made sense to him. Luke just shook his head. What was striking, however, was an enormous tapestry at the far end of the room. It covered the entire wall. At its center was what seemed to be a stunningly beautiful woman with long golden hair. She was draped in long white ropes that glowed slightly. Her ropes and hair seemed to be blowing in a slight breeze. Her face seemed perfect to everyone. To everyone but Luke, there was but one word printed beneath the figure, "Sire."

At first, Luke didn't understand that only he was able to see the script beneath the word "Sire."

"Do any of those words under the word 'Sire' make any sense to anyone?" Luke wondered out loud.

"What words?" Selwyn replied.

"Yeah," Abi agreed. "What words?"

Luke raised his figure and pointed. "You don't see the words under 'Sire'?"

"Nope," Katie said.

"No," Selwyn and Abi said.

"OK," Luke said slowly with a question in his voice. "Now for something new and different," he continued as if thinking out loud. Luke was getting used to having to face surprises all the time. If nothing else, it taught him how to think and react quickly. He was forever reminding himself that had he thought and moved faster when that snake god attacked, then Aunt Elizabeth and Mr. Finch wouldn't still be in the hospital.

"What does it say?" Katie asked.

"I'm trying to figure that out," Luke responded. "It seems like very old writing. But this wall rug doesn't look that old. What I am making out seems like fragments of ancient Celt."

"Maybe a base language?" Abi wondered.

"Base language?" Luke glanced over at her.

"Yeah, something that evolved into Celt?"

"How do you know about these things?"

"My dad likes documentary TV programs, so I watch with him," she told him.

"Oh," Luke went. "A base language? Like Old English? Like William Shakespeare?"

"No," Katie said. "That would be more Middle English than Old English."

Everyone stared at Katie.

"What?" she said with her hands raised upward. "I watch documentary programs too! I like MTV too, but to each her own!"

Luke nodded his head first with an odd look on his face and then shook it as he went back to what he called a "wall rug."

"Why would someone hang a rug on the wall instead of laying it on the floor?"

"Maybe they wanted to keep the wall warm!" Katie blurted out.

First Abi broke into a giggle and then Selwyn, followed by Luke. When they all looked over at Katie, she was giggling also.

Luke turned back to the wall and shook his head with a smile and said to himself, "Keep the wall warm? Strange stuff in those documentaries you watch!" Then he laughed some more. "OK, where was I?" he wondered out loud.

Luke stared at each word in the script beneath the portrait of the woman. He said each individual word in Celt as he made them out. Finally getting to the end, he said them all together in Celt.

"Ancient One of Mythic Time, I Summon You Now to My Side."

All the symbols carved into the wall of the room began to glow. A chorus of voices sounded. Then the woman in the wall rug came to life and stepped out and into the room!

"Maybe reading the whole thing together wasn't a good idea," Abi suggested with the distinct sound of fear in her voice.

"Oops," Katie said.

"Wow," Selwyn insisted.

"Now what?" Luke wondered. "I'm not waiting this time!"

Luke summoned the Sword of Princes, and the other three summoned their swords. The woman stood as tall as the room. With her arms outreached, she bowed her head. Then her glow went away as she shrunk down to the size of a normal person. She kept her head bowed as she went down on one knee and said, "Blessed be your name and house, My Lord Robin."

The woman didn't move. Luke stared at her for a moment and then looked over at Abi. Abi gave him a glance that reflected her frustration with him turning to her when he wasn't sure what to say or do.

"What?" Abi said.

Luke shrugged his shoulders.

"She doesn't seem dangerous to me," Abi told him.

"Right," Luke responded as he put his sword away. The others followed.

"Who—or what—are you?" Luke asked the woman.

"I am a fallen Angel, My Lord."

"I thought all fallen angels were dropped into hell," Abi said. But the woman on her knees who was staring at the floor said nothing.

Luke gazed over at Abi and then back to the woman. "Why do you not answer the question?"

"I am bound to the Robin's house only, My Lord. The words of common mortals do not reach me."

"These are my friends, and when they are with me, you will answer their questions," Luke insisted. His tone of voice was calm, not rude or unfriendly.

"Those who rose up with the archangel Lucifer, called Satan by God, fell from heaven and were cast into hell. I am fallen, but I serve no evil."

"Why did you fall?" Luke asked.

"I refused to bow to and serve God's creation in heaven, so I was condemned to serve it here."

"How long have you been here?" Katie asked.

The angel said nothing.

"Answer her!" Luke insisted.

"I know no time. Time is a phantom of the mortal imagination. It has no basis in reality, as you understand it. I experience what you call time as a single idea not separated by moments."

"How do you serve us here?" Selwyn asked.

"Stand up and look up at me and open your eyes," Luke insisted.

The angel complied, but her eyes were black against a white glowing face. She was quite startling to look at.

"Answer Selwyn's question!" Luke insisted.

"It is my wings that sit on the shoulders of the White Robin. It is my sword that dark creatures fear and wish to possess or destroy."

Luke and his friends looked at one another, completely surprised by this revelation.

"Pershard wasn't after the sword; he was after her!" Luke insisted as he gazed at his friends.

"How is that possible?" Abi insisted.

"She just said she serves only the Robin and only your House!" Katie agreed.

While looking at Katie, Luke got a terrible sinking feeling inside of himself. An awful look came over him as he turned back to the angel.

"Is Pershard a Robin?"

"Yes, My Lord."

"How is he a Robin? He's a Darksider!"

"The dark is dominated by the light so long as the two are in balance. They are not in balance. There are two Robins of the same house: one dark, one light. Because of the lack of balance, they both rule."

Luke was really starting to feel ill now. It was just as if a Darksider had come too close. "How is he a Robin of my House?" Luke demanded to know.

"He is Rajay Rama Pershard of the Cohan, the firstborn son of Martin Cohan. You are Luke Rama Pershard Carter of the House of Cohan. He is your cousin. He is the natural firstborn of the natural White Robin. You are the firstborn of the consecrated White Robin. Until you were born, Rajay Rama Pershard was the natural successor of the House of Cohan and the next White Robin. Your birth broke the balance. The consecrated Robin agreed to no man-child as a sire. When you were born, the pax was broken. Although he didn't know it because he was just a boy, Rajay Rama Pershard turned to a dark lord, an Englishman, who Rajay believed to be just an older member of the Realm. The man owned an estate near the village in India where he grew up. Rajay asked for his help to restore the balance. In exchange, he promised my sword to the dark lord. Without Rajay knowing, the dark lord attacked, but you survived, so the imbalance survived. Now the darkness can roam at will and can corrupt almost anything it wishes because there is no balance between the two sides. God granted mortal men free will, which means your own lust for power can destroy you."

Luke turned pale and stooped onto his knees. His friends were stunned by this news. Luke couldn't believe what he was hearing.

Luke gazed at the floor and shook his head as he said, "Did my uncle know he had a son?"

"A son and a daughter, Magda, yes."

"He kept all of this a secret?"

"Martin was an outcast, My Lord Carter. He lived many years in India, hiding. He knew, as did his father, what would happen to the balance of good and evil if both he and his brother had a man-child, and so did the wizards of Ireland. When your grandfather failed to either castrate or kill Martin, they tried to kill your grandfather before he could sire more children. That's why he was forced out of Ireland. Martin believed that if you failed to become centered by age 16, then the balance would be restored and Rajay would be First Lord."

"My line cannot be corrupted by the Darkside. How did this happen to Rajay?"

"Basically," the angel answered, "Rajay has not been corrupted. He has taken no lives. He has surrendered nothing to the Darkside. He is absent malice, but he lusts after his birthright. He has done everything possible short of turning to the Darkside himself. Even the snake he summoned after you was a third party that by nature was already part of the Darkside. What he believes he wants is justice. Unfortunately, that means you must be vanquished. He can't do it himself, so he manipulates others to do it for him. He's been very clever."

"Did Laura know this? Did you tell her?" Luke asked.

"Laura was a woman. Only a Robin of your House can summon me. Women cannot lead the Realm."

"Why?" Abi demanded.

The angel said nothing. "Answer her!" Luke insisted.

For the first time, the angel broke her stare at Luke and turned to Abi and the others.

"What you call the Realm was formed thousands of your years ago. There was no such thing as a female leader then. Even in your reality now, females make up the smallest number of leaders. I had only one pair of wings to give up. I had to surrender them to the line of mortals most likely to succeed at fighting to keep the balance between the darkness and the light. I cannot change what you call the past."

"How did my father decide to have a boy instead of a girl?" Luke asked.

"There are endless spells available to him and all members of the Realm. They are quite common."

"And he did it deliberately?"

"Yes. Technically, the White Robin is a king. Kings decide life and death all the time. It is their prerogative to do so."

Luke stood up still pale and feeling ill. "What about you now, Angel? What happens to you now?"

"When you leave the room, I will return from where I came."

"Do you know where the Sword of Kings is?

"No, your father blinded me from knowing. I think he worried that Rajay might come in here some day and ask me for it."

"Do you know how I can find it?"

"The Griffin Pass has a large cave on its eastern wall. Your princely sword was forged with a fragment of the Sword of Kings. Inside the cave is the soul of the valley. It is a map carved into its floor. Raise your sword over it at sunset and the light your sword reflects should find its father."

Luke walked up to the angel and looked into her face. "Is there no way you could return to heaven? Is there any way you could be forgiven?"

The angel smiled. Her smiling face absent of eyes was most peculiar to look at.

"We all have our swords that we must carry, My Lord." She touched Luke's face and brushed back his hair a little. "Hold to a trust that I once failed to. Trust in God. Hold onto your faith because I can tell you that Rajay doesn't believe in anything but himself. When you are confused as to what direction to go in, make a leap of faith."

"What is your name?" Luke wondered.

"I am called Sharafin."

"Sharafin, the direction I go should always be to the light? Will I always find what I need?"

Tears began to drop from Sharafin's black eyes. "For your friends and all other mortals, yes. But not you."

"Why?" Luke said with fear on his face.

"You are gray, Luke. You stand between the light and the darkness. You draw a line with your sword. You say this far and no farther. If you walk toward the light, the darkness will fill in behind you. If Rajay stands there, the darkness will just pass through him."

"I have to go find the sword before Rajay does, Sharafin."

"Yes, I know."

"Good-bye, Sharafin," Luke said as he turned to walk away.

Sharafin kneeled on one knee and bowed to Luke as he left. His friends followed. He stopped in the doorway and turned back at the angel. He stared at her for a moment. He had never seen anything like her. If someone had told him about her, he would have thought that person to be crazy. Yet there she was. Luke turned and walked out. Sharafin disappeared, and the image on the tapestry reappeared.

THE SWORD OF KINGS
CHAPTER 21

LUKE AND HIS friends walked out toward the main room of his family's home. He was quiet. He needed time to think, so he stood in the main room. The others were still looking around. They knew Luke was not well, and they were concerned. Luke's friends were just as surprised as he was about the news the angel had given. The unusual pale color of Luke's face reflected the deep emotional impact the revelations about his family had on him. He felt like he had just woken up in the middle of a game where everyone knew what the rules were except him. He looked out the window. The day was getting long, and he had to find the soul of the valley before it ended.

Staring and daydreaming out the window, Luke began to feel anger swelling up inside of him. Soon his pale face was replaced by red when he realized that he must have been manipulated since the day he was born! Uncle Martin had never told anyone what he intended. Luke understood now that he was never to be centered in magic or become part of the Realm. The Darkside never knew this, so they kept searching for him. Laura never knew of Uncle Martin's plans, which is why she sent the leprechauns in an effort to avoid trouble. They caught Uncle Martin by surprise. They wrecked his big plan to save the family. Luke understood now. Uncle Martin could have fought off the Darkside attack in Sugarloaf. He was that powerful of a wizard and practitioner, and like his brother, the Darkside would never have survived an encounter with him. If he hadn't been neutralized, the attack would have failed. But Jimmy took him completely by surprise. Then Uncle Martin knew he had to choose between his son and his nephew.

"That's why he insisted I take his sword," Luke thought. "He chose me. But why? He knew me better than anyone. He had to know I didn't want it!'

Then Luke thought back to lunchtime and the conversation with the leadership. He was in such a big hurry. He wanted the board to go away and didn't want to have to answer their questions. Luke closed his eyes. He ran through the conversation in his mind. Even though he wasn't looking at them when the events happened, he could use magic to see their faces and check their reactions. It was Dickelbee's question about what if anything he might have remembered. He thought about the look on Dickelbee's face. Dickelbee wasn't trying to find out what he remembered. He was wondering whether Luke had discovered anything new! Luke had never bothered to notice this while it was happening! He was worried Luke would discover the house.

"Why is that?" Luke wondered. "Because I can trust them? I don't know them. Why should I trust them?"

Luke turned around and summoned his trunk. He pulled out his cloak and put it on. The other three summoned their trunks and did the same.

"No," Luke insisted. "This is going to get drastic! You guys need to stay where you'll be safe!"

Luke's friends ignored him. They put their cloaks on too. Luke walked back into the museum and pulled one of the charmed swords off of the rack. He put it away with his other sword. Then as he went to walk out, the others followed. He turned around and said, "You guys have to stay here!"

Each one of them told him "Nope!"

"I am going into the Griffin Pass. Believe me, you don't want to come!"

They crossed their arms, and each one said, "We're going!"

"Look, I am the First Lord, and I am giving you an order to stay here!"

Abi, Selwyn, and Katie just stared at him with their arms crossed.

"This is a family matter! You guys can't help, and most likely you'll just get hurt or end up dead!"

Tears ran down Abi's eyes as she told him, "We are family, Luke!"

"Right!" Katie shouted. "And where you go, we go!"

"Right!" Selwyn told him.

"Listen to me guys! You don't understand! You now know something you're not supposed to know! You know why these Darksiders want me dead. Now that you know, they will be coming for you too!"

It made no difference. The three stood there with their arms crossed as they waited to leave.

"God, this is like talking to a wall! OK," Luke agreed very reluctantly. "But you've never faced a whole army of Darksiders before! I have! This is going to get really nasty!"

They all nodded their heads in agreement as if they had any idea at all of what they were getting into. Truly, not one of them had a clue what was going to happen next. Abi wiped her eyes as the four led by Luke headed out. They walked out into the hallway and headed for Luke's grandfather. As they did, several upperclassmen came around the corner and started moving right at them.

The lead upperclassmen shouted out, "You four are not allowed in the Citadel!"

Luke drew the Sword of Princes. Abi, Selwyn, and Katie drew their swords. Luke raised his sword right into the face of the upperclassman with the big mouth. He raised his hands in front of him as if he wanted to surrender. The others with him did the same.

"You," the upperclassman said with his voice stuttering, "you cannot draw on other members of the Realm! It's against the law!"

"No, I can't," Luke agreed. "But I can vaporize any Darksider I cross paths with!"

"We're not Darksiders!" the boy insisted. "We just heard there were Freshers in here. We just came to enforce the rules!" He and the ones behind him all nodded their heads in agreement.

"Really?"

"Yes, My Lord!"

"I don't like being called that!"

"Yes, Master Luke. I'm sorry, sir! I heard the announcement about that. I'm sorry."

"Draw your sword!" Luke told him.

The upperclassman just looked at him with fear and bewilderment.

"Did you hear me?"

"Yes, sir."

The upperclassman drew his sword.

"Tap your sword against mine!" Luke told him.

The upperclassman knew Luke's sword was charmed. He knew what was going to happen, but he did as Luke told him, and he went flying backward against the wall. He barely missed the portrait of Luke's grandfather, who had a look of very uneasy bewilderment.

"Well?" Katie asked.

"He's not a Darksider," Luke responded without looking at her.

The upperclassman picked himself up off of the floor, and he limped back to Luke.

"What's your name?" Luke asked him.

"I'm James Starr, sir."

"Are you on the centurion training track?" Luke responded with hesitation.

"Yes, Master Luke."

"And these others are too?"

"Yes, Master Luke."

"Well, you've made it! By my order, you have a—" Luke looked over at Abi.

"I knew you were going to do that!" she told him.

"—a field commission!" Abi said.

"Right! What she said! And you're a corporal!"

"Aye, sir!" the upperclassman responded with a bit of confidence.

"And these others, they are also field commissioned, and they are your squad, and you are their leader. Understand?"

"Aye, sir!"

"Good! Follow me!"

Luke went past them and right up to his grandfather. He raised his sword right at him. Everyone was startled by this and didn't understand what was going on. With his sword in the old lord's face, Luke told him, "You knew! You knew all this time I have been passing you—even the first time I spoke to you! You knew, and you didn't tell me anything!"

The old man just nodded his head.

"Why?"

"I didn't want my grandchildren killing each other!"

"Who else knew?" Luke demanded. "Did Aunt Claire know?"

"She suspected, but she never really knew."

"Laura?"

"She also suspected and asked me many times, but she never knew, and I never told her."

"Dickelbee?"

"Dickelbee knows everything," the old man said. "Nothing happens in this valley without his knowledge and approval. The only reason Laura did anything was because he said so. Well, it's more likely he manipulated her. His charms and magic seemed to have worked on just about everyone but you!"

Luke lowered his sword. He looked into his grandfathers eyes and said, "Better hope they get me first, grandfather! If I make it back, I'm going to have me a bonfire! I'll let you guess who's going to be in the center of it!"

Luke moved off down the hall and headed for the exit. Everyone stayed close behind him. Fifteen minutes later, they were nearly at the exit door when Katie asked Luke, "Are we heading for the pass now?"

"No, I need help from someone I can trust, someone who has experience with Darksiders. We're heading for the medical center."

"But Thronbasa is too ill to help!" Abi asserted.

"I know," Luke told her.

Just then they turned the corner to head into the medical center, and there stood the board and the First Caldron with Dickelbee at its center. When Luke saw him, he froze for a second. Then he moved forward, with his sword pointed at the ground. He was going to just walk around them when Dickelbee spoke.

"Is there something we could help you with, Master Luke?"

Just hearing his voice enraged Luke. Luke turned toward him with his sword pointing down. His rage sent energy from the sword flowing to the foundation of the building. The building began to shake as if an earthquake was happening. Luke raised his sword and pointed it right at Dickelbee.

"You knew all along! You weren't asking questions at lunch to get me to remember things! You wanted to find out whether I had discovered anything new!" Luke began to take steps toward the High Chancellor. The High Chancellor stood with his arms reached out as if he wanted no trouble. The others began to back away from Dickelbee—in part because they thought he might have turned and because being in front of Luke's sword wasn't a very safe place to be!

"I know now, Dickelbee! I know why this valley was attacked! I know why all those people lost their lives! I know why both my uncles are dead! I know who's responsible, and I know you knew what was happening all along and did nothing to stop it! You didn't even bother to tell Laura—the girl who you called a daughter! You are scum!"

The angrier Luke became, the brighter his sword glowed.

"Surrender your sword, Dickelbee!" Luke ordered.

Dickelbee drew his sword and tossed it at Luke's feet. Luke gazed at it for a moment. It wasn't a charmed sword!

"I want your charmed sword!" Luke told him.

"I don't carry a charmed sword," Dickelbee responded. "I am a member of the Diplomatic Corps and a priest, not an Alfa-Omega."

Luke glanced over at one of the centurions, and she came over and picked up Dickelbee's sword.

"Mr. Starr," Luke said.

"Yes, sir!" Starr replied.

"You and your centurions will escort Father Dickelbee to his room. You will watch him pack, and then you will escort him out of the valley!"

"Aye, Master Luke!" Starr replied. The new centurions drew their swords and pointed them at Dickelbee as they escorted him to his room.

Luke turned to the other leaders as he lowered his sword to the ground and said, "Thronbasa is now High Chancellor!"

They all nodded their heads with respect as Luke walked past them and into the medical center. As he entered, he put away his sword, and the others followed his example. The doors on most of the wards were closed. Thronbasa had no idea what was going on as Luke passed. In fact, she was sleeping. Luke headed right for the security wing of the hospital. As he approached the big locked door, a tall man dressed in doctor's clothing stepped out from behind a desk.

"May I help you?" the doctor said in a snobby voice.

"I'm going in to talk with Marta," Luke responded in a friendly voice.

"I'm sorry; visiting hours are over. You have to come back tomorrow at noon."

"Do you know who he is?" Selwyn insisted.

"Yes, First Lord," the doctor responded, gazing at Luke. "But I am in charge here, and I say who can come and who can go. That is my responsibility."

Luke gazed at Abi, who leaned over and whispered in his ear. Then Luke turned back to the doctor.

"You are cited for contempt. Three days in jail," Luke told him, acting like he had any idea of what he was talking about. He had no idea what "contempt" meant! He did think it was interesting how the smug expression on the doctor's face disappeared.

Abi leaned over again and whispered in Luke's ear. Then Luke turned back at the doctor and said, "Oops, sorry! That's three months in jail!" He still had no idea what Abi was talking about, but he liked the effect it was having!

The doctor sneered at Luke in frustration. He stepped out of their way, and he was not happy about it.

"I don't have the keys, and the centurion on duty is on his rounds and will not be back for at least an hour," the doctor told him.

"Don't bother about the keys," Luke told him as he walked up to the door and said, "Oscailte Cead Caite A Fhail Mo Diol!"

The door unlocked itself and opened. Luke and his friends went walking in under the sneering eye of the doctor. As they walked, Luke reached into his pocket and pulled out a little black book.

"What's that?" Abi asked.

"This is my little black book where I copied some of the spells out of your book," Luke told her.

"Out of my book?"

"What else am I supposed to do when I'm sleeping? Sit there and look at myself? I tried to be productive."

"Yeah, OK," Abi replied. "Maybe you should try asking too!"

"What?" Luke told her. "You mind?" Luke had a smile on his face.

"No! Duh! Just nice to be asked!"

"Right!"

"What are we going to do?" Selwyn asked.

"I am going to introduce you to Marta. She's a real warrior witch. You've never met anyone like her."

Within moments, Luke was looking in through the one-way mirror attached to Marta's room. He couldn't see her right away. The room was long and had many parts, and where Marta slept wasn't in front of the mirror. Luke unlocked the door and entered slowly calling Marta's name. She peered from around the corner, and when she saw Luke, her eyes and face lit up. She reached out with both arms. The tall redheaded woman lifted Luke up in a huge hug, and when she put him down again, she gave him a hug kiss. Luke's friends smiled at Marta's delight in being with Luke again.

"Finally!" Marta said as she held both her hands and looked at him. "You've lost so much weight! You're so thin! Don't they feed you?"

"Yes," Luke told her. "The food is rather good here."

"Aye, it always was, wasn't it? Look, you brought your whole crew with ya!"

"Crew?" Katie wondered.

"Aye, you four are quite famous after you took out that snake god! That was brilliant work, now, wasn't it? Let me guess; let's see. Obviously the tall, dark, and handsome one is Mr. Kidney, now, isn't he?"

Selwyn smiled and bowed to Marta.

"And let's see. This one looks like the outdoors type. I would be guessing you're the famous Katie Gardner who dashed through the Great Hole in the Wall!"

Katie smiled, and she also bowed to Marta.

"And this lovely Lady must be Miss Bishop. Abi isn't it?"

Abi smiled and nodded to Marta.

"What a lot you four are!" Marta put her arms around Luke's shoulders. "The newspapers are full with all you've been doing since last week when that dopey identity spell was broken! What kinda name is Amade anyway?"

"We improvised!" Abi said with a smile. Luke also smiled.

"Miss Marta," Katie wondered. "If you don't mind, may I ask why you are here?"

Marta sat down on a chair next to Luke. "Aye, it's a long story, now, isn't it, Katie? The short of it is I am an alcoholic, and when I drink, I go into what the doctors call a psychosis, which means I am not myself." She took Luke's hand as a tear came to one eye. "The reason I am locked up is because when this lovely boy and his uncle needed me the most, I was off bending my elbow instead of watching their backs! Justice has been done," she said with her voice breaking. "Speaking of which, where are the guards?"

"They aren't here," Selwyn told her.

Marta looked up at Luke as she wiped her eyes and asked, "Is this a jail break?"

Luke had to smile and laugh just slightly.

"No," Abi told her. "Your sentence has been commuted."

"Right," Katie agreed. "But you're restricted to the valley, and you have to finish your treatment."

"Really? Who arranged that?"

They all stared at Luke, who had a big smile on his face. He didn't say anything. Without getting up, Marta wrapped her arms around Luke and said, "Have you really forgiven me, boy?"

"I never blamed you, Marta," Luke insisted. "Neither would Uncle Martin. You keep blaming yourself, but there's no point to it."

Luke sat down next to Marta and stared at her. "I have to ask you some difficult questions, Marta. Uncle Martin is gone now. That leaves me, and I am telling you that you have to answer, OK?"

Marta replied slowly and nodded her head very slightly. She was surprised at how much the lovely, sweet boy she knew had changed. "Aye, Luke, whatever you want."

"You knew about Rajay Rama Pershard, didn't you?"

The question really surprised Marta. She took a deep breath and put her hand to her mouth. "My God, boy, how can you know that?"

"The White Robin's sire told me everything"

"You've been in P.J.'s house? Luke, we have to get you out of this valley! You're in grave danger if you know this! You all are!"

"Marta!" Luke insisted. "Who else knew about Rajay?"

Marta's shoulders dropped down, and her face became long with disappointment. "Martin knew about his children, obviously. His brothers knew. I am positive Jimmy knew."

"Aunt Claire?"

"No. I am certain she had her suspicions, but no, she never knew. Harry was too scared to tell her. He was afraid she wouldn't marry him if he did."

"How can you be sure Uncle Harry never told his own wife?"

"For the same reason Martin ordered no one ever to share what they knew! If Claire had known, Martin would have come home one day to find that she ran off with you. Also, if Claire had ever found out that the reason her husband was dead was because of Martin's lifelong stupidity, there's no telling what she might have done. Claire Cohan is a very dangerous witch!"

"Is?" Luke responded with surprise. "You mean 'was.'"

"No way," Marta responded. "No chance an army of Darksiders or some warlock, not on their best night, would have survived the sunrise if they had been stupid enough to cross swords with Claire Cohan! And your sister, I was on the receiving end of her magic, remember? She is her mother's daughter that one is! When provoked, your mother was the nastiest Alfa-Omega that had ever entered the valley!"

"Where are they?"

"That I don't know. But they didn't find any bodies. There's no way they are dead."

"I have to go," Luke said as he stood up and started to walk away.

"Go?" Marta said with a question in her voice. "Go where?"

"Rajay is heading for the Sword of Kings," Luke explained. "I'm going to get it first before he does!"

"How?"

"I am off to the Soul of the Valley. My sword will reflect the sunset and show me where to look."

Marta started laughing a little.

"What?" Luke said.

"The Soul of the Valley is in the Griffin Pass! You think the griffins are going sit around just because you show up? This isn't our valley; it belongs to them!"

"Well," Luke insisted, "they are just going to have to relax!"

"They have to, is it? They are more likely to have lunch or dinner, and you might be a little of both, but griffins don't relax!"

"I have to go!"

"And you're taking these friends with you? You're a bit cocky for a 12-year-old, aren't you?"

"They fought the snake god and won! How much worse can a griffin be?"

"Luke!" Marta shouted. "If we put the four of you together, you would be 49 years old. A 49-year-old who was highly educated, had lots of magic, and years of experience wouldn't be stupid enough to walk into the Griffin Pass!"

"Well, then, I need someone with more experience, and I need them now!"

"Right," Marta shouted. "Thronbasa isn't going anywhere soon, and the sun will be long gone before you can find anyone!"

"We already have," Abi said.

"We told you your sentence has been commuted," Katie pointed out, again.

"It doesn't look like you're all that busy anyway," Selwyn commented.

Marta stared at Luke wide-eyed. "You trickster, you! You've kissed the stone for sure! You didn't come to talk with me! You came to get me!"

Luke smiled a big smile and started to giggle slightly.

"Your mouth might be American, but your blood is as green as Ireland!" Marta shouted. "I walked right into that! You've been hanging out with those bloody leprechauns too much!"

Luke lifted his little black book and recited an incantation at Marta. Bright sparkling lights surrounded her as Marta's magic once again became centered.

"That feels good, now, doesn't it?" Marta said as she wrapped her arms around herself.

Luke reached out with his hand and summoned the charmed sword he had taken from his father's home.

"Oh, my! What a beautiful sword!" Marta said in amazement. "Where did you get that?"

"I took it out of Dad's house!"

Luke flipped the sword into the air, which surprised everyone but Marta. She caught the sword perfectly. She spun it forward in her hand and then backward. The sword was moving so fast that it was almost impossible to see. Then she switched hands and did it again! Then she threw it over her head, and finally she tossed it spinning in the air right in front of her. It was impossible to tell where the handle began and the blade ended! Marta caught it perfectly by its handle.

"Brilliant balance!" she told Luke. Then to everyone's continued amazement, Marta transfigured right in front of them. She changed into tight brown leathers and boots. Her hair had returned to a perfect shade of red, and her face didn't have a wrinkle on it. She looked brand new!

"Holy lord, she's a changeling!" Selwyn shouted.

"A what?" Katie asked.

"Someone who specializes in magic transformations. She's a shape shifter!" Abi said.

"That explains the dopey cat!" Luke blurted out.

"What cat?" Abi asked.

"And what do you mean by dopey?" Marta insisted. "It's a beautiful and lively and friendly cat!"

"Marta likes to spend her days as a cat," Luke told his friends.

"Oh," all three said at once.

"Come on!" Luke said. "If I don't find this sword before the bad guys do, we're all going to have to live our days as cats!" Luke walked out the door, and the others followed. Marta took one more look around, and then she went too, mumbling to herself, "Nothing wrong with being a cat. Don't understand what the boy's problem is."

Luke, Abi, Selwyn, and Katie walked right out past the doctor. Then Marta came out, and she stopped for a moment in front of the doctor. His gazing eye first spotted the brown leather, and as he made his way higher, he realized who it was.

"Marta?"

"Aye, Doctor Sydney!" she said with a smile.

"You look very good. I've never seen you like this."

"Aye, you've never seen me happy, have you? I've had my sentence commuted!"

"Commuted?" the doctor responded with bewilderment.

"Yes, but not to worry! Suren if I survive the day, I'll have to come back for my treatment, so I'll not be going anywhere soon!"

"Survive?"

"Aye, doctor. You need to grab a sword or your walking boots. I have a feeling things are going to be getting a little difficult really soon! I'll see ya when I see ya, and if I don't, thank you for all your help. Bye-bye!"

The doctor had a slight smile on his face when he was thanked for his help. He kept his eyes on Marta as she left. This was a side to her he had never seen before, and he was rather impressed. As Marta walked off, Luke, Abi, Selwyn, and Katie walked right out past the members of the board. They all nodded their heads to him, but Luke was annoyed with that group. He nodded back, but mostly he just kept walking.

When Marta walked out, they were all surprised. Many had presided over her case, and none had ever seen her looking like this. Marta bowed to the leadership and then kept walking after Luke.

"She's been centered," one of the older female chancellors remarked.

"We never agreed to that," the tall male chancellor insisted.

"We should go and speak with Thronbasa and make certain she knows!" yet another chancellor said.

The whole group of them walked off into the medical facility.

Luke and his friends walked out of the Citadel and over to the broom racks. Freshers were not supposed to be flying without supervision. That didn't stop Luke from raising his hand and summoning a broom to himself. The others did the same. Then Marta walked out and saw what they were doing.

"Oh, Luke," she said, "have you any idea how long it's been since I was on one of those things?"

"The sun is on the move, Marta," Luke told her. "We have to go!"

With that, Luke launched himself into the air, and Abi, Selwyn, and Katie followed.

"Bloody hell!" Marta asserted as she summoned a broom and leaped into the air. She quickly caught up to Luke and told him to slow down.

"I can't!" he shouted. The wind was too loud to hear well. "I have to get to the map!"

"You can't fly into the Griffin Pass!" Marta shouted back.

"Why?"

"Because its part of the valley's boundary! There's no magic at the borders there!"

"Oh," Luke said with a surprised look on his face. He had forgotten about that little fact. "OK, you lead the way, Marta!" Luke insisted.

In no time at all, Marta led the four to the mouth of the Griffin Pass. They all landed safely. "It's been a long time since I did that!" Marta said with a loud exhale. She laughed a bit. "It brings back a few good memories, and considering how many bad ones I have, that was truly grand!"

"What should we do with these brooms?" Katie asked.

"Just put it away like your sword or clothing trunk," Marta replied.

"You mean practitioners carry brooms and swords together?" Abi asked.

"Aye, sure, when they are here!"

"Why not everywhere?" Selwyn wondered.

"It's much easier to jump through a looking glass than to jump on a broom and avoid thunder storms, volcanoes, tornadoes, and airlines, isn't it?" Marta told them.

"That's why you're not used to flying," Luke commented.

"Aye, I had forgotten the feel of it! OK, boys and girls, this is the mouth of the pass," Marta said as she put her broom away and pointed forward. "Luke, are you really sure about this? Because as soon as the griffins spot ya, they are gonna come for ya!"

"Right," Luke agreed. "That's why everyone should stay here while I go and read the map."

"No!" Abi, Selwyn, and Katie shouted.

Marta started sniffing the air about her. "Do you all smell that?"

"Smell what?" Katie asked as they all sniffed the air.

"I think someone is burning a martyr nearby!"

Everyone laughed but Luke.

"Oh, ha, ha, ha," Luke told her. "Real funny, but I'm no martyr!"

"Right, so stop acting like one! If you are going to lead, Luke, do it with your head, not your emotions. You see on the far wall of the pass there where I'm pointing? That's your cave. It doesn't look far away, but the face of the pass there is huge. So it's much farther than it looks—at least five miles and those griffins can smell blood 10 miles off!"

"Right," Luke said as he understood and turned to his friends. "This is what we do: we don't run from the griffins. No matter what, don't run. Keep walking, and no matter how aggressive they seem, just ignore them and keep walking! They are going to be confused by individuals wearing these cloaks in their pass. These uniforms are considered friendly to them. If they come toward you, split up in two different directions, and then come together and split again. Stay among the trees. The griffins are too large for woodland. To keep them off of our backs, we need only keep surprising them. We don't have to hurt them to do that. Simple, abrupt moves are all it takes. If they get too close, then give them a quick swipe from your sword to startle them. Then keep walking like nothing happened. And no talking!"

"How do you know all of this?" Selwyn insisted.

"Griffins are basically big flying cats," Marta told him. "Luke is an expert on cats! He's been surrounded by them constantly since he was a baby!"

"And they never left me alone until I came here!" Luke added.

"That makes sense!" Selwyn replied.

The group drew their swords, and into the Griffin Pass the five of them went.

At the medical center, the board members and the First Caldron gathered around the sleeping Thronbasa. She opened her eyes and realized she was encircled.

"Hmm," Thronbasa commented. "I didn't know it was

visiting hours. To what do I owe the honor of such a majestic visit of the honorable Board of Trustees?"

Thronbasa pushed a button, and the back of her bed began to lift her up a little. At first they said nothing. Thronbasa thought it was an odd situation.

"Lillian," Thronbasa addressed one of the chancellors. "Why are you here?"

"It's about the First Lord, Elizabeth!"

"What about him?"

"He's made you High Chancellor!" one of the men told her.

"First," Lillian continued, "at lunch time, he made you our newest chancellor because we asked him to. Then he and those friends of his that follow him everywhere went and visited his family home!"

"Luke went into P.J.'s house?" Thronbasa was surprised by this.

"Yes," one of the men added. "Then he came out, threatened to vaporize Dickelbee, made him surrender his sword, and then threw him out. Sent six self-appointed centurions with Dickelbee to watch him pack and leave!"

"Oh, my God!" Thronbasa said as she began to sit up.

"Elizabeth, you shouldn't be getting up!"

"I have a bad headache, Lillian, but I would rather have a sore head than be dead!"

"Dead? Why?"

"Mason!" Thronbasa said as she quickly changed the subject.

"Yes, my Lady!" the tall chancellor answered.

Thronbasa looked up at him with surprise. No one had ever addressed her as "Lady" before.

"You know who I am?"

"I guessed, my Lady! There had to be some reason why the boy promoted you twice in one day."

"Who are you, Elizabeth?" Lillian asked.

"I'm Claire Cohan's sister."

"Why did you keep this a secret?" another chancellor asked.

"When I first came to America, blacks were still second class here. The brother of the White Robin was courting my sister. I didn't want to interfere with that. The American Realm wasn't ready for a black first Lady then."

"Well, we damn well are now!" Mason told her. Several of the other chancellors said, "Yes! And we have been for a while!"

"Mason," Thronbasa cut them off. "How many Alfa-Omegas are in the valley?"

"A little over 60, maybe. There are 24 who have duty and 12 that are on duty."

"Summon six of them and lead them off to find Dickelbee. If those students Luke sent with him are still alive, bring them here for treatment! Send all the rest to me!"

"Yes, my Lady!"

"Elizabeth!" Lillian insisted. "What is going on?"

"Don't you get it?" Thronbasa told her as she stepped behind a curtain to dress. "Luke discovered something! I don't know what. Whatever it is has to do with the Darkside, or he would never have drawn his sword! He identified Dickelbee, the chief officer of the Realm! For him to be involved with the Darkside requires some kind of conspiracy. Luke knows what it is! He went into his father's house, he kicked over some proverbial rock there, and black snakes were hiding under it! Now they are going to come racing out to protect whatever the conspiracy is all about!"

"Oh, my God!" Lillian said with a gasp.

"Fiona!" Thronbasa said.

"Yes, my Lady!"

"Go to the training grounds! Have the upperclassmen and the Freshers form ranks!"

"Form ranks, my Lady? They are all 12-year-olds!"

"I know that, thank you! Go!"

"Yes, my Lady!"

"Lillian!"

"Yes, Elizabeth?"

"I want anyone who cannot carry a sword out of the valley before sunset, understand? That means no children in the valley at sunset!"

"Yes, my Lady. I'll see to it!"

"Everyone else, go and find every practitioner in the valley! Then form ranks on the main parade ground in one hour!"

They all said, "Yes, my Lady!"

Luke and his friends were doing rather well making their way across the Griffin Pass. They had been following the edge of the woodland and had made it more than halfway. There was a clear straight line to the opening of the cave. Luke also noted that so long as they all stayed in the middle of the pass, his and Marta's swords glowed and hummed normally. It was only when they approached the cliff walls of the pass that they fell silent and didn't glow.

They finally reached the eastern edge of the pass where there was a last clearing before the cave. Well, it wasn't exactly clear. It was full of large boulders that had fallen off of the cliff face. Luke stopped and looked around. Then he whispered, "I don't understand this. Where are they?"

"It's almost sunset," Marta whispered back. "They usually hunt at sunrise and sunset on the other side of the valley. If we are to make our way through the clearing, I suggest one at a time because if they come, the others can distract them while you have a look at the map."

Everyone nodded his or her head in agreement. Luke stood up and began to make his way across the opening toward the cave entrance. A kangaroo came flying past him! It was acting as if it were being chased. Then another roo came and another, all in a big hurry to get someplace other than where they were. Luke kept walking toward the cave. He had taken only a few steps before he heard growling noises. A great shadow appeared over him. It was obvious he was in deep doo doo. But he kept walking like nothing was there.

His friends watched as the powerful griffin observed Luke walking. The creature growled louder, perhaps thinking it had yet to be noticed. But true to his plan, Luke just kept ignoring the creature. He acted as if he was in the middle of the valley and there was nothing to worry about. Unfortunately, the creature's noises drew the attention of more of its own kind. They started landing around the area where Luke was walking. He had almost reached the cave when he vanished behind one of the larger boulders. He was completely out of sight of the griffins. They all just stood there waiting for him to come out, but he didn't.

Marta whispered to the others, and they split up in two directions and moved along the tree line. To make sure they were noticed, they let their swords scrape along the ground. The griffins turned around and started moving toward them. The distraction had worked. Everyone was walking, not running, and acting as if nothing unusual was going on. This had the griffins looking at one another wondering what was going on. As Luke had predicted, the creatures didn't see the cloaks they were wearing as hostile, so they didn't view the people wearing them as threats of any kind.

Peering from around the rock he was hiding behind, Luke saw the others make their distractions. So, with as little noise as possible, he made his way up into the cave. The light from the sun had gone yellow as it sank to the horizon. It was nearly already shining into the cave.

Luke stepped into what seemed to him to be a living rainbow. The light of the sun reflecting in the cave bounced off of the walls and created an endless volume of sparkling colors. It was as if colored lights surrounded him. He looked at his hands, and even they were reflecting light. He was completely enchanted by the experience. He hadn't expected it and couldn't help but smile as he looked around the cave.

Outside, Marta and Katie had gone north and Abi and Selwyn south along the tree line. They kept walking like nothing was going on. The griffins were clearly as confused by this activity as Luke had expected. A couple of griffins stepped into Selwyn's and Abi's path. Then the two made an abrupt about-face and kept walking like nothing had happened. The same happened with Marta and Katie. But when one griffin dropped its talon right next to Katie, she gave it a poke with her sword. This surprised the griffin, and the creature backed off with a shocked look on its face!

Luke moved toward the center of the cave. He was drawn there by soft blue light. When he looked over the edge of a rock to see what its source might be, his eyes became very wide. There, in an impression on the floor of the cave was the Soul of the Valley. It wasn't just a map. It was a complete and time-accurate reflection of the valley and the people and creatures in it.

Luke could see the Freshers forming ranks and moving off to the main parade grounds. He could see the practitioners gathering there. He could see large groups moving out through the Great Hole in the Wall. He could see the beasts on the far northern highland. This area was heavily populated with creatures the world thought were long gone and extinct. He could also see Marta and the others distracting the griffins outside. At the far edge of the map, where the end of the Griffin Pass should be, stood what looked like a shadow burned into the rock of the cave. It was of a person holding a sword above his head and pointed upward. It was obvious from the map that the sun was about to hit the horizon.

Luke climbed up and onto that rock. He raised the sword above his head just like in the shadow. The light from the sun came to the horizon and filled the area surrounding the map. The shadow in the wall turned to gold, and spirits taking the form of wisps of moving smoke revealed themselves. They sang a song like monks in a cathedral. Luke couldn't understand it. They circled and examined Luke, perhaps trying to understand why he was there. Then they gathered in front of him and bowed to him as the sun struck his sword and projected into the map.

There on the map, on the far side of the valley, nearly to the top of the high, flat ground, was a sword sticking out of a very large stone on a cliff. It was invisible until the light from Luke's sword revealed its location. Then the light was gone! The ceiling over the map changed to a star-filled night with all the constellations in the heavens revealed. "It is so brilliant to look at," Luke thought to himself. His amazement was cut short by the sound of a single pair of clapping hands.

"Well done!" a voice said. Out of the shadows stepped Mr. Pershard. "I must say I am truly impressed with the way you got past those griffins out there."

"Hello, Rajay. I was wondering when you would show up again."

"You know who I am?"

"Yes, cousin, I know who you are and what you are!"

"It's a shame, really. Under different circumstances, we could have been family—even brothers—but there can be only one, and that's not you!" Rajay told him.

"That's not the biggest shame."

"No?" Rajay wondered.

"Nope. The biggest shame is that had I known about you six weeks ago, I would have walked into this valley and given you this sword. I would have walked out again, and neither you nor anyone else would have heard from me ever again!"

"That is a pity. Perhaps had you not changed your identity, it might have happened!"

"If he hadn't changed identity," a new female voice from behind Luke announced, "you would have had him murdered by now!"

A girl with sword in hand stepped out of the shadows. She was from India, like Rajay. In fact, she looked a lot like Rajay!

"Hello, Luke," the girl said as she bowed to him. "I've been waiting a long time to meet you."

"Really?" Luke replied. "How long?"

"Most of my life," she told him.

"Magda!" Rajay shouted. "What are you doing up there?"

"I am taking sides, Rajay! Until this moment, I had the luxury of not having to choose! Now time is up!"

"You are taking sides with that abomination? Against your own brother and your house?"

"No Robin of my house, not Rama Pershard or Cohan, would have made a pact with a devil! Certainly not someone who claims to be heir to the throne of the White Robin! No one who calls himself my brother would either. Luke is my only brother now. You can go to hell, Rajay! You're going to wind up there sooner or later anyway!"

"Maybe you should just leave, Rajay," Luke told him. "No one seems to believe in you."

"I still have believers, Luke. I think you have already met one of my stronger supporters."

Rajay lifted his hand and pointed toward the other side of the cave. Out of the shadows stepped the warlock that had attacked Sugarloaf. There again stood the blood-red eyes, the sharp pointed teeth, and the very vision of what evil meant. Luke went down in pain on one knee and supported himself using his sword. The shock of seeing the creature again made him physically ill.

"Ah, yes, I see you remember him!" Rajay said with delight in his voice.

"I remember it! That's the thing that helped murder your father!"

"My father was a self-serving coward and a disgrace!"

"You should have showed up in Sugarloaf!" Luke responded. "No one would have dared call him coward to his face. They would have quickly learned how good a person he was and how much time had changed him. He was no coward! But you wouldn't know that, would you? Too scared to face him yourself, Rajay? Couldn't do your own dirty work? Had to have something else do it for you?"

"I am a Robin! Why soil my hands when I have such willing supporters to handle it?"

Then the warlock made a hissing sound, and the chanting that Luke had heard the night of the Sugarloaf battle began all around him and Magda. Within moments, Darksiders dressed in red cloaks stepped out of the shadows. Luke was surrounded!

Outside, everyone turned toward the sound coming from the cave. Even the griffins knew that sound. One of them roared, which forced Marta and Luke's friends to cover their ears.

"What was that?" Luke asked Magda.

"Griffins! They can hear the chanting!"

"That was a griffin?"

"Yes! I can't believe you just walked in here past them," Magda told him as she looked around. "I hope they trained you how to fight this summer because there's no magic to help us inside this cave!"

"Not to worry! I learned to fight years before I knew any magic! I am going to make my way to the exit."

"Right!" she agreed.

But just as they began to move toward the exit, two huge rocks came crashing down in front of them!

"Rajay!" Magda shouted. "Stop it! You've lost!"

Luke glared at her in total surprise. "I thought there was no magic in here!"

"There isn't!" Magda told him. "Rajay is a powerful levitator! It's a body power, not a magical one!"

"Right!" Luke shouted. "Why can't I remember that?"

Luke focused his mind and lifted one of the huge rocks and sent it flying at Rajay. He lifted the other and sent it flying at the warlock! Then he took one look at the Darksiders blocking his way and sent them flying in every direction!

"Run!" Luke shouted.

Luke and Magda came running out of the cave. Luke told her to stop and not to run at the griffins. He told her to walk and not look at them. The two slowed down, and the griffins that had gathered outside of the cave were confused by this behavior. But then the Darksiders came running out of the cave after Luke, and again he shouted, "Run!"

As they ran, the griffin closest to Luke let loose with another roar! The sound brought the Darksiders to their knees, but it forced Luke and Magda to the ground as they held their ears. Luke found the noise so painful that when the creature finally stopped, he leaped up and began shouting at the griffin!

"Will you cut that out, you big noisy rug? Do you have any idea how much that hurts?"

Luke was pointing his sword at the griffin with anger.

"Luke!" Magda shouted with a surprised look on her face. "What are you doing?"

Luke turned to her, looked around, grabbed her by the hand, and said, "Come on!"

The two ran past the griffins, whose attention was completely focused on the red robes of the Darksiders. They ran right past all the boulders and right into the woodland. When Luke reached his friends, he stopped.

"Guys," Luke told them. "This is Magda! Magda this is—"

Magda cut him off and said, "Selwyn Kidney, Katie Gardner, Abi Bishop, and hello, Marta! You are looking very different from the last time I saw you!"

"You two know each other?" Luke said.

"Aye!" Marta replied. "Magda is the kindest nurse in the medical center!"

"No time for talk!" Luke insisted. "Girls pick the dumbest times for a conversation!" he thought.

The group ran off toward the middle of the pass. Marta shouted and demanded to know where they were going. Luke told her that they needed only to get to the middle of the pass. Once their swords started glowing, they could switch to brooms and leap out of the pass.

In no time at all, Luke's and Marta's swords began to glow. They put away their swords and summoned brooms. Luke told Selwyn to head for the main parade ground where he knew from the map that the valley's practitioners were gathering.

"Tell who's ever in charge that I know where the Sword of Kings is and that I am heading for the northeast corner of the valley," Luke explained to Selwyn.

They all leaped on to their brooms and up into the air. When they cleared the pass, Selwyn broke off and headed toward the parade grounds. The rest of the group followed Luke north. The valley was quite long. Even on fast brooms, it was going to take a while to get to where he wanted to go. To make matters worse, the sun was down, and while it was still bright, there was little light left. Luke thought things were going to get bad if he didn't get to the north side before all of the light was gone. As it turned out, he didn't have to wait that long because now a number of upperclassmen, riding what looked like flying snow boards, started closing in on him and the others. These were the upperclassmen who had attacked in the woods the day before the snake came after him.

"Hello, Lord Carter! Long time no see!" the lead boy shouted at him.

Luke ignored him, so he shouted again.

"You know, you can't fly a broom and draw a sword! At these speeds, you have to balance yourself really well or you'll crash!" The boy laughed at him.

Marta and Magda swung out to try and knock the upper-classmen off of their boards, but the boards had been developed for speed and maneuverability, and the brooms were Old World technology. They couldn't compete! So when the upperclassmen drew their swords, Luke and the others were sitting ducks. They couldn't draw their swords without losing balance!

The upperclassmen came flying in on top of them as they swung their swords. Luke and the others moved out of their range just in time! Luke kept trying to focus his mind on them, but every time he did, he started losing control of the broom. Then the upperclassmen started firing bolts of energy at them! All they could do was maneuver to avoid the shots. Finally, Luke shouted, "Follow me!"

Luke dived into the trees. Marta shouted that he had gone mad! But now the upperclassmen were having trouble targeting them. The new problem was one bad move and everyone was going into a tree.

Diving, jumping, and shifting from side to side, Luke and his friends did everything they could think of to keep from flying into the trees. But the boards the bad guys were using were more maneuverable, and even in the tree line, they started to catch up! They fired again and again at Luke! The others were being chased as well. Then after one really bad move, Luke hit a tree limb! He and his broom went crashing to the ground.

Luke rolled over onto his back. "That hurt!" he said to himself. Then he heard the upperclassmen coming back at him. He jumped up and started to head for his broom on the ground nearby, but it was too late! The upperclassman was already charging him. The boy drew back his sword to strike, but just as he did Luke summoned the Sword of Princes. As the boy swung his sword, it shattered into pieces! As he passed, Luke turned and launched a bolt of power. It hit the boy, and he was instantly reduced to dust! Then two others charged Luke, but before they could swing, Luke fired on them! They were all dusted.

Luke started heading for his broom again. He thought he might be safe now, but he was wrong! All the snakes on the ground in the forest began to transform into Darksiders wearing red cloaks!

"Damn!" Luke said. "They're like fleas that jump at ya!"

Luke put his sword away, but before he reached for his broom, he concentrated on the Darksiders, and with a wave of his hand, he sent most of them crashing to the ground. He jumped onto his broom and leaped into the air. As he flew over the tree tops, Katie spotted him and shouted, "There he is!"

Luke headed north right away, and the others caught up as best they could. Below him he could see snakes transforming into Darksiders. At first there were dozens, and then hundreds, and then Luke realized that an army was forming below him!

The group broke north of the tree line and into a clearing and headed for the northeastern rock face of the valley. Marta shouted, "Don't get too close to those eastern rocks! They are part of the boundary! There's no magic there!"

But it was too late. The brooms lost lift, and the group started crashing to the ground. Abi and Katie screamed, and Luke instructed, "Levitate!"

Everyone levitated safely to the ground, and Luke shouted, "Come on! We have to start climbing that rock face!"

"No!" Marta insisted. "We have to go back to the magic zone! We have to get rid of these brooms and summon our swords! We can't climb unarmed!"

"Damn!" Luke shouted as he started running back toward the trees.

As soon as they got back in the magic zone, they put away their brooms and summoned their weapons. But as they did, several dozen Darksiders came charging out at them from the forest. Marta started rubbing her sword a little, and then when she swung it, instead of a bolt discharge, she sent a flat line of energy at the Darksiders. The entire line of attackers went crashing back into the woodland! Unfortunately, the discharge also sparked a fire.

Luke turned and ran for the rock face. The others kept up as best they could. Now, dropping down out of the sky, came hundreds of practitioners led by Selwyn and Thronbasa! Thronbasa could see Luke and his group running for the rock face, but she didn't follow. As soon as everyone landed, she shouted, "Form ranks!"

The practitioners, along with well over a thousand Freshers, began to form for a fight facing the woodland.

It was dark now, but the fire Marta had started in the woodland was making more than enough light to see what was going on. Luke located the steps cut into the rock face next to a small cave. As he headed in to start climbing, Darksiders came charging out of the cave. Just like he did every morning since he was 4 years old, Luke struck the first pose of the dance. He didn't have any magic to fight with, but he knew how to fight!

When the Darksiders got close enough, he reached out with his mind and sent a few boulders crashing down. They sealed the cave behind them. He tried to use his mind to send the dark ones flying out of his way, but they blocked him. Then he began to swing his sword. The Darksiders didn't have a chance! Luke cut them to pieces, and soon Marta and Magda were doing the same! Abi and Katie swung at them when the others distracted them. But Abi and Katie were also doing a lot of screaming!

Through the woodland fire, hundreds of Darksiders began to move out to attack the waiting members of the Realm. Thronbasa shouted, "OK, listen! There is no place to run. The only thing behind us is rock! Stay tight together. Fire your swords in tight team formation! Don't break the ranks! So long as there is no place for them to pass through, they cannot get to the First Lord! It is our job tonight to make certain that they do not get the Sword of Kings!"

Now, from the burning woodland emerged the evil warlock! Many of the practitioners and students gasped in shock. They had never seen anything so hideous! He led thousands of Darksiders onto the field of battle. Thronbasa yelled, "Present arms!" Everyone raised his or her sword and made ready to launch energy at the attacking Darksiders. But just before Thronbasa yelled "Fire!" the warlock drew his wand and launched a barrier of energy right through the middle of the field! When the members of the Realm fired bolts of energy, they hit the barrier and went nowhere! Several of the Alfa-Omegas launched their best shots, but they couldn't bring the barrier down.

Luke and his friends were by now climbing the rock face and were making steps toward the stone in which the Sword of Kings was impaled. They could see what was happening below, and it didn't look good! But there wasn't anything they could do!

Down below, Thronbasa said, "When they come through that barrier, they are going to be very close! Concentrate your fire! Keep it up! Darksiders are weak! Their only advantage is their numbers! If you concentrate your fire and don't break ranks, we will defeat them!"

Rajay arrived at the bottom of the rock face. He could see that Luke and his friends were nearly to the top. He pulled from beneath his ropes the Egyptian Black Book of Shadows. He opened its pages and began to chant. Within moments, five giant snakes leaped from its pages. Hissing, and with their tongues darting out and targeting their prey, the evil creatures began to slither their way up the rock face and toward Luke and his friends.

The Darksiders began to pass through the warlock's barrier that had protected them. The fight was on! Members of the Realm stood shoulder to shoulder as they launched one barrage after another at the Darksiders. Hundreds of them dropped to the ground. The ones hit by the most powerful witches, the Alfa-Omegas, were reduced to dust. But there were too many! The Darksiders launched bolts of energy at the lines of practitioners. The lines began to fall! One after another, members of the Realm dropped to the ground and were unable to continue the fight.

From high above, Luke could see what was happening, but he was powerless to do anything! Finally they reached the high ground. Just when they thought the way was clear, five giant snakes jumped out in front of them!

"Oh, crap! Where the hell did they come from?" Luke shouted.

The snakes were incredibly fast! No one could swing fast enough to strike one. But the snakes couldn't get close enough to bite! It was a stalemate, and now closing from behind was Rajay and several of his friends!

"We have to charge them!" Magda yelled. "If we charge them, we can distract them long enough for Luke to get past them! Snakes hate surprises!"

"Right!" everyone agreed. They charged forward, swinging their swords as they went. Sure enough, a small hole in their defense appeared, and Luke ran through it.

He went so fast that he did see one of the snakes bite into Abi. The snake just backed off. The deed was done. Abi stood in shock for a moment as she dropped her sword. Then down onto her knees she went! She tried to shout Luke's name but only managed to whisper it before she fell limp on the ground. Then a snake bit into Katie and backed away! Katie looked at the bite for a moment, dropped her sword, and then fell limp on the ground.

Below, the fighting was going badly for the members of the Realm. They were nearly half of what they started with, and those who remained were becoming too tired to continue discharging energy. Thronbasa shouted and shouted, "Keep up your fire!" But it was useless. There were just too many Darksiders!

Up on the rock face, Luke finally reached the sword. Even in near darkness, lit only by the reflecting fire, Luke could tell the sword was beautiful. He was stunned. He had never seen anything like it. As he approached, the sword began to glow white. Then he reached out and wrapped his hand around its handle, and it began to glow a bright white. Suddenly, there was a tremendous thud! A feeling of numbness came over Luke as he look down and saw the head of a sword sticking out of his left side. Then it was abruptly pulled out, and the world went black for Luke as he crashed to the ground.

There standing over him from behind was Elizabeth Cole, the former chancellor. Her sword was stained with Luke's blood. Magda arrived and screamed as she charged Cole. She swung her sword again and again, but Magda had been fighting the snakes, and she was tired. Cole wasn't. With just a few well-placed moves, Cole's sword went flying into

Magda's stomach. The pain stunned Magda as Cole pulled it out. She dropped onto the rock face.

Below, Thronbasa ordered everyone who was left to retreat into the no magic zone. She would try to fight them hand to hand without power.

On the rock face, Rajay arrived. He saw his sister lying there. He had a painful expression on his face when he looked over at Cole.

"I'm sorry, Mr. Pershard," Cole told him as he knelt down next to his sister. "But she charged me, and I had no choice!"

"That's all right, chancellor," Rajay told her slowly and sadly. "She turned into traitor anyway! I never saw it coming. I always thought she would be there for me. But it was all a lie!"

Rajay stood up and walked over to where Luke was lying on the ground. He saw the sword and was just as impressed as Luke had been. As he approached, it didn't glow at all. He reached over and was able to pull the sword from the stone. He held it up and said, "Finally, after all these years, I have what was always supposed to be mine!"

He turned to show Cole as Cole's sword came flying into his neck. His head went flying off, out, and over the cliff! His body stood there a moment, and he continued to hold the sword. Then the sword dropped down by Luke's side, and Rajay's body fell the other way!

"Finally!" Cole said out loud. "Finally, the natural line is dead! No more boys to be born to subjugate the rest of us! Now we make our own government and live as equals!"

There was no sign of Marta or Abi or Katie. Below, the practitioners fought the Darkside sword to sword. There were very few left. The dark warlock watched in eager anticipation of the final blow being struck.

Cole walked over by Luke and reached down to pick up the Sword of Kings. She couldn't lift it! She dropped her sword and tried to use two hands to lift it. It could not be moved.

"You can't lift it," Luke whispered to her. "The sire had but one set of wings she could give. She had to make the best decision she could. She didn't choose you!"

Cole spoke with surprise as she went to pick up her own sword again. "That's too bad, Mr. Amade! She made a terrible mistake, and now I am going to make it right!"

Cole raised her sword to strike Luke, but as she reached high, a sword tip came flying through her heart on a downward angle. Magda, kneeling on the ground behind her, made her last move!

Cole turned and saw who it was and said, "Stupid bitch! You've condemned us!" She collapsed onto the ground, and then Magda collapsed.

Luke stared at the sword. Behind it, a ghostly figure of a woman appeared.

"Hello, boy!"

Luke saw in the aberration a familiar face. But he wasn't sure it was real.

"Mama?"

The woman nodded her head yes with a bright, brilliant smile.

"Have you come for me?"

"No, Luke," she told him. "It's not your time!"

"I'm hurt, Mama!" Luke told her with tears in his eyes. "I've never tried to hurt anyone, but people keep trying to hurt me!"

"I know, baby," she said as tears rolled down her cheeks. "It wasn't supposed to be this way. Your father was supposed to bare the burdens until you were old enough. But we were surprised, and now you are left with all this pain. I'm so sorry, Luke!"

"What do I do, Mama?"

"You have to finish what you started, boy! Pick up your sword, Luke! Pick it up!"

The woman disappeared. Luke struggled toward the sword. The closer he got, the brighter the sword became. Finally he wrapped his hands around it, and Luke began to glow white. The light consumed his whole body! The pain went away, and so too did his wound and blood. The light from Luke shined on Magda, and she too began to recover. All of her wounds disappeared.

Below, the fighting stopped. The bright light from above could be seen by all. Then Luke stepped out onto the cliff's edge. Like a lighthouse with the power of the sun, the glow from Luke and the Sword of Kings turned night into day.

The dark warlock screamed in pain as he burst into flames. All of the Darksiders began to burn. All of the practitioners began to recover and stand up.

Everyone turned to the light. The soul of the First Lord of the Realm had been revealed, and against this gift from God, no Darksider could survive! Luke had fulfilled his destiny!

As the Darksiders burned beneath them, what was revealed after the smoke cleared were the bodies of the people who had either turned or who were the victims of the Darkside. Luke, Magda, Abi, Katie, and Marta safely climbed down off of the mountain face. When he was finally convinced that there was no more danger, Luke, whose sword was so bright no one could look at him, put the sword away.

There, standing on the last battlefield of the Realm, and without the bright light shining, everyone began to approach Luke and hug him. Each hug was said with a thank you, and most had tears in their eyes for having survived the battle. Off in the distance, Thronbasa stood over the body that was once the warlock's. Luke and his friends approached. As they got close, the identity of the man on the ground was clear. It was Dickelbee!

"We won," Luke said to his Aunt Elizabeth. She turned and hugged and lifted Luke into the air. She then hugged Abi, Magda, Marta, Katie, and Selwyn. It was grand to be alive, and Thronbasa wanted everyone to know it!

The group looked down at Dickelbee in total disbelief.

"How far the mighty have fallen," Marta remarked.

"This is very strange," Thronbasa said.

"Why?" Luke asked.

"He wasn't in the valley during the first attack 12 years ago. It doesn't make sense!"

"He's not English either," Magda said. "The Dark Lord who started all this was from England."

Luke spied the warlock's wand and approached it.

"Careful, Luke," Thronbasa said.

Luke stared at the wand for a moment, and then he stepped on it and crushed it. Unfortunately, the parts left began to glow! Then thunder could be heard and then more thunder and a strike of lightening!

"Damn it, Luke! I said be careful!"

Luke started to back away. He also made a promise to listen first and act second. What was left of the wand began to get hot. Then discharges of energy fired from it. Sprits appeared as wisps of white smoke, and others appeared as wisps of red smoke. They heard the sounds of angels mixed with the hideous sounds of demons. Everyone was frozen, not understanding what was happening. The red and white sprits fought with one another as the ground trembled and lighting struck again and again. Then there was an eerie silence. Doors of energy spontaneously formed, and out of those doors, human bodies began to fall. Live but very naked human bodies began to fall! Most of the people no one recognized. But then they spotted the faces of Claire and Laura! What a surprise and a very happy sight! Thronbasa ran to her sister Claire. Luke ran to Laura. They took off their cloaks and wrapped them around them. What had been one of the most horrible days of Luke's life turned to celebration. The skies cleared. It was all over!

THE FIRST LORD OF THE REALM RETURN OF THE SWORD OF KINGS

CHAPTER 22

MANY DAYS HAD gone by since the battle was over. To Luke, it now seemed like just another bad dream. He stood on the roof of the Citadel and stared at the sky. In the southwest, a full moon was moving below the horizon. It was a brilliant sight. In the east, the first hints of sunrise could be seen from behind the mountains. Like tiny spotlights, beams of sunrise broke across the horizon, while stars could still be seen twinkling behind them.

"What am I doing here?" Luke wondered as the scene dazzled his mind. "What else is there that someone hasn't yet explained to me that I am supposed to know yet decided I am not old enough to know?"

The sight of his mother coming to his rescue was something that Luke couldn't get out of his mind. "To have found me when I needed her most must mean she is watching," Luke thought.

The sky grew bright as the animals of the woodlands moved out to feed in the fields. In the small town below, farmers could be seen tending their herds. Life was going on, and Luke could not help but wonder how different this day in the valley might have been, how different it would have been if they had not won the battle. It all seemed a bit too much, really.

"All in all," Luke thought, "I'd rather be in Sugarloaf!"

Luke moved back inside. The hallways were lit with a brilliant rainbow of colors as the sunrise shone through the tall old tinted windows. All the portraits on the wall nodded their heads to Luke as he passed by. He wasn't in a hurry. The rainbow of colors dazzled him, and there was something very friendly and comfortable about the light that made its way onto his face in the mornings. It reminded him of Sugarloaf. He strolled slowly toward his family's home in the Citadel. Luke even took the time to read some of the captions of the portraits of the people on the walls. Some of them were hundreds of years old. All of the portraits waited on the possibility that Luke might address them. It was a kind of contest between the former members of the Realm. But Luke had already learned his lesson. He wasn't talking to the old people on the walls unless he had to.

As he made his way toward his house, he could see in the distance that Elizabeth Thronbasa was standing in front of his grandfather's portrait. By the movement of her arms and her body language, Luke could tell she was having a very serious conversation of some kind. He could hear the old man consoling her, but he didn't know why. "I shouldn't listen in," Luke thought, "but there are lots of things I should not be doing, and I wind up doing them anyway."

"I have to tell Luke that I cannot be the High Chancellor, grandfather," Elizabeth told the old lord. "Laura and Magda are first ladies by birth. I am only by marriage, and it's my sister's marriage that connects me to the first family, not my own marriage! The White Robin's brother was my brother-in-law. My sister married a prince of the Realm, not me! Claire is 10 times the witch I am! Laura is a fully consecrated master of the elements! Magda soon will be! It's just a matter of months. I cannot run things here with people who have more authority than me by birth. They will be second-guessing my every decision. And I have a family to take care of. I don't have the time to be the person in charge. Marcus is proud that I am now High Chancellor, but my oldest is just 7 years. How can I give my family the time they need if I am in charge?"

"I understand," the old man in the picture told her. "But we do not choose these events in our lives; they choose us, Elizabeth."

"Luke chose me because he had no one else to choose from. Now he has some of the most powerful witches who have ever lived to choose from. No one will question their decisions. Certainly they wouldn't question Laura's decisions, and if they did, they would do it just once. As God is my witness, that girl possesses the same personality as her mother!"

"Elizabeth, those superpower witches didn't win their battles against the Darkside; you did! I really can't see Luke changing his mind."

"You've got that right," Luke said as he stepped into his grandfather's view, crossed his arms in front of him, and leaned up against the granite wall.

The old man had a look of concern come over his face. The change was enough that Thronbasa noticed.

"What's wrong?" Thronbasa insisted.

At first, the old man said nothing. Obviously Thronbasa could neither see nor hear Luke, so his presence was a secret.

"Tell her," Luke said to his grandfather. "Tell her I didn't choose her. Tell her my father chose her."

"Luke didn't choose you, Elizabeth."

"What?" she responded with surprise and bewilderment.

"Philo John chose you," the old man continued.

"That's impossible, grandfather! P.J. never even knew I existed! I made certain of that! To protect Claire!"

"If my dad could walk around like I am now, there's no way he didn't know!" Luke told his grandfather.

"Philo John was a soul walker, Elizabeth," the old man explained. "If he said nothing, it was because he respected your decision to remain anonymous and almost certainly because he loved his brother and Claire. I know for a fact that he admired Claire. You two have nearly the same personalities. I am sure he saw the same qualities in you."

"But he said nothing? I can't believe it, grandfather! You're making this up to encourage me!"

"Tell her if she doesn't believe to go down to the house and walk through the barrier and command the door to open. There's just no way my dad didn't know everything about her!" Luke insisted.

"If you don't believe me, then put my word to the test," the old man said.

"Test?" Thronbasa said with bewilderment again. "What test?"

"If what I say isn't true, then you will not be able to pass through the barrier and command the door to the family home to open."

Thronbasa stared at the old man with surprise but said nothing.

"Go on with ya! Give it a try if you don't believe," the old man insisted.

"If you're telling me this, you're telling a secret, grandfather! You can't do that!"

"Don't worry, Elizabeth. As I understand it, I am to be the subject of a bonfire anyway!"

"Luke would never do that!" Thronbasa insisted.

"Oh, yes, I would!" Luke interjected.

"He just blames you for Martin," Thronbasa insisted.

"That much is true!" Luke agreed.

"Go on with ya," the old man told her. "See whether I am right!"

Thronbasa walked slowly off down the hall with a sense of wonder on her face. She wasn't sure what was going to happen. When he thought she was far enough away that she couldn't hear him whispering, the old man said to Luke, "So, when is my fiery demise scheduled?"

Luke thought for a moment. "I understand that when the sports season starts up here, the tailgate parties include a large bonfire that everyone dances around. I figured I would wait until then! That way everyone could share in my revenge!"

Then Luke lifted the picture off of the wall and followed Thronbasa.

"Just a minute, boy!" the old man insisted.

Luke ignored him and kept walking.

"Luke!" the old man said again and again. When he realized Luke wasn't going to pay attention, he sat back in his chair and mumbled to himself, "What the bloody hell is a tailgate party?"

Thronbasa stepped to the edge of the magical barrier and moved her hand through it. Her face lit up with wonderment as to how much P.J. had really known. Only those who he considered family could pass through the barrier. Luke knew she could do it. He stood behind her with a big smile and took delight in his Aunt Elizabeth's amazement. Thronbasa stepped through the barrier and commanded the door to open. She almost cried when it did. She raised her hand to her mouth as she slowly stepped through the door.

She moved through the corridor and was possessed by complete amazement as she first stepped into the main great hall. She looked around, and Luke could only smile with delight at his aunt's happiness. They both noticed two female voices, and Thronbasa walked toward them and into a kitchen that was brightly lit by the morning sun. At the table, reading newspapers and talking, were Claire and Laura.

Thronbasa moved into view as Claire said, "Good morning, Elizabeth! Did you sleep well?"

"Good morning, Aunt Elizabeth," Laura said with a smile.

"Yes, I slept well, I suppose," she responded as she leaned over and first kissed Claire good morning and then Laura.

Neither Laura nor Claire was surprised to see her.

"How about some breakfast?" Claire asked Thronbasa.

"No, but, perhaps a cup of Earl Gray tea would be nice!"

Thronbasa had no sooner finished asking for tea when it appeared right in front of her.

"My goodness!" she said. "Isn't that leisurely?" Thronbasa had to laugh just a little.

"This is Daddy's breakfast table," Laura explained with a smile. "One of his favorite caldrons in County Antrim gave it to him as a wedding present!"

"Let's hear it for the Irish!" Thronbasa said with a smile and surprise. "Can we ask for anything, or is it just tea?"

"Anything your heart desires in the way of food and drink, and when you're done, it cleans everything off itself!" Laura said.

"Amazing! The perfect home product for any woman with a career and family! How about some warm fresh corn muffins with whipped cream cheese to dip into?"

Muffins and cheese appeared right in front of her. Both Thronbasa and Luke laughed with delight. The women talked like old friends for quite some time. They shared the latest gossip and thoughts about what the new school semester was going to be like. Luke was getting bored listening to the women yap at each other. He was about to leave when Laura said, "Aunt Elizabeth, you have to talk to Luke about traditions!"

"Me talk to him?" she responded. "About what traditions?"

"The school staff is returning. I have talked to quite a few, and they say everyone is upset about this nodding instead of bowing rule! They are complaining that after 5,000 years of tradition, a 12-year-old shouldn't have dropped it on a whim!"

Luke leaned against the wall with his arms crossed and listened intently.

"You're his sister. You should tell him," Thronbasa replied as she sipped her tea.

"But Aunt Elizabeth, you're in charge. He listens to you."

"Aye," Claire agreed, "you're in charge. You should explain it to him."

Thronbasa spread cheese on her muffin as she said, "You're his mother, Claire. You're the one he respects the most. You should tell him!"

"Aye, but I have to do it with a loud voice or threaten to put my foot where the sun won't ever shine before I get his attention!"

Laura added, "And I have to hit him with something before he listens to me! And everyone wants to see the Calibur sword!"

"I have to admit," Thronbasa replied in a very agreeing tone of voice, "I have wanted to put my foot where the sun doesn't shine a few times! I also have to remember he's still a boy."

Luke stood with his mouth wide open feeling insulted as he turned and walked out into the hall. "I can't even see the dopey sword!" he mumbled to himself. "I have to close my eyes every time I pull the damn thing out! And I don't like being called 'boy'!"

He walked toward his grandfather when suddenly he began to fade in and out. He was waking up. In a moment more, Luke opened his eyes. He was lying in his rack. Standing over him, taking turns pushing on him, were Katie and Abi. They were wearing full dress uniforms and cloaks. They even had makeup on.

"What?" Luke asked in a grumpy tone of voice.

"Come on, your majesty!" Katie told him.

"It's time to get up, Luke! The sun has been up 30 minutes already! What's up with you?" Abi insisted.

Luke sat up in his rack. He shook his head, rubbed his eyes, and scratched his head, and then he said, "I think I was having a nightmare! What have you guys put on your faces?"

"It's called makeup," Katie told him.

"Where did you get makeup from?"

"The upperclass girls showed us last night and then came and helped early this morning," Abi explained.

Luke glanced around and noticed everyone was all dressed up. "Oh, boy," he thought. "This is gonna be a long day!"

It was graduation day from first trials. It was also the day in which Luke was to be consecrated as First Lord of the Realm. More than a thousand Freshers had passed their first trials. Thronbasa said that everyone who fought in the battle had graduated first trails, which meant everyone had qualified for admission to the fall semester of the academy.

Luke adjusted his tie in the mirror. He had a full dress uniform on and white gloves. "I look so different," he thought. When he walked out of the boy's room, everyone who had spent the summer with him in the barracks was waiting. They all nodded to him and then looked at him with big smiles. Even Mr. Finch, wearing a dress upperclassman's uniform, was waiting and smiling. Luke nodded and smiled back.

"What?" Luke asked when his friends looked at him oddly.

"You lead the way," Selwyn said to him. "We're all waiting on you!"

"OK," he said with a little hesitation as he slowly walked toward the main door opening. When he walked out of the barracks, he found a huge crowd waiting. When they saw him, they erupted into cheers and applause. Luke stopped. He was stunned by a sea of people cheering him. He had never seen so many happy people in one place. Katie and Abi walked up from behind. Katie took his left arm and Abi his right. Luke gazed backward and said loudly so he could be heard above the crowd, "Are you there, Selwyn?"

"Aye!" he responded with a big smile. "Right behind you! I think I shall always be here too. I've got your back, Luke!"

"Thank you, Selwyn!" Luke told him loudly, with pride and a smile.

Luke and his friends stepped out into the crowd. The people parted and nodded as he made his way to the Cathedral of the Valley. Luke nodded back, and he stopped, only to be greeted by Katie's and Abi's and Selwyn's families. Each time a new group of people saw him coming, they broke into applause. They were all so very happy and even proud to see him. Some were even crying. More than a thousand Freshers walked in precession behind Luke and his friends. The line stretched nearly the entire mile and a half from the training grounds to the cathedral.

Luke was not prepared for who and what awaited him at the cathedral. He knew they would be there, but not like this! When he saw it, he couldn't help the tears that came to his eyes. On top of the marble steps of the cathedral stood his family. There was Aunt Elizabeth, who stood first, and then Aunt Claire, Laura, Magda, Marta, and Sam! They were all dressed in the formal robes of the Alfa-Omegas. They looked brilliant! Luke had never seen anything like it in his life! Aunt Elizabeth also bore the insignias of High Chancellor. Next to Sam stood Sonny, Boo, and Loraine! They were dressed in the formal robes of the centurions. Sonny wore the insignia of First Centurion. They all looked so brilliant!

As Luke drew near, they all went down on one knee and bowed to him.

"Oh, come on!" Luke insisted.

As they all stood up, Claire said to him, "We have to do this properly, My Lord!"

"Aye," Thronbasa agreed. "Everyone is watching!"

Luke walked up to Thronbasa and gave her a hug. The crowd broke into applause. Luke hugged everyone there. When he got to Sam, he called his friends over.

"Abi, Katie, Selwyn!" Luke had excitement in his voice. He held Sam's hand and announced to them, "This is Sam! She's the one who taught us the dance!"

His friends first bowed to Sam, as they had done to the whole first family, and then they shook her hand as Luke gave Sonny, Boo, and Loraine each a hug.

"If all the greetings are finished," Claire asserted, "the elders of the Realm are waiting. Not to mention two cardinals, two bishops, and three dozen other priests!"

Luke took the lead with his friends at his side, followed by his family and the whole Fresher class. As they moved toward the entranceway, uniformed trumpeters raised their instruments and began to play. Everyone inside stood and bowed, and a chorus began to sing. The cathedral was decorated inside, and the sounds of the music reverberated against the walls. Luke was overwhelmed.

As they approached the altar, Katie noticed that the Great Stone of the Caliber sword had been placed off to the far left side of the altar stage.

"What is that stone doing here?" Katie asked Luke.

"I had it brought here," he told her.

"Why?"

"I am going to put the sword back in it and leave it here."

"The Darksiders will know where it is!" she insisted.

"They already know where it is!" Luke told her. "This is holy ground. They can't come in here. Besides, the priests said that there's a charm on it. Once the sword is impaled in the stone, it can't be moved."

The ceremony began with a service by the senior cardinal. The first family, with Luke at its head, sat on the right side of the altar's stage. Katie, Abi, and Selwyn sat in the first row, and they kept smiling at Luke. The rest of the Freshers took up all the rows nearest the altar. When he finished speaking, the cardinal walked over to Luke. Luke stood up as the cardinal took from a small box a ring. It was gold with a light blue stone in its center, and the coat of arms of the White Robin was carved into it. He placed it on Luke's left hand and said, "Welcome to the Realm, Lord Carter."

Luke thanked him and then sat and watched as three dozen priests entered from the sides of the building. They placed a ring on the left hand of each Fresher. Now the Freshers were all members of the American Realm.

"Do you see the podium with the stool and microphone, Luke?" Laura whispered to him.

"Yeah," Luke responded, wondering what she was talking about as he looked to far left side of the stage.

"The stool is for short people!"

"What does she mean?" Luke whispered looking up at Thronbasa.

"After the ceremony, you have to go up and say something to the people," she told him.

"What?" Luke whispered with alarm in his voice. Then he leaned over and whispered to Laura, "Remember what happened last time you called me shorty?"

"Will you two be nice?" Claire insisted.

Laura just smiled as Luke glanced up at Thronbasa and said, "You never said anything about talking!"

"I didn't want you to get nervous or lose sleep."

"What if I don't want to get up there and talk?"

"You have to, Luke. It's not enough that these people see you," Thronbasa explained. "They have to hear you as well."

"No!"

"Why not?" Claire told him. "Suren you can face an army of Darksiders but not say a wee hello to your friends!"

"What am I supposed to talk about?"

"Whatever comes to mind," Thronbasa said.

"Aye," Claire agreed. "Talk about the future or the past. Talk about things you know. Remember, when these people thought you were lost, they were filled with fear. When they thought you had survived, they were filled with joy! They are not just happy to have you here, Luke. They are afraid you will not be here tomorrow."

"This is so mean, you guys not telling me this before now!"

"Oh, go on with ya!" Claire told him. "The sun will come up tomorrow, and you'll still be here!"

"Maybe not," Luke told her, which drew a bewildered stare from the whole first family.

The final part of the ceremony began. Everyone stood up as Luke walked to center stage and a priest removed his cloak. Then the two cardinals came, one on each side. A bishop handed one cardinal a formal robe and the other a formal hat. They placed them on Luke. Then another ring was lifted from a golden box. This was also a gold ring but with a large brilliant square diamond mounted in its center. It bore the crest of the White Robin, and carved around the gem were the words "First Lord of the Realm." It was placed onto Luke's right hand. Now that Luke was properly dressed, the cardinals gave him their blessing. They bowed to him and then left him standing alone at center stage. Everyone then bowed to Luke, and after he finished bowing back, the cathedral both inside and out erupted into an ovation. There was so much joy that many people cried.

When Luke had heard enough clapping, he drew the Sword of Kings and the room fell silent. The sword was so bright, even in the daytime, that it was hard to get a clear look at it. First Luke held it above his head. Then he walked to the Great Stone and drove the sword into it. As he stepped away, the sword's blinding glare faded, and everyone stared in awe of the beautiful sword in the stone.

"Well, they wanted to see the damn thing," Luke thought. "Now they can stare at it all they like!"

Luke made his way across the altar's stage to the far side where the podium was waiting. Laura gave him a silly smile as he stepped up on the stool. Luke's eyes glanced upward at his hat. He felt stupid wearing that hat, so he took it off and sat it on the podium. Now everyone had a nice clear view of him.

"Good morning," Luke said, and everyone replied, "Good morning." Luke thought he was just talking to everyone in the cathedral, but in the Voodoo Pub of New Orleans, there sat a man wearing worn-out cloths, an uncut black beard, and an old-style hat sitting low on his brow. He was drinking a pint of brew and watching on a magical screen. Everything that was happening in the Griffin Valley could be seen and heard. This was Jimmy, the man who had betrayed and murdered the First Lord of the Realm. Luke had no idea that everyone in the Realm was watching and listening—least of all the man who had killed his uncle.

"If I had known I was going to talk before I came here," Luke told the crowd, "I might have written something. Not that I could read and speak at the same time very well, but I might have tried. My Aunt Claire, Lady Claire Cohan, she thinks I should just speak my mind." Luke paused for a moment.

"Since the fight in Sugarloaf, I have had nothing but a mind full of unanswered questions. You know, it has only been 10 weeks—10 weeks since I knew there was a Realm and only nine since Uncle Martin, Lord Martin Cohan, was murdered and I learned I was left in charge. I have to say that being in charge and just 12 hasn't been any fun. I don't really make any decisions; I just make guesses, and then pray I made the right one." Luke paused again to think.

"The one thing I have noticed is the changes. I don't seem to be afraid all the time anymore. After what happened in Sugarloaf, I was alone and afraid of everything and everyone. Now I know I am not alone.

"I also have seen the changes in others. When I first came to the valley, I was lucky enough to run into three friends who, for reasons they have never shared with me, stood by me even when they didn't want to. I also watched them pay the price for my friendship. They were treated very badly during the first week. In the week before the last battle here, Darksiders attacked them. They were attacked because they were my friends. Still, they wouldn't walk away even when I ordered them to. I want to say thank you to my friends, Abi Bishop, Katie Gardner, and Selwyn Kidney."

Everyone applauded Luke's friends. Luke applauded too, and they smiled at him and each other.

"Lady Claire Cohan has said I should speak about the future. If I do, I must make only my best guesses again and hope they turn out to be good decisions. First, I understand that my best guesses as to how I should be addressed and on the subject of bowing were not well received. I grew up an American. I know little about very old traditions. I do know I should respect others and their ways. My Uncle Martin taught me that. So I now remove those decisions. I will wait until I am older to decide about traditions and the Realm." Again Luke paused to think.

"I have brought the Sword of Kings here. I now place it into the care of all practitioners of the Realm. It is your sword, not mine, and it is now returned to you. Its safety is now your responsibility. Before I brought it here, I used it one last time to cast a spell. When the sun rises tomorrow, most of you will not know who I am."

There was a tremendous sound of surprise in the crowed as they reacted to this news, and Luke paused again as he waited for the talking.

"I am sorry if anyone doesn't like this decision. There are two reasons for it. First, and most important, I must somehow find my father. I cannot do this with everyone knowing who I am. Second, when I came here, I did not believe I belonged here. I still feel this way. Not having everyone know who I am lets me fit in better. Everyone can be certain for now that I am not going anywhere. I will remain among you, and if something goes wrong, I will be here for you."

The crowd continued to talk among themselves with surprise.

"Finally, my Aunt Elizabeth, from this day forward, shall be known as Lady Elizabeth Thronbasa Cohan, first Lady of the House Cohan, first Lady of the Realm, and High Chancellor of the Citadel."

The crowd spoke loudly now, and Luke's family gazed at one another. Thronbasa was stunned to hear his words, and Laura was shocked.

"Someday it might be Lady Laura or Magda. But for now, when Lady Elizabeth speaks, she speaks for me. Her decisions are my decisions. If I am to be the one who makes the best guesses he knows how to, then this is what I have decided.

"Lady Claire is appointed as chancellor. She and the High Chancellor shall choose two others to be members of the board. Then elections are to be held in the fall. Four individuals from inside the Griffin Valley and four from outside the valley will be chosen by all of you as members of the board. Lady Laura will head the First Caldron. Lady Magda is appointed as her second. With the consent of the High Chancellor, they shall choose from among the best of us to stand against the Darkside.

"I do not know what the Darkside is planning next. But from this day forward, if they threaten one of us, they threaten all of us!

"I congratulate all the Freshers who have qualified for admission this fall."

All the Freshers applauded, and some even screamed with joy!

"I know that I am alive today because many of you came running when you were needed the most! Believe it or not, the reason I survived Sugarloaf was because people, not members of the Realm, my neighbors, came running to help. In the end, we are all standing against the Darkside! Thank you! Thank you all very much!"

The crowd rose to its feet in a standing ovation as Luke stepped down and walked to his family. The noise from the ovation was so loud that two griffins landed outside to investigate. Laura wasn't too happy about not being first Lady of the Realm, but she was very proud of her little brother. He had proven himself to be a tiny bit more clever than she thought he was. Luke stood holding his hat in one hand and Aunt Claire's hand in the other. He felt very nervous. Claire could feel his hand trembling. She bent over and whispered into his ear and then pushed him out into the middle of the stage. She stood there applauding like everyone else, and insisted Luke bow to the crowd. When he finally did as she asked, the noise only got louder, as many people decided that it was now a good time to start some very happy screaming.

Luke stood there as his family lined up behind him. He took a few steps forward but stopped after stepping off of the stage. He stood waiting for his friends to join him, and when they did, they helped Luke lead everyone out of the cathedral. Everyone headed for the valley town. The townsfolk had prepared a festival. There was food and drink for everyone. Bands played, and people danced. After a brief meal, Luke and his family stood and shook hands, met people from all over the world, and had their pictures taken.

The day was long, and in mid-afternoon, all of the Freshers wanted to go and explore the Citadel. Now that they had their Realm rings, they were allowed to go anywhere. The sun headed below the horizon as Freshers continued to search the seemingly endless hallways. After dark they all wound up in the corridor outside Luke's family home. All the portraits lining the walls were full of tales to share with the young people. There were endless questions, and Luke's grandfather delighted in the attention.

Luke didn't need to survey the Citadel because he did it every night in his sleep. So Katie, Abi, and Selwyn lost track of him when they went out to explore. On their return, they made their way to the portrait of the old First Lord.

"Good evening, sir," Abi said and then Katie and then Selwyn.

"Suren if it isn't the brave Fresher First Lord Crew themselves!" the old lord replied. "So how is our First Lord holding up?"

"We don't know," Abi told him. "We were hoping you might know where he is."

"They all came through here a while ago. They headed out onto the balcony. It's the third door down on the right if I'm remembering correctly."

They said thank you and were about to move on when the old lord said, "Miss Gardener, is it?"

Katie stopped and looked at the others, amazed that the old lord knew her name.

"Yes, sir, but everyone calls me Katie."

"I understand that you grew up in the Bennie world."

"Yes, sir."

"Would you be telling me what a tailgate party is?"

"A tailgate party?" Katie was surprised by the question. "It's a sports party. Americans are fond of pick-up trucks, and the door at the rear of a pick-up is called a tailgate. They arrive early before a sporting event and cook on the open tailgate. Then they drink a lot and go off drunk and stupid and scream at their favorite team for three hours. It's mostly a guy thing. Why?"

"Our new First Lord is saying he's going to have one this fall with a bonfire. He's planning on burning me in front of everyone!"

Katie looked at Selwyn and Abi and said, "He is not!"

"Don't worry, Grandfather Cohan," Abi told him. "We'll protect you!"

The three walked off and Selwyn said, "I thought Luke was kidding!"

"Me too," Abi said.

"He'd better be kidding!" Katie added. "If he's not, I'm gonna wait 'til he's sleeping and hit him with something! Tailgate party? What is that all about? Most people here wouldn't know a tailgate if they fell over one!"

Out on the balcony, the Cohans stared off over the valley. Claire was lying on a settee, and Luke was lying on her shoulder with one of her arms wrapped around him. Elizabeth was sitting with her husband, Marcus, and she had her 5-year-old daughter, Tara, on her lap. Her 7-year-old, Thia, sat next to her. Around the balcony was everyone from Sugarloaf. In came Abi, Katie, and Selwyn. They waved at everyone as they made their way to Luke.

"Luke," Abi said.

"Luke," Katie asserted. Selwyn just stood looking innocent.

"Yes, my ladies?" Luke said, a little on the snobby side.

"Your grandfather thinks you're going to have a tailgate party and burn him in a bonfire!" Katie asserted.

"Yeah, so?" Luke replied.

"What's a tailgate party?" Elizabeth said with and annoyed tone of voice.

"Aye," Claire added, "and why are you picking on your grandfather?"

"He lied to me!" Luke answered.

"What did he lie about?" Laura demanded.

"Rajay," Magda told everyone.

"Oh," Claire said.

Then 7-year-old Thia walked over to Luke and with a very sad look and a sweet tone of voice said, "Uncle Luke, are you going to burn up Grandfather Cohan?"

Luke had an "oh no" look on his face as everyone went, "Aww!"

"Yeah, Uncle Luke," Claire asked as she hugged him a little.

"Yeah, Uncle Luke," Elizabeth said.

"Yeah, Uncle Luke," Katie said, and then Abi and Laura chimed in.

Luke gazed at Thia as he said, "No, I'm not going to burn him up!"

Thia gave him a kiss on the cheek and then went back to her mother.

"If I brought a pick-up truck in here, the griffins would try to eat it anyway! But we could move him, I think!"

"Move him where?" Elizabeth demand.

"No way!" Laura told him.

"I think he should be moved to the men's room in the jail!"

"No!" everyone said in unison. Then everyone stared at Luke, waiting for him to say something.

"I don't know why everyone wants to protect him. I don't think he's worth the time of day!" Luke said.

"You need him!" Claire asserted. "Maybe not today or tomorrow or even next month. But you will need him! And don't worry about not getting along with him. Your dad almost never did either!"

"Aye," Marta muttered.

"You can say that again," Laura agreed.

"Why not?" Luke asked.

"Why not, indeed," Claire said. "I doubt there was any one reason why. There were hundreds. Your dad also had a unique way of annoying the hell out of your grandfather!"

"How?"

"Your dad loved words," Claire told him. "In fact, he was an English professor. That's how he made his way in the world when he wasn't out saving it. Your dad and grandfather had their first real fight when P.J. was your age. When they fought, your dad would write a poem and then keep reciting it around your grandfather. It drove him nuts! But if you wanted to be P.J.'s friend, student, or family, you had to learn his first poem by heart."

"What was it?" Luke asked.

Everyone from Sugarloaf, and Laura, said spontaneously together, "'Pineland Breeze.'" Then everyone laughed at the chorus they had created.

Up above the group, high atop the edge of the Citadel's ramparts, sat three black condors. In the darkness, they were impossible to make out except for the blinking of their blood-red eyes. They stared and listened intently at the first family and their friends on the balcony below.

"How did it go?" Luke asked Laura.

Laura stared and smiled at Luke for a moment and then said:

I walked along a woodland path,
'Twas near the sand where the sea is at.
Salt filled air mixed with cone-filled trees.
Here I thought, began the Pineland Breeze.

The Breeze I thought a heavenly smell,
And so a part of the place I dwelled.
When I left, the Breeze filled my mind,
Reminding me always of other days and other times.

Time has taken me so far away,
The sound of the sea no longer passes my days.
The sturdy trees and woodland so deep,
'Tis only in my mind the breezes still sweeps.

In the darkest of nights when I sleep,
My mind will drift back to that sandy beach,
To the strong cone filled trees, filled with the scent of the sea,
In my mind there is always an eternal Pineland Breeze.

Luke Carter had survived his first weeks in the Griffin Valley. He, his friends, his family, and neighbors had triumphed over the Darkside. Now summer was nearly over. School was about to begin. New challenges awaited Luke, but the Darkside wasn't far away. Luke would have to continue to prepare to meet them wherever they decided to make their next move.

"Time for bed!" Elizabeth said profoundly. "Tomorrow is another day!"

As they walked toward the door, Luke said to Elizabeth, "I think we should arrange to import some packs of mongooses."

"Import?" she replied. "Don't you think we have enough creatures living here already?"

"What's so special about mongooses?" Laura asked him.

Luke replied, "They like to hunt and eat snakes."

Everyone said, "Oh!"

First Lord of the Realm
Níl eagla orm roimh éinne ach Dia amhain